REPLACE YOU

Andrew Ewart was born in Chester in 1983. After teaching in Denmark he studied English at Cambridge, then spent ten years in London. He now lives in St Albans with his wife and daughter. He works as a production journalist and is overly fond of a pun headline.

Also by Andrew Ewart

Forget Me

REPLACE YOU

ANDREW EWART

ORION

An Orion paperback

First published in Great Britain in 2021 by Orion Fiction,
an imprint of The Orion Publishing Group Ltd.,
Carmelite House, 50 Victoria Embankment
London EC4Y 0DZ

An Hachette UK Company

1 3 5 7 9 10 8 6 4 2

A CIP catalogue record for this book
is available from the British Library.

ISBN (Paperback) 978 1 4091 8973 2
ISBN (eBook) 978 1 4091 8974 9

Typeset at The Spartan Press Ltd,
Lymington, Hants

Printed and bound in Great Britain by Clays Ltd,
Elcograf S.p.A.

www.orionbooks.co.uk

For Laura – irreplaceable

I

The White Prison

Trapped. Trapped again. When I woke up in this white place a
few hours ago, my first thought was that there might have been
another one of my little episodes. Slightly too deep this time?
I pull up my sleeves – while I was unconscious, an unknown
person dressed me in a medical smock as colourless as the small
room I've found myself inside – and inspect my arms. The scars
on my forearms are old and familiar; thin white brushstrokes
intersecting and dividing on the ochre canvas of my flesh. There
are no obvious recent wounds. Pills, perhaps? No, my stomach is
settled. There is none of that raw, reamed-out sensation that I've
felt before when toxic sludge has been aborted from my belly.

There are no edges or corners in this room. Its internal
geometry is perpetually curving, the walls very slightly sloping.
Could I be in a cave or an underground bunker? There must
be a reason for the room's strange shape. There must be a reason
that there are no doors.

There must be a reason why I'm trapped here.

My room. My cell. White; everything is white except for
a black video screen set into one wall. There is a humming
sound, almost sub-audible, that may be coming from that screen.
With no sign of the outside world, the screen is my window
into whatever existence lies beyond this prison. Feeling brave,

I touch the screen and it winks into life. I see an unlovely marshland painted in smears of brown and green, a breeze knocking the stocky heads of bulrushes together like drunks at last orders. This scene does not change, even though I study it intently as if revising for an exam. Nothing changes. Nothing changes for what could be hours. Eventually, growing restless and somewhat spooked, I tap the screen again. The scene flicks to blackness once more.

I've woken up before in places I don't recognise, after what I call my Great Waves. My tongue tracks over the broken incisor in the top of my mouth, a remnant of when I passed out in the bathroom at home – I thought I saw something move behind me in the steamed-up mirror, something familiar yet monstrous – and hit my face on the sink. I think that was the first of the Great Waves, or was it the second or third? This is how it happens: first, there is the despair, a sadness that swarms around my brain and makes me feel as if nothing will ever be good again and all hope is lost. There's a smell; a boggy, decaying odour. Then I feel an enormous rushing sensation, like a tide big enough to swallow the world. Then I go away for a while.

Right now, sitting in my holding pen, I feel no fear. Not yet, not quite yet. Because this is a mistake. Everything will be sorted out soon. I judge that I woke up here three or four hours ago – although obviously I have no way of telling the time – and I feel remarkably clear-headed. There is neither the threat of an oncoming Great Wave nor the memory of its passing. In a perverse way, I feel better than I have done for many years. Maybe the worst has happened. Whatever the worst might turn out to be.

My name is Amaya Gemma Dala, or just Mya. There are a worrying number of gaps in my memory, like an autostereogram that never swims into focus no matter how hard I stare. If this place is a psychiatric hospital – the most likely scenario if it really was a Great Wave that washed me up here – the doctors wouldn't leave hazardous items in the room. And they haven't left that to chance. Maybe I could knot the bedsheets into a noose, but the covers are papery and fragile – and anyway where could I hang my slipknot on these smooth, smooth, smooth walls? I might try beating my head against the curvature but frankly I don't have the energy. I think someone has their eye on me anyway. There are no visible cameras in the cell but I'm sure they are watching. Surely they wouldn't leave me here alone.

They. They? Who are they, Mya? I think of faceless men in white coats and that's when the first jolts of panic race through my body. My heart begins to larrup and sickly sweat prickles out beneath my arms. Why am I here? Who put me here?

'Hello?' I call out to the empty room. 'Anyone there? Anyone watching, listening? Hello, anyone?'

Silence, but for that scarcely audible buzzing. For a moment, I half expected the screen to smash into life and a hideously distorted voice to drone out of the void. Instead, I smile at the screen. I smile as sanely as I can manage. I wish I could see my reflection in its dead eye. For some reason it seems incredibly important to see my reflection right now. To make sure that I'm still me.

'Hello? Anyone?' I try again. 'Look, I don't . . . You don't understand . . . there's been a mistake.' I let out a casual, not-fussed-at-all laugh that splinters viciously like a broken glass. 'It's not a problem. But you've got the wrong girl. I shouldn't be here. Right?'

My nails dig into my palms. Trapped. Trapped again. Why am I here? Who put me here? So many questions, too many questions. It's a mistake. It's a terrible mistake. I shouldn't be here. I can't be here. I've got to get out. Get out. Right now.

'How long do I have to stay here?' I yell at the screen, my control slipping as a tremendous pressure builds behind my eyeballs, feeling my entire body shaking. 'What do you want from me? What do I have to—'

Then the panic overwhelms me and I am on my knees, holding my head in my hands, rocking back and forth, whimpering to myself. No, no, I can't lose control. I can't let them believe I'm the person someone clearly *thinks* I am.

I concentrate on breathing. Low and slow. Self-hypnosis. Get the fans going to cool down that overloaded hard drive of my brain.

Breathe … breathe, Mya, breathe. Breathe. Nice and deep and slow. Breathe and calm. Breathe and calm. Calm. Calm. There. Well done.

I've always had a tendency to lose myself in my own head. My brain has got me into this trouble. That means my brain must get me out. Turnabout's fair play. My brain has taken me so very far in life and yet almost killed me a number of times. I can't control my thoughts. Being in my head is like strapping yourself into an aeroplane seat and waiting to soar above the clouds or crash in fiery oblivion. *She's either a genius or a lunatic,* one of my father's colleagues told him once. Terribly unprofessional, but I think Dad was secretly quite proud. *Why can Mya not be both?* he had replied, a hint of a smirk playing around his lips. That was when we could still joke about my mental state. Right now I think I'm an unfixable problem for my father. I don't mean to be. I hope Dad knows where I am; he cares about me so much.

No, this won't work. I'll upset myself again. Think about the good times, Mya. The good times that will come back around so very, very soon. Once this silly mistake has been sorted out. Think about Marco, think about how you found one another and everything seemed brighter. He really is incredible, in his amiable and unassuming way, at easing out the knots and kinks in my psyche. Patient, serene, calming. God knows he needed to be. Some people said it would never work out. That I'd grow bored of him. *Does he provide you with enough intellectual stimulation?* my father asked once after I brought Marco home for the first time. There had been a mildly excruciating family dinner and then Dad had played one of his stupid psycho games. *A remarkably uncomplicated fellow*, my father told me the next day, as if I didn't know already. *Devoid of reckless emotions.* This from the man whose obsessions had driven his own wife to a breakdown. I retorted that I'd seen the damage a stimulating, complicated, reckless man did to my mother. Dad sighed, scratching his whitening moustache, and fixed me with those limpid, hurting eyes. *It was not an insult, Mya. You of all people should understand how great a compliment I have paid young Marco.* I can't remember why his remarks needled me so much. But I was angry. Marco's not stupid. Not stupid at all. Okay, book learning isn't his thing, and you won't find him at an art gallery or the opera. He speaks one language and rarely eloquently. He has absolutely no idea what my job entails, what happens at the Academy. He is not, by any stretch of the imagination, a man who stretches his imagination. But his emotional intelligence is staggering. I've always found it difficult to be in unfamiliar places but I've never felt safer than when I woke up in his bed after our first night together and saw that close-cropped head on the pillow beside me, his powerful body at complete peace. He may look like a thug but he loves like an angel. He comforts, he listens, he consoles. He knows when a Great Wave is coming and shields me from the worst of the dark swells. He tries. He tries so hard.

But did Marco try hard enough this time? I wonder. Have I pushed him away one too many times? Am I beyond his help, a lost cause?

A lost cause. Those words could be etched on my tombstone.

I feel drowsy. There is nothing to do here but wait, so I might as well sleep. At least my memories seem to be returning sporadically. A comfort blanket to wrap around me in this cold and colourless place. If I can hold on to the memories of those I love, then I can hold on to hope.

Another thought strikes me as I pull the sheets over my head to block out the incessant glare of the white light. A thought that I expected to terrify me but instead find strangely soothing.

Is this place heaven?

Slept for hours, I think. A miracle under the punishing glare of the lights. My saliva is rancid – the usual sleep-grot, the product of a diminished saliva flow allowing bacteria to proliferate. But is there also a tang of something chemical? A sharp taste, weirdly tantalising, like nail varnish or aniseed. It could be paranoia. I don't feel doped.

Even though I could stay here forever in my bed sheet cave, I decide to face my future. I've always needed a reason to wake up in the morning. Marco. I think of Marco. I think of his lost-little-boy smile; how it slices ten years off his age and softens the crueller lines of his cheekbones and jaw. I fantasise that this has been a hilarious mix-up – oh, how we'll laugh – and Marco is waiting outside this white room, grinning, waiting for me to wake up, waiting to spin me back to the flatlands on the pillion of his Suzuki Bandit. We'll race home and he'll take me up to his bedroom and hold me and comfort me and kiss me, and do whatever else he pleases, so long as we are far from this white place. This white prison. Anywhere will do. Anywhere but here.

No. No more fantasy. It's time to face the world, Mya. Face your future. Surely it won't be so bad.

If only I could believe my own lies.

Biting down on my lower lip, I shove off the sheets. The whiteness almost blinds me, wiping out my vision with migraine-inducing intensity. I press my fingertips against my eye sockets and wait for the worst of the headache to pass.

When my sight returns to normal, I see that there is a gaping hole in the side of my room. A door, I realise to my bemusement. A wide-open door. Where the hell did that appear from? I could have sworn I checked every single inch of my room for exit points. The door must have been set so neatly into the curve of the far wall that I hadn't even noticed it. Now it is open.

Is this a trap? Tentatively I push myself out of bed. My bare feet slap on the plasticky tiles. The floor is warm and seems to thrum gently beneath my toes, pulsing like a heartbeat. The light spills out of my room – no, not my room, *the* room, there is nothing of me in this place, nothing – and merges with the light from outside.

My heartbeat is skittery. My mouth is dry. The tiny hairs on my forearms have pricked up to attention.

Holding onto the doorframe for support, I peek outside the cell. I see a long corridor that curves away out of my line of sight. There are no windows, no other doors. No people, no signs of life. There are no sounds but for the blood rushing in my ears.

My fingers find purchase in the wall. First there is flatness, then my nails sink into small gullies. I trace the indentations and carefully slide around to view the marks.

Sickly panic sweat springs out on my skin as I see what has been carved into the wall. A name is chiselled by my door: *Amy G Dala*. They know me here, even if they've misspelled my name. This was no mistake. They have been expecting me.

I should run. Who knows when I might have this chance again? But an aching weariness has settled into my bones. Worse, though, is the fear. I'm scared to see what lies beyond this room. I'm scared of who I might meet in that curving corridor. I'm weak. I'm weaponless. I'm barefooted. There is a strong urge to step back inside the cell and pull the sheets over my head and let what's happening to me simply happen.

No. I need to get out. I need to escape. I need to get back to Marco.

Glancing back into the cold safety of my room, movement catches my eye. The screen has turned itself on. I stop shock-still, thoughts of escape obliterated. The scene of the flatlands is the same. But now two figures are walking together through the bulrushes. They are a young couple in their mid-twenties. Their body language – hand in hand, stepping in time, wrapped up in one another's warmth – tells of total devotion. The couple are going to pass right by the static camera that feeds to my video screen. As they come closer, recognition flares and my breath catches in my throat.

The man on the video screen is Marco. He is wearing his usual black leather jacket and a T-shirt with the logo of the Damned, one of his favourite bands. Shaved head and ripped jeans and cherry-red Dr Martens boots; it is unmistakably him. This is the Marco I know, the Marco I love. But who's the girl with him?

Who is that girl?

I know her. Of course I know her. How can I not know her? This must be a joke. A fucking set-up. I'm on a reality TV

8

show or at some mad party, or this is immersive theatre or a carnival attraction, a haunted house maybe, because this isn't real. This can't be real. Surely this can't be real?

As the couple walk past the camera, their faces come into focus. They are gazing into each other's eyes, caught in a freeze-frame of shared intimacy. The girl beams up at Marco. And he looks back at her with such, such love. Because that girl is … oh God, that girl is me.

She's me.

Or, at the very least, a girl who looks identical to me.

2

The New Intake (fresh meat)

On the viewing platform at the top of the tower, the gentle autumn breeze teased her hair. The sun, when it managed to bully its way through the clouds, set about tinting her bare shoulders. She was staring down at the tiny specks of people two hundred feet below; humanity reduced to scuttling insects. Like kicking over a stone and disturbing an ants' nest, exposing the chaotic industry. But there had to be a pattern somewhere.

She watched the new intake of students emerging from the coaches, wheeling their suitcases or lugging rucksacks. They began to proceed across the white-and-black marble squares of the front court towards the main lecture hall. The glass doors were flung wide open, beckoning them inside. Some strode confidently – public school followed by Oxbridge, you could always tell – while others, more nervous, hung back or clung together in hastily formed pairs or trios. Mostly young, mostly enthusiastic, all curious to know what was inside the great edifice that loomed above the flatlands. The secrets locked away.

The Academy looked better when you were perched on top of it, she thought, rather than staring up at that vast red-brick block. The building was shaped with two wings that curved around into a semi-circle, tapering like pincers, fiercely guarding the tower at the heart of the complex. Residents of the nearby town called it The Crab. There had been plenty of opposition to its construction almost a decade ago. A carbuncle, as the furious letters to the local newspaper had branded it, a monstrosity, an obsolescence. In the minds of nature enthusiasts, the silty marshes – mostly used for burning tyres, teenagers' illicit parties and fly-tipping – had suddenly taken on the charms of the Hanging Gardens of Babylon. There had been arguments and there had been counter-arguments. The finest scientific minds in the country, the world, would soon be flocking to this undistinguished corner of East Anglia. The councillors insisted the Academy would provide jobs, transport links, the financial security of heavy government investment. Her father, who never had time for rows, had seen it slightly differently: the Academy needed to be built so the Academy would be built. You couldn't halt progress – every empire had to start somewhere. New Yorkers were probably outraged when the first skyscraper shot up in Manhattan.

She rarely troubled herself with the impact upon the surrounding countryside of the Academy, or – to give it its full title – the Meinhof-Dala-Smithson Academy of Science, Research and Learning. To her, it was simply home.

Footsteps sounded behind her. A hand fell on her shoulder and squeezed affectionately. His scent was both slightly sickening and delightful; suffocating yet all-embracing. The rank residue of cigarettes, which she hated, and his heavily spiced aftershave – like exotic fruit that had fermented into boozy sugar – that she adored.

'New arrivals,' she said with a smile starting to fray at the edges. The sight of the coaches arriving, crawling across the landscape towards the Academy like a wagon train in an old Western movie, caused anxiety to cramp her heart. This was her time. Her intake. Her new friends.

'Fresh meat,' her father replied.

She turned away from the new students milling below and stared at him. His glossy moustache and impeccable hounds-tooth suit were at odds with the wild sproutings of grey hair either side of his bald head.

'God, that sounds creepy,' she said, digging him in the ribs with an elbow.

A delta of incomprehension formed between his thick salt-and-pepper eyebrows. She thought, hardly for the first time, that while Dad charmed everyone he met in his politely baffled fashion, human nature would remain a mystery to him forever. 'That is what they say, isn't it? Fresh meat?'

'Oh,' she said with a slight laugh, 'you mean freshmen. First years are called freshman students in America. That's what you meant, isn't it?'

'No doubt,' Gurdeep Dala replied. 'In fact, we have a number of American friends joining us this year.'

'You won't be weird with the students?' she asked. 'Promise?'

'My dear,' her father said grandly, 'no more weird than normal. Of that you have my word.'

'You really should shave your head,' she said, flicking a finger-nail at the whorls of hair above his ears. 'Those things are totally out of control and bald guys are very hot right now. You look like you've got radio antennae sticking out of your head.'

'Tuned in to the celestial dial,' he said, removing his gold-rimmed glasses and polishing them on his tie. 'Calling occupants of interplanetary craft.'

She huffed. 'You said you wouldn't be weird, Pops.'

'That was a last hurrah, I promise.' He placed his glasses back on his nose and beamed at her. 'A final wild fling with abnormality. Consider me chastened.'

She tried to smile, then stared nakedly at him. 'Do you think

I'll be okay?' she asked. Her voice fractured upon the final syllable.

The grip on her shoulder tightened reassuringly; she sank into his embrace and began to shake a little. 'My dear, why ever wouldn't you be? I can assure you that for the past eight years of accepting students – many quite fiendishly accomplished – not one of them could match your skill or aptitude. I should very much like to meet the prodigy who could best your talent. And in that case, I promise you, there is always nepotism to fall back on.'

'It's not that,' she said, flapping her hands hopelessly, 'I just want them to think I'm normal. Don't look at me like that. I know you hate normal people. I don't care. I'm worried I won't fit in. I'm worried they'll realise I'm different.'

'What makes you say that?'

'Cambridge,' she said in a small voice. 'Cambridge was a disaster.'

'You were so very far from home,' her father said. 'Now... you are home. This time everything will be better.'

She bit down on her lower lip. They both knew she had been barely fifty miles from home but she appreciated his efforts to make her feel better. With an effort of will, she shunted away the dark cloud that had begun to enshroud her thoughts. Instead, she concentrated on the real sky. So blue. So, so blue. Not a cloud in the sky. Breathe, Mya. Breathe.

'Shall I leave you alone for a few minutes?' he asked. 'At eleven o'clock, Frank Baumann will conduct the orientation in the main lecture hall. I would say that is an ideal time to assimilate yourself with your fellow arrivals.'

'Sure thing,' she said, as brightly as she could manage.

Her fingers brushed the rough red-brick surface of the wall that ran around the viewing platform, then clung tight to the black railings. She had grown up around the Academy and knew it as well as she knew her own body; she was so keyed into the building's internal rhythms that sometimes she fancied she could feel it breathing. Her gaze tracked down once more to the students. The front courtyard with its chessboard pattern was almost deserted. The last of her new classmates were dutifully filing through the entrance foyer. A flash of vibrant colour caught her eye.

'Oh gosh,' she said, almost to herself, 'would you look at that?'

The boy was walking alone across the courtyard with an exaggerated swagger. Despite the warmth of the day, he was wearing a black leather jacket. The colour that had distracted her was the Mohican haircut, dyed neon pink, that screamed up from his scalp. His heavy boots thumped on the concrete like a bass drum. She realised that the booming was matched by her heart.

'Behold, Mya,' her father said solemnly. She had quite forgotten he was still there. 'I spy a time traveller.'

'More like a throwback,' she snorted. For some reason it seemed extremely important to set herself as far away as possible from the boy with the stupid punk rock hairstyle. There was a taste of trepidation on her tongue and it felt as if an iron manacle of pressure had clamped around her chest, restricting her breath. What the hell was wrong with her? She couldn't prise her hands from the guardrail for fear her father would see them shaking. 'He doesn't look like a student. He looks like he might mug one of the students. Where are his bags, anyway?'

Gurdeep Dala seemed remarkably unconcerned about the trespasser into his personal fiefdom. 'You know we take all sorts, darling. Maybe he's Kolstein's selection. Or perhaps one of Frank's local care-in-the-community projects. It isn't like you to be so judgemental.'

'Maybe I've changed,' she said, pulling her gaze away from that strange intruder. His rough dress, his pink spikes, his swagger, were utterly incongruous in the ascetic and intellectual perfection of the Academy; the life's work of her father. 'This is the new me, after all. A fresh start.'

'The first day of the rest of your life,' he agreed, offering her his arm. She linked with him and they took their leave of the tower and the mellow glow of the September sun. The lift, she knew, could descend twenty floors in as many seconds, and as they dropped together, she felt like she was falling forever. 'Shall we begin?'

3

The White Prison

Depression is a cancer of the mind. A predatory presence. We need to eradicate it entirely. Hunt down those bad, rotten, stinking cells and cut them out. Inside this vacuum ... something wonderful may bloom.

Who said that? The voice is familiar, an echo in my dreams. I must have dozed off again. Rising and stretching on my cell's single bed, I feel determination steel my spine. I was floppy before, listless and limp. My mind felt as pliant as soggy dough. I couldn't think straight. I could barely think at all. A combination of whatever toxic shit I might have ingested before my Great Wave, and whatever equally toxic medically approved Big Pharma shit they pumped into my body to cure me.

Cure me? Hah. I'm sure I've destroyed more psychiatrists and psychologists, shrinks and head-peepers than I care to count. In another life I think I was a jailbreaker, a criminal who couldn't be bound by mere chains and bars and concrete walls. I'd always find a way free. Only now, the prison is not my mind. My prison is, in fact, a prison.

Let's get things straight. Set out the facts. I was brought here yesterday ... or maybe the day before ... surely not the day before that? Time is impossible to judge. What I can say for sure is that I haven't seen anybody and I haven't been fed. There is a water cooler set into one wall – but no cups, so I have to lap at the

16

tap like a pet hamster in a cage. Humiliating. I hope the people watching – and there are people watching, of that I'm certain – are enjoying the show. Ablutions and evacuations take place in a small tiled cubicle, hidden by a sliding door set into one white wall. I found this miniaturised *salle de bain* by accident: I leaned on the wall, my elbow hit a spongy panel and the door opened. The shower is operated by a plastic button, the water a warm but thin spatter. I can't alter the nozzle and there is no plug for the plughole; obviously they don't want me to drown myself. The toilet is similar to those found on aeroplanes. No escape hatch, no convenient girl-sized hole to crawl through. They really have thought of everything.

The door that opened before – if it really did open – has remained shut and I can't even make out the joins when running the tips of my fingers along what I think is the crack of the doorframe. I may have missed my one opportunity to escape. But whoever constructed this white-walled prison left nothing else to chance. It seems more likely that they – the indefinable and unknowable *they* who watch – were testing me. Waiting to see what I do next. Making notes, watching the progress of the procedure. My mind conjures up images of tall men in white coats with dark glasses that conceal eyes – or at least conceal blank spaces where eyes should be. Men with long fingers and greyish skin, men who have seen suffering and heard screams and made tiny notations as they analyse the lab rat's struggles. Men who cannot be reasoned with, men invulnerable to bribery or seduction or tearful pleas. Men who live for a solitary grim purpose. Men who ... oh, for Christ's sake, shut up, Mya. Where are we going with these flights of fanciful horror? Shut up that frustrated-gothic-novelist voice right this second. Breathe deeply. Breathe and calm, breathe and calm. There, that's better.

My mind got me into this trouble. I shouldn't let it wander

off its too-short leash. I've decided that I imagined seeing Marco with my doppelganger on the video screen the previous day. My thoughts were all over the place and my imagination tricked me.

'Enjoying this?' I call out, addressing the screen. 'Waiting to see if I have another panic attack? Want to see me curl myself up into a ball on the floor again? Nah, I'm not giving you that satisfaction.'

No response. Do I really want a reply? Part of me wants to speak to whoever's in charge here – demand answers, find out what happened to me, convince them I'm sane and need to be let out, right this moment. But I'm scared too. I'm scared they won't believe me. Because I'm still not totally sure how much of this is real. Whenever the cliff edges of reality begin to crumble and my footing slips, my father and Marco are great at pulling me back to safe ground. But neither of them are here.

Seeing Marco on that screen was a dream, obviously. Dad always says that dreams are like a psychic emetic. My subconscious was simply processing – then regurgitating – a situation it can't comprehend. That girl on the video screen, I knew she wasn't me. For one thing, I've never seen the marshlands as a perfect spot for a romantic stroll with Marco. And I've never worn one of those floaty, floral dresses like a silly little fairytale princess. But that's not it; there was something wrong about her. The way she looked, the way she moved. I've been videoed before – for my father's funny games – and I know my own posture, the expressions that cross my face when I think no one is watching. She didn't walk like me. Her expressions were not the same. I've never looked so carefree, so blissful in ignorance. She was a stranger wearing my skin. A replacement.

No, I'm starting to scare myself again. My doppelganger was a dream. A stupid dream.

Despite my confusion and paranoia, I still feel remarkably

clear-headed, physically fitter than I've felt in months. What did I think yesterday? That the worst had happened. Now I have to deal with the aftermath. I have resolve, determination. Better to feel anger – who put me in this place, who, *who?* – than the miserable drifting sensation that always overcomes me before a Great Wave hits. I can get through this, I can endure this, I can beat this.

I will not stay here. This isn't a place in which I can get better. It's a White Prison and that's what I shall name it. I will not live here. I will not die here. I will not accept my future lies here.

The door to my cell slides open.

Suddenly I am unable to move. I feel a strange itching sensation. I smell that dangerous odour again: a children's sweetshop tang like aniseed. Nausea curdles in my veins, coating my limbs in sickly sweat. Too little oxygen, I'm drowning... I'm gasping for air...

There is a squeaking sound and a trolley is pushed into the room. My imagination flexes like a muscle and I think they – whoever *they* might be – have come to take me away. Slap me on the gurney like a slab of meat and do whatever those clever, pallid men do to messed-up people like me. Then I realise it is too small, far too small, to be a stretcher. It's only a food trolley, pushed by a dumpy, dark-skinned woman in a salmon-pink smock. The door whines shut behind her.

'Good morning, Miss Dala,' she says.

The sheer relief at seeing another human floods my vision with tears. I push back the rush of gratitude as if kicking against a warm current.

She sets the trolley up against my bed. Two plastic domes are on the tray, one steaming from a spout at the top. I stare at the woman, who must be this unhappy place's equivalent of a hospital orderly. Her eye sockets are set deep in her skull, craggy alcoves gouged out of a rock face. From the thick-cut lines on her forehead, I judge her to be in late middle age. The name-badge on the front of the orderly's uniform reads: *Anna*.

'What pills are in the food?' I demand.

Maybe I shouldn't have dispensed with small talk. The woman – Anna – just stares at me. Her eyes are tired yet kind. 'No call for pills,' she says quietly. 'We don't hold with that sort of thing here.'

'Seriously, what are your doctors giving me?' I say, with a light laugh to convince Anna that I don't blame her in the slightest. 'I'm only curious. What medicine are they making me take?'

'How are you feeling today?' Anna answers my question with a question. Although somehow that's the answer too. I'm experienced enough in these situations to know when I've been knocked out, rendered incapable of committing harm to myself or anybody else; mostly myself. I stare closely at the orderly. There is no lie in those caves of eyes. They haven't drugged me.

'I'm really hungry,' I tell her.

She smiles. I have pleased her. 'Then eat.'

I feel that same treacherous gratitude. All captives end up loving their captors; I read that in a book once. I repeat my mantra under my breath: *I will not stay here … I will not accept this future.*

The orderly removes the plastic domes and I stare at the food. There is a pile of brown sludge on one plate and a sponge smeared with jam on the other. Surprisingly, I have cutlery – I was expecting to have to eat with my fingers. There is a metal fork, a knife and a spoon wrapped in a paper towel. I eye up the knife. It's blunt but it's still metal. Metal that could be sharpened.

'What's in the casserole?' I ask.

'Beef stew,' she says. 'Very tasty.'

'I'm Hindu,' I tell her. 'I can't eat this. No way. Cows are sacred to me.'

A wrinkle of confusion appears between Anna's eyebrows. 'No one tell me that in the arrivals form,' she huffs.

Arrivals form? This is interesting. Forms need to be signed; bureaucracy requires consent. Who agreed for me to be imprisoned in the White Prison? Who signed away my life?

The beef stew smells inviting and my stomach cramps. I don't think I've eaten in days. I'm starving. My Hindu claim is bullshit – it's my father's heritage but he's far too clever for religion, and he passed on his atheism to his only child. But I can't eat, not yet. Not when I have a plan.

'You not eat?' Anna says, exasperated. 'Very good. Made fresh specially.'

Apologetically I shrug, but make no move to touch my food. I want to see what happens next. I sit silently with my hands clasped in my lap. I can wait. I have all the time in the world.

Finally, the orderly reaches into the top pocket of her pink uniform and pulls out a small plastic intercom. She presses a red button and snaps a couple of words into the receiver. She fixes me with a glare that suggests I have been deeply unappreciative, then steps back and leans against the wall. I sit on the bed and rock back and forth. We remain in uncomfortable silence in our uncomfortable positions until I hear a knock on the door. Anna turns away from me.

There is a short conversation at the door, blocked by her considerable bulk. This is the moment. I grab the knife, pulling it free from its comrades inside the paper napkin. The weight of metal in my hand is reassuring. It's too late to wonder whether I am being monitored through the video screen – I'll know soon enough. Perspiration springing out under my arms, I stow

21

the knife under my mattress. The napkin looks untouched, if you don't notice the missing cutlery ... Oh, who am I kidding? I've mucked this up. I should have been patient. At the doorway I see Anna is being passed another dish. The door slides shut. Anna stumps over with the bowl and sets it on the trolley with a clatter. I stare at the food. It looks like a bowl of blood.

'Paneer,' the orderly announces sourly.

Anna's paneer. Why does that seem fitting? Momentarily I consider telling her I'm vegan but decide not to push my luck. My heart is still pounding and my face is guilt-flushed. Obediently I bend to my food. The tomato sauce is acidic and the cheese is chewy nothingness. I don't care. I don't care so long as the orderly doesn't notice that the knife has vanished. I finish the whole bowl then start on the pudding. The jam roly-poly tastes as if the flavour has been sucked out with a straw. I finish my dinner with long draughts of water, which has a stale taste and a vague whiff of camphor. Slightly too late, I wonder whether the water has been drugged.

'Good?' Anna asks.

'Very good,' I agree. 'Thank you. Thank you so much.' Good Mya, polite Mya. Docile and calm Mya. I'm a decent enough actor, I can play this role for a while. Any possibility of escaping the White Prison may depend on it.

Anna clears away the plates and turns to leave. Again my luck holds and she doesn't spot the missing knife. The door opens and she heads out, the trolley's sticking wheel squeaking in a high-pitched rubbery gasp. If I had to listen to that sound every day, I think I would go insane. *Even more insane?* my mind-voice whispers, and I have to bite back a smile.

As the orderly reaches the corridor, I remember the question I wanted to ask. 'Where am I?' I call after her.

I don't expect Anna to answer. I'm so surprised to hear her

respond that later on I wonder whether I've imagined her words.

'You're safe, Miss Dala,' she says gently, turning to face me, offering me a small smile soaked with pity. 'You're home.'

Then the door to my cell slides shut and I am alone once more.

4

The New Intake (fresh meat)

'It's all in your head, Mya,' somebody behind her hissed.

Blushing, she refused to acknowledge the source of that sly voice. She tried to concentrate on the man talking on the stage of the lecture hall. She jotted down a few notes but the words were meaningless. It was hardly surprising; she couldn't understand anything the professor was saying. Maybe if she had been concentrating from the beginning of the lesson, her pad might be scored with something more elucidating than half-formed doodles. It was difficult though. Her attention had been captured, as it was every day, by the young man sitting three rows away. The young man with the pink mohawk. The young man whose taut forearm muscles writhed like snakes as his pen sped across the paper. The young man wearing a ripped white T-shirt emblazoned with a crossed-out swastika and the words: *Nazi Punks Fuck Off.*

'He wasn't looking at you, Mya. Don't kid yourself,' the voice whispered again.

'Didn't say he was,' she hissed back. She caught a word that sounded like *signifier* from the stage, saw her classmates frantic-ally scribbling in their notepads. No, she was hopelessly lost. She wished she could pay more attention to Dr Baumann's class. She liked him far better than most of the tutors at the Academy, with their white lab coats and unsmiling faces. Chubby, self-deprecating and never seen without his worn-out tweed blazer and colourful bow tie, Dr Baumann was more her idea of how a traditional college professor should look. Plus, she enjoyed the Morals and Ethics lectures. Her father had his truths, deeply held and incontrovertible. But to Dr Baumann – or Uncle Frank, as she had known him since her early teens – the world was a messy miasma, stuffed full of contradictory arguments and jumbled understanding and the impossibility of certainty.

Yes, she went to Morals and Ethics every day. It was a shame that Marco Pellicci also went to Morals and Ethics every day. He was – she had to admit it to herself now, after three weeks – somewhat distracting.

'But you were looking at him,' the girl behind her continued. She had folded her arms on the chair in front of her, resting her chin on her forearms, not troubling to take notes.

'And you were looking at me.'

'I've looked at you five times in the past hour, Miss Samsara. Each time you were looking at him.'

'Suppose you got lucky?'

'*You* might get lucky. If you ever work up the courage to talk to him.'

'No thanks. I'm happy staring.'

'I can see why. He's a modern art masterpiece. Everything in slightly the wrong place.'

'Piss off, Clare.'

'Ah come on, I only want what's best for you, Mya. In fact, Geraint and I were saying last night that—'

A whine of static drowned out her friend's words. The vast screen behind the lecturer blossomed into blue life and Dr Baumann stepped back from his podium.

'So, gang,' said the professor, 'since I've bored you long

enough with words, here's a pretty video from the Guru which touches on a few of these ethical conundrums. You might find it diverting.' The bounce of his Australian accent turned the statement into a question. Baumann's gaze fell upon her and, as his eyebrow raised, she felt herself blush again. 'Even those malingerers in the back rows who prefer chatting to listening. Shame on you.'

A few titters. Shuffling to the side of the stage, Dr Baumann fiddled with the remote control in his hand. The auditorium fell silent as the screen faded to black.

'Shame on you indeed, Miss Samsara,' murmured the girl in the row behind, her breath tickling her ear. 'Talking in class, you little rebel.'

'Me?'

'Didn't see him looking at anyone else.'

'Remind me why you never get caught.'

'I screw the lecturers, remember?'

'Even Dr Kolstein? With the cleft lip?'

'Especially Kolstein. The cleft lip's pretty sexy.'

'You're sick.'

'You're shallow. Go leer at Jimmy Rotter or whatever his name might be; I shan't judge.'

Rolling her eyes, she conceded defeat – as she generally did to Clare Key. The girl had hair the colour of autumn leaves, usually worn in pigtails that framed a pale, heart-shaped face. Her appearance was slightly doll-like, almost angelic; although frequently she couldn't believe the jokes and obscenities that spilled from that grinning cupid's-bow mouth. Clare's accent veered wildly from scouse twang to cut-glass vowels to braying cockney, sometimes in the same sentence. *It's a Cheshire upbringing, darling,* her new friend had told her early on. *We haven't had any culture of our own since the Romans buggered off, so we have to appropriate it from absolutely everybody else.*

They had been inseparable for more than a fortnight now, having met while Clare was kicking at a vending machine in one of the endlessly winding corridors on the Academy's lower floors. It had been four days into her new life and still she hadn't worked up the courage to talk to any of her new classmates. The girl was banging on the glass, stabbing at the buttons, chuntering under her breath. She approached. *There's kind of a knack to it*, she explained, almost apologetically. As she swiped her passcard against the touchpad screen, the mechanical arm swooped out and grabbed the packet of chewing gum, then slid it down the tube into the pick-up slot. *Hark at the smartarse*, the girl groaned. *Don't tell me you've figured this weird place out already. It's messing with my head, I'm telling you.* Then she smiled, pulling a stray lock of Titian hair over one ear. *I've seen you around. You seem to know where everything is, so I'd best stick with you. Care for a Juicy Fruit?* Feeling only slightly queasy, she had smiled back at the girl who introduced herself as Clare Key. *What the hell do you think we're doing here, anyway?* Clare asked. By way of answer, she merely shrugged shyly.

She knew that Clare, just like the other students at the Academy, had received a letter precisely three months ago offering a salary, accommodation and the promise of a generous research bursary should their progress be judged sufficiently impressive. A golden ticket for young adults who wanted to change the world but hadn't the slightest idea how to go about doing so. Her father still remained frustratingly vague about the selection procedure. What she had managed to ascertain so far was this: they were young, they were talented, they were creative and they were troubled.

Fortunately, Clare never seemed to worry too deeply about why her friend Mya always knew exactly where to go and exactly where to be at the Academy. The other students blundered from testing labs to lecture theatres to consultation offices, stumbling into the wrong rooms and coughing apologies. None of them knew that the building's layout was designed to encourage exploration rather than obedience. No place was forbidden. It was part of her father's plan – to uncover the free thinkers, not ciphers who parroted the thoughts of greatness while never once questioning them. She was happy to play a part in his work, although she had to admit the past couple of weeks had been a little, well, distracting. Life was fine. Life was good. There had not been a Great Wave in some time.

She turned her attention to the screen. A few coughs rang around the hall. Then there was a huge bang and a scream of twisted metal. Startled, she matched the sound with her own small shriek. As the din died away, she heard Clare chuckle.

The screen lit up to show a mellow, hazy woodland vista. The low evening sunlight was dappled by the branches hanging overhead. It had been raining and water glistened on the road that cut through the forest; the water shone on the wheels spinning in an upside-down car. Judging by the black smears of the tyre marks, the vehicle had flipped as it skidded off a tight bend, soaring through the evening air, before its flight was halted by a copse of pine trees. Now the car rested on its crunched roof, rocking back and forth. There was the faint sound of the radio playing a soft rock ballad. Finally the tyres stopped spinning and the camera zoomed in to peer inside the car, probing voyeuristically. Two people hung in their seatbelts, unconscious. Blood ran from the neck of one of the passengers – it was impossible to tell the gender – and pooled on the cracked glass of the sunroof.

She winced. She wished the Academy's film crew wouldn't make these Morals and Ethics videos so damned dramatic. Her father would get a complaint one of these days.

The camera's perspective flipped to the driver of another car, peering over his shoulder as he negotiated the bend successfully, pulling up beside the crash scene. The unknown driver killed the engine and stepped out. There was silence but for the tweeting of birds. Then a voice, slightly clipped as if the language was not the speaker's first tongue, filled the auditorium.

'You are first on the crash scene. You see two people inside the car. They are wounded. Time is running short for both of them. You have a sweater that you can use as a tourniquet. But wait... you look closer. You see that the driver of the car is your partner. And the passenger is their lover. What do you do?'

More nervous laughter scattered around the lecture hall like buckshot. A few seats away she heard Clare snort, muttering something that sounded like *Let the bastard suffer.* The camera focused on the drip-drip-drip of blood on the sunroof.

'Your partner is wounded severely,' the narrator continued, 'perhaps fatally. The carotid artery has been severed. Your makeshift tourniquet may well fail. Meanwhile, their lover has a wound to the femoral artery. They are far more likely to survive, but only with immediate medical assistance. What do you do?

'You have two choices. Tie the tourniquet around your partner's neck, even though they betrayed you, even though their chances of survival are remote. Or tie the tourniquet around the thigh of your partner's lover. They have a far better chance of survival. But you know all too well what they have done.

'So, class – what would you do? Just what would you do?'

The lights went up in the auditorium. She could see the rest of the Academy's new intake blinking, rubbing their eyes, staring around as if the answers might be daubed on the shining white walls of the lecture hall. She was the only person in the crowd who knew the voice of the narrator.

Her father.

5

The New Intake (fresh meat)

The group took shelter from the harsh sun in the gargantuan shadow of the Academy building. The grass beneath them was yellowed and brittle to the touch. The summer had spilled the whole way into the middle of September and rain was only a memory nowadays.

'I say let the bastard suffer,' Clare announced, her eyes concealed behind a pair of huge sunglasses. She tossed her red pigtails as a murmur ran around the circle. The five females among the eight of them nodded appreciatively. The boys grinned sheepishly. Courtney, clad from neck to ankle in dark drapes despite the heat of the day, tapped out applause on her palm with purple-painted nails. 'He made his bed. Now die in it.'

'I heard you whisper that while we were watching,' she said. Clare smiled back at her. No one else seemed to have heard her speak. This happened a lot during the after-class discussion circles. Somehow she couldn't quite make her presence felt.

'But isn't it a wee bit more complicated than that?' said Alec. His Scottish burr was so quiet that a mild gust of wind could have carried it off, but the gaze of the whole group was immediately upon him; the skinny boy with a blond quiff like a 1950s teen idol possessed a nervy charisma. He fidgeted with his plaid shirt tails, his seawater-grey eyes fixed on each of them in turn. 'Your girlfriend – or boyfriend's – lover … well, don't they deserve a chance? They might not know. Might not be aware you even exist, like—'

'That's what I'm saying,' Clare broke in. 'Who cares about the other person? They mean nothing. But the twat who cheated on me … yeah, I'd want to see them suffer. I'd let the other person live, just to spite whoever betrayed me.'

'Hold on now.' Alec raised his hands in a placatory gesture. 'Who's saying you're the good guy or gal in this whole mess? You might have been a bad partner. Pushed them away. Driven them into the affair, aye? Maybe there was a reason for them cheating on you, and if you save them you'll find out why. Otherwise you might end up torturing yourself for the rest of your life.' He spread his arms out wide. 'More than that, think of how long you've been together. You still love them, despite what they did. Don't they deserve a chance to, eh, patch things up? Bad turn of phrase, I admit.'

'You're too soft, McTavish,' Clare smirked, popping a stick of Juicy Fruit gum into her mouth. 'They had their chance. Save the random bitch, let your partner die. That's the only answer. Baumann's losing it. Easiest M&E puzzle he's set us so far. Too bloody easy.'

'Not much of a discussion,' said a new voice, 'if you're telling everyone the answer.'

Her head snapping over her shoulder, she followed Clare's irritated gaze and stared up at the source of that voice and felt as if she might pass out. He was standing right behind her, his face concealed by shadows, the false perspective making his pink mohawk reach higher than the Academy's tower. His cherry-red boots glinted like the blood in the video.

'I beg your pardon?' said Clare, removing her sunglasses and staring pointedly at the new arrival.

'Just saying, we ain't got the full facts, have we?' said Marco Pellicci, brushing a hand through his neon spikes. 'Look, there's a boy in your missus's car. How do you even know they're shagging your girl in the first place? Might be an innocent explanation. Hitchhiker. Or an old school friend.'

She felt her jaw working soundlessly – she had to say something, she needed to say something, because she had the answers, her father had given her the answers. Marco noticed her and paused, gesturing for her to speak. Struck dumb, she shook her head, blushing horribly for a record-breaking third time that day.

Marco cocked his head, waiting for her until the silence grew uncomfortable, then shrugged and picked up his spiel. 'Yeah, anyway, we was told *lover* in that video. But how can we know for sure? Ever heard of an unreliable narrator? Maybe it's your own paranoia talking.' The boy grinned wolfishly. 'Maybe you did know. Maybe you've been stalking them, driving right on their tail. They're running scared and took the corner too fast on a slippy road. In fact – you're a psycho and you caused the crash.' He clicked his fingers, forming a pistol with thumb and forefinger and pointing at her – at *her*, no one else, at her – as if aiming at her heart. 'Now that, boys and girls, is a real moral and ethical fucking dilemma.'

There was silence. Even Clare was lost for words, her gum hanging from her lower lip. She gawped up at the boy; the brutish boots, the leather jacket, the obscene T-shirt, the ludicrous hairstyle. His dark eyes were like coals, his upper lip curled as if daring anyone to challenge him. Then Marco looked at her again and his expression softened, his sneer smoothing into a gentle smile.

'That's an interesting way of looking at things, big man,'

Alec said at last. 'Why don't you sit on down with us and, eh, expound your theory, as Dr Baumann might say.'

'Sweet,' said the boy with the mohawk. She saw both Clare and Courtney shuffle over to make room for him and felt a stab of jealousy. But Marco ignored them and sat down next to her. His proximity was dizzying; apprehension and excitement entwining around each other. Synapses popped like fireworks as the rough cuff of his jacket brushed against her bare arm. 'Pleased to meet you crazy kids. I'm Marco, yeah?'

She already knew his name, unlike the others in their discussion circle. She also knew that Marco Pellicci didn't belong here. He wasn't a student at her father's Academy. He was a trespasser, a fraud, an imposter.

But that didn't seem to matter right now.

6

The White Prison

You know those movies or television shows where they show the prisoner banging on the doors, kicking the walls of their cell, howling their head off? *Let me out! I'm innocent, man, I didn't do it! There's been a big mistake. You got it all wrong! Let me out, I'm telling you. Let me out, let me out, let me out!* Such bullshit. Don't let fiction fool you. When you're locked up, you simply sit there and wait. You are still and quiet. It's a prison, even if they dress it up with euphemistic words like *psychiatric ward* or *secure hospital*. It is designed to hold you there until they are ready to deal with you. Until then, you're not leaving. No one is coming to let you out. No matter how loudly you shout or scream.

Seconds slide into minutes. Minutes slide into hours that slide into days. In this colourless place I have become obsessed with time. I've tried to monitor the beats of my heart; 80 beats per minute, 4,800 beats per hour, 115,000 beats per day. Even if I could count the whole way to 115,000, it would not prove the passage of one day. I can't tick off my heartbeat while I am asleep, and here I sleep often – far, far more than I'm sure is normal. If I had to guess, I would say I've been here for six days because I've been fed on eighteen occasions. I wake up and within minutes along comes Anna with the food trolley.

But do they feed me because I have woken up, or have I timed my sleeping to coincide with mealtimes? Questions without answers; these are my obsessions.

Inside the White Prison I am free to do as I wish, so long as my activities do not extend outside these gently sloping walls. I am clean, perpetually first-date clean, because the shower is soothing and when the water runs into my eyes it blurs my vision and I can pretend I'm somewhere else, anywhere else. It's better to dream. I imagine Marco's hands around my waist, the muscles of his forearms binding us together, his lips pressing against the droplets on my shoulders. It's almost too much to bear.

After showering I often find a clean smock has been slid under my door. At first I changed demurely beneath my blanket, conscious of unseen eyes, but now I'm happy to pad around naked. At times it still crosses my mind that I might be on reality TV and the slack-jawed audience is voting to keep me in my cell for cheap thrills. Or maybe I'm the star attraction on an online porn channel. I doubt any viewers are getting their money's worth.

My video screen still flicks between blackness and that gentle, lulling scene of flatland bulrushes. No sign of any human life after that first frazzled day. Only the marshlands and the breeze. There must be deeper meaning in that utterly unremarkable vista. I stare at the fenland panorama for hours when it's there, taking in every angle – even standing on my head, or walking away then casting a quick glance back to catch the screen unawares. I have seen nothing, but that doesn't mean there is nothing. There are answers, I'm certain there are answers, but I just can't see them yet. Sometimes, I remind myself, the answers appear if you look for them long enough. I remember when I was in my early teens and my parents took me to the Salvador

Dali museum in Girona; unimpressed by anything, expression set to perma-boredom. But even my sulky little thirteen-year-old self was taken aback – not a little awestruck – by the giant painting in the centre of the gallery. The man made from rock, encased to his waist on a craggily sinister shoreline, a tree sprouting from his chest, a deep fissure splitting his bowed bald head. I stared at the vast artwork for what could have been hours, entranced in a way I have never been before or since, every moment finding new ways to assess and interpret the image. No such luck with these marshes and bulrushes, the countryside nothingness. No hidden meanings, no secret codes, no optical illusion. They are marshes and bulrushes, that's all they are, I'm sure. But still I keep staring. Will Marco come back? Was Marco ever there? Did I just imagine him and my doppelganger walking hand in hand?

It was a dream. Surely it was a dream. I shouldn't torture myself this way. But I can't help it.

I'm still staring at the video screen when my door slides open. I imagine it will be Anna-of-the-paneer, Annapurna. Instead I see an unknown man standing in the doorway. He has an upright bearing, almost military, and unlike Anna there is no name-badge on his claret tunic. Obviously a different breed of White Prison employee from my favourite orderly. A guard? Immediately I think of the knife concealed beneath my mattress. They've rumbled me. I've been such an idiot. Oh shit.

'Exercise,' says the stranger. He has gingery crew-cut hair and a blandly handsome face, the eyes a fraction too close together. His short-sleeved shirt displays tattooed forearms, ropy with muscle. Surely he must be a guard. 'Please follow me, Miss Dala.'

A new development. Perhaps an opportunity to find out a little more. I flap the baggy sleeves of my smock like a broken-winged albatross. Here's an opportunity to have a little fun.

'Oh gosh, not exercise – I forgot my Lycra,' I tell him. 'I'll get my clothes all messy and sweaty.'

'Exercise,' he repeats.

I sigh theatrically. 'I can't exercise in this. It's too baggy, the trousers trail on the floor. No one will want me on their dodgeball team, I'd be a liability.'

'Exercise.'

'Do you not have some jogging bottoms and a football shirt?' I don't know why I'm winding this man up, just like I irritated the nice woman who brought me the beef stew. I suppose it's a way of wresting back power, if only for a few moments. 'If you've got a kit handy,' I tell him, thinking of Marco, 'I'm a big West Ham fan. Claret and blue. Two world wars and one World Cup, I'm forever blowing bubbles.'

I hate football, I know almost nothing about West Ham United, but Marco lives for his beloved Hammers and I feel warmed after bringing a tiny sliver of his presence into this coldly impersonal place. But in my memories, I can't see Marco's face properly. He's blurry … out of focus … a shadow figure. But I can feel what he means to me deep inside myself. I remember how he made me feel when we were together. Marco came closest to making me better, of that I'm sure. I even allowed myself to believe he had cured me. That's why being stuck in the White Prison feels like something of a betrayal; because being locked up here proves I had only ever been in remission.

'Please, Miss Dala,' the guard says patiently, 'would you follow me to the exercise yard?'

'Oh no, not the exercise yard. I've seen prison movies.

Everyone gets stabbed there.' I pluck at the hem of my smock. 'You simply can't get blood out of white cloth.'

'Replacements will be provided.'

My head snaps up. Was that a joke? I stare at the guard but see no trace of humour on his face.

'Follow me,' he says. 'Please.'

Well, manners maketh man. So I follow.

The corridor seems to slope as we pass a string of doors identical to mine. Are we going up or down? It's impossible to tell whether my cell is above or below ground. Sometimes it seems we are at quite a high altitude, other times I feel as if I have been buried.

There's someone else in the passageway with us now. A figure – young, slight, male – is sitting slumped against the wall. He is holding his head in his hands and all I can see is tousled straw-coloured hair. He glances upwards and I stare into pale, hopeless eyes, the same grey shade as his smock.

'I knew I'd see you here,' he whispers, 'sooner or later.'

'What do you mean?' I ask him, caught between intrigue and fright. There is an alkaline taste on my tongue and my pulse is beating out of time. 'Do I know you?'

'I was hoping that you wouldn't sink too,' he tells me. His voice – a conspiratorial Caledonian accent – is low and soaked with empathy. 'But I'm afraid it takes one to know one.'

'Move along,' the guard orders. 'You shouldn't be out here. You're risking your special privileges.'

The young man pushes himself to his feet and sidles away from us down the corridor. I think I hear laughter; a softly despairing titter. I try to crane my neck around to see him but the guard blocks my line of sight, steering me firmly forward. For a while the only sound is the whisper of our rubber-soled sneakers on the floor. My shoes are fastened with fabric straps.

The purpose is obvious; no laces to weave into a hanging noose. The guard has a loping stride that is deceptively speedy and I have to hurry to keep up. There is a faint clanging sound ahead of us.

'Who was that guy?' I say to his broad back.

No response. Not that I expected one. We take another few corners – the floor is curving now, like a racetrack – and the clanging has grown much louder.

'I'm sure all the patients tell you this,' I try again, 'but I shouldn't be here. Honestly. There's been a terrible mistake. If you point me in the general direction of the exit, I'll see myself out. No trouble.'

No response.

'How long have you worked here?'

Nothing again. The sound of clanging is now a metronomic boom. The guard is pretending not to hear. Or maybe he can't hear. I'd imagine that working here, in the White Prison, you need to be able to block out a lot of unpleasant sounds.

'How's this place for job satisfaction?' I continue, straining to make myself heard above the din. 'Competitive salary, long-term career prospects, private dental care?'

His squared-away head turns slightly towards me. 'We are here to help you, Mya,' he says. 'We're here to keep you safe.'

A variation on what Anna told me. The employees here must have a stock list of responses. We stop by a set of double doors. The guard swipes a pass at a small blue light glowing in the wall. He turns to stare at me. Despite the muscles and the tattoos, he doesn't look like a tyrant. His eyes are red and rheumy like an albino rabbit. I am sure there is pity in his expression.

'Now we wait for the lift,' he says. A tic is flickering below his left cheekbone. The sound is spooking him.

'Chill out here and listen to the drum solo? Is that Buddy Rich you've got locked up down the hallway? I hear he can be quite a handful.'

The banging sound is very close now. There is a doorway at the end of the corridor – seeing an end to the corridor is surprising in itself – and a small round window, similar to a porthole on an ocean liner.

'What's down there?' I ask.

The guard's weak eyes flick towards the door.

'Who's down there?'

'No one who should concern you.'

'Well, I am concerned. I shouldn't be concerned. I'm here to get better and now I'm worried. Frightened, even. This could set my treatment back months.'

'Miss Dala—'

'You know what? I'm going to check it out.'

Before he can stop me, I'm away down the corridor, walking quickly – almost running – towards the source of that endless clanging. I'm sure the passage is growing narrower the further I go. When I was walking behind the guard it was the width of a train carriage, now the walls brush my shoulders. There is nothing in my head but that tribal boom.

Finally I reach the door at the end of the corridor. I stare into the porthole window. I see nothing but an empty white cell identical to my own. The same bed, the same slightly curving walls.

The clanging stops. In the silence I can hear my heartbeat, my ragged breath.

Then a face appears in the window with shocking suddenness. I let out a small scream. I can barely make out any features, only furiously burning eyes. The eyes are black, the shading between pupil and iris indefinable.

Those eyes are quite, quite mad.

The guard's arms lock around my waist. I am pulled back down the corridor. I am dragged away from the sight of that awful, inhuman glare — and I don't resist.

7

The New Intake (fresh meat)

The motorcycle bucked and roared and Marco Pellicci tore away in a puff of smoke. They watched him bent over the handlebars, pink mohawk bobbing in the wind, as the bike sped across the flatlands and left the Academy building far behind. She wondered, only for the merest moment, what it would be like to clamber aboard that huge snorting beast with Marco. Wrapping her arms around his waist, listening to the fabric creak in his leather jacket as she laid her head on his shoulder, nestling into his heat. Feeling the pulsing of the engine beneath them as the bike picked up speed. Trusting him with her life.

'Not really like the rest of the students, is he?' said Alec wryly. 'Do you think he won a competition to be here?'

'I think he applied for one of the janitor jobs,' Clare sniffed, 'and this is a great big mistake.'

'Ach, don't be so cruel. The big man's smart. Rough around the edges, but smart.'

It had been two weeks since Marco joined their group after Dr Baumann's lecture. The boy with the spiked pink hair and the lip curled in an ever-present sneer remained the main topic of conversation.

The three of them wandered towards the bus stop with hands clasped over their folders. It had become an unspoken tradition to have their end-of-day coffees in town rather than the canteen; talking just felt easier out of the shadow of the Academy tower. It had been one of their less interesting days. Three hours of staring at slideshows of the temporal lobes of mice illuminated by alternating stress stimuli. Maybe later she would ask Dad the relevance of that part of the course. She still hadn't told her new friends about him. She was worried that Clare and Alec would look at her differently if they knew her father's identity. Unlike her friends, she wasn't living in the Academy's student accommodation. Her backstory, almost true, was that she was a local girl and stayed at her parents' home in the nearby town to save money. It wasn't too far from reality – Frank Baumann enjoyed bringing local residents into their projects: *The battle for hearts and minds*, as he never tired of informing them. The real reason she lived off campus was she was afraid a loose-lipped member of the Academy domestic staff might spill her secret. She didn't like to lie to Clare and Alec, the first two real friends she had made in years, but she was desperately nervous that they wouldn't accept her if they knew how connected she was to the inner workings of the Academy. She needed to be liked. She needed to be normal. She needed to be just like everybody else.

'See, none of us really know why we're here,' Alec went on. 'I mean, I know some specky gadge came up to me at a graduate recruitment fair and asked me how much I really knew about myself. How much I wanted to know about myself. Screw that – I just saw the figures. Twenty-five grand a year to keep living the student life? Sign me up. And I'm pretty sure the same thing happened to you and you.' He jabbed a forefinger at them to illustrate his point. 'Because that's what happened to everyone here. We're all pointy-headed wastrels with nothing better to do with our lives. But Marco … eh, I don't see him as the university type.'

Clare nodded. 'I reckon the only time he's been in a university is to steal library books.'

'Sure. Bet he reads them, though.'

'Oh, why don't you just bang him, McTavish?'

'I can dream. Don't think I'm his type. Seems keener on the wee beauty to my left.'

She rolled her eyes, feigning disinterest. Clare wasn't fooled. Her friend's face creased into an oddly sad smile, but Clare said nothing and she was grateful.

'Mad Marco,' Alec chuckled, spotting the bus chugging down the road towards them and flagging it down. 'You know, sometimes I think the biggest mystery of this whole project is what the hell he's doing here.'

She was lying on her bed in her father's house later that evening, thinking of nothing much – or maybe thinking about Marco, just a little – when the rolling sensations started up in her brain. The awful currents. Not now. Oh God, not now.

She bit down on her bottom lip. She tried to wish the feelings away.

Her hands went to the tops of her thighs. Through the thin fabric of her leggings, she felt the indentations in the skin; the criss-crossed track marks that mapped out the path of so many past Great Waves.

A nauseating sheen of sweat had already sprinkled out onto her forehead. She wiped away the perspiration and her hand came back bloody. Her palm was shredded and torn. She stared at the penknife clutched in her right fist, its blade winking red. She had carved her left hand into pieces. No, no, that wasn't real. She blinked rapidly, gripping on to the bedsheets, and the horror vanished. No blood, no knife, no illusions. But she knew there would be more.

'Please,' she whispered to nobody. 'Please help me.'

Rivulets of black water began to ebb into her bedroom. Through the door jamb, the cracks around the windows, from underneath her bed. First a trickle, then a stream, then a flood. Soon her floor was covered with a sheet of shimmering opaque water an inch deep and rising. The water was a mirrorless surface that trapped rather than reflected light. She felt her eyes rolling back in their sockets and dug her nails into the calloused flesh of her upper thighs, willing herself to remain anchored in reality. The black waters were rising and she could smell them now, a damp and flat odour that choked any joyful thoughts. Only a few minutes ago she had been wondering – again – how it might feel to sit on the back of Marco's motorcycle, her arms wrapped around him, her head resting against his back as he rode faster and faster. The fantasy had been drowned by the dead-smelling water that had reached the bed and was lipping around her fingers and toes. Now she could only sink. She moaned and squeezed her eyes shut. Her body immersed, the alien cold bit into her and she gasped. In a few seconds the water would reach her face, swamping her mouth and stuffing up her nostrils, and she was paralysed.

Come with me, Mya.

A familiar voice. A familiar touch. She opened her eyes and saw a figure that had once lived standing over her, unaffected by the freezing lake in her bedroom. Her mother reached out a hand. Her mother beckoned.

She didn't want to take hold of that grey and shrivelled hand. She couldn't bear the clammy, grasping touch. But what was the alternative? Her room had started to roll sickeningly, the still waters churning black plumes. The waves were coming.

It's not so bad further down, said her mother. Her voice was so soft, so reasonable, so missed. *Here we sink.*

Then there was a booming sound like an earthquake that shocked her back to the physical world. Retching, she pushed herself up from the bed, scrabbling free of the blanket's grip. The ghost of her mother had vanished. Her clothes were dry. There was no water, no waves. Leaping to her feet, she stumbled to the window and pulled it open, taking huge breaths of the evening air to rid herself of that awful brackish taste.

It took a few moments to realise that Marco Pellicci was outside her house. He was sitting astride his chuntering motor-cycle. She realised that the earthquake sound had been the bike's engine backfiring. Marco had saved her from a Great Wave without even knowing. Grinning, he waved up at her.

Barely thinking about what she was doing, she careered down the stairs, rushing past her startled father as he emerged from the kitchen with a tall glass of lemon tea, grabbing the first coat she saw from the pegs in the hallway. She threw open the front door and ran outside, only wanting to put as much distance as possible between herself and the house. Marco's eyebrows shot up in concern at her bedraggled appearance.

'Jesus,' he said, 'are you okay?'

'Take me somewhere,' she whispered, swinging her leg over the motorbike's pillion and grabbing hold of him. His body felt so warm, so solid, so real. 'Anywhere.'

8

The New Intake (fresh meat)

'It's a puzzle,' Marco said later, tracing a forefinger around the rim of his pint glass. 'I can't figure it out for the life of me. But I'm not that clever. Maybe you can.'

Again he smiled at her. There was an engaging shyness in his expression, a vulnerability that she knew Clare and Alec and the rest of their friends would scarcely believe. She managed to smile back. She couldn't believe how normal she felt; sometimes it took hours after a Great Wave for her mind to settle, even days. But she had never been shocked back to reality before, and there was nothing she could say to this boy that would convey her gratitude because he couldn't possibly know. She didn't want him to know – she wanted to keep her weirdnesses from Marco for as long as possible. She stared around the shabby pub, the Grey Goat, and wondered if any of her fellow drinkers realised how different she was to them, as if they might smell something strange off her. No, she told herself, the only thing they might smell was body odour. Her hair was a mess, she hadn't bothered to change since her three-mile run earlier that evening and her last shower had been that morning, but she didn't care. She was out, away from the waves, away from that sombre, beckoning figure. Away from her mother's drowned touch.

Here we sink.

She didn't want to sink. She wanted to stay on the surface, fighting the undertow. Maybe Marco could keep her afloat.

'You and me are the only locals,' Marco continued when she didn't speak. 'At the Academy I mean, not this pub, there's loads of locals here. The other students are from far away. We're the flatlanders.' He laughed and took another swig of his drink. 'Maybe like the flat-earthers. Me, at least. I can't speak for you.'

'How ...' she started. Her throat closed and for a second she tasted that horribly familiar dank water. Swallowing hard, she tried again, 'How did you find me?'

Marco pursed his lips. 'I'm a dangerous stalker. But at least I'm honest about it.'

She allowed herself a tiny taste of her rosé wine. She didn't want to get too drunk, but the sheer relief of being out of the waves had spiked her body with adrenaline, turning every sip into a quadruple shot of high-tension liquor.

'Why?' she said again. 'Seriously. Why bother with me?'

'You don't say much. Everyone else says loads. Only proving they know the square root of fuck-all.' Marco shrugged. 'Maybe you got the answers, I don't know. Someone must.'

'It is a puzzle,' she agreed. She realised she needed to tread cautiously in this conversation. She didn't want him to know about her father, not quite yet. 'How ... how did you get in? Into the Academy, I mean. You must have had a test ...'

Marco shook his head. 'Just a letter through the door. Asked if I wanted a chit-chat with some geezer with a load of letters after his name. Said they was looking to offer places for people around the area and I fitted the bill. *We're changing minds*, that's what they said. Could end up with a top job and plenty of cash. My mama was pleased. The last official letter we got was my bro Tony's court summons.'

Those two words: *changing minds*. Her father had been very pleased when he dreamed up that catchphrase. She remembered Frank Baumann slapping Dad on his shoulders and telling him, *That's why we call you the Guru.*

'My other brother Roberto reckons it's a tax dodge,' Marco went on, draining his pint. 'Like, get the scummy locals into your posh college and nail a big charity grant. He's probably right. But hey, what other chances have we got in this benighted and beshitted corner of England?'

'Do you live with your brothers?' she asked, trying to steer the conversation away from the Academy.

'Used to be five of us in one tiny terraced house – big crazy Italian family, you know? Now we're getting smaller and smaller. Tony flew the nest ages ago and Robbo left last year, shacking up with his missus Saskia. An old missus that's now the new missus, a schoolyard-sweethearts-reconnecting kind of thing. Our little sister Sofia is going off travelling too – she's a hippy chick, but we allow it. So for the first time in forever it'll just be me and my mama.' Marco's eyes lit up with a sentimental glow. 'But my Uncle Giuseppe lives round the corner. I hope you get to meet him, he's some character. About a hundred years old and still drinks like a sailor on shore leave.'

'What about your father?'

'Dad's dead.' A tic dragged up the corner of his mouth. 'Lung cancer got him. I was eleven. Shit luck.'

'My mother died when I was young,' she blurted out. Despite the alcohol, she still recalled that grasping grey touch.

'That must be how we found each other, you know? You pick up on it.'

She blinked. 'Maybe. I'd ... I'd never thought of it like that before. Is that a superstition?'

'Nah, human nature, innit?' he said with certainty. 'You merge with people just like you – and you don't even realise.' He looked at his watch. 'Hey, you want another drink?'

She must have nodded agreement even though the wine was fuzzing her brain. He picked his way through the maze of cheap wooden tables and chairs, waving to a couple of old men nursing half-pints in the far corner. Since he was distracted, she allowed herself to stare; she had never seen anyone quite like him before. The heavy boots, the red tartan trousers, the low light glinting off the metal studs in the lapels of his leather jacket. He was the sort of man she imagined people would cross the road to avoid. Yet she saw the way he had waved to those old men, how he was courteously nudging the barmaid's attention towards two women even though he had been waiting longer. Finally, holding their fresh drinks, he turned back to her. His gaze was on hers and the pub lounge had constricted to a tunnel, and the sounds of laughter and gurgling beer pumps and the click-clack of pool balls was quelled, and there was no one in existence but her and the boy with the pink mohawk.

Then a middle-aged man with slumped shoulders and reddened eyes barrelled straight into Marco, spilling their drinks down the front of his T-shirt. Marco stared at the man, his lips drawing back from his teeth, an unsettling blankness in his expression. She saw his knuckles whitening on the stem of her wine glass and her mind conjured up a horribly vivid image: the glass smashing into the drunk man's face, blood-flecked foam soaking the carpet.

'You've had enough, Clive,' Marco said. He was at least twenty years younger than the man in the stained cardigan but there was no doubting the dominance in his voice. 'Get gone before you do some damage to yourself.'

'Okay, okay, Marco,' the man called Clive said. There was a

wheeze in his voice and his rheumy eyes were open wide in alarm. 'I'm away right now. Just ... just keep yourself relaxed, eh?'

Clive backed away, open-palmed in supplication. He bunted open the door with a meaty hip, then he was out into the night.

She realised the jocular sounds of the pub had fallen silent. Marco returned to their table bearing their half-full glasses. His breath was coming with an odd catching sound. She realised she was sweating. He sat down, placing their drinks on the table with prissy good care, and stared at her. His expression was impossible to read. Then he smiled and it was as if he was a different person. His eyes were twinkling, filled with merriment – how could she have imagined that strange dark blankness?

'Silly old bugger,' Marco said, alive with good humour once more. She tried not to think of that emptily hungry expression when he confronted the drunk. 'Never seen him sober – he can't hold his whisky. Top boy in his day, Clive. Inter City Firm, but he got old and slow.' He drummed his fingertips on his thighs. 'Anyway, you heard the whole story about my family. What about yours?'

She smiled weakly. 'Not much to tell.'

'Ah, come on.' He winked at her. 'I love family histories.'

'It's pretty sad.'

He spread his hands wide. 'We'll make it less sad together. I promise you this works. It's therapy, swear down. Your mum's dead – that sucks, don't remind me. So tell me something great about her. One way she always made you laugh. What was the funniest thing your mum ever did?'

She thought of the colourless and disquieting figure that glided through her subconscious. Her brain twisted her memories, reducing her mother to a nightmare. But that hadn't been Mum – how did Marco know this? Her mother, when she was well, had been full of joy and love. She would never want to hurt her daughter, scare her daughter. Maybe after tonight she wouldn't see her mother's ghost rising from the dark waves again. She felt another rush of gratitude towards Marco.

'No one's ever asked me that before,' she said quietly. 'I think I'd like to talk about her a little, if that's okay.'

So she talked and she barely knew what she was saying, but Marco listened and nodded and laughed in every one of the right places, and he held her hand briefly when the tears sprung to her eyes. More drinks went down and the alcohol further stoked what was already kindling between them. Before she knew it, the bell had tolled for last orders and they were the only two people left in the pub. They emerged into the brisk snap of the night air, Marco holding the door open for her and draping his jacket over her shoulders. The leather was heavy but felt beautifully safe; a protective shield. Their hands were close but not quite touching.

'I'm not safe to ride the bike, otherwise I'd drop you home,' he said apologetically. 'Look, I'll call you a taxi. I got just enough cash left. Don't worry – I'll walk back to mine.'

Marco was already reaching for the phone in his pocket when she stopped him. In that moment she felt she was on a film set. She was tear-stained, her make-up smeared, and even through the febrile clouds of alcohol she could smell herself, but she knew what she wanted. What she needed. *Or I could just go home with you?* she said, then laughed at how wonderfully corny the line sounded. *So long as you have a working shower.*

But that never happened. She wasn't brave enough to ask him; maybe she never would be. Instead, her mind took a short sojourn from reality and before she quite understood what was going on, she was stepping unsteadily into the back seat of a minicab and he was waving at her from the doorway of the pub. At least, she presumed that dark figure standing there with his hand raised in farewell was Marco. The lights behind him had cast his face in shadow and through the alcohol mists she could see only a silhouette. As the taxi pulled away, she wondered whether that person could have been anyone at all.

9

The White Prison

Arms out, arms straight. Reach up. Stretch. Bend down, keep going, touch your toes. Hold, hold, rest. Breathe. Shoulders back, pull. One foot in front of the other, right knee forward, pull, tense. Left knee forward, pull, tense. Rest. Straighten up, hands on hips, push forward. Hold, hold, rest. Breathe.

Rest. Breathe. Rest and breathe.

There are at least two hundred strangers in this exercise yard. Maybe three or four hundred. Maybe more. I'm not that tall and around me I can see only a sea of grey tracksuits and perspiring faces. My ears are resonating with the communal chorus of puffs and pants. There is fake spongy grass beneath my trainers, the rubber soles squashing down the rubber stalks. Effort has gone into making the yard look like a garden, but it's still a walled garden. I wonder what would happen if I made a sudden break for that wall. The bricks are stacked around twelve feet high; easy enough to vault over with the aid of an accomplice. They can't hold us here against our will – or can they? We're not criminals. I doubt some of us are even that insane.

We take our orders from a ruddy-faced woman who wears a green uniform. She has close-cropped blonde hair and looks to be in her early fifties. Occasionally I sneak glances at my fellow residents of the White Prison as we stretch and lunge and rest and breathe in unison. No one resists but no one smiles either. I am conscious of the eyes of some of the men flicking over at me, particularly when I lunge forward in a sprinter's crouch upon the leader's instructions. Enjoy the view, gents. It is strangely heartening that whatever pills they're pumping into us here haven't dulled the senses completely.

Talking of senses, I'm not totally convinced that we are outside. The nose knows best. Yes, there is sky above me and a faint outline of the sun through the grey pillowy cloud cover. But the air smells wrong; too warm for an overcast day and faintly medicinal. There is a light breeze but I'm sure it hasn't changed speed or direction in the half-hour we've been exercising. For verification, I lick the tip of my forefinger and hold it to the wind. The blonde woman spots me and her eyes narrow. Quickly I drop to my haunches, concentrating on bending and stretching, resting and breathing. No unwanted attention, Mya. The sooner I slot in seamlessly, the sooner I shed my newbie tag and lose the guards' natural suspicion of the fresh arrival, the sooner I can work out why I'm here in the first place.

My memory is still so fuzzy. It feels as if I'm shining a torch into the haunted house of my brain and the light is feeble and flickering. There are nooks and crannies full of secrets that I can't make out. What have I done to myself? I rarely remember the onset or aftermath of a Great Wave but this time it feels different, far more powerful. If I overdosed before I was taken here, I must have taken something pretty strong. Or maybe they gave me something pretty strong when I arrived. Or both. I can't remember… I just can't remember… I just can't…

No, stop. I remember Marco. I remember how much he loves me. Hold on to that thought, Mya. Does Marco know I'm here? Is Marco working to get me out of here? Is Marco with a girl who looks like me but isn't me, isn't me at all... No, no, that was a dream. A lurid fantasy. A nightmare.

'You're not crazy.'

My head jerks round. I see rows of strangers performing limp attempts at burpees. Not one of them is looking at me. Certain that the gaze of the blonde leader is again tracking in my direction, I stare at the heels of the woman in front.

'Hey there.' That female voice echoes in my head again. It is impossible to tell which direction it is coming from. 'You don't have to look. It's better if you don't look.'

'What did you say?'

'I said you're not crazy.'

'Oh yeah? How would you know?' There is truculence in my voice. Do I want to be crazy? Do I want to be here forever? My father used to think my depression was teenage attention-seeking. At least until the first accident. Then, finally, he understood.

'You're too sane for your own good, Mya.'

Suddenly my legs won't work; I have to concentrate on putting one foot in front of the other and my heart is jarring arrhythmically and my lungs are imploding and I'm choking in the unnatural air.

'What?' I manage to cough out. 'How do you know my name?'

'You heard me, dummy. You're too sane for this place.'

'Is this an internal monologue? Because that means I really have gone crazy.'

'Are you speaking out loud?'

'I think so.'

'Then I'm no more a voice in your head than you're a voice in mine.'

'Maybe we're voices in each other's heads.'

There is a low chuckle. 'Well... I suppose you're right about that.'

For a few moments I hear nothing but the huffing breaths and I wonder if my new friend has gone away. If she was ever really there in the first place.

'In twenty seconds,' the stranger says, and I feel oddly relieved that she hasn't abandoned me, 'the instructor will tell us to place our hands on our calves and bend down towards our knees. When she tells us to do that, Mya, turn your head to the left. And say hello.'

My muscles twitch in anticipation. This person knows me. She knows my name. What matters most is that she knows I shouldn't be here. What else does she know? Does she know how to get out of this place?

'Now, team,' the blonde instructor announces in her reedy trill, 'place both of your hands onto your calves and reach down towards your knees. Bend and stretch. Are you ready, team?'

There is no acknowledgement. This group doesn't seem the sort for *hoo-yahs* and high-fives. But everyone complies. As I clap my hands around my legs and bend forward, I look over my right shoulder and see a row of sagging, uninterested faces.

'I said left, dummy.' The voice is amused. I pull my gaze to the opposite side – *just keeping the neck muscles nice and supple, Ms Gym Class Leader* – and see someone staring back at me. The girl's face is thin and wry, a shaggy dark fringe hanging over her forehead. One startlingly green eye drops down in a broad wink. Then the cheery expression vanishes immediately, disquietingly, and the girl's face is as blank and incurious as the rest of the group.

We rise and stretch, rest and breathe. Rest and breathe. In the past minute I think I have forgotten how to breathe.

'You didn't say hello.' The dark girl sounds disappointed.

'I was scared,' I admit. 'Everyone else would have heard us.'

'No, not them.' There is an edge of contempt in her voice. 'They're too far gone.'

Too far gone. The flatness of those three syllables clanks like the door to a tomb closing. How far is too far gone? How long will it take until I'm too far gone as well? How long will it take for this place to grind me down? I want to ask this green-eyed stranger endless questions. Maybe I shouldn't ask her anything. For all I know, this is some sort of trap – although seeing as how I'm trapped already, how could it be any worse?

'How long have you been—' I'm struggling to find the right word. A resident? An inmate? A prisoner?

'I've been a patient here for almost five years.' For the first time I pick up a trace of accent, a matter-of-fact but cheery timbre that brings to mind woodlands and chilly winters and roaring fires, possibly Nordic? 'I don't mind telling you, I've been very patient.'

The wordplay in her sing-song voice makes me smile. It may be the first time I have smiled since I've been locked in the White Prison.

'What's your name?' I ask. 'You know mine. Somehow. So turnaround's fair play.'

'Johanna,' the girl says. Is that a memory emerging or just lactic acid tingling in my muscles?

'Give us hope, Johanna,' I say involuntarily, remembering a song that my mother used to dance around the house to when slightly drunk.

I hear a stifled cough, perhaps a laugh. 'Oh, what was that?'

'Sorry. Nothing.'

'You're strange, Mya. But I know you're not mad. There is a mad boy here but that's all in the future.' Another titter. 'Or maybe the past. It doesn't matter now. You're here at last.'

'I don't understand you in the slightest. Why *am* I here?'

'In a sense you're not here because only some of your senses are still here and outside these walls, I doubt too many have spotted any change in you. It's disappointing how people view physical health as the sole signifier of sustained lifeforce, isn't it? It comes down to brain cells. You see, your brain is a cell.'

Just my luck. I meet the one person who seems as though she could be an ally in this awful place and she turns out to be a lunatic. Friendly and loquacious and charming, but still a total lunatic. 'You're not making much sense,' I tell her tiredly. 'I don't mean to be rude, but have you ever wondered whether you're the crazy one?'

'Uh-uh-uh.' Her ragged black fringe whips back and forth across her face. 'I'm thinking clearly in this place, Mya. Ever since I came here, for the first time that I could remember. Thinking very, very clearly.'

'If you know all the answers, then how do I get out of here?'

'Ach, such a question. Well now, My-My, I'm afraid no one can help you with that one.'

Fortunately, my exasperated sigh is drowned by the heavy breathing of the other patients as the squat thrusts begin. 'Wait – so if you can't tell me how to escape, how are you going to get out yourself?'

'We won't ever leave. We can't.'

Her words set off a sickly plunging sensation in my stomach. 'I don't believe you.'

'That was the sacrifice I was willing to make.' There is a resigned melancholy in her voice. 'A sacrifice for those most important to me. You made a sacrifice too, although I fear your situation was pretty far removed from coherent consent. But you have to remember that you made that sacrifice for yourself – and for Marco.'

Oh God. She knows Marco too. I'm close to fainting. The group moves into a series of ponderous lunges, grinding as one in a gasping ballet, and I try to keep up even though shock has sapped the strength from my legs.

'What?' I ask muddily. 'What did you say?'

'I'm doing this for you and Marco. This is the best way. Trust me on this one.'

'Does Marco know I'm here?'

'He doesn't think he does.' She lets out a giggle that straddles the cracks of sanity and madness. 'Although he's closer than you think, Mya.'

'Oh great, another riddle.'

'It will make sense soon, I promise.'

It seems that Johanna is about to say more – probably more infuriating riddles in that clipped, bouncy accent – but the instructor claps her hands and the girl's words are lost.

'And stretch and stretch and... rest!' she announces. 'Well done, team. Class dismissed.'

We turn in unison and the orderlies split our phalanx into a string of smaller lines. My last sight of Johanna is the back of her head as her group is led towards a door in the far corner of the complex. As I join my own line and walk in step with the rest of the zombies, I think about our conversation – probably the longest human interaction since I've been here and certainly the strangest.

That ragged-haired girl knows something; that much is obvious. She must have known me – perhaps known both of us – before I ended up in the White Prison. But I have no memory of her and so much of what she told me made no sense. She's been here for years but didn't seem surprised to see me. That means someone must have known I was coming.

Someone must have been planning my incarceration for a very long time. All of these thoughts are deeply troubling.

Does Marco know I'm here? I asked her. Johanna believes he does, at least in some way. She knows more than she's letting on but it seems she wants me to figure it out for myself. That's fine. In this blank place, stripped of everything I once possessed, my only wealth is time.

As we are led from the exercise yard with its unnatural grass and unnatural sky and unnatural air, a new thought slams into my brain with the force of a blitzkrieg.

Did Marco put me here?

IO

The New Intake (fresh meat)

They were racing but it seemed as though they were barely moving. She was laughing, laughing – and if a shriek of absolute terror had converged with her laughter, who was around to hear it? The faster he drove, the more miles he put between herself and her former fearful existence. The motorbike growled like a wild creature but they were riding that tiger with arrogant ease. She was shaking wildly, juddering to the twinned pulses of the machine and his movements. *You have to lean with me . . . your body has to follow mine.* Each time he tried to ease off the throttle she would slap her hand against his chest as if to kick-start his heart, clamp her thighs against his, and he would send them hurtling forward at even greater speed. She seemed to be turning the motorcycle through him, guiding his course with her natural motion. Faster, faster, further, further. She never wanted this journey to end; it wasn't just the speed, the thrill, the feeling of thumbing her nose at fate and flicking V-signs at mortal peril. It was his presence – the sensation of herself locked into Marco's frame, like a jigsaw puzzle where the pieces had fallen into place completely by chance.

The motorbike's headlamp illuminated each road sign a

millisecond before disaster. He banked heavily on the corners, leaning up against the curve of the carriageway, trusting physical instinct not to spill them and shred their bodies on the concrete. The countryside road was ill-lit and deserted, low-hanging branches of craggy trees rushing past before she had time to register their existence. Any obstacle – a vehicle pulling out of an unseen junction, or a fallen branch lying on the road – would send them spinning over the handlebars. An accident would probably be fatal.

There was no logic to any of this, she realised in a rare moment of cohesive thought. Marco was only riding so recklessly because she kept urging him on. She wondered whether she had a death wish. Did she really want them to end up at the bottom of one of the drainage ditches that ran around the flatlands? Broken bodies twisted around each other; her rewritten cover version of that old doo-wop ballad of doomed romance her father used to play all the time when she was a child. 'Leader Of The Pack,' that was the one.

She couldn't bear to imagine the journey ending. That jagged rush of adrenaline would dip. Their heartbeats, racing as one, would slow to a trudge as the speedometer ticked down towards zero. White numbers on a stark black dial counting away the moments in which they could feel so wild, so carefree, so together. Everything from now on between them would be a disappointment compared to this lunatic twilight ride.

So they rode on.

Less than half an hour earlier she had heard that now-familiar scatter of gravel against her bedroom window. She pulled up her bedroom blinds, cracked open the window and stared out. There he was, resting against his idling motorbike, arms folded nonchalantly, the streetlight his spotlight. He could have knocked. Of course he could have knocked. But Marco Pellicci had a taste for the dramatic arrival.

'Why don't you come down?' he called up to her. 'I know a fun place we can go.'

He ran a hand through his neon pink spikes, sending them shivering like porcupine quills. The studs on his leather jacket gleamed. His jeans were more rip than actual denim. And – good grief – that really was a toothpick dripping from his bottom lip. His overconfidence in clichés should have been laughable. Instead she found it intoxicating, irresistible. He was a man completely out of time; either one step behind or ten leaps in front of the world. He didn't care what anyone else thought of him. He only cared about her.

'Okay then,' she hissed back. Her father was still working at the Academy, but it was late and she had seen a few neighbours' curtains twitch as the engine shredded the silence. 'Keep your voice down, though.'

As she locked the front door behind her, she saw Marco was fiddling with something at the back of his motorcycle, the word *Suzuki* shining whitely on its frame. It had been as if he was ignoring her. Well, wasn't that romantic, she thought sourly. To think of how her heart had thrummed as she frantic-ally dressed up for him. That was Marco Pellicci alright. So arrogant, so detached, more interested in his bloody bike than her…

Then he turned towards her, smiling proudly as he held up a dark piece of fabric. For a moment she mistook it for a cowl, and she thought of her mother and her vision threatened to swim. Then the lamplight glistened off the leather and she understood, and near-painful twinges of pleasure spread out from her chest through her whole body, leaving her glowing as if she had immersed herself in a warm bath. It was a lover's gift.

Not ten dozen roses or a gemstone ring. But a gift nonetheless. His sort of gift.

'For you,' he announced. 'Custom fit from my pal Nettles.' She was dumbstruck as he placed it around her shoulders like a royal's ermine robe. 'Tarmac will shred your skin to hell if we spill. Trust me, I've done it enough times. You come off that bike at seventy miles an hour, you're going to need some serious padding.'

The leather felt immensely heavy on her shoulders yet somehow it wasn't weighing her down; she felt strong, impervious. Haltingly she found her voice. 'You've crashed it how many times? You know, that doesn't inspire confidence.'

'Years ago,' Marco said with a wink. 'My road-rash days are long gone, baby girl. This time I got precious cargo.' Proprietorially, he rapped on the pillion. She sighed. It was ridiculous, it was reckless. It was also just what she needed. She swung her leg over the machine and he revved the engine. More lights winked on down the street. She hoped no one would complain to Dad. The motorbike began to move and as they took the first corner, banking like an aeroplane, she clung on tighter and felt his muscles stiffen beneath the leather.

'Do I get to know where you're taking me, then?' she yelled back above the buzzsaw din.

'The funfair!' he yelled gleefully, removing one hand from the handlebars to place it on her leg, his fingertips drumming polyrhythms on her thigh. 'Do you want to go to the funfair?'

'So long as the rides are fast,' she said.

'We can go fast,' he agreed. 'Oh yeah, like you wouldn't believe.'

So now they were racing. Marco twisted the throttle once more, and she squeezed tight against him, laying her head between his shoulder blades. In that moment she imagined she felt first one wheel, then the other, taking flight from the road. No longer prisoners of gravity, their bodies were carried upwards on an unearthly gust of air. Leaving the solid ground behind forever, they aimed for the horizon.

II

The New Intake (fresh meat)

The funfair was just about to leave town and the site was deserted. She saw the unlit structures of the big wheel and the chair-swings in the near distance, like skeletons of long-dead dinosaurs, and could have wept. There were no bright lights. She had hoped for music and laughter. Here there was only silence.

He killed the engine and the motorcycle puttered to a halt next to the security fence. There was a brightly coloured poster attached to the metal mesh. *Calisto's Ultimate Funfair,* she read. *Waltzers, dodgems, haunted house. Only £1 a ride. Thrills 'n' spills guaranteed.* Or not.

'Damn it,' said Marco, bashing a closed fist against the handlebars. Frustration distorted his voice into a growl. Ill vibrations shuddered through her. 'We're too late.'

'It doesn't matter,' she said, placing a conciliatory hand upon his shoulder, 'I enjoyed the ride.'

He shook his head, obviously angered, as he helped her from the motorbike. Her sneakers squished into the soft mud. For a short while they stood in front of one another in silence that quickly grew oppressive. His lips were downturned in a surly moue. Desperately she searched for something to say. 'Nice bike,' she said approvingly, as if she knew about such things. 'Fast. Does it have a name?'

Marco shook his head. 'I think you name ships, not bikes. It's a Suzuki Bandit, for what that's worth.'

'So it's a Bandit – why not call it Smokey?'

He grinned and the clouds on his brow evaporated. He had a great smile, boyish and disarming; it was a shame he utilised it so rarely. 'I like it. Really like it. Surely you're too young for that sort of movie reference?'

She matched his grin. 'I am. I am far too young, you're quite right. But Dad came to Britain in the Seventies and couldn't get enough of Western trash culture. He loved showing me those old chase films. Burt Reynolds and Tom Selleck were his idols. He even grew a great big moustache in tribute. You must see it sometime, it's truly ... luxuriant.'

'Luxuriant,' he repeated. 'Now there's a word I love. One of those words where you can taste the syllables oozing out of your mouth. Sweet and unctuous. Like marshmallows and melted chocolate.'

She stared at him, biting on her lower lip. He had wrong-footed her again. 'Of course,' she continued, as casually as she could muster, hoping the tremors wouldn't show in her voice, 'since Dad and his moustache lived on through the Eighties, he looked less like a macho ladykiller. More a regular at a Soho gay bar.'

'Are you sure he wasn't?'

She exploded in laughter, leaning on the bike for support. Patiently he waited for her giggles to stop. 'You don't have much of a circuit-breaker, do you?' she said wonderingly. 'Whatever you think, you just ... just say.'

'Say what I want, do what I please,' he told her with a wink. Now his eloquence had evaporated and childish boasting had filled its place. It should have irritated her, yet there was an appealing artlessness to his braggadocio. Marco turned back to the fence and kicked at it with the toe of his boot. The rattle of metal sounded awfully loud in the empty landscape. 'And what I really want to do right now,' he went on, 'is ride the funfair rides.'

She laughed and shook her head. 'However would you suggest we do that?' she asked, although somehow she already knew.

'Up and over, baby girl,' he said, hunkering down on one knee and forming his hands into a cradle. There was a manic urging in his dark eyes. It seemed as though for Marco Pellicci, vaulting her over a ten-foot fence was as easy as, well, falling off a bike. 'Up and over we go.'

Her muscles tingled and her breath came in a tight-chested whine. She followed him as he picked his way past the carcasses of the fairground rides, his jacket shimmering in the moonlight. Past the waltzers, round the hotdog and candyfloss stands and the popgun stalls. Finally they came to the big wheel. She cast a nervous glance around.

'Do you think anyone saw us?' she whispered.

'There's nobody around for miles. Who'd see us?'

'Security guards . . . CCTV . . . dogs?'

'They've taken the night off.'

'How do you know?'

He shrugged. 'Instinct. That's all.'

'Instinct?'

'Instinct,' he agreed, as if the point had been proven long ago. 'Only thing that's never let me down in this world. Just like it was instinct to come over to you that day at the Academy. Despite the way your friends were looking at me, like I might cannibalise them given half the chance. Earlier this evening it was my instinct to take you for a motorcycle ride. Right now it's my instinct for us to go on that big wheel. Together. This very moment.'

'Pity there's no one around to work it.'

There was a direct challenge in his gaze. 'Well, every problem has a solution, don't it?'

She was about to reply but he had already hurried over to the small control booth next to the big wheel. He fiddled at the bottom of the glass screen with what looked like two long hairpins, while she stared on open-mouthed.

'I'm pretty good at this sort of thing,' Marco explained.

'Should I ask why?' she asked.

'Ask no questions and I'll tell you no lies.' There was that rakish grin again. 'Come on, nice and easy. There … there … oh, oh … oh yes. There we go.'

There was a creaking noise then a crunch. He slid the screen of the control booth open and slipped the pins into the pocket of his jacket.

'Wow,' was all she could think of to say.

'Wow indeed,' agreed Marco. 'Now – lights.'

Reaching into the booth, he fiddled with something in the darkness. Then her vision was blasted into a spectacular kaleidoscope by a thousand multi-coloured lights beaming down from the big wheel. The slumbering attraction had burst into life. A spacecraft landing in the field could not have taken her breath away more effectively.

'There,' he said proudly. 'Ain't that a pretty sight?'

Marco fumbled inside the booth once more and there was a whiff of oil and a clanking of machinery and the wheel began to turn. The carriages swung and dipped in the night sky. She shook her head. She felt utterly bemused, a little afraid, almost unbearably excited – and scarcely able to believe that this was happening to her.

'Hop on with me,' he said, offering her his hand. 'You'll never believe how high we can go.'

12

The White Prison

This is the shadow ball at the silhouette sanatorium. Oh God, how did I get here? I remember being led back to my room from the exercise yard, where I had spoken to the girl called Johanna. The landscape had appeared again on my video screen, the heads of the bulrushes still nodding smugly in the endless breeze. I suppose it's meant to be a calming scene but it's anything but serene, because I'm forever watching for what I saw – or what I dreamed I saw. I decided I wasn't going to torture myself with thoughts of Marco and my doppelganger any longer. There was nothing to do so I lay down on my bed, pulled the papery sheets over my head, and I must have drifted off.

Then nothing, until I return to hazy consciousness, alone in what appears to be a vast ballroom. I'm not in my dreary inmate smock. I'm wearing a flowing white evening gown cut to my exact measurements. Wondering whether this is another dream, I rub my eyes and my fingers come back smudged with kohl. The unknown people who dressed me like a fucked-up Cinderella have even painted my face. My heels clack on a marble floor, squared into black-and-white segments like a chessboard.

'What the hell is this place?' I murmur to myself.

Then the fuzziness in my vision clears and I see dancers.

Hundreds – even thousands – of dancers. A delicately yearning motif is struck up by an orchestra hidden I know not where. The sound is hypnotic, looping. The dancers, every one of them wearing white, begin to revolve in their pairs to the gentle waltz. The music is slow and soothing, so very close to beautiful, but there is a strangely warped quality to the violin notes that sickens the sweetness. Out of tune, out of time? I know nothing about classical music but there is a wrongness in the refrain that sets my nerves jangling. I spin around, looking to leave, but there is no sign of an exit. Maybe Johanna is here? I try to pick out her dark fringe in the whiteness. Instead my vision alights on a red stain. A figure – definably male, a stranger – is slipping through the crowd. He moves amid the revolving revelry with uncanny grace. The redness that caught my attention is sprayed across the front of his pleated white shirt.

This doesn't seem real. None of this twisted fairytale makes any sense. I feel like I've fallen into a horrible dream and pinching myself won't do the slightest good. But I'd better start believing. There is a man walking across the dancefloor towards me. That man is covered in blood.

He is coming for me, I know it. I need to get out. I can't move. My feet are stuck to the chessboard floor.

I've been scared before: when I was seven and a schoolfriend and I went cockle-picking on the beach in Whitby and nearly got stranded by the tide, or the night at my Cambridge college when the ex-boyfriend of a fellow student broke in drunk and furious and tried to force open my door. Yes, I've been scared before. But never scared like this. I've never been so scared that my entire body feels as if it has turned to stone, my heels encased in cement. My body has betrayed me. I couldn't move even if I wanted to. Do I want to? Because something – some dark, unknowable instinct – wants me to stay. Let what is about to happen simply happen.

The stranger is very close now. The moment the dancers form a barrier between us, he slides through the infinitesimal gaps. I think I can even smell him. I remember reading somewhere, maybe in one of Marco's dreadful crime-thriller paperbacks, that born killers have a defined odour – like raw meat and charcoal. This man's scent is different though. Familiar.

Sidling out of the last row of dancers, he steps forward towards me and I gasp. His face has no features. No lips, no mouth, only empty space. Then I realise he is wearing a mask. The sort you see actors wearing in Greek tragedies; only there is no upturned smile or downcast pout, just blankness. The skin around the mask is so pale it seems translucent. I can see his scalp through his buzzcut hair. He is wearing a white tuxedo and his shirt is spotted with rose madder droplets. But it's not the red-sprayed pattern on his shirt – surely blood? – that truly frightens me. It is what I can see through the eyeholes of his mask. In his gaze there is only darkness. If I fell into that black glare, I doubt I could ever claw my way out. This is the coldly burning stare I saw when I looked into the porthole window of his cell. I remember Johanna's words: *There is a mad boy here but that's all in the future.* My future has arrived far too soon. The man standing in front of me is quite insane. This is the Madboy.

And he's asking me to dance.

I want to wake up. Most of all I want to wake up in my bed with Marco next to me. But I'd settle for waking up in my solitary little cell, the only sound that constant mechanical drone. Every time I think I'm getting a grip on how to cope with living in the White Prison, it rips understanding away from my grasp with another dirty trick. The sliding door that seems to disappear into the wall ... the enormous communal gym class... the screen that shows me images I dare not believe... and now this crazy ball.

As the stranger drops to one knee in mocking deference, he proffers a hand. The Madboy never breaks his gaze. Barely able to believe what I'm doing, I hold out my own hand – what else can I do? There's no escape – and he clasps my fingers and pulls me into the whirling throng. There is phenomenal strength in his grip but his touch is warm and gentle. The music picks up pace. A drum beat thumps over the nimbly sliding strings. I realise that it is the pounding of my heart.

'You've been looking for me,' he says.

Mutely I shake my head, my teeth clenched to stop them chattering. Terror has stolen the words from my tongue. He's wrong though, not that I would dare to tell him. Why would I be looking for him?

'You can get me out of here,' he continues, 'and I can—' Then he turns, the eyes beneath the mask widening. Over his shoulder I see two guards in their claret tunics push through the crowd, heading towards us. I stop dancing and raise my hand, beckoning them over. I should feel relief. They're coming to save me. My dancing partner spits out a low obscenity, sweat popping out on the top of his brow, staining the tragedy mask.

'Dance,' he says. 'Dance, if you want to find out why you're trapped here. And if you ever want to get out.'

The guards are very close now. Not running but converging rapidly upon us. In less than ten seconds they'll have their hands on this madman. I'll be safe – for a short while – but I'll never hear what he wants to tell me. Whatever the hell is happening in this moment, it will be over.

The music rises to a horrible crescendo; the strings shrieking like torture victims, the drums descending into splintered arrhythmia.

'Dance!' the stranger snaps.

My body obeys him despite the frantic yammering of my brain. I drop my hand and he grabs hold. Quickly he yanks me into the crowd and we are whirling among the shadow figures in a chaotic embrace, our footsteps somehow in time, and the music eases into a lullaby and I feel strangely at peace. Until I stare upwards at my dance partner and see there's no light of sanity in those black eyes. Instead I try to concentrate on what I'm hearing instead of what I'm seeing. The music is beautiful. Slow but compelling, powerful yet tender.

'I love this song,' he says as if reading my mind. 'There's usually lyrics. But they tend to scrub those things out here. Don't want the inmates getting excited by a *soupçon* of humanity, do we?'

'What do you mean?'

'We always dance to this,' he says. 'I wish we could dance to this song every night. But... circumstances, you know?'

He really is totally insane. 'I don't understand. Please... please... I think you've confused me with someone else.'

'I think that's impossible,' he says. 'Do you trust me?'

He is staring intently at me. He'll know if I'm lying. I shake my head. 'No,' I tell him, my words barely a whisper. 'Not in the slightest.'

He tilts me backwards until my hair brushes the floor and I'm powerless to resist. 'Fine. You don't have to. I trust you, you know.'

'You trust me?' I say faintly.

'Oh yes.' The mask warps in the corners. I realise he is trying to grin. 'I've trusted you with my life.'

'Why? Do you know me? I don't know you.'

Impatiently, he shakes his head. 'Keep dancing. They're still searching for us. The guards.'

'Good,' I tell him. 'I'll scream and they'll grab you. Just like you grabbed me.'

'I wouldn't do that.' Again there's a smile in his voice. His right hand slips upwards from the small of my back to my neck, the fingertips trailing over the tiny hairs. Then his grip closes around my throat and I gasp. 'From this position I could snap your neck in a second. Half a second, actually. I wouldn't want you to suffer.'

I feel tears coat my eyes. 'Why do you want to hurt me? I've never done anything to you.'

'You have, though. You destroyed me. You just don't remember.'

His grip loosens but his hand remains at my throat. I think of ways to distract him, trying to stop myself looking around for my saviours in claret coats.

'I didn't see you earlier,' I say.

His eyes narrow, his posture stiffening as he turns me against the tide of the crowd. 'What were you doing earlier? Were you looking for me again? Spying on me again?'

'In the exercise yard,' I gabble, 'we were all doing ... exercises. Earlier. We were told to by this gym instructor woman. We were all doing it together. Running, jumping, squatting, lunging. Synchronised. In ... in the exercise yard. I saw a display like it on TV one time, somewhere like Korea or Taiwan, and they're all moving in perfect harmony. That was us. In the exercise yard. Earlier.'

'In the exercise yard? Earlier? Yeah, I gathered that.'

'You weren't there.'

He laughs softly. 'You missed me? I'm flattered. No, I was ... indisposed.'

'Do they not let you out?' The words are out of my mouth before I can push them back in.

'Not if they can help it.' Was that a catch in his voice? For

a second his eyes seem to moisten too. 'But this evening...
well, I had to come. I wouldn't have missed this night for the
world.'

'Why not?' I ask, then wonder whether this was exactly the
wrong thing to say.

'Ah, come on.' His eyes are different now, twinkling with
merriment. His tone is light-hearted, teasing. 'The night. The
song. Us. The way we're dressed. It's so perfect.'

A shrilling choir of alarm bells ring in my mind. He's delu-
sional. He's obsessed. He thinks that I'm someone else. 'Please,
I'm not who you—'

'You really don't remember.' His tone is desolate. Then it's
as if a switch has flicked in his brain and the mellowness in
his eyes has been replaced by that burning darkness. His grip
tightens on my neck again as he pushes me backwards, forsaking
any charade of dancing. 'No, you're lying to me. Yeah, I see it
now. Everyone fucking lies to me here. Why should Mya be
any different?'

The stranger pushes me backwards and my bare shoulders
connect with the curve of the wall. He has pinned me into the
corner of the room. I see no way of escape and whimper in
fright. I'm trapped. I've always been trapped here, right from the
moment I woke up, however many days or weeks ago. Maybe
there's some solace in knowing this will be the last time. There's
no sign of the guards. They've let a lunatic loose in this asylum
and I'm his target. The one I was warned against: the Madboy.

'One kiss?' he says. He bends closer to me, the mouth-slit
in his mask against my cheek. I had expected his breath to be
foul but instead he smells of peppermints. 'For old times' sake?'

Again I can't talk. Miserably I shake my head. But he doesn't
seem angry, only saddened. He lets go of me and I slump to
the ground.

'I don't blame you,' the Madboy says. He stands before me, his great shoulders heaving like a bull conquered by the matador's cunning. 'No, not in the slightest. I'm sorry. I'm so sorry. I'm not ... I'm not really myself in this place.'

That makes two of us. I don't know whether they're doping the food or piping sedatives through the air-conditioning system, but I haven't felt like myself ever since I arrived here. We have that much in common. Why am I being drawn into complicity with someone so dangerous? We feel like allies now and that's worrying, because this man is covered in blood and clearly insane.

But he's calmer now and I need answers.

'What's with the blood?' I ask, unable to stop myself. 'You ... your shirt.'

He stares down at the red-speckled fabric, scraping the blood-stains with a fingernail as if to erase any trace of guilt. 'That was from some time ago,' he says. Is that regret thickening his voice? 'It really was a night to remember. Blood never washes off. Not all the way.'

'Not all the way,' I repeat, wondering what he means.

'You need me,' he says quietly, 'if you ever want to be yourself again.'

Then the Madboy slips back into the throng, merging among the whirling bodies like a ghost, and he is lost to me.

13

The New Intake (fresh meat)

Suspended in the sky, they sat in that swaying carriage for what seemed like forever. Time was meaningless. They were static and the world itself was turning around them. His arm was draped almost but not quite chastely across her shoulders. The night was so balmy they had removed their jackets, now puddled together on the floor of the carriage. The gondola swung back and forth like a metronome and each time it reached the apex of its arc, his fingertips would brush her bare skin. The tick-tock touch sent shockwaves through her system. She almost dreaded that sensation; the anticipation of the thrill was so great it was nearly nauseating.

'What can you see?' he asked.

Puzzled, she turned to him. 'Blackness, mostly,' she said tartly, fighting for a measure of self-control, 'on account of it being night-time. A few lights in the distance.'

He laughed lightly. 'That's not quite what I meant.'

'So what do you mean?'

'From the moment I met you, you seemed like someone who wasn't really there.' Troubled, she stared at him and he grinned disarmingly, his hand slipping across to the nape of her neck, stroking her hair. 'Oh, I mean that as the highest compliment. Like this reality is a silly distraction and there's a greater purpose. As if you were looking through people, seeing what most people can't see. I found it fascinating. Still do. It's as if you know a great big secret about the world. But you're not letting on.'

'And you took me up on the big wheel to find out my great big secret?'

'Absolutely,' he said. 'We're up here way away from everybody else. Just us two. So there's an element of trust already. Otherwise ... well, it's a long walk home, baby girl.'

He let out a laugh and she echoed it, only slightly troubled. It occurred to her — just then, oh so late, that she barely knew this man and there was no other person for miles around. 'Hate to disappoint you,' she said, 'but there really isn't anything to tell.'

'Everyone has a story,' he went on implacably. 'God, most of the other students can't stop telling their stories. Spewing out their whole autobiographies before the first drink's even gone down. I felt like I knew their whole lives within minutes. I try to smile and nod and be polite, but ... you know, it's boring. Tiny triumphs, minor disasters, empty revels.'

'What makes you think my story would be different?'

'Because when you think no one's watching,' he said, 'you look like the loneliest person I've ever known. And I want to know why.'

There was only empathy in his eyes. She turned away from him, finding something incredibly fascinating in the twinkling lights of the town in the mid-distance, not wanting him to see her cry. She thought of her disastrous few weeks at Cambridge. Her impersonal little room with the single bed; more like a cell, really. The walls were white, stained in places with the Blu-Tack of previous occupants' posters. That room became her prison, because every morning — after a night of fitful sleep and recurring dreams of being trapped in an enormous oily, stinking machine that threshed and clanked and wheezed and came ever closer – she felt a fear so paralysing it took most of her strength simply to push off the blankets. Leaving the room was quite beyond her. Her window opened out onto the college's front court and night after night she heard groups of new students gather there – talking, joking, forging new friends or fresh romances. Each shriek of laughter caused a needle of anxiety to twist and grind against the base of her spine. She received an email with her lecture timetable but attending would mean a walk of almost half a mile to the site; that would mean different people, unknown situations, danger. Sometimes she heard knocking on her door. But she knew she had waited too long, so she never answered – the thought of human contact sent jolts of panic shuddering through her chest. One time a note was slipped under her door; glittery purple writing on pink paper inviting her to something called a *bop*. She tore up that pink slip and flushed the pieces down the toilet. She hated her room but at least she felt safe there. She only went down the two flights of stairs to the communal kitchen when she was convinced the college was sleeping. When she did pass somebody else on the corridor or the staircase, she tugged her grey hooded sweater further over her face and pushed her frame into the brickwork on the furthest side of the wall and waited until that shadow figure had passed on by. Late one night, when she was starving and had convinced herself that no one would be around, she opened the kitchen door to see a girl on her knees in front of a rangy boy with a sheaf of straw-coloured hair that fell fetchingly across his forehead. The boy winked at her and his face crumpled into a demon's leer. Dropping her packet of instant noodles, she fled back to her room, her heart jouncing in her chest.

Days slipped into weeks. It seemed as if she had been

forgotten by the university. Her world had constricted almost entirely to the safety of her room. She passed her time watching old movies on her shiny new laptop, studying course textbooks for lectures she would never attend. Eking out the food supplies she had brought down with her, making occasional scurrying trips to the 24-hour convenience store across the road from her college. So long as she never replied to the emails in her university account inbox then no one troubled her. She slept for up to fourteen hours at a stretch and – with the curtains drawn and the nights closing in – she started to become uncertain as to whether morning and evening had swapped places. She couldn't say whether she was happy or miserable because her existence had been reduced to mindless drifting. She was standing on the edge of a river, and it was impossible to tell whether the current would be kind and the water balmy – or if she would be caught by an undertow and drowned. Better to stay on the safety of the banks.

Then one day there had been a great banging on the door that jolted her from her reverie; a male voice demanding that she opened up, that it didn't have to be like this, that they could talk it through. *Please don't do this ... don't do this to me, you bitch ... oh God ... sorry, I didn't mean that ... I don't know ... I don't ... I didn't mean it, okay ... don't do this ... please don't do this.* She guessed it was mistaken identity. What she did do was shunt her bed up against the door and pile her heavy coursebooks on top of the blankets, weighing it down in case that stranger forced the door, cowering in the corner until he stomped away. The next day she had fled. After a sleepless night she called the earliest available taxi and left Cambridge forever. She didn't even trouble to pack; she left her college room as a memorial to her failed attempt at a regular life. She went home to her father and the Academy. Back to normality, or whatever passed for it.

'I try really hard to be normal,' she told Marco. The words came in a rush; spouting like a tapped oil well, pouring from her throat before they could choke her. 'I put on normal person clothes and use my normal person voice and wear my normal person mask. But I'm always scared, so scared, that someone will find me out.'

'Then don't be normal,' he said. 'Enjoy being a freak. Celebrate the fact you're a weirdo. People stare at me all the time. Sometimes they shout or throw things. I love it.'

'You're different, though,' she said. 'You're ...' She spun her wrist in a spooling motion, eloquence deserting her. He was confident, assertive, uncaring what anyone else thought of him. He was everything that she was not. Yet somehow their differences seemed laughably tiny.

'You can say it with your hands if you like,' Marco told her with a smile. 'You're talking to an Italian, remember. I can translate.'

'You're different,' she said. 'I'm the same. Same difference, if that makes sense.'

'Totally.' He nodded. 'Maybe that's what connected us in the first place.'

'I thought I'd blown it when I quit university,' she admitted. 'Thought I'd ruined my whole life.'

'So go back,' he said. 'Quit this course, or whatever the hell it is we're doing here in these godforsaken flatlands. Go back to university tomorrow. I'll drive you on the back of my Bandit if you like. You'll only beat your problems by confronting them. Cheesy but it's true. And tomorrow's the first day of the rest of your life. Again, sounds cheesy – one hundred per cent ripe whiffy Camembert – but ... you know ... that's true too.'

'You really believe that?'

'Sure. I believe everything I read in greetings cards.'

The air was coming in cooler now and he retrieved his leather jacket from the carriage floor to cover her like a blanket.

'I'll pass on your kind offer,' she said. 'I'm done with that life. It wasn't mine.'

He squeezed her hand hard. 'Honestly, I was praying you'd say that,' he told her. 'I'm not sure I'd have let you go, anyway. Can't risk losing you to some Eton fop with floppy hair. His family might have a castle. How could I compete?'

She managed a laugh. 'How indeed?'

'Is there anything else I can do?'

'Hold me,' she replied. 'Nothing more... I can't cope with anything more right now. Just hold me.'

'Of course,' he said. Craving comfort, wanting only to forget what she had told him, she nestled into his body. Her mind was a maelstrom of confusion. She barely knew him but felt she could tell him anything. Although there was so much about herself that she would not dare reveal.

'Reckon I could stay like this for forever,' he said. 'You?'

His voice was that now-familiar Marco Pellicci mix of glottal stops and easy humour, but the yearning lurking beneath his words unnerved her. She stiffened against his touch and shifted away, her heart hammering, her skin tingling. He stared quizzically at her; her face was aflame and she hid it in her hands. She felt his desire for her – not so much physical as mental – and it had an elemental power. She could sense that force thrumming in the space between them. She felt so inexperienced, so uncertain. Was she ready for this level of passion? Was she capable of controlling it?

'Please don't tease me,' she almost whispered. 'Please don't let me down.'

His teeth shone in the darkness, brighter than every one of the funfair lights. 'I wouldn't dream of it, princess. I just can't lose the chance of a million more moments like this. That's all I'm saying.'

'This is all very ... very new for me,' she tried again, 'I'm not used to ... I don't know ... I'm not even sure what I'm saying right now. Everything in my life's changed these past couple of months. You'd never believe me if I told you how much. And now things are changing here. And I'm not used to life racing so fast.'

He held up his palms in a gesture of surrender. 'Cool. Cool. Whatever makes you happy. I'm happy to go slow if you want.' Again his grin glittered in the moonlight. 'Except on the Bandit.'

His lips brushed her forehead. The gesture was as chaste as a gentleman offering a lady a turn around the ballroom in a Regency romance. She snuggled back into his warmth, marvelling at how his taut and muscular frame could feel so welcoming, wondering how she could feel so safe sitting with an almost-stranger at the top of a big wheel in an abandoned funfair. It was instinct, she supposed; she trusted him. She supposed she was already falling in love with him. But another part of her brain – that cowardly, untrusting part of her psyche that she hated – warned her against surrendering herself totally to Marco Pellicci. She felt a strange certainty that once she had let him in, it would be far, far harder to push him out again.

14

The New Intake (fresh meat)

Looking back later, after everything went wrong, she couldn't remember the moment she felt herself give in to him. There was a sensation of loss yet something much greater gained. She knew she would never be her whole self again – but neither would she be complete without him. The distance between them was reduced to nothingness. A fragment of her soul had flung itself free of its shackles and twinned with a splinter of his own. The memory of the moment itself had evaporated but the sensations abided.

She did remember their trip to Cambridge a few weeks after the night at the fairground. His day of exorcism. Not with a Bible and holy water, but with cheap wine and laughter.

It had been the warmest November on record. They were floating on the River Cam. The steering pole of their punt dug into the riverbed and sent their vessel on a shaky trajectory towards the willows draped over the muddy embankment. Frantically trying to right their course, standing at the stern, Marco pushed the stick hard into the mud. The impact wobbled the flat-bottomed boat and nearly toppled him into the murky river.

'You look very fine up there,' she called up from her seat,

swigging from a bottle of cheap sparkling wine. 'But you are beyond useless at punting.'

'Everyone's a critic, Minnie.'

She was wearing a gingham dress that fell to slightly above her knees, huge hipster sunglasses with red plastic rims and a red bow in her hair. When he had met her outside her house that morning – the familiar scatter of gravel against her bedroom window, even though she had been listening out for the chug of the motorcycle engine for at least an hour – his first words to her were that her outfit reminded him of Minnie Mouse. *Don't push your luck*, she shot back. *You're the one dressed like a Seventies throwback*. He had laughed and dropped to one knee to kiss her hand in mock deference. Would the Mya of only a few short months ago have said something like that? Of course not. She wouldn't have possessed the nerve. It was funny how she was dressed as a cartoon mouse because hadn't she once been mousy little Mya, scurrying into the corners away from the light? But now she was with Marco, her entire life had changed. It felt as if she had inhaled his devilry, absorbed his fearlessness. Sometimes she felt she had just been born again. She felt like a completely different person.

She was confronting her problems head-on, just like that boy with the pink Mohican and the leather jacket and the vast clumping boots had told her to. She was facing her fear. Since she'd dropped out of her course, her mind had built Cambridge into a horror-movie citadel. Now, with Marco by her side, she saw it for what it really was – just a pretty town, crawling with geeky-looking students and tourists trying to take pictures of them.

'Anyway, I got to push and steer at the same time,' that strange boy protested, wiping the sweat from his brow. 'It's difficult.'

'Jesus, why are men totally incapable of multi-tasking? Here, you sit down and have a drink, and I'll show you how it's done.'

'No, I'm getting the hang of it. Really.'

'Move over, Captain Crash. This is women's work.'

'You'll take my punting stick only when you prise it from my cold dead hands.'

The bubbles of the wine rose to her brain. 'Challenge accepted!' she shouted. Setting the bottle back in their picnic bag, she jumped to her feet, meaning to push him into the water. But the sudden momentum set the boat rocking again and she pinwheeled her arms for balance, her chic sunglasses flying off her face. 'Shit! Marco—'

Dropping the stick, he leapt forward and caught her before she tumbled head first into the River Cam. They watched as the punting pole bobbed away from the boat on the mild ripples of the water, slightly too far out of reach.

'Lost the stick,' he said, 'and those damn shades are in the drink too. Oh hell.'

The boat meandered beneath the willow trees, their branches hunched like old men weighed down with heavy baggage. A green curtain blotted out the light. She rested her head against his chest and breathed in the scent of his sun-warmed skin. She had barely tasted the wine but felt drunk by his presence, the overwhelming realness of him.

'Let's just leave it,' she said. Again his reckless emotions were passing through to her by that strange osmosis. Her instinctive terror about breaking a rule – any rule, no matter how petty – was quelled when she was with him.

'I'm mad jealous of you for studying here,' said Marco, gesturing at the stone buildings reclining elegantly back from the river. 'Even though it didn't work out. All those books, all those brains. People who changed the world with their minds.'

She shook her head firmly. 'My dad came here on a scholarship. Full term, unlike his useless dropout daughter. He has the letters after his name but knows less about human nature than anyone I've ever met. Knowledge is overrated, Marco.'

'How can you say that?' he protested. 'I love how you know so much more than me. I get less dumb every second I spend with you.'

She bit down on her lower lip. She thought of what her father knew, and what he was teaching her, and what she was concealing from the man next to her. 'Learning never did me much good. There's a lot I think I'd like to forget, actually.'

'From schooldays, yeah?'

'Sort of.'

He pushed back her hair and stared intently at the exposed nape of her neck, before placing a kiss just below her earlobe. 'School and me didn't fit either,' he said ruefully. 'Found the classes easy enough but never applied myself. My brothers Tony and Robbo – they was bad kids, proper tearaways. By the time I arrived my card was marked. So school was a busted flush for me. Everything important I learned, I learned afterwards.'

'The more you learn, the less content you are,' she said with quiet fervour. 'You get greedy for knowledge. You always need to know more; nothing will ever be good enough. My dad told me so many high achievers hate themselves for not being good enough. Because you'll never be the very best. Knowledge doesn't make you a better person.'

'You seem like a great person to me,' he said. 'But maybe I'm too stupid to know the difference.'

'I find . . .' she started. She didn't want to ruin their day, the special day he had planned out for her, but he deserved to know this at least. 'I don't know how to say this. I'm sorry. I find things get dark sometimes.'

'How do you mean?'

She took a long drink of the wine before continuing. 'I'm a little afraid to tell you this. Because after I've finished, you might not want to be with me anymore. You've probably worked some of this out yourself – Jesus Christ, despite what you keep saying, you're anything but stupid. I have problems. I wish I didn't and I wish they'd go away. I'm fine right now because everything is balanced and I'm with you and I feel safe. These things happen to me and I can't control them. I call them Great Waves because they crash down and swamp me and drown the person I want to be. I wish I didn't have to tell you this. But you have to know in case it happens again, and the more time we spend together the chances are it *will* happen again, and it's pretty scary when that tide washes me into those dark places and I don't want you to blame yourself. I only wanted to let you know that ... that it's not your fault.'

He folded his arms. He bit down on his lip. His mouth had hardened, almost in anger, but his eyes were wet. 'It's not your fault either. Yeah? Any of those clever-clever people you know ever tell you that, Mya?'

She blinked, her defences blown apart by the simplicity of his argument. 'What do you mean? It is me. How could it not be me?'

He shook his head solemnly. 'The girl I know is you, and she's great. So the person you're telling me about ... that must be someone else. A total fucking nightmare character who's lodging in your brain. Some werewolf, some banshee. If that bitch keeps telling you that you're a loathsome individual who deserves to die alone, then sooner or later you're going to believe it. I don't care how strong you think you are. Everyone sinks sometimes.'

A flat echo: *Here we sink.* She shook her head to rid it of those thoughts.

'So it's a puzzle. A conundrum. A real brain-teaser. How are you going to get rid of her?'

'I don't think I can,' she whispered. 'I think whatever it is … it's in me forever. Now I've said my piece. We can … we can go … I don't know where.'

'I think we should just drift downstream for a while,' he said equably. 'Maybe that's a metaphor. But … you know … any time you need to talk, I can listen.'

'I know,' she said. 'I feel like I can tell you anything. I feel like I *have* told you everything.' Although that felt like a lie. She had told him more than she had once dreamed of telling anyone. But there was so much she could not reveal. Not yet. Most probably not ever.

'So here's another conundrum, princess,' said Marco. Distracted by the punting stick floating away, he had failed to notice the darkness drifting across her face. So – with an effort of will – she made that expression vanish and beamed back at him, a sunny girl without a care in the world. 'We're going to get fined for losing that bloody shillelagh. How do we get it back?'

'What are you suggesting, hotshot?'

Immediately, he pulled his T-shirt over his head and her tongue flickered over her lips as her gaze tracked down his lean frame. Marco had a great knack for distraction.

'Swim for it?' he suggested, grinning wildly, balancing on the edge of the boat, poised to spring into the opaque soup of the river. 'Go on, race you!'

15

The White Prison

My double is sitting on the sofa in our apartment at my father's Academy, wrapped up in Marco's arms. The warped normality of the scene steals the breath from my lungs, paralyses my tongue. I want to scream through the screen. I need to let him know that she isn't me.

But all I can do is watch.

I've been staring at the video screen in my cell for the last hour. I can't believe it. I have to believe it. Everything is happening right in front of my eyes.

My head was a mess when I stumbled back from the shadow ball. I've never felt that mixture of fear and disappointment before. I was scared of the Madboy, definitely. The way he turned from charm to aggression as if flicking a switch, the humanity fading from his eyes as the furies took hold. But he knows something – and somehow he also knows me – and I'm pretty sure he has a plan to get out of this place. When he left me I felt weirdly bereft. It was the first time I had seen true emotion, as frightening as it might have been, from someone here. Rather madness than that unsettling blank expression on the faces of the other inmates.

Groaning, aching, I had pulled the bedsheets over myself and tried to sleep for a hundred years. But I was woken by a mild hiss and burble like the static of an untuned radio. The sound was low but insistent. Pacing around my room, I realised that the source of the sound was the digital screen. The marshlands were darkened, the only light was the moon's rippling reflection on the stream. I peered closer.

Then the image fuzzed and there was a loud cracking sound and I fell back with a gasp, my heart booming. The marshes dropped away like glass from a shattered mirror and I was staring at our room. There were two people on the settee watching television. One of them was Marco. The other was me. Us, or almost us. I didn't recognise the dress I was wearing. I didn't recognise the calmness in my expression. I don't ever remember either of us being so silent, so still. It was like staring at two mannequins.

Unable to look away, I watched. I watched Marco and my doppelganger together. I watched them for what seemed like days.

Eventually he spoke. To her. Me? No, her.

'Would you like a glass of wine?' Marco asks. 'Or beer, maybe?'

'I'm fine, thank you,' says the girl with my face and my body and my voice. 'I'm perfectly fine.' No, she definitely can't be me. Since when have I ever turned down alcohol?

'Do you want to see if there's something else on?' says Marco, gesturing towards the television.

'Oh no, I'm fine with this. Only if it's alright by you.'

'Yes, it's alright by me.'

'Great.'

'Great.'

The channel they are watching is showing some execrable

95

reality show. This doesn't happen to us. Marco watches football or boxing, I prefer classic movies. Otherwise we sit and talk, we have discussions, we make each other laugh. I've always hated the couples who slump in front of the TV and block each other out. Now we're just like them. The girl with my face is content to sit and soak up this brainless mush. Surely Marco realises this isn't me? Can't he see? Can't he see?

'It was a nice day, wasn't it?' my boyfriend says.

'Yes,' the Mya-double agrees. 'It was nice to see your family. Your Uncle Gi is very sweet.'

'They said you seemed happy.'

'I am happy,' she says. 'So very happy.'

Oh God, it's like they've sucked every drop of emotion out of her. Someone has siphoned off all my intelligence and humour, all my rage and despair, all my complexities. What's left is a pretty little empty shell.

'Uncle Gi told me you looked different,' Marco tries again. I feel a spark of hope. Uncle Giuseppe. He adores his nephew; Marco's dad died when he was a child and Uncle Gi became the father figure. Even in my shattered memories, I do remember how proud Marco looked when he first introduced us at a family party. I know Marco's uncle and he knows me. Now Uncle Gi has realised I'm different, that I have somehow been changed. I've been replaced. This is proof.

The tiniest line of concern appears between this new Mya's eyebrows. She lays a hand on his forearm. The gesture is so intimate that I gouge my nails into my palms. That's my boyfriend she's touching and she's stolen him and he doesn't even know it yet.

'Do you think I look different?' she asks, batting her eyelashes.

'You look different because you are different!' I yell at the screen, not caring if I seem mad. Who cares, they've locked me up for being mad so why not give them what they want? 'Everyone can tell you're a fake – you imposter, you fucking fraud. Everyone can tell … everyone can …'

I tail off, my angry words swallowed by shock as I witness what is happening on the screen. Obviously I'm wrong. Not everyone can tell; Marco can't tell because his lips are on hers and I have to watch – wanting to claw my eyes out but unable to look away – as my partner kisses the girl who's pretending to be me.

Finally – after far, far, far too long – they break away.

'You're the best thing that's ever happened to me,' this girl – this imposter – says. How wonderful, a platitude. Marco must remember this isn't the way I speak; like an adult-sized version of those kiddies' dolls that gurgle *I love you* and *You're my best friend* and *We'll always be together.* But Marco doesn't understand. I can see it in his expression. She has tricked him. He can't see that she isn't me and I'm trapped in the White Prison and there's nothing I can do but watch. So he kisses her again and something inside me snaps and I let out a howl. Socking my fists against the screen, I call out even though I know they can't hear me.

'Marco … please,' I beg him, 'Marco, don't … don't … please. Don't let her in. Don't believe her. I'm here … I'm here …'

Marco glances upwards and I wave frantically, battering his image with my fists, fooling myself that the video screen is a window and somehow he can see me. Then he turns back to my doppelganger. Her gaze is happy and serene and maddeningly incurious. He stares at the girl intently and the moment stretches out and I wonder whether somehow I've managed to get through to him.

Then he smiles and tells her, 'I love you, Mya.'

His words hit me like a hammer blow to the chest. I fall to the floor of my cell, sobbing, crying out for him and what I've lost.

The screen winks to black.

There is a knocking at my door. The pillow has grown damp and swollen with my tears. Was that a dream? The video screen has returned to its normal scene of windblown scrubland. No Marco. No Mya doppelganger. Just a dream. Again? Again. Surely.

The knocks come again. Three brisk raps. Carefully I lever myself off the bed, my brain feeling as if it has been rolled like dough by a sadistic baker, and stumble across the room on unsteady legs. The door slides open and I stare into a pale face framed by a heavy black fringe.

'Hey there, sleepyhead,' says Johanna. 'Good grief, you look terrible.'

My vision scopes and contracts. Her face is enormous, a hydrocephalic balloon, then it's as if she is a hundred yards away. I'm still caught halfway between realities. I'm not sure whether I can believe what I saw on the video screen last night. Rubbing at my eyes, I mumble a few words that may or may not constitute a greeting. Johanna is holding a key card in one hand.

'Good news,' she announces brightly. 'I've been given permission to take you for a little walk outside.'

Who died and made you queen of the loony bin? I think it, but I don't say it.

'Certain privileges, My-My,' she says. Did I speak those words out loud? 'I've been here for so long they've started to trust me. Poor misguided fools.'

One eyebrow raises slyly. Mischief thrums through her words. I like this girl. Shaking my head to clear it of thoughts of my replacement – it must have been a dream, surely it was a dream – I follow her. The opportunity to leave my cell, maybe see the sun again – the real sun, not the artificial light of the exercise yard – is exciting. Johanna leads me along the sloping corridor. We walk briskly, purposefully, even though I have no idea where we're going. Two elderly cleaners are mopping the white walls. One turns towards me, sensing our presence. The eyes that squint out of his wizened face are milky, shrouded with cataracts. The other cleaner is wearing overlarge sunglasses. They're both blind. I wonder why the maintenance staff here are hired for their blindness. What don't the people who run this place want them to see?

'You knew me, didn't you?' I whisper to Johanna. 'Before I was locked up here.'

'You're not one for small talk, are you, Mya?'

'When we get out, we can shoot the shit about music or films or boyfriends,' I snap. 'Until I can live free again, apologies for being a tad terse.' The girl blanches and I feel a needle-prick sting of guilt. 'I appreciate you trying to help me,' I say, laying a conciliatory hand on her arm. 'I just … I don't know what I'm doing here. Who put me here, how they put me here and why they put me here.' More silence from Johanna. Still, I press on. 'What even is this place? No one will tell me. I know I have problems. But this … this isn't the answer.'

Her brow furrows. 'Don't say that. Please. You never know who's listening.'

'The other patients,' I continue, 'are they … are they the same as me? Are they the same as you?'

'We should be here,' she says. There is a certainty in her

voice that chills me. Again she seems to believe she deserves to be locked up in this awful void, this empty hell. 'It's better for everyone. You … I've been thinking plenty about you, My-My. You're not quite what I expected.'

'So what happened to me, then? How should I be? Where should I be?'

'Mistakes are always made. They put people in the wrong places sometimes. I'm sure it happens everywhere. You might be a bug in the system, Mya. A glitch in the program. You can't spell *sanatorium* without *sane*.'

I contemplate her remark. 'Hang on, that doesn't work. You're missing a letter.'

'Doesn't matter,' Johanna says. Her perky demeanour has returned. There is a dancing light in the depths of her eyes. 'My silly joke. What I'm saying is that you're not how I remembered you, My-My. You're different. For better or worse.'

I stare at her closely but she's either telling the truth or is a completely convincing liar. 'Sorry, how did we know each other out there? Where did we meet? Why do—'

'Yeah, you certainly changed people's lives out there,' Johanna says, cheerfully ignoring my questions, then lets out a high titter that jangles my nerves and pricks up the hairs on the nape of my neck. 'That's right. You changed lives alright. You did. And Marco did too, from what I've heard.'

'Marco,' I breathe. She knows him. I knew it. 'Is he okay? What's happening to him? Is he—' I stop short of asking whether he is living with a perfect double of me. 'Does … does the screen in your cell show you anything?'

Johanna looks honestly perplexed. 'What do you mean?'

'You know … things. Images of people. People you know. People you love.'

Her smile is faltering again. 'There are no screens in our rooms, Mya. You might be a special one but not even you can wangle those privileges. The less we know about the world outside of here, the better. It's better for everyone. It's better for ourselves.'

'You sound like a convert.' Again, I'm pressing her. Am I opening an ajar door or kicking at a bricked-up barrier? 'You seem totally sane to me, yet you don't want to leave. Forgive me for feeling a little confused.'

Johanna sighs. Her tongue flickers over her front teeth, seemingly caught in an internal debate about how much to tell me. 'This isn't about me any longer, Mya,' she says. There is an unexpected coldness in her voice. 'The worst of me is in here, that's why I'm happy to stay. Even help them. They were right to do what they did with me. But you ... the more I think about it, the more I think they replaced the best of you.'

More riddles. I decide not to press her again. Johanna is the only person in the White Prison who has even hinted I should not be here. It would be reckless to take her faith for granted.

We keep walking in silence. At last we stop at a white door with a black rectangle set into its centre.

'Here we are,' says Johanna. 'The viewing platform.'

She beeps her card against the black screen and the door whooshes open and a rush of wintry air fills my lungs. The colours, oh my life, the colours. After the endless unnatural white of my prison, the vibrant red streaks of dawn carving through the night sky overwhelm me. An earthbound constellation of city lights glows in the mid-distance, a beacon beckoning me home. It's too much. I stagger backwards and Johanna holds me, steadying me. I feel sick and gleeful and wonder pulses through my body and I can't wipe an enormous grin from my face.

I look out at the world beyond the White Prison, the free world. The darkness illuminated. The lights. So many lights. I've never seen anything so beautiful in my life.

16

The New Intake (fresh meat)

The room was hazy with tart, acrid smoke. She held her fingers up to her face, marvelling at their slim perfection, as a spectral guitar riff drifted through the fog. She had no musical knowledge, had barely mastered the recorder at primary school, but now she could visualise the chords in her mind. To play them would be childishly simple. Her fingers would dance a tarantella on the steel strings. If there had been a guitar in the room, she could have played it, definitely; played it like a demon. There was so much she could do these days. She would scarcely have believed it possible three months ago. She could walk out onto the balcony right now and take flight.

'So you're a thing now, Miss Samsara?'

'A thing?' she repeated dreamily.

'Yes. A thing. It's so bloody obvious.'

'Confess! Confess!' a male voice boomed across the room. 'Repent now or burn in everlasting hellfire, goody wife.'

Affecting nonchalance, suddenly conscious of the nausea swirling in her gut, she picked her way over to the window and took great draughts of fresh air. The marijuana buzz dissipated with speed. She chewed down heavily on her lower lip – the flesh was calloused from repeated bites over the years, it was often a way to fight against the milder waves that threatened to overwhelm consciousness – and now the room was back into focus. There, that was better. Her brain felt sharp, her tongue crystalline. Her words could cut and sever like a surgeon's blade. She turned to her friends with a smile.

'Gang? Can you hear me, gang?' She mimicked Dr Baumann's inflections. 'Miss Key, with an English degree from a world-renowned university, resorts to using the word *thing* when a plethora of alternative terms are at her disposal. Is that really the optimal use of her talents, gang?'

'Stop evading the question. You and Mr Hunky Punky, the bloke who still thinks it's 1977 – are you or are you not a thing?'

The crystal in her skull shattered, she lost her private battle against the high and burst into hiccuping laughter. 'Well … yeah, I suppose we're a thing.'

'Congratulations!' Clare kicked back on her bed and took another toke, letting the smoke plume out through her nostrils. 'That wasn't so hard. Is he all pink and spiky downstairs too?'

'Why don't you let your imagination run wild?'

'Oh, I shall, I shall.' Clare passed over the joint and she braved a quick puff, hoping she wouldn't cough again and embarrass herself. She saw the psychedelic drapes hanging on the walls of Clare's dormitory bedroom pixelate like an old computer screen. 'Good impression of Baumann, by the way,' her friend added.

She nodded her thanks, more concerned with looking as if she knew what she was doing with the joint, then passed it back with some relief. Three months ago she couldn't have imagined smoking weed. She couldn't have imagined herself with so many friends, especially ones like Clare. She certainly couldn't have imagined herself going out with a strange boy with pink hair and an attitude that dared the world to take their best shot at him.

'You're in love with him, right,' Alec said from the armchair in the corner of the room, not troubling to look up from his mobile phone. 'That's a statement, not a question. I'm not looking for verification.'

'You're always looking for verification, McTavish. Last lecture you were so far up Kolstein's backside I thought we'd have to send a search party.'

'Hand me that spliff and I'll agree with you.'

'You must agree with me – no one gets hurt that way.'

'Are we mobbing out tonight's guest lecture?' Alec asked, turning his attention to her. 'Should be good. That Dr Calvin fella from Ree-Mem. Heaps of intrigue plus free wine. Almost certainly bad wine. But free wine.'

She shook her head. She couldn't tell her friends that Dr Cal had visited her house twice in the past year to discuss a future collaboration with her father. 'Can't, sorry. I'm … well … Marco's taking me out. Down to London, actually.'

'Ooh, do tell. Michelin-starred meal? West End show?'

'Umm, no. West Ham United.'

'West what-the-hell?'

'The football team. I mean, it's one of his big loves, and I thought—'

'Jeepers, don't tell me.' Batting her eyelashes, Clare tilted her head to one side and made a pillow of her hands, creasing her face into a gooey smitten expression. 'It'll be so romantic. I can see him there in his very best home shirt, with only three splodges of ketchup and a few bloodstains on the front. Just the two of you and thirty thousand bald psychopaths. He'll let you share his meat pie then you can give a rival fan a drunken kicking, together. Then a quickie behind the away end.'

Alec snickered. 'Bit strong, aye?'

'Bit strong? From the laddie whose country invented poetic

obscenity? Whose entire culture revolves around booting the shite out of snivelling Sassenachs?'

'That's barbarian history, Miss Key. You're looking at the face of modern, sensitive Scotland.'

'Oh, for Christ's sake, grow some—'

She barely heard her friends as they bickered. Slightly spangled, she pushed herself up from the bed. The marijuana had coated her vision with a silvery sheen. She wondered if Marco would notice or even care. *Live fast, die young and leave a beautiful corpse*, was his motto. She said her goodbyes to Clare and Alec and caught the bus from outside the Academy building. An unwritten song, with a rhythm so sweet it couldn't possibly be played on earthly instruments, was ringing in her head. She couldn't ever remember feeling so happy.

17

The New Intake (fresh meat)

The football match was fine, if not exactly enjoyable. She tried not to let the alarm show on her face as she saw how Marco's emotions swung with his team. His anger frightened her. In fact, she spent more time watching her boyfriend than she did the players in claret and blue running about on the pitch. West Ham went a goal down early in the first half, and as the opponents in white congregated in a pile by the corner flag below them, she could see the veins popping out on his arms as he slammed his fists on his thighs again and again. She stared at Marco as he howled at the players, wrenching at his hair, spitting insults at the referee. There was a poisonous mood in the stands as the last minutes of the match ticked away. She was worried that their evening would be ruined. Then West Ham equalised with a last-minute penalty – the tension close to unbearable as the player wearing the number eleven shirt stepped up and calmly stroked the ball into the bottom corner of the net, far beyond the goalkeeper's reach – and the crowd exploded into a heaving, leaping mass, similar to the mosh pits at the gigs they went to some nights. Marco was hugging her and kissing her and telling anyone who would listen that she was his good luck charm, his rabbit's foot and four-leaf clover rolled into one, and seconds later they were tumbling away from the stadium in the centre of a happy, chanting throng.

There were more drinks than she could handle in more bars than she could count and she was introduced to people she would never remember. What she did recall – and she was quite spaced out by this point – was the unmistakable pride on Marco's face as he introduced her to his friends, who all seemed to be *top boys* or *solid geezers* or *total legends*, and their affable but uncertain reactions to her. She supposed she wasn't the sort of girl these men would expect Marco to go out with or had gone out with in the past. She knew she was different, and though Marco's friends were good-natured and charming in a rough sort of way, they knew she was different too. Perhaps she simply smelled wrong to his friends; they didn't realise it, but animal instinct had picked up some nasty otherness upon her.

Those thoughts played on her mind later as she lay awake beside him. She slept over at his house most nights – since his brother Tony moved out, he had most of the top floor of the house to himself, and his mother, while as silent as Marco was loquacious, seemed content to have her around. She couldn't sleep now though. Staring at the blue display on the digital radio on his bedside table, she watched the morning hours grind from two to three to four.

'You asleep, princess?' he mumbled, turning over in bed.

'Yes.'

'Wake up then.'

'Okay.'

Naked, he slid out of bed and padded towards the ensuite bathroom. She heard him splashing water on his face. She reached for his West Ham home shirt atop the puddle of clothes on the floor and pulled it over herself. He loved her to sleep nude, but she found certain aspects of intimacy – she had only been with two men before him – a struggle. At times she wished she could be one of those cool girls like Clare or Courtney who treated sex as casual entertainment. But Marco didn't want Clare or Courtney, she reminded herself. He wanted her and that was everything.

'I get like that sometimes during the game,' Marco explained when he reappeared. 'Just totally … wired. Your blood's up, yeah? Ready to fuck or fight. No surrender. Then it's over and after the rush, there's the crash. So you fall asleep. But you can't rest properly. Like soldiers on the battlefield, ready to leap up and take arms at any moment. Know what I mean?'

'I guess so,' she said uncertainly.

He sat down beside her on the bed. He was staring at her face but not into her eyes. Raising a hand, he gently swept the hair back from her forehead. 'Can I ask you something?' he said, then before she could reply he continued, 'How did you get those scars?'

She shrugged off his touch. She had always felt self-conscious about the row of white pinpricks that ran around her hairline. She couldn't remember when she had first noticed those small circles of pocked flesh; the scars had been there ever since she could remember, an unavoidable side-effect of her father's work and her own education. But she didn't want Marco to know about any of that quite yet, so she sought for a distraction. The light from the bathroom had fallen upon a row of cups and placards on the top shelf of his wardrobe, tinting the mementos golden. 'How did you get those?' she asked quickly. 'The trophies?'

'Fighting,' he said with pride. 'Here. Feel this one.'

Reaching up, he took down a carving of a boxing glove then passed it over. Unprepared for the weight, she almost dropped it. 'Onyx,' he explained. 'Heavy as hell, ain't it? Won me two of those bad boys. Eastern youth championships, five years back.'

She traced her fingertips over the stone carving as electricity crackled through her nerves. The trophy felt dangerous, like playing around with a loaded gun. Wetting her lips with her tongue, she passed back the glove and he tossed the weight easily from one hand to the other as she admired the popping curve of his biceps.

'I was good at fighting,' he went on. 'Boxing, I mean. Proper boxing, not street-brawling stuff, that's for mugs. It's a family thing. My dad battered Tony so Tony battered Robbo so Robbo battered me. We're a fighting family. Like you get dynasties of actors or writers.'

'You're pretty special at writing too,' she said. She thought of the poems he wrote to her. The tiny scraps of paper he would leave inside her notepads or slip into her pigeonhole at the Academy. Some of the poems were long and florid, as if his thoughts were bleeding over the pages. Others were terse and brutally minimal yet elegant. The discovery of a new one flowered roses in her cheeks. 'You're really good,' she told him, even though he looked away as if ashamed. 'I don't know whether they'd be seen as good in the way university professors see things as good. Rhyme and meter, iambic pentameters – that sort of nonsense. Technically, I'm no expert. But I do know what they make me feel inside. Like I'm being carried away from this world. Just for a short while.'

Marco shrugged. Was he blushing? Refusing to meet her enquiring stare, he set down the onyx boxing glove and picked up a dumbbell from the rack beneath the trophy shelves, flexing. 'Nah, it's not anything. Not anything special. Don't know where it comes from. Think I steal what I write from proper authors, then forget. That's what creativity is, innit? All these people who everyone says are geniuses, they're just great at remembering what geniuses said.' He was speaking too quickly; there was a sensuality in seeing him uncomfortable for the first time. That fleeting glance at his vulnerable side sent a thrill through her body. 'If you think my poems are weird or creepy or whatever, I'll stop, yeah?'

'I don't want you to stop,' she told him, laying a hand on his forearm. 'I only ... They mean a lot. That's all I wanted to say.'

'Want to know a secret?' he said, recovering some of his poise as he transferred the weight to the other hand and began another round of bicep curls. 'I got in a lot of practice before we both pitched up at the Academy together.'

'You wrote poems for another girl?' she asked.

'Never, baby girl,' he said. 'I wrote them for you.'

She stared quizzically at him. 'What do you mean?'

'You was in my school, weren't you? Back in the day. Had the biggest crush on you. Started writing you poems about that time. Proper soppy stuff. I'd have rather died than let anyone see them.' He grinned, recovering some of his cocksure attitude. 'If any of my mates had found them, I couldn't have taken the shame – I'd have had to leave school, leave town, probably the country too. But you left instead. So you saved me.'

She shook her head. 'No-no-no, we can't have been at school together. I was home-schooled,' she told him. She tried to keep her tone light even as faint recognition chimed in her mind. 'You must be remembering another Indian girl who you thought was me. Don't worry, it doesn't mean you're racist. Much.'

'Nah, it was you, defo,' Marco said with certainty. 'I thought you was called some different name back then but maybe I'm wrong. Whatever, I couldn't forget your face. Never got the courage to speak to you but I'd never mistake you for no one.'

He set down the dumbbell on the rack and stared at her. 'Then you went away. No one knew why and I did plenty of asking. Thought I'd lost you forever. Not until I saw you ... not until I got accepted at the Academy and caught your eye in the lecture hall. Nearly fell off my chair. Could be fate, who knows?'

'Who knows?' she repeated. There was a puzzle here that she couldn't hope to solve. She had never been to a normal school. Her father wouldn't allow it. Normal people went to normal schools and the Dala family was anything but normal. Her father had some unusual ideas, and one of those unusual ideas was that contact with regular people would reduce an intelligent person to their level of mental tedium; an intellectual cross-contamination. So she had grown up alone but surely not lonely, because Daddy was the most interesting man in the world and he was friends with people who were almost as interesting, and one day he would tell her every single one of his secrets.

'There's one thing I can't work out, Mya,' said Marco, sitting down on the bed and wrapping an arm over her shoulders with a peculiar half-smile. 'What do these people at the Academy do? What do they want with us? This ain't like a regular university, I'm sure of it. Why the hell are we here? Who's in charge?'

'Ask my dad tomorrow,' she said as casually as she could manage.

'Huh?'

'My dad. I'm using a fake surname here, so no one treats me any differently. My real name's Amaya Dala. My dad's Gurdeep Dala. We're students at the Meinhof-Dala-Smithson Academy. Do you see where I'm going with this?'

Marco's mouth gawped open then closed. He looked like a fish drowning in air. 'You ... your dad's ... your dad...'

Now he was baffled and uncertain, the way she had been at

the start of their relationship, and she was relishing the switch in control, the power she now held over him. 'Yes, that's right, my dad,' she said carelessly. 'You wondered who was in charge – well, it's my dad. So you can ask him all the questions you like. I told him we'd be meeting tomorrow for dinner. That means today. And that I'd be bringing my boyfriend too.'

She had never believed she would see him speechless. 'Jesus,' he said at last. 'That's … it's … there's a lot you haven't told me about yourself, Mya Samsara – or should I say Mya Dala? I thought that—'

'You thought I was sweet and innocent? As if I didn't have secrets.' He laughed shakily and shook his head. 'What was that song you played me? 'No One Is Innocent.' So there you go.'

'Wow. Jesus. God.' He blinked. 'Never thought I was the sort of geezer who got introduced to parents. I suppose we'd better get our heads down. Beauty sleep. Not that you need any.'

'I'm not going to be able to sleep,' she admitted. 'Just like you said – too wired.'

Marco grinned. 'In which case,' he said, placing a gentle kiss on the nape of her neck, his fingers trailing almost casually across her thigh, 'should we find a way to while away the hours?'

18

The White Prison

We are close to home. We're so, so close I can't believe it. The reddish glow of the early morning light has fallen upon the skeleton of the fairground wheel in the mid-distance. My eyes moisten as I stare out at the closed-down funfair that Marco and I broke into on our first date. The funfair, reduced to toytown dimensions, looks almost close enough to reach out and touch. I make callipers with my thumb and forefinger and compress the scene into inches. I can get there. I know I can. But first I have to find a way out of this place. We are at the top of a tower block, an insane distance above the earth. Below me I can barely see the well-known, little-loved flatlands. Wisps of cloud float below us. This tower is impossibly tall. I doubt any other building has ever been built so high. Shining silver railings loop up from the guardrail of the viewing platform to high above our heads, locking into the white brick of the building's roof. Evidently the bars are to prevent suicide attempts, but I reckon you would pass out from oxygen deprivation or terminal velocity before you hit the ground. No one wants to die unconscious; a sack of meat tumbling gracelessly to explode upon impact. Whether or not you're suicidal, everyone wants to know the time their life finally stops, right down to the final millisecond. It's the only way of taking back control.

'Great view, isn't it?' says Johanna. The wind tugs at her hair, pulling it away from her face. I had thought she was at least a decade older than me but in that moment she looks so youthful and carefree, as if the air — at our incredible height — has blown back the years. Perhaps it's the taste of freedom; it's so sweet. If you squint hard enough you can't even see the thick wire mesh that stops us climbing onto the ledge and flinging ourselves off. The bars that keep us safe and keep us trapped.

'The best,' I agree.

'I feel alive again when I'm up here,' says Johanna. 'We could be out in a normal place, two tourists way up high in a sky-scraper, sightseers admiring the view. The Seattle Space Needle, maybe, or the Burj Khalifa — if it wasn't for the guardrail and the disappointing absence of a sky bar.' She offers me a shy smile and I feel an urge to hug her. 'We can pretend though, if you want.'

'What do you mean?'

She pouts, hand on hip, tossing her hair. 'Cocktail, Miss Dala?' she asks. In that moment I can see how Johanna used to be, stuffed to bursting with humour and vivacity, before they locked her up and crushed her spirit. 'Strawberry daiquiri?'

'My favourite.' I grin, understanding the charade. She poises her fingers as if holding an invisible flute and passes it over. I mime drinking. 'Why, thank you,' I tell her, 'most refreshing.' It is. Oh wow, it really is. I can taste the sharp sugary fruit and the burned piquancy of the spirit.

'Olive? On a little cocktail stick?'

'Don't mind if I do.'

'We have a reservation later at that restaurant you can't stop talking about. Hottest joint in town. Every table was booked out months ago. But –' she pauses theatrically '– they made an exception for us. Of course.'

'Of course.'

'Then later drinks and dancing. Superstar DJs. Champagne on the house. Devilishly attractive company.'

'And that's just us two.'

'It doesn't get better than this.'

'It simply doesn't get better.'

We collapse against each other in laughter. Johanna feels nearly weightless in my arms, as fragile as a baby bird. Beneath the hanging folds of her regulation smock, she is so thin it seems she could slink through the metal bars and take flight. Anger flushes through me; I hate the faceless strangers who have done this to her, who reduced her to this state. She needs to get out, she needs freedom. But does she want it? From the moment we met on the exercise ground, she has been entirely accepting of her fate. They've broken her down until she genuinely believes she needs to be here. What sort of monster would do that to her? If she was stronger she could find a way out of the White Prison by herself, I know it. Perhaps that's why she needs me.

'I thought we could talk properly here,' say Johanna, 'now that we're alone.'

'Of course,' I tell her with real gratitude. This girl has given me something to aim for. The taste of fresh air, at long last, has flung my senses into disarray. For the first time since I've been locked up in here, I feel certain I will get out. They won't break me.

'Do you know why you're here, Mya?'

Resting against the railings, staring up at the endless blue of the sky, I decide I might as well try honesty. I owe Johanna that much.

'I think... I think it was a suicide attempt,' I tell her, picking my words carefully. 'I'm not lying, my memory's a total mess. If I knew what happened to me, I'd tell you. I've done silly things before. I'm not proud but I'm not exactly ashamed. I'm sure I've woken up in hospitals. But I've never woken up somewhere like this, where no one will tell me what's going on, how long I'm going to be here, whether I'm down for treatment or just being held like a rat in a cage. I've had no contact with the people I love. My dad, my boyfriend Marco. I've heard nothing from them. That's what scares me.'

Johanna's hand tightens on mine. 'What do you remember about him, this Marco of yours?'

I feel a prickle of uncertainty. 'First of all, I need you to tell me how you know so much about me. Put your cards on the table. I like you and I want to trust you. But someone trapped me here. And outside, someone –' I try to figure out how to convince her that what I'm saying is the truth, seeing as how Johanna doesn't believe I have a screen in my cell '– God, I know it sounds insane, but I... I've been replaced. They replaced me. Out in the real world, there's someone mimicking me. A girl who looks like me but isn't me in the slightest. A doppelganger. So I'm not good at trusting right now.'

'Fair enough,' Johanna nods. If she's concerned by how insane my words sound, she's not showing it. 'In the spirit of honesty and friendship, I'll tell you. I read your file.'

Swallowing hard, I can barely believe what I'm hearing. 'You did... you have... there's a file on me?'

The girl laughs. 'Of course, dummy. There's a file on you, there's a file on me. None of us are anything more than files. Personalities reduced to lines of code. There's a file on Magda the fitness instructor. There's a file on Lianne the cook,

Tristram the head porter, Duane who runs the guards. Don't you understand, My-My? We were all mad once. At one point in our past, we were totally, completely, painfully mad. But we were cured. That's why we have to stay here. So others can be cured too. So we can help cure them. That's the idea. That's the principle upon which this place is founded. That's how it sustains itself.'

My mind reeling, I cling to the guardrails for support. I feel as if I've lost my grip on this world and I'm tumbling an infinite distance through the atmosphere. 'What, you're part of this? You're in on the system? You're one of... one of them?'

'I'm one of them,' she agrees. 'But don't fret, my dear.' She steps closer and impossibly I can smell the sweet tang of strawberry daiquiri on her breath. 'I knew *they* were going to bring you to this place, Mya. You were slipping beneath the waves. It was no surprise at all to see you here. That's why I want to help you.'

'What do you mean?'

The girl folds her hands as if in prayer, staring out at the flatlands. The new dawn has tinted the unremarkable landscape into magical shades. 'You're important to me. You helped me live again. There's a lot of history between us, Amaya Dala, and that counts for plenty in my book.'

'So you're going to help me get out of here?' Apprehension scrabbles in my gut. I wonder who *they* are and how close she is to them; she has some special privileges, after all. Please don't tell me that I've misjudged her. 'Right? Right?'

Johanna shakes her head. She laughs lightly. 'No one gets out of here, Mya. Don't be silly. You looked alone and I thought you needed a friend. I felt like I owed you for how you helped me before.' Tenderly she strokes my cheek. Her eyes are earnest, glazed with the blank zeal of the convert. 'I'm sorry for what

I said earlier. I won't fall prey to those doubts again. This is a good place, Mya. You might not understand it at first. But in here you're helping people. You're changing lives.'

'You don't mean that. This is hell.'

She shakes her head, her black fringe whipping back and forth. 'You were in hell before. So was I. But you can't remember and I can. Trust me on this one.'

'How can I trust you when you're one of them, when you're complicit in everything?' I snap. 'They're all zombies here, Jo-Jo.' *Jo-Jo.* Where did that pet name come from? She actually flinches when I say those two short syllables, so I use them again. 'They're zombies, Jo-Jo. Just zombies. I was getting through to you before – wasn't I, Jo-Jo? Some part of you knows this isn't right. This isn't the answer. No matter what you tell yourself. You're not a zombie. But you're a liar. You're faking it. You trust *me* on this one.'

Her eyes are enormous and hurting. 'I can't listen to this anymore. I only wanted to help. Tell you it's not so bad, that you have someone here for you. I thought you understood, Mya. I mean, Jesus Christ, you talk to me about complicity? Seriously? I thought you knew. I thought you were—'

Then she spins on her heel and flees the tower, her hands clapped to her face. I feel a guilty sting but, worse, the utter coldness of isolation. She is institutionalised. Johanna is the same as the rest of them. I'm more alone than ever.

Reeling from betrayal, I don't even remember returning to my cell. The television screen on the wall is flickering again. *There are no screens in our rooms, Mya.* Is that so, Jo-Jo? I know what I'm seeing. The wind-knocked bulrushes wave goodbye as the marsh scene dissolves into somewhere else entirely. The milky sunlight has been replaced by a harsh electrical glare. Oh God, it's happening again. It's happening again and I am not sure that I can bear it.

The screen is showing a small room. The décor is a mixture of office and hotel suite. I see filing cabinets and an imposing desk in one corner, but there are abstract art prints on the walls, and an armchair and comfortable squashy sofa. There are two people sitting together on one of those couches, staring into one another's eyes, their fingers entwined. It is obvious that they love one another very much, that they are happy to be together, that they are grateful for every moment they share. Those two people are Marco and the girl who looks identical to me. They are definitely us. Only we've never been in this room before.

A door opens and the couple look up. A man, a stranger, walks in and smiles at us – no, he smiles at *them*, that girl is not me and she never will be – before perching on the desk. He has a patchy auburn beard, horn-rimmed spectacles and an intensely friendly expression. He is wearing corduroy trousers, a brown tweed blazer with leather patches at the elbows, and an absurd polka-dot bow tie.

'Good morning, gang,' the man says. His voice is soft with a faint Australian twang. 'How are you both feeling?'

'Fantastic,' I say. The sound of my own voice startles me. No, it's not me speaking; it's the girl on the sofa with her fingers clasped in my boyfriend's hands. She is so convincing. Surely Marco must know she's not me, though? He must realise that I'm not her? But there is no suspicion in his gaze. Only love.

'We're doing great, Dr Baumann,' Marco agrees. *Baumann.* I know that name. I definitely know that name even if I can't place his face just yet. Friend or enemy? He does look friendly, like a big cuddly bear, but I can't help feeling as though everyone is an enemy.

'Miss Dala,' the Australian man says. I beam up at him as if
I'm back at primary school and he's my favourite teacher. That
is definitely not me. That's not how I look at people; I don't
trust them enough. 'How have the past three months been for
you?'

Three months. Three goddamn months. So that's how long
I've been trapped in the White Prison. The days drag endlessly,
so how the hell have those weeks flown past? Three whole
months since I was replaced. Replaced by her. The woman on
the sofa holding on to Marco, that's not me. She's my doppelganger. My double. My replacement. I'm finding it hard to
breathe and my palms are slicked with sweat. I want to howl,
scream, smash my fists against the digital screen until the image
of her is splintered and warped. Because she can't be me. She
can't be with Marco. This can't be happening. But it's no dream.

The stranger with my face lets out a little sigh of utter contentment. 'It's been ... just ... bliss,' she says. Her eyes are shining
with tears of gratitude. 'That's the only word I can think of.
Bliss. I wake up every morning and I can't believe the world's
so full of wonderful things for us to do together. I go to bed
every night and I can't wait for the next day to begin. Not just
the next day – the next week, month, year. I'm looking forward
to the rest of my life. I feel alive again.'

'Any adverse sensations? Nausea, headaches?'

'None whatsoever.' She beams.

The professor sitting astride the desk – he's called Dr
Baumann, I must remember that name, it might be important
later – nods smugly. His tongue flickers over his lips like a snake
tasting the air. In that moment I don't think I've ever hated
anyone more.

'That sounds most promising,' he says. 'I'm so glad you've

found our work to be beneficial.' He turns towards Marco. 'And what about you, buddy? How are you adjusting?'

Adjusting. What a loaded word. But strangely fitting. I've been adjusted. There is no question about that. I know that I'm jagged and cracked. This woman is so smooth, so malleable, so polished and gleaming. But if she is me then who am I?

'Mya's happy, professor,' says Marco. 'That's what I want. That's all I've ever wanted.'

He doesn't know. He doesn't understand. He doesn't recognise that this girl is not me. Again I feel like screaming.

'Excellent, excellent,' Dr Baumann says. 'No further questions, gang. Bossman reckons I should run a few more tests but I'd say, with the greatest respect, he can go whistle. You're discharged. Free to go. With my blessing.'

He offers a thumbs-up with both hands. The couple on the sofa giggle. They stand up and walk arm in arm to the door. The professor opens it for them and drops his left eye into a matey wink. Marco offers his hand and they shake.

'Thank you, Dr Baumann,' my boyfriend says. 'Thank you for everything you've done for us.'

'All part of the service,' the man replies. He's talking to Marco but staring directly at me, or rather my replacement. 'You look after this one, y'hear?'

Marco drapes his arm over my shoulders – no, my doppelganger's shoulders – and squeezes her tightly. 'Of course,' he says.

'We'll check up on you again in another three months. Only a formality, no worries. Do keep us informed of any changes.'

'Well…' Marco says. The Mya next to him blushes and giggles again, her gaze demurely on the floor.

'Well, what?' Baumann asks, grinning indulgently. 'Come on, buddy, I'm a busy man.'

'We're going to get married,' Marco says, pure innocence glowing in his eyes.

'We're going to get married,' repeats my double.

This time I do scream.

19

The New Intake (fresh meat)

Her father greeted Marco at the front door with a firm hand-shake, then pulled him into a hug. Beers had been opened and the conversation was flowing pleasantly enough. Marco had surprised her by arriving in a slim-fitted navy blue suit with an open-necked black shirt. The combination of smart apparel with shocking-pink mohawk was striking, to say the least. Her father's face had been a picture as he took in the sight of this imposing stranger standing on his doorstep; an involuntarily pace backward, his nostrils flaring in surprise.

'Nice suit... did you rob a maître d'?' she asked while her dad was in the kitchen fetching cans of Red Stripe lager.

'I'm Italian, baby, fashion's in my blood,' he replied with a smirk. Then that familiar wriggle of an eyebrow to tell her that while he might be joking, he still meant every word. As he whispered in her ear, she could smell a cologne that was evocative, somehow old-fashioned – pine and leather, a scent an aged banker might slather on his skin. If his intention in dressing up was to make her feel more comfortable, he had failed badly. Slightly too late, she wondered whether this get-together might have been a mistake.

But the evening had been fine so far. Her dad seemed simul-taneously distracted yet elated. She just hoped he wouldn't be

too weird. She had spotted at least four beer cans crumpled
the bin, soldiers vanquished before the war had even begun, ar
there were two cigarettes burning in the ashtray.

The two men were talking about football and she zone
out of the conversation. The armchair was comfortable and
she hadn't slept in far too long. Running purely on nerves and
caffeine, she began to fret about how she had lied to Marco.
Thankfully, he appeared to have taken her explanation with
good grace. *I just wanted to be normal,* she told him. *I didn't mean
for this to happen. I didn't expect us to happen.* They had walked
together that morning from his house to the Academy, hoping
the fresh air would blow away the cobwebs, strolling hand in
hand past the bogs and bulrushes. The scenery wasn't beautiful
by any stretch of the imagination, but it was the place they
both belonged. *It's no big deal,* he replied, squeezing her hand.
*I get it. At my school there was a kid whose dad taught science. Mr
Edwards, his name was. Real bastard – the teacher I mean, not his
kid. So whenever Mr Edwards took one of us to pieces in class, we'd
give it back to his son in spades. Yeah – spades, rocks, broken bits of
wood, lots of nasty stuff. Sins of the father sort of thing, proper biblical.
I don't blame you for not wanting the same.* He had laughed and
she harmonised, albeit uneasily. Her dad had committed no sins.
His work was about changing people for the better. Changing
the world for the better. Changing minds.

'...their anger little more than sublimated homosexuality. The
caveman mentality is the recourse of the erotically uncertain.
The failure to connect emotionally results in physical explosions.
I refer you, obviously, to the Spartans and ancient Greeks, who
accepted that the pleasures of embracing another man's flesh
were identical to piercing it in battle.'

Blearily she raised her head and saw, with a sinking sensation,
that her father had folded his fingers into the shape of a steeple.

The way – oh no, oh God – he always did when he had made an important point during a lecture and expected agreement, possibly applause. Marco was staring back at him with a curious expression; he was smiling yet perched at the edge of his chair, as if poised to leap forward at any moment.

'What you're saying, right,' her boyfriend began, 'is that football hooligans don't really want to punch each other. Those geezers scrapping on the pitch last night actually wanted to … well … screw each other instead?'

She tried to work out what the hell they were talking about. The fight, of course, the fight at the football game. It had made the front pages of the newspapers and the morning news bulletins. The battle in the crowd during the televised England international. Some fans even invaded the pitch. The newsreader had called it an unpleasant regression to the dark days of the Eighties.

'West Ham United, isn't it?' her dad asked. Marco nodded assent. 'The gallant claret-and-blue, gentleman captain Bobby Moore, forever blowing bubbles. Or is the true image that of the gangs on the terraces? Fists into faces, knives swiping at tattooed forearms, bottles smashing against sweating bald heads. Fascinating to watch those lager-sodden troglodytes arrange themselves in formation. Irrational violence organised with the precision of a military strike. The Inner City Firm hooligan crew, am I right?'

'Inter City,' Marco corrected him. She groaned inwardly. It had been a trap.

Her father leaned forward, an eagerness in his expression. 'Your sort of game, is it?'

'Know a few boys from the old days,' he grunted. 'Don't run with that crowd anymore. Mug's game, innit? Cameras

everywhere now, lifetime ban or a prison cell. Technology always catches up with you.'

Her father drummed his fingers on his thighs. 'Indeed, my young friend. How acute of you. But let us bring ourselves back to the unpleasant scenes yesterday. It is my true belief that those angry young men last night were not fighting each other, oh no. They were fighting their own taboo desires.'

Marco's eyes had squinted almost shut. There was a strange and unsettling emptiness in his expression. The temperature in the room had dived towards freezing and her father, her bloody dad who knew so much and so little about human nature, was oblivious. Marco was about to say something, his mouth was opening and she feared what might come out of it, so she jumped in before he could speak.

'Keep up, Pops. Taboo desires? Seriously?' she stammered. 'No one's totally gay or straight or anything. Sexuality's a sliding scale, you're not anointed from birth. You need to be dragged kicking and screaming into at least the nineteenth century, maybe even the twentieth. But we'll get there, I promise.'

'She only calls me Pops,' he said, winking at Marco, 'when she realises I have led her down a path she wishes to tread no longer. She believes it irritates me. Essentially, she recognises my argument to be correct, but her liberal sensitivities prevent her from acknowledging a disgraceful reactionary viewpoint.' He smiled happily. 'I hope you don't think I'm cruel, young Mr Pellicci, but I cannot resist toying with my daughter's mind.'

'Your call, boss,' Marco said. He leaned back in his chair and took a long slurp of lager. 'My mama says I'm never too old or too big for a clip round the ear. She's right, too.'

'True, true.' He nodded. 'But as we saw from those regrettable incidents at Wembley last night, the bad old urges are not sleeping but simply dormant. All it requires is a little spark to wake them up. Sometimes those tiny explosions spark ... oh, something monstrous.'

'Is this going anywhere, Dad?' she asked. She had managed to form her expression into one of studied boredom, but she was picking at the skin around her fingernails. 'You know I hate football talk. I'm hungry, too.'

'You enjoy punk rock as well, don't you, Marco?' her father asked, ignoring her. She could have protested but would they even have heard her? She doubted it. Her voice was lost to them. 'I can see by your hair and by the most ... ah ... interesting band T-shirts you wear to our lectures. Such brutal music. So loud. So furious. So vibrant.'

'Oh yeah!' her boyfriend exclaimed, amiable and enthused once more, and she tried to relax. 'Punk saved my life, I reckon. First time I heard the Pistols or the Damned or the Clash or the Ramones ... oh man, I didn't even know music was allowed to sound like that. Blew me right up inside.' He thumped a closed fist against his chest. 'That's why I look like I do. Even though some people round these parts hate me for it. It's a mark of gratitude. Like if I'd had a heart attack and they'd stitched me up, I'd show it proudly. Wear my scars right on the outside.'

'All that sound and fury, signifying ... well, you tell me. Yet you seem such a pleasant fellow. Sitting here, politely smiling at my poor conversational gambits as if you couldn't think of a finer evening. Such a gentleman, I thought, as you walked into the house, shook my hand and kissed my daughter chastely on the cheek. Yet you find pleasure in such macho, even blood-thirsty pursuits.'

'Well now,' Marco said, 'I suppose I'm a man of contrasts.'

'Indeed you are!' Her father laughed. 'A complete man, alpha and beta impulses harmonising beautifully.' He clapped his hands together. 'But now we must eat. I trust your appetite has been set ablaze by the kindling of lager, Mr Pellicci, for tonight we have for you a plethora of the very finest dishes from the Indian subcontinent – prepared by myself, of course.'

He rose and gestured grandly towards the dining room, motioning for them to follow.

'It's all from The Bombay Bazaar on the high street,' she whispered in Marco's ear with a lightness she didn't truly feel, relieved they had stumbled through that conversation. 'Look out for the takeaway bags under the kitchen table.'

20

The New Intake (fresh meat)

If she thought the evening's discomfort was over when they sat down to dinner, she was sorely mistaken. Because Marco had evidently decided the time had come to pose some searching questions of his own.

'You know, I only found out you and Mya was connected yesterday,' her boyfriend said, washing down his forkful of jalfrezi with the remnants of his can of lager. Her father immediately replaced it. She rarely saw Dad drunk – he couldn't possibly work with a hangover, he told her, and he was always working – but they had already ploughed through at least a six-pack each. 'She told me she didn't want anyone else to know you were the boss. That people might treat her differently.'

'Understandable,' Gurdeep Dala agreed. 'No wants to be the teacher's offspring. It is terribly embarrassing.'

'We're still mostly in the dark though, aren't we?' Marco said. There was a worrying eagerness in his expression, a hunger in his voice, and she felt nausea as she choked down another gobbet of her slightly greasy murgh makhani. 'Been here months now. How I see it, you got a whole load of kids down here all dewy-eyed and hopeful, and you're stringing them along. Like a movie where you don't know where the plot's going and you only stick with it cos you already paid your money. Only here you're paying the money to us. For reasons I ain't worked out yet.'

'Did you not receive the letter of admission? Surely that would have put your mind at rest and quelled any troubling questions?'

Marco took another drink, finding interest in the water-colour painting of the African veldt on the far wall. 'Oh yeah, yeah-yeah-yeah, course. I got the letter to come here, just like everyone else. What did I have to lose? A few months' pay on the building site? Your Academy shebang sounded loads more fun.'

'Indeed.' Her father smiled sunnily, again steepling his fingers beneath his chin. 'Indeed.'

'My old mates are fascinated by this place,' he went on. 'Always asking me in the boozer what goes on in that dirty great big tower. What sort of show you're running here.'

'The best show in town,' her dad replied, still beaming. 'Our Academy attracts the brightest and best, the great and good. If I may permit a touch of arrogance, I believe we offer hope to humanity.'

Marco sniggered then hiccuped. She laid a hand on his shoulder as if she could restrain him from speaking further and he shrugged it off, the snub almost graceful. 'Brightest and best? Can't say I've ever been called that before. Teachers used to tell me I got a head full of rocks. Punk rocks, I reckon. So the joke's on them.'

'Oh, you do have potential, young Marco. Your school grades were – before your unfortunate lengthy absences from education – quite intimidating.'

'Not sure about that,' he muttered, busying himself with tearing up keema naan. 'Nah, not sure about that at all.'

'Are you ashamed of your intelligence, Mr Pellicci?'

'Can't be ashamed of what you ain't got.'

A low chortle. 'Such modesty.'

'Just the truth.'

'Do you always tell the truth, Marco?'

He nodded fervently. 'Big time. Say what I want. Do whatever I please. If people don't like hearing the truth, that's their problem.'

'And what if I decided to bring an unpleasant truth to light? Right here, as we dine on my wonderful cooking, having invited you into our home and our lives?'

She raised her hands in a *Stop* motion. She didn't like the track this conversation was taking. Not one little bit. 'Dad, maybe we should—' she started.

'I'd welcome it,' Marco told her father. Again neither of them seemed to be able to hear her. Had she spoken? Could she speak? Her boyfriend's grin was too wide, too white. 'Tell me anything you like, Mr D. I'm a boxer, or used to be anyhow. I'll take it on the chin.'

She was performing a frantic mime and her dad was pretending not to notice. 'What if I told you,' he continued implacably, 'that I happen to know you are an imposter at our Academy? There was no letter. You remain here only upon my say-so. You are a welcome guest, do not mistake my sincerity here. But an uninvited guest. A most vivid and fascinating ghost at our feast.'

Time seemed to stop. She looked from one man to another. Then Marco burst out into a huge crow of laughter and her father joined in with his familiar whinnying giggle and she stared at the pair of them, baffled. She had feared a scene, a confrontation, and now they were beaming at one another like long-lost brothers.

'Busted,' Marco said, still laughing. 'Yeah, you got me, I been stealing an education. I ain't seen this little raver for more than ten years. Thought I'd lost her forever. So when I realised she was at the Academy, I followed her in.' He snapped his fingers. 'I guess now you got to either call the police on me or shake my hand. Cos you knew right from the very start I was blagging this whole thing. And you know what? I think you like it.'

'How right you are, Marco Pellicci,' her dad said, warmly wringing his hand. He raised his beer can and Marco knocked it with his own in a rough toast, beer pattering on the tablecloth. 'How can I fail to be impressed by such braggadocio? Such recklessness in the pursuit of love. Indeed, I am so very, very pleased you are part of our lives now.' He dropped an eyelid into a roguish wink. 'I must say, I am also extremely impressed by your poems.'

Marco blinked. The laughter stopped like a shut-off tap. 'What poems?' he asked coldly.

'The poetry you wrote for my daughter. Wonderful. Quite wonderful.'

Only moments ago the room had been charged with bonhomie. Now the atmosphere was arctic. Her boyfriend's shoulders were heaving like a bull readying its charge. 'That was us ... that was between us ...' he stammered. 'You got no ... no right ... you can't just ... just break that trust.' Standing up suddenly, he slammed his fist down on the table and she let out a short shriek. 'Fuck this, I'm out.'

She grabbed for his arm and he pulled away. The suit fabric left a rasp like sandpaper on the flesh of her palm. Then he was gone, butting the table in his haste to be free of her. His nearly full can of lager toppled to the floor.

They were alone in the dining room. The beer glugged onto

the carpet, filling the atmosphere with its yeasty stench. She stared over at her father in mute reproach, horrified at how the evening had ended. He stared back at her. He appeared to be strangely satisfied.

21

The White Prison

It is parade day. A celebration for the founder of this institution. Everybody is expected to attend. It's a small mercy that we patients don't have to perform one of Magda's gym routines – a synchronised dance of broken souls – in honour of whatever sick bastard constructed this hellhole.

They must have taken down the walls of the exercise yard because where we are standing is at least the size of a football pitch. There are ranks upon ranks of blank-faced people in their smocks. A vast army of the lost. Looking to my left and right, I am unable to see the end of my row – and there are hundreds of rows. Oh God, how many of us are trapped here? I'm standing next to Johanna in the centre of this rigid mass of humanity. We have made our apologies to one another and, while I gave mine with good grace, I most definitely did not do it in good faith. Despite our fight on the viewing platform, despite what she said, I still feel as if I can get through to her. Surely I *was* getting through to her? I need an ally here and she knows more than anyone about the workings of the White Prison. More importantly, if I ever escape and make it back to Marco, then Johanna may be the only person who can vouch that I am the real Mya. So I need her on my side.

A hush descends upon the crowd. I suppose we are staring

towards a stage but all I can see is a phalanx of broad pastel-shaded backs.

'He's here,' says Johanna. She's a tall girl, only a couple of inches below six feet, and she is craning to look over the shoulders of the men in front of us. I have no chance. 'He's on stage right now.'

'Who is he? What does he look like? What's he saying?'

She doesn't respond. Something is wrong with the speaker's microphone – I can only hear screams of feedback, the drone-like fuzzing of an untuned radio. But no one else seems to have difficulty making out the words. The crowd appears entranced.

'What's he saying?' I ask again.

'He's saying… he's… he's saying…' she starts then stutters to a stop. Are her eyes wet? Oh please, surely not. 'He's saying that when his work is done, we can go back to being ourselves. Once we're cured, we can be ourselves again. That's what he's saying, Mya.'

She can't fall for that confidence trick, can she? Somebody please turn off the gaslight. I'm scared for both of us. Because I can tell that she believes him.

'Your sacrifice has allowed yourselves to live again.' Finally I can hear the man on stage, although his voice is heavily distorted as if echoing from forty fathoms deep. I gaze around at the faces of my fellow patients, expecting to see anger or at least disgust. Instead there is only acceptance – even tearful smiles. It's so obvious that the satanic hypnotist on stage has brainwashed them. 'You are the pioneers. Never forget that, my friends. Your work shall allow humanity to reach a higher plain. A plain of peace, a plain of contentment, a plain of hope. We will get there. I promise that. With your help we will get there. This day, we are ascending.'

There is applause. A great swelling that flows and churns

and shakes the ground beneath my feet, and I press my hands against my head, trying to block it out. Trying to block everything out.

The next week – I'm timing my breaths again, determined not to let the days slip by unnoticed as I did before – passes unremarkably. I have a plan. My time is coming soon. Until then I have to stay calm. I'm surprised at how little my escape worries me. I'm more scared thinking about what will come afterwards. For now though, I'm crawling the walls, sticking to the outskirts of this institution, scrutinising the faces of my fellow inmates. Wondering if they are suspicious because I don't look as blank as them. There are no mirrors in this place but I'm sure I can make out a hint of my reflection in the black eye of my wall screen, and I'm grinning madly.

Stuck here for any longer? Not a chance. I've committed the plan to my mind, reciting it six times before bed and six times when I wake up. Mya's catechisms, or maybe my vedas. The White Prison is only vulnerable when its routine is disturbed; with so many patients, it's impossible to track every one of us at the same time. There are cameras fitted into the walls but they will be blinded by smoke and flames. If the plan works then there will be too much else going on for those cameras to focus on me. There will be running, there will be shoving, there will be confusion. Chaos. Panic. Screaming.

I'm ready to be me again. Not just because I hate being trapped here. It's because of Marco. He's with someone who looks the same as me and he hasn't realised it yet, and this woman might well be dangerous. In those bursts of video activity he seems so placid and calm. Has he always been like that? Something tells me not, but I can't trust my memory.

What would Marco think if he saw us both together – two

Mya standing in front of him? Which one would he trust? I don't think we'd even come to that moment. He would just think he was losing his mind, obviously. Therefore I have to get him alone. Somehow.

The fairground is so close. If only I had some way of summoning Marco to the fairground then I think I'd have a chance. Because this girl, this other Mya, she wouldn't have seen what I saw. She wouldn't have felt what I felt when we kissed at the top of the big wheel.

The other girl, my double – how does she feel? Does she understand love? Does she know what she took from us? Does she know about me? Surely she must. Surely that simpering, giggling clone must at least sense that she is a replacement. Not the original. I can't begin to imagine who or what she might be. If she is even human at all.

On a purely instinctive level, surely Marco has to be suspicious too? She must move wrong, taste wrong, smell wrong. Even if Marco's mind refuses to send out any warning signs, maybe his body is reacting differently to her. It makes me sick, physically sick, to think of them together. In my brief glimpses of her on the video screen, my double appears so different to me in life that she must be different in bed, too. She can't share the intimacy we have treasured; I can't let myself think of that, I won't allow it. Does Marco ... does Marco ... does Marco notice that she's fucking him all wrong?

Oh God, I've got myself into a state again. I'm backed up against the bed, as near to a corner as I can find in this endlessly curving room. Whimpering and shaking, twisting clumps of lank hair around my fingers, I shake my head to clear it of the frazzled static that is threatening to blot out rational thought. Too much of that sort of behaviour and I'll never be able to break free and get back to Marco. My plan relies on appearing calm, placid, normal. No threat whatsoever.

Breathe. Breathe, Mya, breathe. Think of the escape plan. Think of how incredible it will be to taste fresh air, freedom air. Think of how you'll make everything right. Think of holding Marco in your arms again.

Breathe. Think of something good. *Think happy thoughts*, a deranged cartoon voice shrills in my ear. *Happy thoughts, Mya, and you'll float away.*

So I try to float away. I think of Christmas. Our first Christmas together. I never celebrated the holiday with my father; culturally he's Hindu but he holds contempt for every religion equally. No Diwali and no Christmas either. Marco and I used to love Christmas, though. Think of Christmas, Mya. Think of the good times. Think of the good times we'll share again. Soon, so soon.

We are still in our pyjamas even though it's late afternoon because no one is going to intrude; this is a Christmas just for us. Okay, so the turkey is a little dry and I've blackened the pigs-in-blankets and the parsnips are so underdone they could be used as cudgels. It doesn't matter because we have each other. We have dragged our kitchen table into the living room so we can watch Christmas movies while we eat, and now it's an Arnold Schwarzenegger comedy where he's dashing around like a lunatic trying to find a last-minute present for his son, and we're laughing even though the film is pretty terrible, because we have drunk six snowball cocktails each and we are giddy with happiness. Or at least I was. One minute I'm fine, the next minute ... I'm gone. Because a Great Wave has struck me, taking me completely unawares. I'm under the table, sobbing and howling, rocking back and forth, praying for an end to everything.

Now Marco is with me. He holds me. He hushes me. He whispers soothing words in my ear and I can barely make out what he's saying, fighting against the current that aches to drown me, because he always says the same words when I'm under the waves: *Everything will be alright. Everything will be alright. Everything will be alright.*

Eventually, everything is alright, or as near to alright as it will ever be. A Christmas miracle; it has been only the smallest of Great Waves. Barely a ripple. I am fine. Thanks to Marco.

I come out from beneath the table. For the first time I realise Marco is wearing a silly wig – his hair stands up in a strip of bright pink spikes tracking down the centre of his skull – but when I touch his Mohican, needing to be certain he's real and not a hallucination, it feels like actual hair. Since when did he have a crazy hairstyle like some punk rocker from decades ago? This is wrong.

Something else is wrong too. Because when I emerge, clasped in his arms, we are not in our little flat. Now we're in Marco's home and I'm being embraced by his whole family, whose faces are whitened and creased with concern. His mother and his brothers and his Uncle Giuseppe don't know what to say. I've scared them. Marco is explaining that I'm prone to terrible cramps; it's a bad time of the month. I am both impressed by his ability to lie on the spot and irritated that he couldn't think up a more delicate deceit. I'm being hugged by Sofia – his sister, a bouncing bundle of curly dark hair and hooped earrings and overwhelming perfume – but I'm sure I've never seen her before. She's been out in Australia, travelling with her boyfriend, for as long as I've known Marco. Sofia is holding me as if she deeply cares about me, as if we're old friends. Did this really happen? We shared last Christmas alone, just the two of us, I'm sure. I don't understand. Something's wrong with my memory.

It doesn't matter. I have distracted myself, that's the main thing. I'm calmer. Now is not the time to succumb to any Great Waves. Not when I'm so close to getting out. And I will get out.

Pushing myself up on my bed, I realise that in my hysteria I've shunted the mattress away from its moorings, uncovering a secret treasure that I stole and buried on my very first day in the White Prison. Caught by the low light, the knife winks up at me. Blunt but sharp enough. I hold it in my right hand, testing its weight. Wondering whether I will ever use it – and who I will use it on.

Who or what: maybe my replacement isn't even human. Has plastic surgery gifted her my features? Is she wearing a Mya mask, her face carved and sculpted into my likeness? Or has she been artificially created in her entirety? Everything else that has happened to me is so insane that I can't rule out any possibilities.

The key question is: does my double bleed like me?

If my plan works, we might find out.

Sliding the knife back into its hidey-hole, I allow myself a slight, tight smile.

Time passes. Faster now. Faster.

22

The New Intake (fresh meat)

The months passed quickly. Was she dreaming? It felt as if a kidnapper had made off with the old Mya and slipped a replacement into her little corner of the world, hoping that no one would notice. The shy home-schooled girl had become a confident, self-reliant young woman with friends and a busy social life and a boyfriend who adored her. Her change was so complete that she doubted her younger self would even recognise her. She went to punk gigs and boxing bouts with Marco, and while she disliked the violence of both the music and the sport, she loved him and wanted to understand his obsessions. During the concerts she stood at the back of the crowd nursing a plastic cup of cider while Marco threw himself into the mosh pit, the stage lights picking out his bobbing spikes. He bought her an acoustic guitar and taught her chords so they could play along together to Blitzkrieg Bop and White Riot, and after a few weeks she was starting to master fingerpicking and even crafted a few simple songs. She thought of asking him to write lyrics for her, but the confrontation with her dad was fresh in her memory. Marco had apologised, in his own fashion, for fleeing that night. *Those poems ... that soppy shit ... that ain't me, you understand?* She understood, even though his response saddened her. He simply couldn't bear for anyone else to see his softer side. She supposed she had to be grateful that he had let her clamber inside the shell he had built to shut out the world.

So they never talked about the disastrous dinner. Her father was out of town frequently, charming backers for a new project, and no one else seemed to be aware of Marco's illicit presence among the students. She was simply relieved that life was continuing much as before. But the Academy no longer felt quite as safe so she spent more and more time in Marco's world. She was introduced to his brothers Tony and Roberto, who treated her similarly to his West Ham buddies – with amiable uncertainty. But she was also introduced to Marco's Uncle Giuseppe, whom she adored.

The party conversations had floated past her like the helium balloons bobbing against the ceiling. Those balloons were in honour of Giuseppe – seventy-eight years old that day and still running two miles each morning through the local woods, Marco told her proudly. That had been before he was yanked into the kitchen by Tony and Robbo for a private drink. As she craned her neck to stare through the open door, she knew the siblings were talking about her – translating the chuckles and nudges and fist-bumps, they were judging her but kindly – and she felt at once reassured and self-conscious. She was happy enough hiding in the furthest corner of the living room, eking out her glass of red wine, the voices spiking in volume as the drinks went down. No one seemed to notice her. Her thoughts drifted to a place close to contentment.

'Hello there, pretty stranger.' She stared upwards blearily. Uncle Giuseppe had perched on the armrest of his chair. The old man's face – twinkling little coals of eyes buried deep in a face that was constructed of wrinkles within wrinkles – swam into focus. 'Cheer up, eh? You cannot spend the entirety of my birthday party pining alone. In fact, I forbid it. Here! I go ...'

Springing up from the armrest with astonishing vigour, Giuseppe departed then returned moments later, dragging Marco by the arm. 'Listen now,' he began, then immediately lost his train of thought. They waited patiently while the old man tapped his fingernail on the rim of his wine glass, before his eyes lit up once more. 'Ah yes, listen. You shame me, young Marco. Your girl, sitting here by herself while you drink beer with your layabout brothers.'

'I couldn't help it,' Marco protested. 'You know Tony.'

'I know Tony and I know you. Tony has no romance in his soul. Why do you run away from this vision?' Hooking an arm around her neck, the old man pulled her close, his breath a nimbus of chianti and denture paste. 'You love this girl?'

Marco rolled his eyes. 'Oh come on, Uncle Gi, don't put us on the spot. We barely know each other.'

'Painted,' his uncle said enigmatically, forefingers making brushstrokes in the air. 'Painted all over your face. You can't fool me, boy.'

Marco shrugged, shuffling his feet, crimson blotches appearing on his cheeks. No doubt he would attribute his blushing uncertainty to alcohol. She could not help but feel offended by his indecision. Where was his overbearing confidence now? Where was his romantic recklessness?

'If I had such a girl,' Uncle Gi went on, 'I would not hide myself away. In a kitchen, of all places. I could not bear to miss her for a moment. I would be brave, I would be bold, and if I should expire at the very sight of her – ah, sweet death! Far better for a heart to become so stuffed with emotion that it bursts, than that heart never beat at all!'

Clapping a hand to his chest, the old man contorted his face into a lovestruck grimace that looked more like he was suffering severe constipation. Conceding defeat, Marco burst out laughing and she joined in diffidently.

'Uncle Gi has a gift,' he told her, 'for very bad poetry.' Gazing fondly at one another, uncle and nephew clinked glasses. 'That's how he won over Ciara all those years ago,' Marco added, gesturing across the room at the woman with kohl-stained eyes and hair dyed an unlikely aubergine shade. 'Some say wooed, others say battered into submission, with his poetic bullshit.'

'Bullshit glazed with honey,' agreed Giuseppe. 'Words are our only weapons, boy. Women have a great many weapons at their disposal. We men have a very ill-stocked armoury in this battle of romance. But do we have our words. Look at Cyrano. But then Cyrano was a coward anyway. I have no sympathy. A coward hiding behind a solitary ugliness. If it were not his nose, it would be another feature – weak men forever find a way to justify their lack of bravery. And what is a big nose anyway? I have a big nose, you have a big nose, all Pellicci men have big noses. A family heirloom, a badge of honour. You know what the classical philosophers say? Giant nose, giant...' He pursed his lips, pumping his forearm in an unmistakable gesture.

'Let's keep it clean.' Marco grinned, and now it was her turn to blush. 'There's ladies present, yeah?'

Uncle Gi held up his hands. 'Apologies, my dear.' He waved over at his wife and blew a kiss across the room. Ciara rolled her eyes and shook her head as her lips tilted upwards; in that fleeting expression she witnessed the frustration and adoration of a decades-long union.

'She was seventeen,' the old man said, his eyes clouding over as he lost himself to memory. 'Black hair and a simple white dress. Every boy in Catania wanted her but she chose me. We went to England with the clothes on our backs and a handful of coins in our pockets. No one wanted us but that was fine, we wanted each other and we endured.' Giuseppe let out a short laugh that was very nearly a sob. 'You keep your dream, boy. You keep this impossible, glorious girl close. There's a special place in heaven that God keeps for dreamers. Maybe one day you realise your dream is reality, or reality is a dream. Is all the same anyway. You understand me, Marco?'

Marco clapped his uncle on the back and the pair embraced. She wasn't sure whether he did understand. Not truly. But she did.

It was only when she was completely knotted into their relationship that she began to notice another side to Marco. Not a good side. A part of his character that worried her. At first, she had thought it harmless, even silly, when she saw him slam a fist against a wall or seat when West Ham conceded a goal – all men got angry at football, didn't they? But there were other times. Scarier times. The time when Marco confronted a neighbour, fists raised, during a pointless and stupid argument about a car blocking his driveway. The time when Marco returned from a night out with his brothers with his knuckles swollen and bloodstains down the front of his Zen Arcade T-shirt. Worse, the time when Marco chased a gang of kids down the high street after one shouted *Paki slag* at her, catching the ringleader and dangling him over the canal bridge, bawling into the teenager's face until – every pretence of street-toughness having long evaporated – the boy burst into tears and begged to be set free. *He won't do that again*, Marco told her afterwards, upsettingly satisfied. *If you'd let go over the bridge*, she hissed back, *that kid would never have done anything again*. Her boyfriend stared at her, his face painted with honest confusion. *It was just shock treatment, babe. I can't abide that sort of racist crap. Especially when it's against someone I love. I only want to protect you, Mya.*

It was only later, much later, that she realised it had been the first time he told her he loved her. All things considered, she would have preferred a poem.

'Boys will be boys,' said Clare after she confided in her friend. 'He's letting off steam, they all do it. Geraint plays rugby, he's always coming back on Sundays battered and bruised. Loves it, the big silly sod. It's war games, pretending they're soldiers. Showing off their big guns and big dicks. I'd leave him to it if I were you.' Her friend tilted her chin with her fingers, staring searchingly into her eyes. 'Unless he raises a hand to you. If he ever does that – ever-ever-ever – then I'll chop off his bollocks with a bread knife. That's a promise, Mya.'

She wished she could believe that Marco was only letting off steam. She knew he would never hurt her. Not intentionally. But still she worried. She thought of how his eyes darkened whenever he lost his temper; she remembered a nature documentary on great white sharks and the creeping dread when the camera pinpointed their black, emotionless eyes. That was how Marco looked when he got angry. Not too often, but often enough to unnerve. Her intelligent, eloquent, loving boyfriend temporarily took leave of his soul and became a predator. She saw those eyes piercing through her dreams. Surely it should be romantic to dream about her partner? It didn't feel that way.

But when he was as sweet as he was being that evening, his arms wrapped around her, his voice soft, his expression one of total devotion, it was easy to forget about that black-eyed, intimidating presence. His alternate persona: Mad Marco.

'You'll never know how lucky I am to know you,' he whispered as they lay naked together in her single bed. 'I'm looking for a word to describe you. A word that fizzes on the tongue, effervescent, the act of telling sets you tingling inside and out. I'm searching for that word, always I'm searching. Hunting down that word which perfectly fits you. I'll find it one day. But then again, it might be a crime to catch it.'

How could a man who spoke so beautifully be capable of causing harm to her? She nestled into his muscular frame and wished away her worries. They continued their lives together. The purpose of the Academy was no clearer to the students but – perhaps surprisingly – few of them quit. They co-existed alongside the white-coated workers even though they had little direct contact. The lab workers' mere presence convinced many of the intake there must be a job at the end of the process; that the lectures and assignments were part of a training regime. Their classes centred around the human brain and they were encouraged to end each day with a personal history lesson, with particular attention paid to their emotional state. *How did that make you feel?* either Dr Baumann or Dr Kolstein would ask, and after the initial spiel the whole class was encouraged to contribute. *Do you feel angry? Sad? Did it disturb the balance of your mind?* Always the questions.

She was alone in knowing her purpose at the Academy: to learn her father's trade. She knew if her other classmates discovered her secret – that her surname wasn't really Samsara but Dala, that her father's name was embossed in gold upon the Academy's crest – the questions would never cease. But she would have been helpless to respond. Still, there were rumours. The theories ranged from a tax dodge, to being guinea pigs for a medical experiment, to being filmed surreptitiously for a reality television show. A milky-skinned boy named JJ, who either never changed his clothes or had several identical monochrome Gary Numan T-shirts, told anyone who would listen that there were thousands of hidden cameras studded across the site. Some students didn't bother digging deeper and simply enjoyed the ride. 'It's just like university, only you get paid,' Clare announced one evening in the pub, her words flecked with finality. 'So why bother trying to cope with reality?' It seemed that most of the students agreed with her.

Her other concern was Alec. He had fallen hard for an Australian bartender called Jonas, and when the feelings weren't reciprocated – or rather, brutally shunned – he fell into a decline that alarmed them all. He stopped washing, his hair grew shaggy and lank, he shuffled through the hallways with an old man's bent gait. One morning, as he shook his left hand free from writing cramps during one of Kolstein's indeterminable lectures, the sleeve of his stained plaid shirt slipped back and she saw a dirty constellation of cigarette burns pocking his forearm. She thought of the criss-crossed lines of razor-blade scars at the tops of her thighs, her hesitation marks, and empathy flooded her body. She wanted to talk to him, she needed to talk to him – if the tender-hearted young Scotsman was floundering in a Great Wave of his own, maybe she could swim through the churning waters and pull him back to the surface.

She was just figuring out the best way to get Alec alone. She knew she could help him. She could save him from himself.

Then one day, in early springtime, Alec disappeared.

'They'll find him at the bottom of the canal with his pockets full of stones,' Clare mumbled in the common room the next morning, her eyes red-rimmed, her complexion waxy. Her boyfriend Geraint reached across to squeeze her hand and she pushed him away. 'He didn't want to die, I don't think. But he didn't want to live enough either.'

When the security guards forced their way into Alec's room, they found the bed neatly made and his clothes folded up inside suitcases. His mobile phone and credit cards lay on the bedside table. An uneasy atmosphere hung over the Academy. The air seemed thick, heavy and starved of oxygen. Conversations collapsed, their true purposes better left unspoken. Everyone was afraid of speaking too loudly, as if a joke or a crass remark might make them guilty of an unspecified crime. Marco was away in Crete on his brother Robbo's stag weekend so she and Clare clung together, needing one another's comfort yet barely talking. Throughout the hideously dragging hours, guilt raked at her conscience. She should have done something. She should have told her father about her fears for Alec. She could have saved him.

Three days later, Alec came back.

'Jesus, it's great to see you guys.' He beamed to an audience of gaping open mouths. The Academy canteen had fallen silent. Even the lab workers were staring. A knife was dropped and clattered on a plate, the shockwaves reverberating around the hall. 'Sorry to worry anyone. Really sorry. I just went away to get my head straight, I think.' He laughed easily. 'Can't remember what I did. Must have worked though, aye?'

His hair was neatly trimmed and there was a lustre in his eyes she hadn't seen for months. Caught between joy and fright, she gawped at him and for a moment it seemed the young man was transparent. She could see right through him to the wall behind. At last, Clare pushed herself up from her chair and paced slowly towards Alec. When they were kissing distance away, she raised her arms and locked them around his slender waist, her head resting on his chest.

'I wanted to see if you were really real,' she said quietly. 'It's going to take me a long while to convince myself that you're not a ghost.'

'No bocan here,' Alec said, stroking the strands of auburn hair back from her face, placing a gentle kiss on her forehead. 'I'm real as real ale. Solid as a politician's principles.'

Clare's upper lip curled. Drawing back her hand, she hit him on the cheek with a hard, open-palmed blow.

'Was that real?' she demanded.

'Yes. Yes, it was. Ow.'

'You selfish bastard,' she spat. There was a low murmuring in the hall, the sound of stools being scraped back. 'Scaring us like that. You selfish fucker.'

'That's right.' Alec nodded. He grinned even as his left eye filled with water and his cheek throbbed an outraged red. He held up his hands. 'She's right, gang. I was selfish. But I won't do anything like that again. Promise. I'm better now. Much better.'

Then Clare broke down in tears and Alec laughed and took her in his arms and the room erupted in a warm wash of applause.

23

The New Intake (fresh meat)

When Marco came back from his lads' holiday sporting a heavy bruise beneath his left eye – which she tried not to notice – she could not make him understand. He didn't see how tormented she had been over Alec's disappearance. How guilty she felt about not reaching out to him before he nearly – so very nearly – tumbled off the precipice.

'Like the boy said, he went off for a few days to get his head straight,' Marco said, draining his pint, drumming his fingers on the table impatiently. She had felt a little put out that their first evening together after more than a week apart was in the Grey Goat, instead of her favourite Italian restaurant in the town square, but tried not to let her irritation show. 'Should've probably told someone. But yeah, no harm done, eh?'

'I was scared,' she said in a small voice. 'So scared.'

Marco leaned over and kissed her. His breath smelled of something chemical. A vein was pulsing in his forehead. His foot was jiggling to an internal rhythm. He hadn't been able to sit still for a minute. 'That's cos you're a good person. You care for people.'

She felt a wriggle of anxiety in the pit of her stomach. 'Aren't you? Don't you?'

He shrugged and sniffed. 'I like the skinny little toerag, don't get me wrong. But some blokes ain't cut out for the rough stuff. If he's gonna try and top himself over some barman who ain't even queer, when he's never loved and lost, what chance does he have when some queen breaks his fragile little heart?'

She blanched. A damp, flat odour assaulted her nostrils. She had yearned for his touch over the past awful week but now there was a terrible coldness emanating from him. The few inches between them felt like a howling void. 'This isn't like you,' she said. 'You... you're not... you don't normally say things like that.'

Marco shrugged again, shaking his head. She noticed white powdery matter around his nostrils and felt a sickly understanding. 'Yeah, yeah, whatever. So, what's the plan, little princess? Couple more drinks –' he grinned but his lips curved too widely, splitting the smile into a leer '– or shall we blow this joint? Christ, it was torture in Malia, hundreds of girls walking around in only a stitch and a promise. But I kept myself pure for you. So... what do you say? Back to my place to, uh, reconvene?'

She stared back in revulsion. 'You're off your head,' she said. 'Was that supposed to be a compliment?'

Marco pushed back the pink spikes of his hair and sniffed again. 'Come on, Mya, I'm only messing with you. I missed you this week. Swear down. Here –' he leaned in to whisper conspiratorially '– later on you can tell me about your little pals and their exciting adventures. Promise I'll listen. Just not now, yeah? Hey ho, let's go.'

'I'm not going home with you,' she said, attempting to gulp down a choking lump in her throat. 'This isn't really you. Is it?'

'This is the best possible version of myself,' he said grandly, lifting his pint glass up to the ceiling and slopping beer down his sleeve. 'Really, you should be honoured.'

'I'm not honoured, I'm bored. You're being a bore. And a boor. See what I did there? You like wordplay, don't you?'

His lips were still perked up at the corners but an arrowhead of irritation had formed on his brow. 'Don't tease me, baby girl.'

'I'm not teasing you,' she snapped. She fanned her fingers beneath her eyes, irritated that her body had transmuted anger into tears, not wanting to cry in front of this man who seemed so much like a stranger tonight. 'I think I should go now. Alone. I don't want to be around you right now. Not when you're being like this. Pretending to be someone else – or maybe this was the real you all along, and I never noticed.'

His gaze went dark and the room closed in on her. 'What's that supposed to mean?' he said. His words were soft but unmistakably menacing; knives wrapped in velvet.

'Oh, figure it out, Marco,' she said, trying to stay the fear from her voice. She realised a number of other drinkers were looking round at them. 'Even pissed-up and coked out of your brain, you're not stupid. You're just trying too damned hard. You're a fake.'

His jaw clenched. His breathing was ragged. His posture was hunched like a bull readying itself to charge. 'What's that supposed to mean?' he repeated.

She laughed wildly. A cruel doppelganger seemed to have taken charge of her tongue and she was powerless to bite back the mocking words. 'You faked your way into my life. You're faking right now. I don't know who you are. You're a poet who's too chickenshit to let anyone see the best side of him. You mangle your own syntax so nobody'll question your working-class credibility – even though you can't hide that you know things, you really know things. Worst, you're a punk who lives with his mama. A pink mohawk and a studded leather jacket in this day and age? Really? Don't you notice everyone laughing at you behind your back? Punk's dead, Marco Pellicci. You're making yourself look even more of a throwback than you already are. It's time you grew up.'

His hand shot out and clamped down on her wrist. 'You'd best watch your mouth.'

Time seemed to stop.

'Or what?' she said quietly. She felt icy water running through her veins. She was not afraid of him; her only feeling was betrayal. He wasn't menacing, he wasn't the Mad Marco ogre as many saw him, he was simply a petulant child who had grown too tall and too strong for anyone to risk disciplining him. 'Or what, Marco?' she asked again, staring down at the hand locked around her wrist. 'What will you do to me?'

A semblance of humanity returned to his expression. Twin flames of shame lit his sunken cheeks. He dropped his hand and closed it into a fist. 'Right then,' he said sullenly. 'Fine. If that's how you feel. Go on. Leave. You'll leave me just like everyone else does.'

Grabbing her bag and coat, she stumbled towards the exit, gracelessly knocking over the table in her haste to be as far away from him as possible.

She had almost reached the doorway when she heard the sound of breaking glass. Then a shriek.

24

The White Prison

The screen shimmers and shakes. There is a howl of static that I match with a whimper of my own. The frazzled mess of blacks and whites and greys is forming into definable shapes.

This is our apartment in the Academy. I can see everything. I remember everything. Our bed with the woven blanket showing the African savannah. My guitar perched in the corner, silently waiting for its owner like a faithful, abandoned pet. Marco's boxing trophies on the wardrobe shelf. I stare through the screen and I'm back in this alternate world; I can't bring myself to believe it is reality. What have I done? I don't want to see. I have to see.

The camera – if that's what it is – focuses and picks out a figure sitting on the edge of the bed. It's Marco. He's awake. There is a dark-haired figure beneath the African blanket that rises and falls with the metronomic rhythm of sleep. Me, or the alternate me.

Marco's head is in his hands. There is no sound but I can tell he is upset. I want to reach out, comfort him, brush my fingers against the tiny spines of his stubble and promise that everything will soon be back to normal. I'm coming back for you, darling. I'm coming back and I won't leave you again. Whoever dragged me from you won't be so lucky again. We'll run away, far away, and they won't ever find us. It'll just be us two, Marco and Mya. We'll live free. Forever.

Things aren't perfect in Marco's life now. The camera tells me so. His fists are clenching, there are veins bulging in his temples. He keeps casting glances over to the slumbering form beneath the savannah. He knows … he knows … he knows she's not right. He knows she's not right. He knows!

This is good. This is very good. He knows she's not right. Maybe some part of him knows she's not the real me. With or without Johanna's help, surely he'll be able to tell that I'm the real Mya, the right Mya – on instinct, in an instant, in a single glance.

Suddenly Marco stands up. He marches up and down the bedroom, his palms clamped to the sides of his head. Up and down, three times, a one-man army at the world's smallest military tattoo. He grabs a photograph from the bedside table and stares at it intently, holding it millimetres from his face as if he's trying to look through the acetate. I can't make out any details but I'm sure I know that picture. We were punting on the River Cam, drinking cheap sparkling rosé from the bottle, choosing which posh colleges we'd turn into locations for all-night raves and paintball games once the revolution came. That was me. I was there. At least I haven't been replaced in those photographs.

Now my doppelganger is stirring. She tosses her hair and rubs at her eyes, yawning. Perhaps she was never really sleeping. Waiting to make her move. I wouldn't put anything past her. She reaches her arms out for him. Her lips move. Still I hear nothing. He turns. She smiles. She's beckoning him.

No. No. No, Marco, don't go. Don't leave me here.

Don't go!

I slam my fists against the television. It explodes into black shards and I jump back to avoid my hands being shredded by the cascading glass. But no – that was an illusion. The screen is unharmed. It is simply a black void. Our room has vanished. Marco has vanished. My double has vanished. I don't have to watch any longer. I never have to watch any longer. I'm getting out. I'm done with this place.

The knife, hidden beneath my mattress since my first day in the White Prison, is attached to my right thigh with a strip of bedsheet. I know I could use it on somebody in self-defence, if I was afraid for my life. I'm capable of that much.

But could I use the knife in cold blood? On the girl who has replaced me? Could I really do it?

I suppose we'll just have to wait and see.

The television screen has been my tormentor for the entire time I have been locked in this white place. It seems fitting that it could prove to be my saviour. Stepping closer to the screen, I prod it dispassionately. My forefinger makes a grey circular indentation in the spongy material before it springs back to blackness. I push it again. The strangest notion takes hold of me – maybe if I could split the screen, I might be able to crawl through the splintered shades of reality and find myself in that peculiar other dimension where Marco and my doppelganger live.

Should we find out?

I unknot the sheet that lashes the blade to my leg. Gripping the knife, I swaddle my fist with the thin bedsheets, wrapping them round and round until my right hand resembles a white boxing glove. Marco always loved his boxing – or did he? Vaguely I remember there was a change in him, how he started to despise combat sports and left his treasured old vinyl punk records to gather dust on his bedroom shelf. It seemed to happen so suddenly, too. It's confusing. No matter. I'll remember more once I'm free, of that I'm certain. What matters more is whether my makeshift bandage will protect me from an electrical shock.

I bite my lip and close my eyes. I offer prayers to a variety of gods I don't believe in that this works. If I can destroy this hateful screen then something, surely, will happen. Maybe there'll be something behind the screen. Maybe they'll send in a phalanx of guards and in the confusion, I might have an opportunity to slip free. It's more likely that they'll cart me off in restraints, kicking and screaming, and slam me into an even bleaker cell. But what's the alternative? A lifetime here? I'd rather die today. *Live fast, die young and leave a beautiful corpse.* I believe Marco told me that one time. But it seems so unlikely, so unlike him. When I get free, I'll find out why my memories of him are so muddled. Once I'm out. Focus on the present, Mya.

I pull back my arm. With a howl that explodes from my stomach and tears my throat, I swing the knife forward. The blade socks into the squashy screen and I pull forwards and downwards, hacking and tearing, every second expecting to feel a bolt of unbearable voltage lash up my forearm and frazzle into my brain. But it never happens. I gouge away. Finally I fall back, panting heavily, then step forward and admire the chaos I have created.

Another dimension? Nope. Just a black hole, a ragged tear in the centre of the screen. I peer inside and the perspective is dizzying. There is something like a metal air vent behind my room; a tunnel that drops for what looks like forever. I see a huge tangle of wires, glowing with neon pulses, connecting out of the back of what is left of the screen and spiralling out in every direction. Wires up, wires down, wires left, wires right. Wires leading to wires leading to wires. Reaching inside the screen, I tug at one of the strands, dislodging it from its nest.

There is a cracking sound and the bright pink wire fades to grey. Faintly, in the depths of the tunnel, I can hear an alarm bleeping. Yanking out a clump of neon strands, sparks spurt out of the empty sockets and more sirens begin to ring shrilly.

Those wires must link to a mainframe, the heart of the White Prison. I think of my science training: catalysts, reactions ... explosions. An idea forms in my brain.

Hurrying into the shower, I hold my blanket beneath the filter's pathetic drizzle until it is soaking wet. Then, bundling the sheets into a ball, I race across my cell and toss the sopping bomb into the hole in the screen, then dive beneath the bedframe to shelter from the blast.

Boom! Boom? Sadly not.

After a short while I emerge and laugh shakily, feeling a little embarrassed. What was I expecting? An action-movie explosion? A gaping hole in the prison's walls that I can scamper through? I haven't blown up anything, I think I've just blown my chance at escape.

Or have I? There is a sparking noise. A fizzing. Anticipation spikes up the hairs on the back of my neck, playing a xylophone chorus down my spine. Is it happening? Then nothing. Absolutely nothing more. Is that the end? Maybe. No ... no ... what's that smell? An unpleasant chemical odour. A wisp of smoke. Smoke means hope.

Again, I shuffle towards the hole in the screen and peer inside, even though the vapours are catching harshly at the back of my throat. Peering through the fug, I stare down at the tangle of wires – popping and sputtering, spitting blindingly white bursts of flame – and crow crazy laughter. The bray of the alarms is almost drowned out by the crackling din of fire. I remember once spilling a glass of water on a live plug socket; that dangerous effervescence of tormented electricity. This sound is the same, only amplified enormously. The wires are melding into a molten mess and I feel a tremendous heat rising from the vent tunnel. The White Prison's guts are aflame.

It's burning. Oh yes, oh yes, it's burning. Everything is burning. They'll have to open the doors now – they can't let the patients choke to death. Surely they'll have to open the doors.

For what I hope and pray is the final time, I stare around my cell. Those curving white walls; the single bed with the slippery sheets, too thin and papery to make a noose; the bathroom with its faint chemical odour. I'm checking out, I won't be staying at this hotel of the damned again. I'm going.

But I don't want to go alone. I need Johanna to come with me. She believes she deserves to stay here – but that's nonsense, dangerous nonsense. She's institutionalised, Stockholm Syndrome or something. She needs me and I need her too. Alone, how could I convince anyone that this actually happened? She is proof that I'm not crazy. We'll break out of here, Johanna and I, and we'll find Marco together. She can vouch that I am the real Mya, the original Mya, and everything will be fine and – given enough time – my memories of the White Prison will exist only in nightmares.

Again I swallow smoke and let out a lung-eroding cough. No more than ten minutes have passed since I tossed my bomb into the tunnel. The fire must have spread so quickly through the air vents. I envisage smoke consuming the corridors, turning the whiteness a shade of dirty grey, causing panic among the guards and inmates. The smoke is choking now and I hear panicked shouts outside my room and the air is definitely hotter in here, the taste of fire on my tongue. The alarms are far louder too; a dawn chorus of shrilling buzzers assaulting my eardrums. I am the catalyst and the reaction is phenomenal, exhilarating, terrifying. What have I done? Just what have I done?

Keep it together, Mya. Stay calm. Stay sane. I count my breaths. I'd count my heartbeat if it wasn't racing so fast. Instead I bang out a regular thump-thump on the television with the palm of my hand. One, two, three, four. Staying alive, staying alive. Breathe, breathe.

But I won't stay breathing unless I get out. My door remains closed. Over and over again I beat my hands against the barrier, trying to swallow down the hysteria swelling in my gullet. But this is taking far too long. It must be twenty minutes now since the first fire and my door is still locked. The smoke is slipping between the cracks and I can hear the sound of running foot-steps and faint screams. Nausea churns in my stomach. I hope no one is hurt. I might be less than stable but I'm not a monster; the inmates of this asylum, these poor dislocated souls, don't deserve to die in a fire. I'm waiting, I'm waiting, I'm waiting. To distract myself, I run through my plan again. Then I remember what I've forgotten. Quickly I rip strips from what remains of my bedsheets and douse them in the lukewarm water oozing from the taps. This will help me breathe once I escape my cell.

There is a heavy thump against my door and a low groan. My eyes are stinging from the smoke. My head is spinning and my words sound as if they are coming from underwater.

'Johanna?' I croak. 'Johanna, is that you?'

Slowly, miraculously, the door slides open and I sob in relief. Then, as the corridor is revealed, a huge plume of smoke barrels into the room like a home invader – followed by a body, and I let out a scream. I leap backward as the figure slumps to the floor. Their arms are splayed out, they are almost unconscious. A patient, obviously male, with a shaven head and well-defined muscles. He has been burned and there is a medical mask plas-tered to his face, obscuring his identity. I try not to look at the red-and-black smudges on the mask. Bloody, burned. The figure on the floor needs help badly but he is blocking my path to freedom. I should step over him. He means nothing to me. I need to go.

The man on the floor of the cell moans. I can smell fresh sweat and a barbecued sweet scent that I think – oh no, please no – must be cooked flesh. But above that smell there is a ripe, sour odour that I know must be the reek of fear. He is almost unconscious but he knows that he's going to die. If his wounds don't kill him, the smoke will.

I need to get out. But I can't leave him here. Not like this.

Wrapping my damp bedsheets around my face, I take hold of his heels and pull him out into the deserted, smoke-soaked corridor. There is no sound but for the insistent beeping of the alarms and the squeak of my slippers on the linoleum floor. Frantically I cast my gaze around, hoping against hope that I might spot Johanna, but I can barely see anything in this grey haze.

I drag. I drag. I drag. The corridors are endless. I can't tell which way to turn. I drag. I drag. I drag. At times the burned patient groans and each one of those flayed gasps sends a shudder through my whole body. It would be too easy to leave him here. He's not my responsibility. But I can't abandon him. My arms and shoulders are singing with exertion and my vision is fuzzing dangerously and I don't know how much longer I can keep doing this.

Then I pull the patient around yet another corner and blinding bright light savages my vision and I go to my knees, sobbing in gratitude. An open door. Sunlight. Natural light. Real light. I can taste the air. I take great gulps of that glorious free air. It makes me drunk.

I'm out. I'm getting out. This is the end of the White Prison. This is the resetting and restarting of my old life. Things will be better, I know it. I never appreciated what I had before. I never appreciated the beauty of life. I thought I was trapped inside my stupid, self-defeating head. Now I know there are far worse places to be trapped.

I push myself to my feet. Ten steps, that's all it will take. Ten steps to freedom.

Then a hand clasps around my wrist like a manacle and I shriek and turn and stare into the face of the patient. The white mask stained with gore. His black eyes are wide, staring, mad.

Oh no. Oh God, no.

I've saved the Madboy. I try to pull free but he's too strong. I can't shake him loose. His blistered lips flap soundlessly. The open door begins to swing slowly shut. The sunlight recedes. I've got no time, nowhere near enough time.

'Take me with you,' the Madboy wheezes, his voice the creak of a haunted house's floorboards. 'Take me with you or I'll drag you back inside and you'll burn.'

Now I'm trapped. Again.

25

The New Intake (fresh meat)

'Okay-okay-okay, worst names for cats, everybody,' the burly young man said, clapping his hands, shouting to make himself heard above the hubbub of the bar. 'I'll kick us off with ... Thundercat.'

'Magical Mister Mistoffelees.'

'Astrophe. As in Cat Astrophe.'

'Furbaby,' Marco said. There were murmurs of approval from the group.

'Tiddles.'

'Tigger.'

'Tiger.' There were a few *oohs* among the crowd but they were waved away. She thought Clare had got away with that one.

'Chairman Miaow,' Alec offered.

'Superb,' JJ muttered.

'Ali. As in Ali Cat.' Groans.

'Pawdry Hepburn.' More groans.

'Oedipuss Rex.' Cheers.

It was her turn. She flushed. She felt the eyes of everybody upon her. 'Uh ... God ... Catty?'

'Out!' Geraint announced. 'Sorry, Mya. It's terrible, but not terrible in the right way.'

'Don't we get to vote?' Marco asked.

His tone was level, almost pleasant. But still she felt a tingle of disquiet. Marco had been quiet that evening. The first time he had spoken was to play Geraint's silly word-association drinking game. She touched the arm of his tuxedo and felt the tension in his biceps. She knew what was hidden beneath the fabric of his white dinner jacket. The cuts on his forearms, a memento of the night he had returned from Crete, had finally healed over. The twisted pinkish marks and the memories remained unseen by others, unknown to anyone except her. They were an upsetting reminder, carved into his skin, of what he was capable of doing – to himself or others.

It had been three months since that horrible evening. When she heard the sound of breaking glass and a scream, she had spun on her heel to see him standing in the centre of the suddenly silent pub, the broken pint glass in his hand. He was reaching out to her in abject apology, his forearms a bloody mess. He had twisted his anger in on himself. The cutting was his apology for how he had treated her; Marco Pellicci's own spin on supplication. He had begged for forgiveness and eventually she had felt powerless to resist. After all, it had been three months. Three months of constantly being afraid of what Marco might do next – to himself or others. Three months of staring at the pink strands of hair on the pillow next to her and wondering how well she knew him. Three months of pirouetting on the edge of a razor blade.

'Get it down you, love,' Clare's boyfriend urged, snapping her back to the present. 'You know the rules. One shot of sambuca, top quality, very good price.'

She felt Marco's gaze upon her as she poured the aniseed-reeking spirit down her throat. She endured the burning sensation, tears springing to her eyes as the group applauded.

She didn't care about them; they weren't real people. The only person she was thinking about was Marco. Was he disappointed? Upset? Angry? He had tried to be good, he had promised to be good, this was him being good. It didn't help.

'Right then, new game,' Geraint said, as Courtney returned from the bar bearing another tray filled with shot glasses. 'Ooh, and it's tequila this time, nice one. Hardcore. No surrender.'

'Perhaps we've played enough games,' Clare said, plucking at the hem of her emerald ballgown, the one she called her Princess Fiona dress – because her nickname for Geraint was Shrek. She felt a pulse of gratitude towards her friend.

'One more,' Clare's boyfriend insisted. 'Come on now, got a good one here... what was it... what the hell was it... oh yeah, I got it. Worst names for punk bands.' Geraint nudged Marco with his elbow, far too hard, but the dig provoked only a flicker of an eyebrow. 'Come on, you should be good at this, Johnny Vicious from the Clash Pistols. Tailor-made for your area of expertise, eh? Eh?'

'You're right, chum,' Marco said. Again, his tone was calm and flat, almost dead. He wasn't rising to Geraint's bait. She should have felt proud of him for keeping control of his emotions. Instead her stomach was tying itself in awful knots of tension.

'Right then, off we go,' said Geraint, clapping his hands. 'Mya, as you ruined the last game, you can kick off the new one. Remember the rules: total improv. Nothing that's real, nothing that you've thought of for more than a second. Even a stutter loses.'

Suddenly she wished to be anywhere else but this bar, with these people, but there was no escape. She stared at Clare's boyfriend – his face pinked from alcohol, his lips creased smugly – and felt for a moment the sort of hatred that burned through

Marco each day. The answer came to her quickly. 'The Total Twats,' she said, directly to Geraint.

There was a ripple of approval. 'Superb,' agreed JJ, smoothing down the front of his black-and-white Gary Numan T-shirt.

'The Paedophile Priests,' said Marco. He smiled sweetly at the uncertain staccato laughter, his hand resting on hers. 'Always thought that could be my band,' he added, 'but never could find anyone else to join. Heaven knows why.' More laughter. That was more like the Marco she knew. She allowed herself to relax a little.

'The Up Yours.'

'Bambi Killers.'

'The Cheesy Weasels.'

'Full Metal Jackasses.'

'Out! Too American.'

Knocking back his shot, Alec withdrew from the crowd with grace, picking his way through the cramped bar towards the toilets. She watched him go – full of confidence, tipping the barman a wink as he passed – and wondered how her troubled friend could have changed so completely.

'Toilet Destroyers,' said Courtney, seized with sudden inspiration.

'The Shithouses.'

'The Gobbers.'

'The Vomits.'

'The Face Kickers.'

'The War Bastards,' said Geraint.

'Out!' Clare cried with possibly false glee. 'Too Eighties metal.'

'Ah, come on,' he protested. 'That was good. Wasn't it?'

'Rules, lover boy,' she said, wrapping her arms around his neck as he drank down the harsh spirit. 'Live by the sword, die by the sword.'

'It was a good name.'

'It was a shit name,' Marco said. Geraint stared at him, his heavy eyebrows knitting together, and her boyfriend's smile extended into a predatory grin. 'That's what I think. And like you say so appositely, lover boy, I'm the expert. Got a problem?'

'Screw it,' Clare's boyfriend muttered, dismissing the confrontation and pushing himself up from his stool. 'I'm next at the bar, what's everyone wanting?'

Grateful for the distraction, she took Marco's hand and led him away from the throng. He went willingly. Out in the smoking area, their breath puffing out converging plumes of frosted air, she let go of his hand with some relief. Holding on to him felt like gripping an electric cable; an unexpected power surge could kill her in a second.

'What's wrong, baby girl?' he asked.

An ambulance shrieked past, its flashing lights momentarily painting his white dinner jacket blue. The Academy students' end-of-year night out was traditional fancy dress. They had bought their outfits earlier that day, giggling in the charity shop, a little stoned as they picked out a tuxedo for him and a ballerina's tutu for her, to be worn over tie-dyed leggings. *I look like a punk rock James Bond*, Marco had grinned as he assessed himself in the shop's cracked mirror, running his fingers through the cerise spikes that she had dyed herself only an hour before. *Licence to get pissed and destroy.* She noticed the middle-aged till lady staring disapprovingly at them and sniggered even harder. It had been a good time. But nowadays with Marco, the good times were always tinged with an emotion she didn't want to admit to herself. Apprehension, certainly. Maybe even fear.

'What's wrong?' he persisted.

'You,' she said simply. 'In there. I saw the way you were looking at Geraint.'

Marco sighed, dragging a hand through his spikes. 'Sorry, Mya. You saw the boy was being wide. Needling at me. Winding me up. But ... we're gonna rise above.'

She chewed on her bottom lip. 'Do you promise?'

'Swear down.'

She hooked one leg behind the other, caught in an agony of indecision. 'We can go home if you'd like?' Suddenly it seemed very important to take her boyfriend away from this place, this company. 'It's starting to rain. Every Bond needs his Bond girl, doesn't he?' she went on, the words spilling out gracelessly. 'I can slip out of this tutu – or keep it on if that's more kinky. We're too cool for this place. Hey ho, let's go. What do you say?'

'Time for all that later, yeah?' He kissed her sweaty forehead. She could smell the aniseed aroma of the sambuca shots on his breath. 'I'm having fun. Aren't you?'

Her reply was suffocated as their friends piled out of the bar and surrounded them in a laughing, whooping rugby scrum. She was carried down the road in a tumble of humanity and they descended into the bowels of an underground club where the lights were either low or blinding and the music boomed with a demonic industrial churn. In the chaos of the night, she lost sight of Marco. The shots of sambuca and tequila kept coming and after a while she slid into a disengaged and fuzzy state, and she was talking to people she had never met before, and sounds zoomed in and out of comprehension – *Alright darling ... Are you lost? ... What's with the ballet dress? ... You gotta fella, eh? ... Are you lost? ... Where your friends at? ... Wanna come with me? ... You lost?* – and she was trapped at the bottom of a tunnel and faces were rushing towards her, slack-jawed with idiot leers but hungry, zombie-like, and she called out for Marco to save her from these slow but relentless predators but he was nowhere to be seen.

She gulped a great panic breath.

Something inside her mind flexed and bent sickeningly.

She knew that feeling. Above and beyond the drunken confusion, she knew when a vital component had slipped out of place in her poor imperfect brain. She wasn't in a tunnel. She was standing on the shoreline, her feet stuck in quicksand. Waiting for the monstrous tide. The black waters that drowned all hope.

A Great Wave was coming.

She needed to get out.

Again and again she called out Marco's name. But her throat had closed in and all that emerged was a pained wheeze. The music pumped and pounded as if she was trapped in the centre of a huge threshing machine. She stared across the dancefloor, watching the silhouettes embrace in a stilted seizure waltz. When the lights fell upon the grinning faces, she saw the dancers were alien and hunched and cadaverous, their teeth thin daggers as they feasted upon one another. She whimpered and turned and ran, butting into a troglodyte in the doorway who slopped beer down her dress, his eyeless face a scrunched parcel of fleshy creases, and he spat an obscenity at her in a language she couldn't comprehend as she escaped the dancefloor.

Now she was in a small black room. She was alone. The walls pulsed with the heaviness of the techno beats, or maybe that was her brain slamming itself off the walls of her skull.

She breathed. She might be safe here for a few moments. Just to recuperate. Convince herself that she wasn't going insane.

Then, with a groan in the voice of her slowly dying mother, the walls began to close in on her. She saw the four walls smooth into an endless, impossible arc. The door was her only hope, but that was shrinking with every passing second, merging into the rest of the curving walls. The green lights above the doorway read *No Exit*.

Clawing at the handle, she threw her whole weight against the barrier with a strength born from desperation. An alarm bell shrilled and she span around in fright and nearly toppled over the safety rail of a spiral staircase that led even further down to hellish depths she couldn't bring herself to imagine. She stared up and saw the stars, natural light at last, and grim determination took hold. The darkness below beckoned her, reaching out with hooked fingers. Instead she climbed up, up, up, her sneakers skidding on the rain-slicked steps, using the moonlight as a guiding beam, pulling herself to safety.

She reached the street, her eyes bulging, her chest heaving as she drank down lungfuls of rain-scented air that had never tasted sweeter. Her vision was flickering like a badly tuned television and her foot caught on the metal lip of the top step. She stumbled. She fell into outstretched arms, pulling the stranger to his knees. She stared up, expecting another horror, but to her incredible relief she saw the man was Marco.

'Jesus, Mya!' he gasped. 'Been looking everywhere for you – thought you'd left on your own.' He stared closely at her and his reddened eyes narrowed in concern. 'Are you okay?'

Miserably she shook her head. If she could get back home, back to where she was safe, the worst of the Great Wave might wash over her. Crawl beneath the safety of the bedsheets and shiver and shake until she was almost completely dry. But if she stayed here, she would drown.

'Go, go-go-go,' she yammered as he held her tightly, both of them on their knees in the middle of the street, the puddles soaking through her colourful leggings. 'Take me home. Please, please, there's monsters in there. I need to go home. The walls are closing in. The wave, the wave, the wave. I'll drown here. I need to go home.'

'Are you mental, love?'

She realised there were other people around them. Her performance had drawn quite the crowd. She saw Clare's boyfriend looking down at her. In her supercharged emotional state, she assessed him in minute detail: the alcohol-puffed face, the cocky grin, the legs-apart poise that assured everyone that he was twenty-five and invulnerable. Later, much later, when nothing could be done, she realised that she had been the last person to see Geraint as the person he had been, rather than the senseless form he would become.

'What did you say?' Marco asked. The rain was beating down on his white dinner jacket with renewed force. His hair was plastered flat to his scalp, pale pink streams of dye running down his cheekbones. He was still staring at her, still holding her, but his eyes had grown dark and she didn't know if he could still see her. 'What did you say about her?'

Too late she recognised that coldly polite tone, so colourless and unsettling.

'Your missus there,' said Geraint. She wanted to stop him, clap a hand over his mouth, stitch up those flapping lips, because Clare's boyfriend was drunk and arrogant and foolish. He didn't know what he was saying, he didn't know who he was talking to, he didn't understand the consequences. 'Bit mad, isn't she?'

Marco let go of her and she sagged to the ground. She wished she could call him back but she didn't have the strength, she couldn't find her voice. Slowly, robotically, he stood and straightened up.

'Fit and all that,' Geraint went on, mugging to the crowd even as a number of their friends – seized by an impulse they couldn't possibly understand, only knowing that something was about to go wrong, badly wrong – began to pace backwards. 'But you got to admit it, mate … your girlfriend's a total fucking lunatic.'

She stared up, her expression pleading. He didn't see her; he couldn't see her. Her boyfriend's eyes were blank. Great white shark in hunting mode blank. She knew what was coming. She was powerless to prevent it.

'No, Marco, no …' Another voice, female. A clatter of heels on stone cobbles. Was it Clare? Too late, too late.

'No one speaks to her that way,' Marco said. His voice was emotionless. 'No one.'

With savagely beautiful motion, the man she loved swung his clenched fist in a deadly curvature. The crunch of bone upon cartilage echoed through the street, harmonising with Clare's scream. The blood from Geraint's burst nose fell in a pretty spray upon Marco's white dinner jacket.

The young man dropped straight backwards like a felled tree. The back of his skull cracked down on the edge of the pavement. The sound was louder than a bomb. The aftershock robbed them of their senses. There was silence for what seemed like forever. Marco stared at her, then stared at his right hand as if it was no longer a part of him, his fist slowly unclenching.

Then Clare was down on her knees in front of her boyfriend. 'Marco, you bastard … oh no, Jesus, fuck … Geraint. Get up, Gez. Get up. Get up!' Clare slapped at his cheeks, beat her hands against his chest. 'Oh God, Marco – what have you done? What the fuck have you done to him?'

Marco sank to his knees too and cradled Geraint's head in his hands. Blood was leaking from the unconscious man's nose and ears. There was a gory Rorschach pattern across Marco's shirt and tuxedo. His lips were moving but no sound emerged.

'What have you done?' Clare repeated, her voice wavering

in panic. She seemed beyond anger. Her nails were clawing at her cheeks, raking her features into a fright-mask. 'Oh Jesus, what have you done?'

'I don't know, I didn't ... didn't mean it, I'm so ... so, so sorry,' he stuttered. His voice was childlike, pleading, begging for an adult to come along and tell him everything was fine, everything could go back to how it used to be, it was only a silly game and it would still be alright in the end. 'I didn't know ... I didn't mean ... I don't know what to do.'

No one else knew what to do either. The boy lay still on the ground. There was nothing but silence as the rain fell into his open eyes.

26

Out of the White Prison/
Into the Bleaklands

Is he dead? The shapeless form beneath the blankets is so still that I can't tell whether or not he's breathing. Surely no one can be so badly burned and live. Infection, sepsis, toxic shock syndrome – there's a rancid package waiting for him if he survives. Maybe I should kill him now. It would be cleaner, kinder. I run my finger over the blade of the knife, dull but sharp enough; more for tearing than cutting. Could I do it? I think I could do it. If the Madboy had turned on me yesterday – when I dragged him out on a stretcher made from our gym jerseys and two mops taken from a storage cupboard, as the building behind us blazed like the world's biggest Roman candle firework – I could have done it. It would have been self-defence. But he remained limp, sometimes letting out a semi-conscious howl that shredded my fragile nerves, and I kept on dragging. I dragged him until dawn. I dragged the Madboy until a milky sun rose above the bleached scrublands of whatever country or world I'm in right now. I can't make out the building in which I was held prisoner any longer, which is a relief, but I can see the smoke drifting from the still-smouldering tower.

I don't want to close my eyes – not only because I'm afraid of what the Madboy might do to me while I'm asleep, but also because every time my eyelids flutter shut, I'm plunged back into my memories of escaping from the White Prison. A dizzying spiral of endlessly winding corridors. His weight draped over my shoulders, heavy as hell. At times during that awful night, I thought I could hear the screams of the other inmates, smell the sweetish odour of charred flesh. But I told myself that the sounds and smells were just in my head; it was the only way to keep myself sane. We stumbled together for an eternity until I came across the store cupboard, its lock smashed, and fashioned a stretcher for him. When we emerged, the smoke was swamping my vision and I couldn't see more than a few paces in front of me, my free hand tracing the line of the wall. For some time I thought I had made a dreadful mistake and had led us further underground, to be either barbecued or suffocated. But then my nostrils picked up a perfumed scent, fragile but amazingly fragrant, and by then I couldn't see anything so I trusted my instincts and followed that lightly exotic aroma and finally my fingers closed around the bars of a metal gate. In disbelief I stared upwards and I could see stars pricking through the gloom, and despite the chaos and the fear and the exhaustion, I felt a supercharged surge of optimism. I would live free ... I would ... I would ...

Then my overburdened mind took a brief trip out of reality and when consciousness returned, I was standing in a barren landscape, the White Prison behind me, the Madboy collapsed comatose at my feet.

I couldn't say why I saved him of all people.

Dispassionately I stare down at my patient. What can I do with him? My gaze flicks back to the blunt knife. Perhaps I wouldn't have to look. Perhaps he's dead now anyway, so my conscience would be clear.

But then I would be alone. Despite everything, despite my fear and revulsion, I don't want to be alone. I have no way of knowing if all or any of the patients managed to be evacuated in time. Treacherously, my mind flashes up an image of Johanna clawing at a locked door; her face blackened, her mouth an open tunnel of horror, her dark fringe singed away to the skull, praying to choke rather than burn.

You see what happens when I'm on my own? My mind plays tricks on me and it has a vicious sense of humour: I'm stuck in a chilly desert, no food other than two cans of fizzy drinks and a box of cereal bars looted from the store cupboard, lost and exhausted, nursemaid to a lunatic. This isn't the freedom I had seen from the top of the tower. This isn't freedom at all. Now I only see emptiness.

The thing underneath the blankets hasn't moved for what I judge to be almost an hour. Shivering in the early morning air, I shuffle towards him, each step a marathon. I hold the knife in front of me like a field marshal with his baton. When I come within a body's length of the Madboy, the blade begins to tremble so violently that I fear dropping my solitary weapon. Gritting my teeth, I will myself to control the shaking and eventually the palsy comes under control. I drop to my knees. The gravelly ground pinches through the thin material of my trousers. My heart is beating so fast it hurts my chest. If I brought the knife down now, through the blanket into his heart, it would be quick. I wouldn't even have to see his face.

'You won't use that,' a husky rasp of a voice comes from beneath the sheet.

With a shriek I topple backwards. I scrabble away from him on my haunches, waving the knife uselessly in front of me, slicing thin air. I wait for him to toss off the blankets and leap at me. My last memory will be the sight of his face twisted in fury, smelling the stinking breath from his scorched throat.

Instead, nothing happens. He stays beneath his covering. I see he is shivering too.

'I will use the knife,' I say, hoping this sounds like a threat instead of an apology. 'I swear.'

'You might.' There is a horrible, hacking coughing sound. He lifts the sheet a fraction and spits a wad of bloody matter onto the earth. 'You might if I came at you. If I jumped up and grabbed you around the throat. You might use it then.'

'Are you planning anything like that?'

I'm amazed at how calm my voice sounds. There is silence for some time. I wonder if the body beneath the sheets has faded back to unconsciousness.

'No. Not right now. This isn't your fault. I could blame you – you're the reason I was locked up in the first place – but, no, I still can't justify saying it's your fault.'

The Madboy doesn't sound mad in the slightest. He sounds rational and resigned. Could this be a trap? I'm letting my guard down… Oh, who the hell am I kidding? He's a huge and insane man, I'm a ninety-pound female holding a knife that would struggle to carve a chicken breast. If he wants to kill me, he'll kill me. Instead he wants to talk.

'What can you see?' he asks. 'What's out there?'

'Nothing.'

'No buildings, no houses?'

'Nothing. Seriously, it's empty. Not even any trees or flowers. Wherever we are, it's totally barren. Nothing on the landscape. Bleak.'

The blankets begin to tremble and keep trembling. There is a low, repetitive huffing sound. Eventually I realise that he's trying to laugh. 'How's this prison break working out for you?' the Madboy asks.

I draw the business end of the knife across my wrist. The

blade barely makes an indentation. So blunt. I couldn't kill him even if I wanted to. I need him. 'Quite honestly,' I say, 'really, really fucking badly.'

'You got a plan?'

'I did have a plan. You messed it up.'

'So you were going to leave me. Leave me in there. To burn.'

There's no point in lying. 'Yes,' I tell him. 'What did you expect?'

'Nothing better,' he says, hacking up another bolus the shade of ripe cherries. The blood looks so vibrant on the unnaturally pale earth. We've replaced a colourless interior for a colourless exterior. 'I didn't expect anything better. I didn't deserve anything better.'

'Why?' I ask, genuinely curious. Also, I feel safer if I can keep him talking. 'What did you do? Why did they lock you up in the White Prison?'

'The same reason they locked you up.'

I shake my head. 'Me ... I ... I think there was a mistake. A terrible mistake. I never harmed anyone except myself.'

'You sure?' He pulls the flap of his covering back and the sun's weak light falls upon him for a moment and I see a blackened, ruined face and gasp. I'm horrified but I can't look away, I can't break that darkly burning gaze. 'You sure about that, Mya?'

My vision zooms and contracts simultaneously, my stomach lurching as if I'm strapped into a loop-the-looping aircraft. 'How do you know my name?' I ask faintly.

'Everyone knew you in that place,' the Madboy says, wheezing now as if talking is costing most of his remaining strength. 'You were ... you were the star of the show.'

He collapses back beneath the blankets. I stare around, as if during our brief and unsettling conversation a miracle might have sprung up behind me. A familiar row of buildings, a battalion of emergency services with sirens blaring, an aid convoy. Even a cool water fountain would be a start. No, there's only emptiness. Even my mirages are disappointing.

'So where do we go from here?' I ask.

'Where do you want to go?' he counters. His voice is weak, drifting.

'Home.' I flap my arms hopelessly. 'If I can even get home. I might not even be on the same damned continent as home. But I'll try. I need to see my boyfriend. There's ... he's ... something happened.'

The Madboy grunts, losing interest. Gradually his laboured breathing grows shallower. Soon he's unconscious again. I think of Marco – how he seems too good for this world, how he tries to see the best in people. He'd struggle with this specimen. Still, the Madboy being asleep gives me time to think. I decide to walk, more to keep warm than out of hope I'll see anything in these featureless flatlands, and I set off at a gentle trot.

Once I'm out of sight of the burned and shivering figure, I feel a little better about my predicament. Firstly, I've escaped the White Prison and no one is following me. That's a great start. Secondly, I've clung on to the hope of seeing Marco again for so long, I'm not going to give up now. Thirdly ... what the hell? The ground has shifted underneath my feet. The earth is disappearing beneath me. Scrabbling away from the hole, my ankle buckles as I slip and nearly fall. The opaque earth has sloped into a tunnel. One second I am on solid ground, the next I'm staring goggle-eyed at a black hole that seems to drop forever.

Crouching down, I peer into the tunnel. It's only just large enough for me to crawl inside. God knows why I'd want to do a silly thing like that. Instead I stay on the lip of the opening, occasionally glancing over my shoulder to assure myself that the Madboy is still comatose beneath his sheets. What could have created such a hole? I think of a gigantic, sightless mole burrowing with claws the size of shovels. It's not a pleasant thought. Maybe I shouldn't look inside this hole. Maybe I should go back...

Then I feel a suction, followed by a great propulsion which I'm powerless to resist, and I'm pulled into the tunnel at terrifying velocity and the blackness swallows me.

27

The Bleaklands (memory holes)

Where am I? I hear raised voices. Anger and resentment are jousting for supremacy. A red lamp above my head stutters into life. I'm sitting on a staircase in a house that I don't immediately recognise but which feels eerily familiar. Somehow I feel smaller. There are paintings on the wall. Watercolours. Veldt scenes, daubed inexpertly but with evident love. Wildebeest at a watering hole; giraffes on a knock-kneed progression across the brushland; hippos – great grey sacks of fat – slumbering in the mud by a lake; a mother and baby warthog rootling together.

In wonder, I realise that it was my mother who painted those pictures. She always wanted to go back to South Africa. She had been a volunteer aid worker there for a year after leaving university. My father had refused to leave Britain; he insisted his visa situation was too precarious, but in truth he never wanted to leave his work. In past times – they had already sacrificed so much to be together, the girl from a small town in Yorkshire and the Indian refugee – they might have split up. Ended it all. Then I came along. My mother never went back to South Africa. My father's dedication to his work grew and grew until it became inseparable from his personality. Their relationship never recovered.

And I can hear the raised voices of my mother and father

right now. I'm a child again, only three or four years old, trembling in my nightgown on the seventh step of our old house's wooden staircase. I always choose the seventh step because the board doesn't creak. I'm listening to them fight.

Somehow every one of these revelations seems very obvious.

'You are being completely irrational,' my father snaps. He sounds different. Younger? More engaged with the world. More engaged with his wife. He is furious with her and that shocks me. I didn't know he was capable of such emotion. He was always too distracted with his projects to be angry with me during my teenage years, though I gave it a good effort. 'This is the only solution. Why can you not see?'

'I can't see because it's your solution, not mine, and you're totally blind to what anyone else wants,' my mother says. My mum has been dead almost ten years. Now I can hear her voice and it takes all my self-control not to burst into tears. Those slightly flattened vowels of the northern accent she never truly shed. 'I need hills, Gurdeep,' she continues. 'Nature, wildlife, freedom. The only thing that makes me feel better nowadays is stepping outside and seeing the Dales. Can't you understand? I need open space.'

'There is plenty of open space where we're going, Alice. You should see where we're building our Academy.' His voice grows strident, messianic. 'It is … it is majestic. Nature to make the heart soar. Green fields and flowers as far as the eye can see.'

'It's just flat,' my mother says disconsolately. 'I hate it. Green fields and flowers – are you joking? It's a wasteland, that's what it is. Where's the life?'

'You sound like a child. You need to set an example to Amaya.'

'Gemma! I thought we agreed.'

My father lets out a sigh. I can tell that he's pinching the bridge of his nose between his thumb and forefinger, the way he always does when he's stressed. 'We decided together on her name.'

'Names. One for you and one for me, and I guarantee she'll be a hundred per cent happier with the one I chose.' My mother's voice has dropped lower, conciliatory. 'She'll be starting school soon, darling. We both know what kids are like. Or have you got forgotten how much abuse you took when you first came here? Those neanderthals who kicked the shit out of you outside the train station? You've told me the names they called you. So much for names.'

'This is her culture, her heritage,' my dad says mulishly. 'There will always be neanderthals. Some never evolve. People such as ourselves must rise above. To higher plains.'

'I guarantee she'll be much happier if she *sounds* like she fits in.' There is resignation in my mother's voice. This is a pact, a contract, and in these marital negotiations she's given away too much. 'Where … wherever we bring her up.'

'You're saying,' my dad starts, his voice suddenly flushed with hope, and I've never hated him as much as I do now, and if I had any control over my younger self's body, I would rush downstairs and try to choke him with my child's hands, 'you're saying you agree, my darling Alice?'

My mother is silent but that passes for acquiescence in this household. My father has won. I knew he would. We'll go to the flatlands. My father's Academy will be built and I will grow up there. I'm the soothsayer. The girl who can predict the future. Too bad I can do nothing to change it.

A brief shaft of light falls upon me as the kitchen door opens then closes again. My father passes me on the staircase. He stares at me for a moment and ruffles my hair. There's such triumph in that simple gesture. I want to be sick.

★

There is a sucking sound and I'm pulled out of my memory with the same vertigo-inducing speed. I'm kneeling in front of the tunnel. Only it's not a tunnel anymore. It's barely an indentation in the bleached earth. As I watch, confused but fascinated, that dark passageway seals itself shut with a barricade of tiny pebbles. The hole in which I witnessed a near-forgotten memory has closed over.

My mother. The first time I've allowed myself to think of her in years. I never even saw her, only heard her voice. It's too much to bear. It's not enough. What is this place? An idea is nudging into my mind but it is so impossible, so insane, that I simply sit and stare at the ground. I want more, no matter what it costs me. I want to know the truth.

Then a tiny, insidious crunching sound reminds me I'm not alone in this place.

I'm quick but he's quicker.

A thick cord, a blanket knotted tightly into a rope, wraps around my throat. I wheeze out the last of my breath in panic. That charred, pained rasp tickles my ear.

'You didn't really think I'd forgiven you?' the Madboy whispers. 'Did you, you deceitful bitch?'

28

New Beginnings

Light was nudging up his eyelids. He wanted to keep them shut, perhaps drift back to sleep, but the room was too bright. He pulled back the thin bedsheets and saw he was wearing a pastel blue smock of the sort worn by hospital patients. Groaning, he swung his legs out of the bed – the thigh and calf muscles throbbing obscenely – and stared around his surroundings. He didn't recognise the place in which he had woken: a clean and spartan room with white walls, unfurnished except for a single bed and a small circular table with two wooden chairs. Not a hospital, more like a particularly unwelcoming hotel. He was certain he had never been here before. God, he must have been drunk the previous night, but he couldn't taste the foul residue of stale booze coating his tongue. His head ached but not with the sickly grind of a hangover. It was his skull that was prickling. Massaging his temples, his fingertips traced tiny dots that ran around his hairline. Those indentations weren't painful, exactly, but the spongy sensation of pressured flesh made him feel disconnected – as if, should he push too deeply, his mind might come untethered from reality and float away like a helium balloon on the breeze.

The door opened and a stranger entered. He stared at the girl and felt a blast of pressure in the centre of his chest. For a few moments he could only stare slack-jawed at her beauty. Inky-black hair that fell to her shoulders, caramel-coloured skin that seemed to glow with inner radiance, enormous dark eyes that stared at him with an expression caught between relief and concern. She knew him, he could tell.

He didn't know her.

'How are you feeling?' the girl asked.

'Fine,' he said, embarrassed at how little he remembered. 'I'm good.'

'Good,' she said. 'That's so good.'

She perched down beside him on the bed and took one of his hands in hers. At her soft touch, his limbs began to tremble involuntarily. 'It's okay,' the girl said, squeezing his fingers. 'You're safe. You're safe now. Everything is fine. We ... we sorted it all out for you.'

'I'm sorry,' he mumbled, 'I don't understand. I don't know who you are. I don't know who I am either. I just woke up here and I don't know what's happening. I'm sorry, but I'm so confused.'

'That's fine,' she said brightly. He plucked up the courage to meet her gaze. She was smiling but those incredible eyes were moist. 'They said you'd take a while to adjust.'

'Adjust to what?'

'You've ... you've been ill, Marco,' she said. 'But now you're better.'

'Now I'm better?' he repeated. He hadn't meant the words to sound like a question. He realised she had called him by his name but felt no recognition at its sound. At least he had a name, it just meant nothing to him at this moment. 'What was I sick from?' he asked. 'How long was I sick for?'

The girl didn't seem to have heard him. She rose and pulled open the curtains, flooding the room with light. She was dressed simply but perfectly in a white blouse and clinging black jeans. A clock-spring of pressure turned in the pit of his stomach. 'I'll ask them to send up sweet tea and toast for you,' she said. 'There's plenty for us to talk about, but I don't want to overload or overburden you. This is simply like waking up, darling.'

Darling. This girl didn't seem the sort of person to throw around affectionate terms carelessly. It felt too perfect to be real. It seemed too good to be true.

'Are we … I don't want to push things here, but … are we together? Are you my—' With his hands he sketched out words he felt too embarrassed to say.

'Oh yes,' she told him with a light laugh, kissing him on the forehead. His nostrils picked up a sweet scent of lightly floral perfume and he felt a giddy surge of joy. 'You and I, darling. Marco and Mya. Don't worry. It'll come back to you, I'm certain.'

Mya. Her name was Mya. Marco and Mya; those names harmonised in a delicate cadence. He fought a brief battle with a cheek-bursting smile and lost. Despite the confusion, he felt awfully grateful to have woken up. His muscles felt oddly weak as if he hadn't used them in far too long.

'Marco and Mya,' he said. 'Wow.'

'Wow indeed,' she agreed. A shadow seemed to drift behind her eyes but that was probably his imagination. 'Marco and Mya. That's us.'

'Then aren't I the lucky one?' He grinned, risking a joke.

She seemed to contemplate the words deeply; chewing them over, tasting them on her tongue. 'Yes, you are, Marco,' she said at last. 'You've been given a second chance.'

★

His memories began to return over breakfast. The girl ate with him, their knees almost touching as they sat around the little table. She smiled frequently and laughed often. Her name was Amaya Dala. They had been together for almost a year. They had met at her father's place of work, the Meinhof-Dala-Smithson Academy of Science, Research and Learning, which was where he had spent the past two months of convalescence. He was not actually meant to have been there in the first place, she told him with a giggle – he had followed her inside the building one day and pretended to be a student. The charade was quickly uncovered and could have snipped the wings of their fledgling romance, but instead he had shown so much promise that her dad had agreed to take him on as a protégé. They had been happy together – so happy, she said. That was until his unfortunate accident: a terrible cerebral trauma that he had barely survived. It was solely thanks to her father's ministrations that his life could begin again. *Dad's the only reason you're still with me*, Mya told him. He knew she wasn't lying – instinctively he didn't believe this girl could lie convincingly to anybody – but he could not make that connection between the man she told him he had been, and the person he seemed to be now. He didn't feel intellectual, he didn't feel special – his mind felt muddled, sludgy, strangely incurious. He had to take her word for who he was and who he had been. The memories were returning – or at least blocks of knowledge were clicking into place in his brain with a satisfying yet oddly hollow thunk, which he supposed was the next best thing.

The girl sensed his uncertainty. 'You're still not feeling like yourself?'

He spread his hands wide. 'I'm sorry. I'm trying to piece it together. It's not you, it's me.'

She huffed out a short burst of laughter. 'Ain't that the truth.'

'What? What do you mean?'

Mya shook her head. 'No matter,' she said. 'Go and look in the wardrobe. I stocked it especially for you. See if there's anything you recognise.'

She tapped a button in the panel set into the white wall and a door slid open. At her urging he rose from his chair and peered inside. He had never seen such peculiar clothes. Ripped T-shirts with violently scrawled slogans. Red-and-black tartan trousers. A monstrous black leather jacket decorated with silver studs. The rancid, smoky smell of the old material made his stomach perform a nauseous somersault.

'Your favourite leather,' she said. 'Never have it off your back. Even on the hottest day of summer.'

He tugged the jacket off its peg then hefted it in his arms. 'Heavy,' he said.

'Needs to be,' she said. 'You come off that bike at seventy miles an hour, you're going to need some serious padding. You have to lean with me – that's what you told me. So we don't spill.'

He barely understood what she was saying. 'I have a motor-bike?'

'Your infamous Suzuki Bandit. Some days I used to wonder whether you loved it more than me. In a failed attempt to bond with your bike, I named it Smokey.'

'We went out riding together?'

She mimed steering then clapped her hands to her mouth in mock horror. 'Oh, did we ever.'

'Did I go fast?'

'Like the most blazing blue of blue blazes.'

His tongue moistened his cracked lips. 'What sort of person was I?'

Again she let out that strange chuffing sound which he

supposed was laughter. 'Don't you mean what sort of person are you? You've not changed, darling. You're still the same devilishly debonair punk rock weirdo misfit I fell in love with. It'll come back to you.'

He nodded, trying not to let the uncertainty betray him in his facial expressions. 'I guess I've got a lot to be thankful for. That you're still here. That your father saved me.'

'We weren't going to abandon you, Marco,' she told him. 'We're just happy you're back with us again. I can't tell you how happy I am.' Mya's lower lip trembled and suddenly she seemed to be on the verge of tears. 'I thought I'd lost you forever.'

'Can I meet him?' he asked, attempting distraction. 'Your father, I mean. I guess I owe him my life.'

'Oh yes,' she replied, raising a hand to his face, her fingertips brushing the bristles on his cheek. 'You'll meet everyone again. My dad. Your family. I hope you'll recognise them all but I'm here in case you feel … you know … like everything's running too fast for you to keep up. It'll take time, Marco darling, but I promise you we'll get there.'

'Together?' he asked, barely daring to hope.

'Together,' Mya confirmed, then suddenly pressed her lips against his with hungry fervour, and his hands slipped into her hair, her sweet scent overwhelming him as he surrendered to instinct, and for a short while there were no questions and no answers – only certainties.

29

The Bleaklands (memory holes)

My eyes are burning, my lungs are screaming for oxygen. Clawing at the burned hands either side of my head, trying to gouge at the darkened flesh with my nails, I feel myself slipping away. Maybe it wouldn't be so terrible to die.

No. There's someone who needs me. I have to get back to Marco. The thought of him has sustained me while I've been locked up. I try to use my love for him to break this hold but the neurons in my brain are switching off like lights on a circuit board winking to black. There's no pain now. Euphoria. I'm floating, I'm floating. I'm lighter than air and bigger than any god and what I know – or what I think I know – can explode the petty nastiness of this world in which I'm trapped. We are so near to each other right now, I'm certain, but I can't let it end this way. I'm out of the White Prison and I'm close to solving the mystery and getting back to my love, my only one. I can't let my doppelganger win. I can't let Marco live a lie. I need him and he needs me.

There's something so familiar in this touch that's killing me. The tender violence. Somehow I know the Madboy doesn't want to do this. It's only happening because I am here with the worst of him. He's not himself... he's just not himself anymore... he's not... he's not who he was...

He's not who he was. That makes two of us.

Finally, the Madboy lets go of the rope he has wrapped around my throat. Retching, I collapse to the ground, sharp stones pricking through my thin smock. I focus on the little stings to ignore the horrible burning pain in my neck.

'Now,' he wheezes, 'now you'll get me out of here. You're the only one who knows, yeah? So you're going to set me free. Or else –' he indicates the noose in his right hand '– you get this around your neck again. I won't stop this time and I won't make it quick.'

Despite my fear, I let slip a shrill laugh even though it hurts my damaged throat. 'How?' I demand, what's left of my sanity crumbling in the face of his own lunacy. 'How can I get you out of here? Where is there to go, exactly? We're alone out here in the middle of a grey desert. What can *you* see, you fucking maniac? Just what am I missing? The Hilton? The airport? Taxi cabs? What can I do, exactly?'

'You're the reason I'm in this place,' he says. There's still menace in his voice but my outburst has taken him aback.

'So you claim. I'm pleading Not Guilty.'

He blinks, as if remembering. I've truly surprised him. Pacing backwards, I put some distance between us. To my left I can hear a pitter-patter of tiny stones shifting. Chancing a glance over my shoulder, I spy another one of those odd tunnels opening up in the ground. I can go in there. Maybe I can hide from him inside my own memories.

He is far enough away. Surely.

The hole is right behind me. It's a hop, skip and a jump away. But as I let myself topple backwards and surrender to the suction of the memory hole, the Madboy lunges towards me with impossibly quick reflexes. He grabs my ankle and

I'm kicking and screaming but I can't shake him loose in this hurricane vacuum and we are pulled together into ... where?

Where are we now in my memories?

The woman lying in the bed is so still she could be a mannequin. Her chestnut hair is lank and hangs like tatty theatre curtains either side of her pale face. Her eyes are open but fixed on nothing. Her eyes don't see the patterns of climbing roses on the wallpaper and the sunlight streaming in through the window. Her eyes don't see the mug of tea steaming on her bedside table, left there even though she hasn't moved by herself for ten days now, as if she might suddenly snap to life and gulp it down. Her eyes don't see the row of watercolour paintings of the African veldt lined up on the wardrobe shelves in front of her bed. Her eyes don't see a fifteen-year-old girl kneeling by her pillow, gently weeping.

Neither can my mother see her own daughter, a decade older now, standing at the foot of the bed wearing a soot-stained hospital smock. Nor can she see a strange man lurking in the corner of the bedroom, an unsettling figure whose face is concealed by a torn, oozing bandage that has been scorched into his flesh.

Wake up, Mum! I want to cry. *This isn't right, this isn't natural. Your daughter's in danger. Yell, scream, tell this lunatic with the burned face to get the hell out of your house.* Silence. I can't speak here. Neither can the Madboy. We can only watch.

There is a knocking at the door. My teenage self pushes herself to her feet and goes to open it. As she passes me, I reach out to touch her – comfort her – but my hand ripples straight through her body. I may be a spectre in this scene but I can still smell the cloying jasmine scent on my younger self's neck, because she has started wearing her mother's perfume; a way to remember her even though she isn't gone, not quite yet. My right thigh – her right thigh – stings. A morning spent tracing the blade of the kitchen scissors up and down the soft brown flesh with prissy care, creating first a noughts-and-crosses grid, then a chessboard of red lines on her skin. Mya's teenage kicks, her funny games.

My father enters. The change in him shakes me. He has aged about a hundred years since I saw him last on the seventh step of my childhood home in Yorkshire. Funny, I'd never realised the hair loss and the deep lines on his brow had occurred after my mother's suicide attempt. I never understood guilt could have such a physical effect.

'That's enough, sweetpea,' he says quietly. 'You have been up here hours.'

They reached her just in time, the paramedics said. I never believed them. The saviours in the green uniforms who came in the ambulance – the woman with the close-cropped blonde hair and a brusquely professional manner, and the muscular young man with tattoos running the length of his arms – reached my mother too early or too late. My father returned from work, an hour or so after he promised to be back, as ever, and found the bathroom door locked.

If I had stayed at home that evening, like Mum asked, none of this would have happened. We could have shared the sofa, cuddling up under the African blanket, and she would have let me have a glass or two of wine, and we would have watched an incredibly crap reality TV show and poked fun at the contestants. Instead I had a different plan. Instead there was an argument. Instead I got my own way, as I always did with my soft-touch mother. Instead I ran out to the park to drink cider with the scummy boys who hung around there at night, spinning the roundabout too fast or dangling from the monkey bars holding a spliff. Childhood left far behind aged fifteen. As I was felt up behind the parkie's hut by a baseball-capped conquistador named Carl, I heard the scream of an ambulance. A siren and flashing blue lights. But maybe it was the wrong ambulance.

My mother is only kept alive by the wires plugged into her. Somehow my father had managed to convince the hospital to let him take her home. It would make no difference; it simply made the ending that much more horribly protracted. He hadn't been able to fix her.

'I'll stay a little longer,' my younger self tells him. 'I have to tell her about what I did today.'

My dad sighs. 'She can't hear you, Mya.'

Angrily shaking my head at his idiocy, I snap, 'You always know how to say exactly the wrong thing.'

Rubbing at his furry greying eyebrows, he smiles at me painfully. 'It's a talent. Your mother used to say the exact same thing.'

'Don't speak of her in the past tense. I hate that.'

'Amaya, we must accept—'

'I said fucking *don't*!' I yell.

The palms of his hands raised, he concedes the point and backs out of the bedroom. The room in which Mum will die – quietly, without fanfare or dramatic exposition – four days from now. An act of mercy? Or an act of God? My father never allowed me to find out.

'I'll be here if you need me,' he says. 'You only have to ask.'

'Right, Dad.'

He pauses. My teenage self wants him to go. My adult, disconnected self needs him to stay – I'm screaming out for him to take me away, to rescue me, as if he is still as indomitable as he seemed when I was a child.

'Mya,' he says slowly. 'Your mother would be proud of you.'

'Right, Dad.'

'If you ...' There is a catching sound in his throat as he com-
poses himself. He pretends to adjust his spectacles but really he's
wiping his eyes. 'If you ever feel like your mother did ... please,
please come and tell me. We can work it out. I can ... I know ...
I think I can make you better. I think I have a solution.'

Then he is gone and so are we.

We watch the memory hole in the desert form back over. Soon
the colourless stones have sealed the tunnel as if it was never
there. Now I understand everything. It is grim knowledge but
at least it is an answer. My body is gone and I'm trapped in my
own head. These are the flash-before-your-eyes moments. Only
they're not like you see in the movies.

'I think I know where I am,' I tell him. 'I think that I'm
dead already.'

The Madboy stares up at me. Somehow I manage to form
my lips into a smile.

'This is like a shit horror movie,' I tell him heavily, 'and the
big twist is we're all dead. That place back there –' I indicate the
smouldering wreck of the institution far in the distance '– that
was purgatory. I was in purgatory. Somehow I got myself out
of purgatory. But I didn't go up. I went down instead.'

'So where does that leave me?' he asks. His tone is fretful, a
self-pitying whine. 'I am real, I promise. I'm really real. If you're
dead then why am I here with you?'

'I should have realised something else too,' I continue, barely
hearing him. 'It was so horribly obvious I didn't want to believe
it. I know what you are now.'

'What? What am I? What do you think I am?'

'You're him, aren't you?' I demand, spreading my arms out
wide, daring him to disagree. 'You're the man I loved. You're
Marco gone insane. So yeah, this must be hell. Someone's taken

the sweetest person I've ever known and turned him into a devil. To torment me.'

He shakes his head, the stained white mask flapping. 'You've gone mad yourself. I don't know anyone called Marco.'

'Do you know why you were locked up in the White Prison? Can you remember anything before that?'

He shakes his head again. I'm sure I can see tears forming in those black eyes. 'They ... they dosed me. I didn't know whether it was day or night. Summer or winter. Years could have passed in there. I forgot who I was ... I forgot ... I forgot ...'

'Here,' I say gently, 'let me show you something.'

Steeling myself, I offer him my hand. After a few moments' thought he takes it, wincing at the pressure of my fingers against his injured flesh.

'What?' he asks fretfully. In that moment he isn't the Madboy any longer, he's the Marco that I knew and loved. 'What are you going to show me?'

'I don't know.'

That's the truth or near enough. Suddenly at least a dozen holes have popped up across this wasted savannah, these Bleaklands of my dying or almost-dead mind. I lead Marco, or at least this abysmally flawed recreation of him, towards a tunnel. We pause on the edge of the opening, our toes hanging over the pitch-dark void, waiting to be pulled inside.

'I don't get to choose my memory,' I tell him, 'but maybe it's our only hope of getting out of this place.'

30

New Beginnings

He walked into the great open hall and the crowd exploded into applause. He shrank back from the light and the sound. He would have fled had it not been for the gentle pressure of Mya's touch on the small of his back. Everyone he knew was there. He remembered them all now – the memories popping in his mind like cherry bombs. His mother, his two brothers Tony and Robbo, Uncle Gi. With a nimbleness belying his years, Giuseppe was the first to reach him. The old man's grip had surprising strength. Tears were streaming down the wrinkles in his face. *It is you, it's really, really you*, croaked Uncle Gi, his voice pitching wildly with emotion. *Ah, Marco, I thought we'd lost you forever.* Then the whole group converged upon him. His back was slapped, his hand was shaken, his cheeks were kissed. He didn't know what he had done. It seemed as if an act so simple as waking up had proven to be a minor miracle. A bottle of beer was thrust into his hand. There were toasts in his honour. Jokes he did not understand whipped up gales of laughter. He was confused but happy to be with these people; they loved him, they had taken care of him, they would never let him go. He just wished he knew why they thought he was so special.

But he tried to put these concerns out of his mind. Instead, he smiled placidly and watched the revelry revolve around him, until – at an unspoken order – the party was suddenly over and Mya took him home.

Time passed; the simplest and most wonderful trick in the magician's repertoire. She fascinated him and beguiled him. In turn, he loved her and made her laugh – sometimes intentionally. They fitted so well together. Her harder edges slotted into the malleable parts of him so very neatly. They woke in the single bed of his family home entwined in one another and he never wanted to let go. Even their clutter had combined on his bedroom shelf: her overnight bag mixed with memorabilia from a pre-Mya history that he could barely recall.

One morning she woke as he was looking at the boxing trophies on his bedroom shelf. Had he once even liked boxing, let alone participated in the sport? It seemed impossible. The thought of violence made his stomach lurch. It was the same as his West Ham United shirt, his punk rock records, his Suzuki Bandit motorcycle in the garage. He felt nothing for any of his past loves. He had watched a video of classic Hammers matches with his brothers and sat silently, slightly bemused, as they whooped and cheered; punk rock sounded like an atonal mess of chugging guitars and shouting; the solitary time he had attempted to ride his motorbike, he had steered it into a neighbour's hedge. He felt no nostalgia for his life before the accident, however, because Mya had endured. The strength of his love astonished him. He couldn't function properly without her. Even the prospect of her going away was like a constricting band of pressure around his chest, drawing ever tighter. When she did have to leave him – she spent three days a week working at her father's Academy – he paced the house endlessly, unable to focus on books or television. Some days he walked out to the edges of town – not risking a ride on that oily, snorting

Bandit – and stared at the great red tower in the distance. The place where his life had been saved.

She had told him about the day he almost died. He had suffered a brain aneurysm during a night out to celebrate the end of the Academy term. He had collapsed in the street. The doctors had not expected him to make it. It was only her father's intervention that allowed him to live again. *There might still be a few loose wires up in that big dome of yours*, she told him with a lopsided grin. *Dad says it's totally normal to feel a little ... disconnected at times. Those wires will start sparking again soon, I promise.*

So he surrendered himself to her. She tended him and cared for him and he was the perfect pliant patient. His muscles were still weak from his months of bed-rest but they went for walks in the countryside together, hand in hand, and he felt the milky sunshine of early spring dapple on his face and felt himself renewed. He was just like one of the green shoots he saw poking through the earth; struggling towards the sunlight.

But whenever he tried to ask her about their lives before his illness, she was oddly evasive. She would only tell him that they had been together, in love, and happy – but she admitted that she had felt something was wrong with him, badly wrong, even before his collapse. He could see the pain of Mya's recollections painted in broad brushstrokes on her face and feared one of her bouts of melancholy was coming on.

That was the only problem he could possibly see with Mya; when her mood darkened, it sucked all joy from life, turning their golden life slate-shaded. So after a while he stopped asking those questions. He needed to see her smile; it was as vital to him as breathing. Instead of wondering about the strangenesses of his new life, he thought of Mya and what she meant to him, and how lucky he was still to have her. Some mornings – he woke often in the night, while she would sleep until noon given the opportunity – he lay beside her and gazed for hours at her face. The sweep of inky hair sprawling out over his pillow, the feline cheekbones, the tiny spray of freckles over her nose. There was no doubt that she was portrait gallery beautiful. But it was the blemishes that made her truly perfect – the diagonal crack sheared off one of her top incisors, the traces of chickenpox on her chin, the peculiar row of white indentations that pocked her skin around her hairline. Without those tiny tarnishes she would not be mortal. She would be a goddess – and he didn't know if he could trust himself to believe in her.

When a man was fortunate enough to start the day gazing at such a face, he told himself, that day began in a state of glory. As Mya often reminded him, he had been given a second chance. He could scarcely believe his good luck.

For some reason the boxing trophies kept on troubling him. He had to admit that there was a dark intrigue too. Especially with the two full-size model gloves – carved from onyx, astonishingly weighty – from the Eastern Counties Youth Championships. He took down the stone gloves from the shelves and examined them owlishly. His name was engraved on the base: *Marco Pellicci*. Was that who he was? Was that who he had been?

He felt arms reach around to encircle his waist. Her lips pressed against the nape of his neck. Her warmth, her endless warmth. 'What are you thinking, darling?' asked Mya.

'I don't remember winning these,' he admitted. 'Don't remember winning any of them, not even sure why I kept the trophies. Most of them are crappy plastic, sprayed gold.'

'Guess there wasn't much money in amateur teenage boxing in East Anglia. Maybe if you'd battled all the way to Madison Square Garden, you'd have a trophy that didn't melt on top of a radiator.'

Again, he turned the onyx fists over in his hands. 'I do like these ones though,' he said. He felt those wires of recollection finally spark in the back of his mind, before the connections came loose once more. 'The stone gloves. They're heavy as hell. Here, feel it.'

He passed one over. Mya grasped it and the weight sagged her arm. She laughed uncertainly. 'Heavy as hell,' she repeated.

Often, he woke early and watched her sleeping and felt almost breathless with gratitude that she was part of his life. He just wished she would stop asking him the same question, Mya's one endless question. Whenever she thought her teasing had strayed into cruelty, whenever she was late after a day at the Academy, she would drop her head and stare at him from the corners of her eyes – a strangely furtive, guarded look. As if he might lose his temper. As if he might fly off the handle at any moment. As if she thought he was a different person.

Then she would ask her question. Over and over again she asked him the same thing: *You're not angry with me, are you?* He couldn't work out why she kept on asking that question, repeating the words like a catechism. *Are you sure you're not angry?* Why was she obsessed with him being angry with her, what possible cause could he have to be angry with her? Maybe she had a previous boyfriend with anger issues. But it still hurt to think she could see him the same way. Sometimes on those early mornings – as Mya lay beside him in bed – he wondered about the peculiar intensity in her eyes when she asked him whether he was angry with her; as if he was being cross-examined. But if it had been a test, he told himself, then surely he had passed that test by now.

So he tried to put those worries out of his mind.

★

There was another strange and somewhat unsettling scene a few days later. They had been passing through the Academy – Mya had some textbooks she needed to pick up from her room in the great tower – and she had left him kicking his heels against the brickwork of the front court. He was enjoying the sensation of the sun beating down on his close-cropped scalp when he realised he was being watched.

It was a Sunday morning and the Academy was almost deserted – he suspected most of the students who lived in the building were sleeping off the previous night's alcoholic or romantic endeavours – so he heard the stranger before he saw her. There was a rapping sound of boots proceeding towards him. At last he saw her. The girl was slightly built, her frame swamped by an overlarge military camouflage jacket. A rucksack was slung over one shoulder. Her hair, pulled into a ponytail that made her look scarcely out of her teens, was as red as the brick wall on which he was leaning. He thought her heart-shaped face would normally have been pretty, but her expression was so murderous that it shrouded dark clouds over the sunny day. He shifted uncomfortably, scanning the surroundings for Mya. What was taking her so long? As the girl approached him, his pulse quickened with rising panic.

'You,' she said. The single syllable word sounded so accusatory.

'Me?' he replied, flummoxed. 'I'm sorry … I don't … do I know you?'

She dropped her bag and the sound cracked around the front court. 'I would say so. What say you?' Dumbly he shook his head. 'You don't have to speak,' she went on. 'I heard what happened. They explained everything to me. Oh yeah. The simple solution. How splendid.'

'I had … I had an accident,' he stammered. 'I don't remember. I don't remember much of anything.'

The girl nodded. She was staring up at the Academy tower as if she could not even bear to look at him. 'Don't tell me. I was there. The other –' she turned her head and spat at his feet, a smear of white foam on the chessboard-patterned stone '– the other person who was in that *accident* with you is still in hospital. Breathing through a fucking tube. I'm going up to see him right now, as a matter of fact. I'd love to tell you more but they would cut my funding. Oh yeah, I sold out. A reformed punk like you should understand that everyone sells out eventually. I shouldn't even be talking to you right now. It's against the rules. But, seeing as how it's just us two old pals here...'

He heard a shout. Staring up he could see Mya above them on the walkway, waving frantically. Then she disappeared from view.

'You don't know what the hell I'm talking about, do you?' the girl demanded. 'Oh God, they really did a number on Mad Marco, eh?'

The girl took a pace forward. They were so close he could smell Juicy Fruit gum on her breath. She raised her hand – he thought she was about to strike him, and flinched – but instead she traced her fingertips around his hairline. Her touch was soft yet unbearable. The way she was staring at him made him feel grubby, sticky, ashamed. At last she stepped back.

'Huh, I thought as much,' the redhead scoffed. Her tone was harsh but her eyes were moist, her expression wounded beyond measure. 'Fixed. Yeah, that figures. Good luck to you both.'

Then she pulled her rucksack over her shoulder, turned abruptly and stalked out of the Academy front court, the heels of her boots click-clacking on the marble flagstones.

Moments later, Mya arrived at his side, flushed and breathless. 'She shouldn't have done that,' she muttered to herself. 'My dad... I'll tell... she should have known better.'

'What on earth was that all about?' he asked.

'A spurned lover?' she suggested, offering him a queasy smile. 'Stud like you, there must be thousands of besmirched maidens knocking about East Anglia. Or maybe just a case of mistaken identity?'

Baffled, he shook his head. 'She looked at me like she hated me,' he said. 'I don't know anyone who hates me. I don't know her. I don't... I don't think I know her, at least... I mean, I thought...'

'Don't worry about her, darling,' said Mya, silencing him with a kiss before taking his arm and leading him away. 'She's out of our lives now.'

31

The Bleaklands (memory holes)

My seventeen-year-old self stares glumly out of her window from her room way, way up in the Academy building. The princess locked away in the highest room of the tallest tower. The girl is watching the new intake of students arrive. There is a knock at the door and she flings on her white lab coat. Dr Baumann stands in the doorway. As ever, sweatily raddled and out of breath, rubbing at the angry shaving rash on his throat. This Mya is aware that she has known Frank Baumann since she was a child, considered him a friend and confidante. But since her mid-teen years he has grown distracted – even wary – in her presence. She supposes it's the way she looks now. Some of the laboratory workers find her distracting too. Gurdeep Dala's sweet little girl, all grown up – and treading on the toes of proper research scientists. How hilariously patronising, she thinks – and I think the same, pleased at how switched-on I was as a teenager. Before she has even been to university, this Mya knows every bit as much about the Academy's work as her father. She knows this because her father tells her everything.

This is his legacy. This is her birthright.

'Guru's about to grandstand in front of our new students.

Give it some big licks on stage,' Frank Baumann tells her. 'Do you want to watch?'

'Big time. I want to see them,' she replies. 'Fresh meat, right?'

Mya grins and I wince. She's so confident, so sure of herself. I know that nothing matters in her mind but the success of the Academy, the glory of her father. This can't have been me. Surely this wasn't me? This really was me.

Ten minutes later they are standing behind the tinted glass in the auditorium, watching the man on stage. Her father looks tiny yet somehow huge. She feels so proud of him. Perhaps he would never be understood in his time, she thinks, but future generations would venerate him like a god.

'Here at the Meinhof–Dala–Smithson Academy of Science, Research and Learning, our goal is to perfect people,' her father tells the crowd, concluding his spiel. 'Our aim is to change minds.'

The students, realising that this is their cue to applaud, bring their hands together – at first tentatively, then with greater fervour. Her father exits stage left, nodding to the unseen observers in the gallery above, the applause ringing long and loud.

They don't understand. This younger Mya doesn't understand either, although she thinks she does. She thinks she knows everything. Not yet.

Their first patient has checked in. There is always one within the first three to four weeks. A student, one of the older ones – a woman in her late twenties named Johanna Ehrlich – has been referred to Gurdeep Dala by Dr Baumann. I know this but I don't know how I know this, because I can't remember any of it. I can only watch the scene spool out like a movie reel. I feel the Madboy's dark glare upon me. Mute in my memories,

I'm unable to tell him that this is as much a mystery to me as it is to him.

Unconscious, Johanna Ehrlich is lying on a gurney, hooked up to machines that whir and hum. There is a silver band around her forehead. Wires are plugged into the veins of her neck. Thick bandages are wrapped over her forearms, the wrists encased in white gauze. An Academy worker greets us as we approach the bed. Obviously, he only sees Mr Dala and his teenage daughter. If he saw Mya's doppelganger and a horrendously burned stranger next to them, he would run screaming from the laboratory.

'Eduardo,' my father says, laying a hand on his colleague's shoulder as he assesses the screens of the chuntering machines with a practised eye. 'You are a wonder. Alive yet not alive. Textbook anaesthesia.'

Eduardo, a slight young man with olive skin, busy eyes and a neat goatee, nods his thanks.

'What is her background?'

'One of the local ones.' The lab worker's mouth curls into a wry smile. 'You know, from your little care-in-the-community project. Two children, preschool age. A boy and a girl.' Eduardo blinks, fastidiously wiping his lips with a handkerchief that he folds back into the top pocket of his white coat. 'This wasn't the first time. But her partner doesn't ... doesn't know she's had an accident here.'

My father *tsk-tsks*, shaking his head. 'A shame. Such a shame. Still, this can be put right. And it shall be put right.' He strokes his chin and I can hear stubble rasping against the pads of his forefingers. 'In fact, I am rather in the mood for a change this afternoon. I shall let Miss Dala take control from here.'

The man's jaw clenches. 'Mr Dala, are you sure that's—'

'Relax, Eduardo,' my father says, radiating bonhomie. 'I shall be guiding her through the cerebral framework, following right behind. It will be a great experience for her. As you yourself know, every one of us must start somewhere.'

'She's only seventeen,' Eduardo mutters.

'And every teenager needs a hobby,' my father chuckles. 'Hush now. Mya knows quite as much as I do. Perhaps even more.'

My father and my younger self settle themselves into the reclining chairs next to Johanna's trolley and pick up shining silver headbands from the cradles set next to them. The thin strip of metal gleams, refracting the light and blinding us for a moment. There is a row of serrated teeth on the underside of the band. The Marco-Madboy shakes his head, muttering under his breath. My past self places the band around her hairline, winces as if struck by a lightning flash of pain, then she is still. Her body is limp, her breathing soft and low, her eyes glassy. My father smiles indulgently down at her, then places his own band on his head, folds his hands across his chest. His eyelids flutter shut. He looks as close to contentment as I have ever seen him.

Then we are inside Johanna Ehrlich's head.

Immediately I know this woman's life. I know everything about her. I see two children: a boy of three who is silent and pensive, worryingly different to the rampageous little lads of his age, and a baby aged nine months who won't stop coughing at night. Johanna feels she is to blame for their problems. I know her exhaustion, I know her worries at never being able to provide for Ronnie and Zelda. I understand her shame at a university education that she believes has gone to waste. Her isolation in East Anglia away from her mother and father in Stuttgart. Her relief when the Meinhof-Dala-Smithson Academy offers her a post – part-time work with childcare facilities and

free accommodation. An answer to her problems. A way out.
A new life.

But the old life is proving difficult to escape. Her ex-partner,
drunk and dissolute for so long, has reinvented himself with
religion and is demanding access rights. She is unconvinced,
she refuses to believe he can change so completely. The children are better off without their father until she can trust him
again. He feels she is being unreasonable. He wants to see his
children. So he is making trouble; his religious fervour does
not extend to empathy. One night, sitting at the kitchen table
in the maisonette the Academy has provided for her, weeping
as she reads another demand from his lawyers, Johanna's gaze
falls upon the bread knife draining on the rack. The children,
for once, are both asleep. She has drunk two bottles of wine,
topped off with a handful of pills. Strangely, Johanna Ehrlich is
thinking clearly for the first time in years. Maybe this would
be a better way.

She reaches for the knife.

I don't want to look. I know how this ends.

When I open my eyes again, we are in a strange place,
shrouded in swirling smoke, neither indoors nor outdoors. The
scene is malleable and ever-changing. Shapes and colours fade
to a featureless whiteness.

'How does it appear to you, Mya?' my father asks, his voice
distorting as if he is both extremely close yet far away. 'What
can you see?'

Before I can answer, my younger self does it for me. 'I see...
I see a room,' she says. 'A large bare room.'

She is right. The four of us are standing in a large bare room.
This is what she sees, so we all see the same.

'No furniture?'

'Nothing. Red walls. A bare wood floor.' There is a touch of frustration in her voice. 'I'm sorry, I just ... I don't know where to go from here.'

'Are there any doors in this room?'

'No.'

'The patient suffers from mild agoraphobia,' my father says. 'Not the root cause of her depression, but certainly a factor. Shall we rid Ms Ehrlich of that unpleasantness, my dear?'

'How do I do that?' my younger self asks, not unreasonably.

'Do you remember what I told you about rewriting the mind maps?'

She nods. 'Uncover and rescind the trigger event in the patient's personal history,' teenage Mya says as if remembering a lesson. 'Then cauterise the negative emotion appertaining to the memory. Remove every trace of trauma. Finally, create a new emotion.'

'The balm for the wound,' he agrees, his eyes closed as if hearing the sweetest song. 'Good girl. Clever girl.'

Mya nods. She scrunches shut her eyes. She is clenching and unclenching her right fist, the way she does – the way I do – when concentrating extremely hard. 'I think ... I think I see where it started. She was seven years old. She was playing at her friend Lucie's house. Lucie called her Jo-Jo and she called her Lu-Lu. She loved her friend Lucie. But Lucie's dad had a fierce dog. A guard dog, an Alsatian. It was tethered up in the yard and it barked like crazy and she'd always scamper past too scared to even look at it. She'd dread that moment but her love for Lucie was bigger than her fear of the dog and once she was in the house everything was okay, she had fun.' My younger self takes a deep breath before continuing. 'One day ... one day the dog got loose. The chain wasn't locked properly on its collar. When Jo-Jo opened the gate, it went for her. Snapping and growling. She ran. She was screaming and screaming. She could smell its breath. She knew it would be the last thing she smelled – that bad dog's stinking breath before it bit down on her throat. Only Lucie's mum had heard the barking and she opened the door and pulled her inside the house. Two seconds later the dog thumped against the door. It took them four hours to get little Jo-Jo to come home. She's hated leaving the house ever since. Because no matter how many years go past, some part of her mind tells her there will always be a bad dog waiting for her outside.'

A sound of barking fills the room. The booming roar echoes around us. There is a reek of spoiled meat. This is not my nightmare but I'm still frightened. The bad dog is in the room with us. I can see it, smell it. The dog is impossibly big, impossibly fierce. The dog that has charged, slavering and snarling, through the darkest dreams of Johanna Ehrlich for the past twenty years.

'Bad dog,' says Mya. At the strident sound of her voice, the huge animal whimpers then shuffles backwards. The mindless fury in its eyes has been replaced by apprehension. Maybe I'm going crazy, but it looks as though the creature has shrunk from its elephantine size to a normal large dog. 'Here, boy. You need to be trained.'

The dog whines again. It is shrinking. It is most definitely shrinking. It's now the size of a rabbit. Then a mouse. Then it is so tiny that the other Mya is able to scoop up the animal and drop it into the pocket of her white lab coat.

'Stage One complete,' my father murmurs. 'Not quite how I would have chosen to complete the cauterisation, sweetpea. Quite possibly better.' Mya, aged seventeen, glows with triumph. 'The trauma has been diminished,' he continues, 'so, if you please, would you show me how you intend to deal with Ms Ehrlich's phobia.'

She drops to her knees and loosens a floorboard. Underneath

is a huge axe. The weapon is cartoonishly big. The blade dwarfs her body. She pauses then takes it easily in her hands, even though she shouldn't have the strength to lift it. She heaves the axe over her shoulder, then, with a huff of exertion, she drives it into the wall. A great split appears in the plaster, which cracks into a chasm. Then the red walls fall apart and crumble to nothingness. We're standing outside – bathed in golden sunshine, smelling the sweet scent of mown grass, hearing the birds tweet in glorious harmony and breathing in the fresh clean air of the outside world.

'Again, a little unconventional,' my father says, stroking his moustache, 'but effective.'

'There's no fierce dog, Jo-Jo,' the younger Mya says. 'So there's nothing to be scared of outside. The world's a good place, a friendly place. It wants you to stay in it.' She turns to her father hopefully. 'Was that alright?'

'Good girl, clever girl,' he says, rubbing his hands together gleefully. 'Now, tell me, what do we do with these cut-out elements of the psyche?'

'We create a computer simulation from their mind map. A digital recreation of the worst of our patients' brains.'

'And where must we keep these unwanted elements of Ms Ehrlich's psyche?'

'The Cell. The Brain Cell. In the safest place inside the Academy.'

My father nods. 'Quite right. And why do we store these simulations in perpetuity?'

Younger Mya pinches the bridge of her nose between her fingers. 'For ... for legal reasons. In case a procedure is questioned or challenged. And, more importantly, for research purposes. So others may one day be saved.'

'Good. Good. Excellent.' He squeezes her shoulder lovingly.

'Now we have conquered the phobic condition, reduced to poor little Fido or Fifi living in your pocket, we shall test the boundaries of your knowledge with Ms Ehrlich's more complicated problem. Let's get to the heart of the matter, sweetpea. The real nitty-gritty.'

'Okay, Dad,' my younger self replies. She smiles up at him with admiration, adoration. I want to be sick again.

Instead we are pulled out of the memory and out of the tunnel and we're back in the Bleaklands and the Madboy is staring at me with a flatly murderous gaze. With a single brutal motion he pushes me down to the sun-bleached gravel, a knee on each shoulder, and I'm helpless. His hands reach out to wrap around my throat. Unable to move, I stare up at him, desperately willing whatever of Marco's sweet nature that is still left inside him to take control again.

'You lied to me,' he growls, dog-like himself. 'You lied.'

I shake my head. 'No. No, please, no. I don't remember any of that.'

'What were you doing?' he almost screams. Even in his rage the tears are rolling down his cheeks, and somehow I feel he understands more than I do right now. 'Fucking around with people's minds? Did you think you were God?'

'Please,' I say softly. I manage to free an arm – not to break loose, but to wipe away one of the tears tracking down his ruined face. I feel like weeping myself because despite the sweat and blood and the horribly sweet odour of burned flesh, he even smells like Marco. It's impossible but I can still smell that pine-and-leather aftershave he used to wear on special occasions. Deep down, underneath the coatings of madness, I know he's the good and pure boy who I love and who loves me. He just doesn't know it yet – and that could be the death of me. What did I do to him? What did I do to Johanna? What sort of person was I before?

'Please, darling,' I try again, 'I'm as confused as you are. I don't remember doing any of that. I don't remember my dad teaching me. I feel … I feel like that was a completely different person. She looked like me, that girl, that Mya. But she's a doppelganger, I swear.'

'So who are you?' he demands. 'Who am I? What did you do, Mya? What the hell did you do to me?'

'I don't remember doing anything,' I insist. 'I told you, I was replaced. So were you.'

With a moan of frustration, he rolls off me and slumps on the ground, breathing heavily. Gently I stroke his cheek, then lean over and – feeling no repulsion, only a yearning to soothe the hurt in his body and the hurt in his head – place a small kiss on the blackened skin.

'You're Marco,' I tell him. 'You're not the Madboy, remember that. You're my darling Marco. And I love you very much. And even if we're in hell right now, or naraka or purgatory or non-space or whatever you want to call it, at least I'm here with you.'

His fingers interlock with mine. How many nights have we lain awake together, our hands entwined in this way? We can get this back. We can make it out of here together. We can make everything right again. Then I realise I've been speaking out loud; there's no circuit-breaker between my thoughts and my words in this blasted place. He is nodding, he is smiling – that tentative little-boy-lost grin I remember so well – and now he's pushing himself to his feet, offering me his hand, leading me towards another one of those bottomless holes bored into the landscape by an unknowable hand. The Madboy is gone. Marco is here with me again.

This is the sweetest nightmare I have ever known.

'Here,' he says, pointing to the tunnel's yawning open mouth. I can only wonder why he has chosen to pick this hole above the dozens pockmarking the landscape. 'For me this time. This one feels right.'

32

New Beginnings

It had been almost a month since he woke up but still Mya's father was a mystery to him. Tonight, though, was the night. It felt as if an insect was wriggling in the pit of his stomach – no, not just one insect, a whole swarm. Mya, realising that he was too nervous to make any useful conversation, suggested he had a drink or two. The gin had helped at first. Then he panicked that her dad would think he was a drunk, not worthy of his intelligent, beautiful daughter. After the gin he gargled half a bottle of mouthwash, scrubbing his teeth until the gums bled. He couldn't fake a smile, he realised. The grin in the bathroom mirror was frighteningly fixed. He looked like a stalker, not a suitor.

Mya's fingers pinched at the skin around his throat as she tightened his tie. She stood back to admire her handiwork, staring at him as if he was an artefact in a museum's display case, trapped in still life.

'Can I at least lose the tie?' he asked. 'It's choking me.'

She sucked at her front teeth. 'Okay. Lose the tie. Probably too much anyway.'

'And the shirt?' he asked hopefully. He had put on weight during his recovery and the buttons strained at his gut.

'Don't even think about it, buster. You want to impress him, don't you? My dad was dressed in a three-piece suit the day he met my mother. He was going for a job interview. Still insists she'd never have noticed him if he hadn't been looking his best. Obviously, an off-the-peg Marks and Sparks suit did the trick.'

'It worked out for them though.' He paused, trying to remember if Mya had mentioned her mother before. 'Didn't it?'

Mya turned her face away, biting down on her bottom lip. For a second it looked as if her mood would darken again. Quickly she knocked back the rest of her drink. 'Hey ho. Shall we go?'

He liked Gurdeep Dala immediately. The man had an amiably distracted air, so different to the intense scientist he had dreaded. He thought of Mya's contrasts – the shifting plateaus of her emotions, her swings from elation to sadness as if her psyche spun on an otherworldly axis – and smiled to himself. They were strange people, brilliant people, and he was grateful that they made time for such a deeply normal character as himself. The conversation crackled between father and daughter and he was unable to keep up. Their words fizzed across the living room as if the air between them was electricity. Knowing he could add nothing of interest to the debate, he relaxed back in Mr Dala's favourite armchair, sipped his can of beer and admired them.

It took a few seconds to realise that Mya's father was trying to attract his attention.

'I was saying, young Marco – would you mind playing a short game with me before dinner? A brief test of psychometrics. Only to make an old research scientist very happy.'

'Oh, for God's sake, Dad,' Mya huffed.

'Humour me, my dear daughter. Humour me.' His girlfriend

shook her head and folded her arms across her chest. 'May I quiz you on a hypothetical scenario, Mr Pellicci?'

'Sure thing,' he said equably, draining his beer. The house seemed oddly familiar to him. Somehow he felt as if he had been here before.

Gurdeep Dala scuttled through to the kitchen for a replacement can of Red Stripe, then pulled over his chair until they were sitting only a few feet apart. He noticed the row of small white indentations that ran around the man's bald head. Then Mr Dala gently tilted his head down until they were staring at one another eye to eye.

'My first question,' he said. 'Imagine a scenario. Say … say you were moving out of your home. Possibly even to cohabit with my daughter.' His tufty eyebrows wiggled roguishly. He couldn't bring himself to look at Mya. 'She persuades you to use a friend − not your friend, hers, a stranger to you − to assist with the task of removal. They carry a box of vintage glassware. A present from a favourite relative. Do you have a favourite relative, Marco?'

'Uncle Gi,' he said, smiling, enjoying the game. 'He's my favourite relative.'

'Uncle Gi's gift,' Mr Dala agreed. 'These glasses mean the world to you. However, this friend is clumsy. He drops Uncle Gi's gift. The glass shatters. It's irreplaceable. How do you feel? Frustrated? Even angry?'

He thought for a moment. 'I don't care. It's just stuff.'

'Very well. So, another scenario. A relative from far-off climes has invited you to stay at their house. A well-deserved holiday. You endure a long, tedious flight. You take a costly cab ride. You arrive at their front door and they are not home. They are away. They have forgotten you are coming. You're stranded in a foreign country. Thanks to their selfishness. How do you feel?'

He blew out the air from his cheeks. He thought about that imaginary family member's home, hammering his fist against the locked door. How would he feel? 'It's a shame. A bit annoying. But ... we can find a hotel somewhere. We can still have a great holiday. It's not the end of the world.'

'I see. Excellent.' Mya's father drummed his fingers on his thighs. 'One more scenario before dinner. You are out on the town with friends. My daughter has left you to your –' here Mr Dala made rabbit ears out of his fingers '– boys' night out. You believe she is at home, safe and sound. Instead you enter a bar and you witness her in the arms of another man, kissing passionately—'

'For Christ's sake, Dad!' Mya broke in. Turning, startled, he saw she was gripping the stem of her wine glass so tightly that her knuckles had turned white. A vein was pulsing in her temple. 'Leave me out of your silly games. What the hell are you playing at?'

Mr Dala held up his hands in apology. 'Only a theoretical test, my darling daughter. A little game to highlight the interesting inconsistencies between your partner's personality and his pec-cadillos. I refer you, obviously, to Malhan and Hessel's epochal research paper *The Human at Play and War*, which clearly states—'

'You go too far sometimes,' Mya interrupted, staring coldly at her father. 'Keep your psycho-games for your patients. Marco's different.'

'It's fine,' he said, concerned that he had been the cause of the family's disharmony. He was anxious for the evening to go well. He desperately wanted Gurdeep Dala to like him. The man was quirky, even strange, but he could attribute that to genius. 'Really, I wasn't offended.'

'It was a joke, sweetpea,' Mr Dala muttered, his voice that of a petulant teenager. 'Only a joke.'

'What do you think, Marco?' she asked, reaching over and placing her hand on his. 'What do you really think?'

'It was only a joke,' he agreed. She smiled weakly and seemed to relax a little, even as she finished off her wine in one great gulp.

Mya had insisted on coming back to his house that night. She hadn't wanted to stay with her father. It seemed that the taxi cab couldn't arrive soon enough. He watched her as she stared out of the window into the rainswept blankness as they crawled through the streets of his hometown. The streetlights flashed in her dark eyes.

'That was a nice evening,' he said.

'Yes,' she agreed colourlessly. 'Yes, it was.'

'Food was good. Spicy.'

'I wish he'd stop pretending he can cook. He always orders a takeaway then says he made it himself. I used to think it was funny. Now I realise it's just another one of his lies. That's what I've had my whole life and I've had it up to here. A lifetime of pointless lies.'

Constrained by the seatbelt, he attempted a clumsy hug. 'No, I think he just wants to impress. Curry's always good when you've had a beer. I'm a little bit pissed, actually.'

'You and him got through fourteen cans. I counted.'

'That would explain it.'

Mya stared at him for a moment. Then she slammed her fist against the plastic armrest of her seat. He recoiled, his mouth hanging open in shock. 'I hate it when he does that,' she sobbed, her fingernails raking at her hair. The cab driver glanced questioningly at him in the rear-view mirror and he could only shrug in response. 'That stupid game. He's so ... so fucking weird. My dad ruins everything. That's why I could never have friends over. That's why the other girls at school thought I was a freak.'

'You are a freak,' he agreed, reaching for her hands, scarcely aware of what he was saying, only wanting to distract her from the melancholy that was shading her brow. 'I love it. It's brilliant. You should celebrate it.'

She stared at him for some time. Her lips moved as if repeating his words under her breath. He wondered whether he had said something similar before. 'Thanks, Marco,' she said, her breath catching as she recovered her composure, 'but you don't know what it's like being constantly analysed. Everything I did, everything I thought, was picked apart and put back together. Like a bug under a microscope – only he was probing my brain. He doesn't understand people, not in the slightest. He wants to know, he really wants to know, but he doesn't understand, and that's what makes him dangerous.'

Confused, he shook his head. 'Don't be too harsh on him. We were only playing a game of consequences. Like a game show on telly, and the host asks if you want the cash prize or to see what's behind the mystery door. A bit of fun. There's nothing to it.'

Mya bit down on her bottom lip. 'You don't understand either, darling. That sort of thing you saw tonight ... it's happened every day of my life. It messed me up. It meant I couldn't be around normal people. I couldn't function in the real world.'

'You seem to do pretty well. You're much better than me.'

She squeezed his hand. 'I felt like a complete failure when I ended up back at his Academy. A princess from a ruined fairytale. Locked away in the tallest tower until my dying day.'

She managed a small smile. 'You'll never know how you rescued me.'

'If I rescued you, then you rescued me.'

'I'll hold you to that one,' she said wanly, leaning over to kiss his cheek. 'It makes us just about equal.'

33

The Bleaklands (memory holes)

The boy is staring at the back of the girl's head. Every fibre of that black ponytail has been imprinted on his mind. His gaze feels white-hot, able to scorch through the walls of her skull, transmitting his thoughts directly into her brain. Surely she would look, surely she would somehow feel his presence. A sixth sense? Psychic transmission? He had read about all these powers in his superhero comics. She would turn, surely, she would turn and he could drink her in. He wants her to look and he dreads her looking. The incomparable reaction she sparks inside him, unwittingly, when he catches a glimpse of her face. That's why he can't take it. That's why his gaze always drops to the floor in her presence. It kills him to look at her, but he can't live without seeing her.

So instead the boy stares at the back of Gemma Dala's head, three desks away, while old Mr Hockley drones on about equations and formulae, subtractions and divisions, linear forms and theorems. If x is Marco and y is Gemma, and x is minus y — almost certainly forever because, oh God, she isn't even aware that he exists — then what hope is there of combining the co-ordinates? Can there ever be a solution?

There was no worse age than fourteen, he had decided. It was the worst number. He remembered his brother Tony, watching boxing on TV one night, describing a fighter: *That geezer's worth the square root of fuck-all.* He didn't really understand what Tony meant but the phrase appealed to him. It seemed that fourteen was the square root of fuck-all. It didn't add, it just took away. Fifteen might be better. Sixteen, he was certain, would be the golden number. But by the time he was sixteen, Gemma Dala could be somewhere else entirely. Obviously, she would still be at his school – there was GCSE coursework, then the exams, and she was so bright, top of the class in everything but English. He was sure she would stay on for A levels and university applications. But by then she would have been stolen away from him, oh yes she would, he knew it. She had grown tall early and her frame was all angles, her movements clumsy as if she was just stepping into her skin for the first time. As stupid as he was aged fourteen, he knew her gawkiness wouldn't last. Right now, he was sure he was the only boy noticing her beauty, but that was because the rest of them were blinded by superficiality. Right now they were distracted by girls who weren't like Gemma. The girls who painted their faces with make-up that looked half an inch thick, the girls who stalked in threes and fours down the school corridor as if it was a catwalk, the girls who stuffed the fronts of their sweaters and wore skirts that barely brushed their knees in clear contravention of the uniform policy, not that many of the male teachers seemed to care. The jackals of his year and the years above – the boys with flashy haircuts and permanent sneers – were distracted by those girls. They could have any of those girls, but he knew jackals enjoyed preying on the weak. There had already been rumours floating about Gemma's mother, how she'd been carted off to the nuthouse, the funny farm, the laughing factory. He wondered whether he could believe that rumour. Amid the jeering, shrieking, shoving chaos of the schoolyard, Gemma Dala was a mute and pensive presence. She floated ghostlike through the throng. She didn't seem to notice anyone around her, but far too soon they would notice her. He ached to protect that girl. The sense of outraged propriety was already kindling. He had noticed her first. Not that it mattered.

So the boy stares at the back of the girl's head and wishes he could be brave. Confident like the bigger boys. Maybe there's a drink, a drug he can take. He wishes confidence could be bottled and swallowed, or maybe injected into his veins. Thrumming with that pure and clean hit, he could stride up to her after class. Ask if she fancies going into town, you know, sometime, maybe see a film, you know, just the two of them, like, together. And the look on her face, the way her eyes flash, her white teeth ...

It's a lovely daydream. A fantasy he entertains during boring classes, a fantasy that slides into stickier territory when he's alone in his bedroom that evening. He wishes he could be brave. Bigger. Confident.

But he knows he's not brave or big or confident. He will never talk to her.

Then one day, that strange and quiet girl simply disappears.

34

The Bleaklands (memory holes)

Fifteen was not better. A year later and the boy hasn't grown as he hoped he would. While most of his classmates have bulked out, acquired muscles and the swagger of manliness, he's still weak and pudgy. He feels permanently out of breath. He hates nothing more than revealing his flabby body after football. He can't run; they always trap him in the showers. The slaps on his pink wobbling flesh, the legs stuck out for him to trip and sprawl on his face in the dirty puddles on the changing-room floor. Fat Marky, they call him, and that's pretty funny until someone comes up with Porkchop Pellicci, or just Porko, and that's even funnier. Everyone's laughing. Everyone's laughing the whole time. So he gives up sports. Instead he sits in his room and plays videogames and watches Eighties action films and internet pornography. He stuffs his face with chocolate bars and crisps, growing fatter still. He sits and formulates elaborate revenge plots against the boys who taunt him. He writes down what he would do to them if he was bigger and braver, the words growing darkly beautiful in their extremities, and sometimes he reads them back and wonders how those bloodily florid words could have spilled from his brain. But he can't stop writing those words because he is trapped in that worthless fat body. He sits and wishes he was someone else, someone else entirely. He sits and hates.

In the absence of his father, his dad's elder brother Giuseppe – or just Uncle Gi – begins to take an interest in his stumbling trudge towards manhood. On Saturdays they usually go to the games arcade on the pier. As he batters away on the machines, Giuseppe sits on the bench on the boardwalk looking out to sea, eking out the sole rolled cigarette he now allows himself each day. His brother, the boy's father, had been killed by the habit four years ago – his lungs blackened through decades of sucking in tarry filth – and Giuseppe Pellicci rations himself to that solitary smoke as both a personal warning and a tribute. Troubled, he stares at the boy, remembering his promise to Franco that he would always look out for his youngest son. Was he respecting his brother's wishes? He never sees the boy with any friends, any girls. Spends the whole time in his bedroom playing computer games. Looks away whenever he asks how school is going. Giuseppe decides something must be done.

So one Saturday, the routine changes. They don't go to the arcade. The boy is driven to an industrial estate on the outskirts of town and they walk in silence towards a metal door set into a block of dirty white bricks. As his uncle opens the door, he is buffeted by a gust of old sweat and cheesy socks. His eyes streaming, he takes in the dank, oppressive room. He's never seen anything like it. So many men. Men doing push-ups and lifting weights. Men punching black bags that swing from the low ceiling. Men fighting, men fighting, men fighting. There is a constant soundtrack of huffing, slapping exertion. Sweat glistening on taut muscles. Eyes rolling in sockets. A thrumming aura of tension that he can taste.

His gaze is pulled to an older man leaning on the ropes of a ring in which two teenagers wearing blue headguards circle one another warily. He wears a tracksuit the colour of dirty ash and thick-rimmed spectacles are perched on the end of his nose. The man has a paunch and below his black baseball cap a few bubbles of silvery hair cling stubbornly to his temples. His appearance is entirely monochrome, daubed in shades of black and grey, as if he has ambled out of an old photograph. The stranger raises his hand as they approach the ring. His uncle mutters a few terse words about a phone conversation earlier. The stranger eases himself down from the ring apron and looks him directly in the eye. Only now does he see the definition in those thick black arms, the bunching of muscles in his shoulders. He feels a little afraid but also strangely fascinated.

'You like boxing, young fella? Want to be a fighter?' The accent is a curious blend of Cockney rasp and Caribbean melody: *Wannabe a fiy-uhh?* A hand is thrust out. The man's palm feels like sandpaper. There is an electric current of power pulsing in that grip. 'Name's Leroy Minto. And you must be Marco. How old you, boy? Eleven or so?'

He blushes with shame. He looks up at Giuseppe and his uncle looks away. 'Fifteen,' he whispers through parched lips.

Leroy Minto sucks at his front teeth. 'Yeah, we'll try him out in the juniors first,' his new trainer says.

He hates boxing. For the first six months he hates every single second. He is pushed around, manhandled, poked and jabbed. The punches don't hurt too much but the insults he endures from the other boys – the bigger boys, so very much like the jackals at his school – sting mercilessly. It is even worse with the younger ones; many of them traveller kids who have been boxing since they were able to walk. He hates boxing and he hates everyone and he hates himself. He's close to quitting, despite knowing how much it would disappoint Uncle Gi. Until one morning, skipping around the ring to keep out of the reach of a bulky but sluggish boy named Sammy Frankham, he swings a despairing left hook, not expecting the blow to land. Instead his fist connects beautifully with Sammy Frankham's cheekbone and the boy's right eye reddens and waters, the skin below immediately marking up. Sammy Frankham stumbles back, his lower lip wobbling. The insult framed on his lips will never be voiced. Seeing the other boy's expression of hurt and confusion is the most delicious sensation he has ever experienced. The sense of power taken away from the strong, invested in the hands of the weaker yet wilier, unlocks an unknown and unknowable part of his psyche.

The bigger boy flails his arms but he lost his heart the second that blow connected. It's going to be easy, far too easy, to take the rest of his body apart.

He has never felt this way before. He feels immortal, invincible. He feels he could dive into the surface of the sun and come out shining.

He steps forward, fists raised, grinning.

Twice a week for the next two years he goes to Leroy Minto's shabby boxing gym. Eventually, perhaps stirred into action by the violence of his hobby, his testosterone belatedly kicks in. He grows and grows and by the age of seventeen he's well over six foot. The other boys at the club, and many of the older men too, take a backward step when he walks into the club. Leroy teaches him his ringcraft that went all the way back to fairground boxing booths in the Sixties – *Dip and slip and rip, Marco* – but by the end of his time at the club he's simply walking through opponents. They're beaten before he ducks under the top rope. There is an array of tournament trophies on the top shelf of the wardrobe in his bedroom. There are rumours of scouts from the British Olympic team tracking his progress at these local tournaments; the rangy cruiserweight whose aggressive swings bely the surgical coldness in his inside work. Now Leroy is saying he could even think about prize-fighting, pro level. *No pressure but you got proper talent, seriously no one in this manor can live with you, what do you say we go down to London, meet my old mate Barry at his gym in Bethnal Green, I've told him all about you, Marco, he's a fella who can make things happen.* There's only one problem: his mother tells him it would kill her to see him box without a headguard, in an environment – however controlled – where accidents could and did happen. She's so frail now. Losing her husband, cancer chipping away at his lifeforce like the cruellest sculptor, has almost destroyed her. He kisses her forehead and makes that promise to his mother: *Swear down.*

It is only a white lie. He never boxes without a headguard. The swift and clean revenge attacks administered upon the three worst of his schoolyard tormenters don't count as boxing because boxing bouts are usually competitive and well matched. As Leroy says, no one in this manor can live with him. He never goes too far, but as he blackens an eye or bursts a nose, he thinks of the slaps on his chubby body in the school showers and wonders whether he might be the bully now. But it's done, it's over. Boxing has served its purpose in his life. He throws away his gloves but keeps the gym weights and his trophies, even though most of them are worthless plastic crap. His favourite trophies are the two onyx gloves from the Eastern Championships, which he sets on the top of his wardrobe and brings down sometimes to polish, hefting them in the hands that bested Sammy Frankham a lifetime ago. The gloves feel heavy enough to drag a man down, but every time he sees those trophies, the stone as unyielding as the muscles of his once-flabby torso, fierce pride soars inside him.

By the time his unremarkable stint in education finishes – he does manage an A-grade in English, somehow, despite barely reading the course books – he has changed beyond measure. He doesn't even recognise the photographs of himself when he was younger, so he burns them. He is a different person now. He has a new name too. He's not Fat Marky any longer. Not Porkchop Pellicci. Definitely not fucking Porko. He's just Marc. Or Big Pell. Or sometimes Mad Marco.

He would never admit it to anyone, but he likes that last name best of all.

Years go by and his life has been sputtering in circles. He's twenty-one and burned out on the world. He takes temporary jobs and quits whenever he fears he might be pushed into a role of any responsibility. He doesn't know why he has stayed in this flat, dreary area of East Anglia but somehow he can't bring himself to leave. He tries to fill the void with drink and drugs, football and fighting. He never goes out looking for trouble but he attracts it like moths to a lamp. The excitement of the late-night brawl makes him feel alive for a short while, but in the morning – his knuckles purpled, his lips swollen – that feeling of aimlessness returns. He wishes he was somewhere else, anywhere else, but he can't shake the sensation that there is something unfinished in this town. If he left, it might pass right on by unnoticed.

Some nights he writes ... well, not poetry exactly, because nothing rhymes or is intended to rhyme ... but streams of thoughts set down in short lines. Always about the same person. A half-remembered figure, a long-ago love with a swinging dark ponytail and a face he can never quite make out. She dances through each one of his words.

One night, he goes with a few workmates from the building site to a punk rock gig in London. They catch the train down, cracking cans and laughing, then stomp up to Camden, the chill night air sending a thrill through his body. From the moment he sees the singer – with his leather bondage vest and tartan trousers and his green hair spiked up like an electrocuted cartoon character – swagger onto the stage, he is intrigued. When the drums begin to thump and the fuzzy bass rumbles and the guitar chords roar through the speakers, he is queasy with anticipation. And when he sees the writhing, leaping mass of humanity in front of the stage, he's utterly lost. The mosh pit seems a little like boxing. Only at the punk rock show, when somebody is knocked down, there are many hands reaching down to pick them up, set them right – and crash into them once more. That night in Camden gives him a purpose. He was once a fat loser, then a boxer, now he is a punk: the three stages of Marco. He grows his hair long enough to tease into a mohawk, then has it shaved around the sides and dyed fluorescent. He relishes looking different. The time traveller from the late Seventies, with his ripped leather jacket and his cherry-red Dr Martens boots and his pink hair. Some people laugh at him, others look away, and he doesn't mind either. Of course, there are those who jostle him in the street, spit and call him names – distant cousins of the schoolyard jackals. But he can handle them.

He's going to leave this town. He has saved up enough money. He wants to move to London, find a cheap houseshare with his mates Kev and Nettles, go to gigs in Camden or Brixton every night, maybe even start a band himself. He can't play any instruments but he has started writing lyrics. Maybe the words are a little sappy for a punk group but if he screams them loud enough then no one will understand what he's singing about. They won't know who he's singing about.

Her. Always her. Forever her.

35
New Beginnings

He found her crying at the top of the stairs one night and nothing he could say would make it stop. The past month had been traumatic. He told himself that difficult times were normal for any relationship; the honeymoon period couldn't last forever. He had already seen her sulking and hungover, sick with flu or grouchily restless with cramps. He loved her regardless. In sickness and in health, he told himself, for better or for worse. But this was different. Nothing bad had happened. There was no great tragedy. But as their days went by together, Mya seemed to find less and less joy in life. He couldn't tell why she felt this way. Sometimes, as they sat on the sofa watching television, he could sense that she was gazing at him – contemplating the row of abrasions that ran around the top of his forehead from a long-ago accident he couldn't remember. But when he stared back and smiled, she looked away and knuckled at her eyes as if hiding tears. It seemed like it was his fault. What had he done wrong? What did she want him to be?

The flashing eyes which had entranced him grew dull and inward-looking, the flesh around the sockets darkly smeared as if bruised. Her hair was lank and unwashed and it took some convincing to get her to bathe. Hours upon hours would pass and barely a ghost of a smile would cross her face. She would stay in bed with the covers pulled over her head, snapping at him whenever he brought up sweetened tea and toast, or suggested a walk outside might do her good. Other times she clung to him like a frightened toddler, her hands clasped around his neck, her whole body trembling. Each day he promised her everything would be better tomorrow, knowing it wouldn't, and he had started to hate himself for offering her false hope.

Now Mya couldn't stop crying.

'Is it me?' he asked, draping an arm clumsily across her shoulders. She had lost almost a stone in weight and her clothes hung limply. Her frame felt jagged, full of unforgiving ridges. It was difficult to believe that their bodies had once slotted together so sweetly.

She looked at him and laughed. There was a wild, desperate quality to her laughter that trailed icy fingertips down his spine. She shook her head and briefly touched his arm. 'God, no, Marco. You're perfect. Absolutely perfect. That's the fucking problem.'

'Is there anything I can do?'

'No. There wasn't anything you could do last time. Or the time before that.'

'I'll keep asking though.'

She placed a kiss on his forehead. Her lips were blistered, like sandpaper to the touch, and he tried to stop himself from shrinking away. 'I know you will, darling. I appreciate it. I appreciate you, even if I'm not so great at showing it.'

'Maybe we should go out?' he suggested. 'I found a nice walk by the canal path the other day. The leaves are starting to drop from the trees. The colours are beautiful.'

She sniffed. 'I'm sure they are for you. I can't see colours anymore. The Great Wave drowned every one of them.'

Sadly, he nodded. He stared around his childhood bedroom

that had become their own little home. He thought of the tiny changes she had made; the vintage film posters on the walls, the fairy lights strung along the banister rail. Before she agreed to move in with him, she had told him about her Great Waves. It had been quite soon after the strange night at her father's house. After a few glasses of wine to steady her nerves, she had sat down with him and explained her condition. *This is serious, me and you*, Mya said, drumming her fingers on her thighs. *It's working. I wasn't sure it would again. I don't quite know why but it's working. My dad was right. So before we go any further, you need to know something about me. It's not a particularly great something.* So she had told him about her problem, the mental imbalances she had suffered for as long as she could remember, and he held her hand and listened. *I don't want to hurt you, Marco*, she finished. *I only want you to know what's wrong with me.*

She didn't mean to hurt him. He knew that. Even when her mood swung from disinterest to irrational anger, he refused to let himself be hurt. When she spat insults, swore, told him to get the hell out of his life and never come back, he endured it. He told himself it wasn't Mya speaking. It was the Great Wave stealing her voice. Instead he built himself a mental shelter – a golden carapace constructed from the memories they had shared before these dark months – and sheltered inside.

She couldn't hurt him. But knowing he was unable to help her? That hurt more than he felt he could bear. Because there was always the fear that one day, those hungry black tides inside her brain might completely wash away the Mya he loved.

'Doesn't it bother you, me being like this?' she asked. 'I'd be … be pretty pissed off if I were you. Can't be much fun having a lunatic for a girlfriend.'

Stubbornly he shook his head. 'I'd rather have you than someone else. Anyone else in the world.'

He hoped his words, sincere and tender, would help. Instead Mya sobbed ever harder. It took her a while to compose herself and he rubbed her back, trying to massage the softness back into her. 'You didn't have much choice,' she said finally, her breath hitching. 'You poor innocent bastard. You didn't have a choice in the matter.'

'What do you mean? I don't understand.'

'I tricked you, darling.' She was blinking rapidly, her fists clenching and unclenching as if she wanted to hit somebody – or herself. 'I wanted this relationship and you didn't have a choice. Doesn't that make you angry?'

He shook his head. 'I'm only angry with this stupid illness that's making you say things you know aren't true. You're not the real Mya right now. The Mya that I know is just … just brilliant. And I love her very much.'

Quickly she pulled herself out of his embrace. She stared at him intently. In a second she had come alive again but not in the way he had dreamed of; her expression was too anxious, too evaluating. 'What did you say?' she demanded. 'What on earth did you just say?'

'That you're brilliant,' he repeated, confused. 'That I love you very much.'

She shook her head. 'No. Before that.'

'I said—' He tried to remember the exact words. 'I said this illness is making you say what's not true. That you're not the real Mya.'

That look of concern now seemed close to horror. Her nails raked at the flesh around her cheeks. 'Please go, Marco,' she muttered. 'I can't … you can't be around me right now. It's not safe. Go out. Have some beers with your friends or go for a ride on your bike or something.'

'I can't leave you when you're—'

'For God's sake, *go!*' Her voice was almost a shriek.

Stumbling backwards, he overbalanced and nearly toppled head first down the staircase. His heart pounding, he clung to the banister railing. The fairy lights winked mockingly. He knew enough from the past two months to realise there would be no reasoning with her. So he left, padding down the stairs away from her, bewildered and more than a little scared. He knew everything about her. He didn't know her at all.

Acting on unconscious instinct or instruction, he found himself in the garage, sitting astride the Suzuki Bandit. The motorcycle still scared him. But Mya's moods scared him more. Unsure of what he was even planning, he caressed the throttle. The oily whiff of the engine unlocked a secret compartment in his heart and he realised he was smiling. Carefully he steered the bike out of the garage and when he fired up the engine and began to ride, his troubled thoughts were whipped away by the night air. He rode for miles and miles, faster and faster. He never wanted to stop.

36

New Beginnings

The next day it was as if a light switch had flicked on inside her head. He had slept on the sofa. The last thing he remembered was arriving home in the early hours and pouring glass after glass of Scotch. He hated whisky but it was the only drink that could kill his thoughts cleanly. Eventually, as he had hoped, unconsciousness claimed him. When he woke – his head buzzing, his vision blurry – Mya was standing over him. Her posture was relaxed. Her smile was conciliatory. That carefree light was back in her eyes.

'I'm so sorry,' she said. She reached out her arms and he crushed her into his embrace. 'I'm sorry about everything,' Mya whispered into his ear. 'I feel better now, so much better. I'm sorry you have to be in love with a weirdo.'

'There's nothing to be sorry about,' he told her, confused but delighted. 'I love being in love with a weirdo.'

They took his motorbike out to the coast and tried to skim stones in the sea. The foaming surf swallowed the pebbles before they had skipped more than once or twice and they giggled at their own hopelessness. They walked along the pier, past the old art-deco arcade with its four wooden turrets piercing the gloomy sky, its roof sloping like a wave. They found a small, empty café and ate a simple lunch of fish and chips that tasted better than any food he could remember. The cawing of the gulls mimicked their laughter and the gentle rush of the waves whispered that everything would be fine, that there was not a single reason to worry, that they had weathered the storm together. They perched their elbows on the railings of the boardwalk, staring out at the endless grey expanse of the North Sea, sharing one another's warmth.

'Do you think there's anything beyond this life?' Mya asked suddenly.

'You're a Hindu, aren't you?' He grinned. 'Aren't you supposed to come back as a variety of animals?'

She dug him in the ribs. 'Behave. Culturally I'm Hindu but inside I'm pure atheist. My dad would disown me if I started spouting off about reincarnation.'

'Well, what do you think?' he asked. 'This is about the closest to heaven I can imagine. Being here with you. No one around us, nothing much to do. Just us and all the time in the world.'

She stared at him, her eyes moist. She took a few gulps of the salt-tinged air and placed her hand upon his.

'When I first tried to kill myself, I thought I saw God,' she said. Her tone was matter-of-fact, almost free of emotion. 'I was only a teenager, messing about with pills. I don't think I even really wanted it to happen. I remember feeling very sleepy. Sludgy. Life was moving a few paces behind regular time. There was this song on a playlist one of my friends had made me and I wanted to stay and hear the end. It was beautiful. Everything I wanted in a song. Pain and hope, love and hate, anger and beauty. But I... I slipped away before the song finished. I was somewhere I couldn't really see. A void or a vacuum. And I felt this presence. This gigantic thing enclosing me. There was silence, peace. I felt this faith I've never felt before. Then – I don't know why – I opened my eyes. I wanted to see. Wanted to see if my mind was capable of experiencing whatever this presence was, or whether it would just … just explode. So I opened my eyes. I saw. Then I realised it was a nothingness. Just blankness. A white place.'

He hugged her tightly, clinging to her with desperation as if the force of his body could stop her attempting such an atrocity again. He knew now that he could do nothing when she felt that way. He was powerless to stop her hurting herself.

'I hate to think of you not being here,' he told her. He stared through the wooden slats of the pier at the waves breaking against the stilts that suspended them above the sea. 'I don't want to imagine a world that doesn't have you in it.'

'You won't have to,' she said.

'Promise?'

'You know what the really funny thing is?'

'Funny?' he said, aghast. 'The funny thing? About suicide? Funny?'

'I've never heard that song since,' she said with a rueful smile. 'The one I was listening to when I almost died. To tell you the truth, I'm not even sure the song exists. Not in this world.'

Her candour made him uncomfortable. Mya seemed fine now, even happy in a strange way, but the suddenness of her plunge into despair had shaken him. He had been watching from the shoreline as her head bobbed under water, so very close to drowning. She had dragged herself out of the Great Wave that had almost consumed her. She was better now but it was no thanks to him. He hadn't been able to keep her head above the waves. He couldn't be her lifebuoy.

'We should go,' he said, rubbing his hands together. 'It's

getting cold. We can drive back, order a takeaway, watch a film, some wine…'

'No, let's stay a little while longer,' Mya insisted, kissing him. Somehow her lips tasted of the briny scurf of the sea. 'I think there's peace here.'

37

The Bleaklands (memory holes)

Then he sees her. He's doing an odd job for Leroy Minto; his old trainer's sideline in window cleaning at the ugly great building on the outskirts of town. The big red monstrosity. It's a university or a research laboratory, maybe both. Locals simply call it The Crab.

Hanging off the side of the Academy building, his gloved hands covered with suds, he looks down and sees her. He sees her for the first time in years. The world flips, his vision spinning and yawing like an out-of-kilter gyroscope, waves of unreality crashing into his brain. This can't be real.

It's so very real. The Academy is opening its doors to a new batch of students the next day and the building is humming with activity and Gemma Dala is standing in the middle of that chessboard pattern in the front court. She's the same as ever; slipping in between groups of people like a spectre, never quite fitting in. She hasn't normalised as he feared she would. She has become even stranger, even more wonderful. She hasn't quite shed her teenage gawkiness, her natural shyness, but her face is still an artwork. He will remember that face for the rest of his days. He feels overwhelmed, overjoyed. The straps of the harness are holding him fast but still he's falling. He never stops falling.

In that moment, hanging above the ground, he realises why he has stayed in the flatlands for all those wasted years. She is his anchor.

The next day he infiltrates the throng of new students filing dutifully out of the coaches and into the Academy. No one questions him, no one calls him out. Why would they? He's about the same age as them and many are dressed as peculiarly as he is, with their kaftans and berets and jeans slung so low he can see their designer underwear. The sort of try-hard intellectuals, striving for eccentricity, that his West Ham mates despise. Now he wants to be part of them because she is a part of them. He even goes to the lectures although he can't understand what is going on, or even what the pupils are supposed to be studying.

Soon after, on a burning hot afternoon in that endless summer, he sees his chance. Gemma is sitting on the fringes of a circle of her classmates in the shadow of the Academy building. After eavesdropping for a while – as a girl with auburn pigtails talks about the lecture, confidently overriding everyone else's point of view – he strides over, trying to look as though he belongs.

'Not much of a discussion,' he announces, his heart booming with frenetic blast beats, 'if you're telling everyone the answer.'

Gemma Dala doesn't recognise him. He can understand why; he scarcely believes the chubby, nervy, defeated-looking child in his old school photographs used to be him either. She has changed too. For some reason Gemma Dala, in the years they have been apart, has changed her name to Mya Samsara. But she is the same person; he would know that face anywhere. The name doesn't matter. He has found her again. The boy has never felt so happy, so alive.

She's the same girl he has always loved.

★

ANDREW EWART

They are a strange couple. Freaks, maybe. But strange is good, freakish is good. Who the hell would want to be normal? The pensive, beautiful girl and the exuberant boy who meets the world with his chin thrust out; they don't seem like a natural match. Others stare, others mutter, but who cares what others think? The others don't understand. The others don't realise that their jagged edges slot together so perfectly.

They are growing up hand in hand, making each other better people. Mya is becoming more confident, more expressive, willing to take risks. Simultaneously his irrational aggression, forged by the sneers and jibes of his childhood, ebbs away in the face of her love. At times the anger seems barely there; a cancer lying dormant in his cells.

There are moments, though, when he's close, so very close, to losing control. Mya can't save him from himself forever. It only takes a scornful glance, a misspoken word, a perceived slight, and that unquenchable rage is rising within him, aching to burst free. His brain grows so swollen with fury that he feels he needs to let it out or his mind will implode. Sometimes he is able to twist the blade in on himself; he punches walls, drives his fists into the muscles of his thighs until the flesh purples. He is scared of what he might do. Not to Mya, never to Mya, but to anyone who puts themselves in his way – an innocent pedestrian stepping into the path of a hurtling juggernaut – when that anger tries to take control. He is scared that if he reveals his true nature, she will leave him, and strives to maintain control. But the worst impulses remain.

He still goes to the Academy, carrying on the charade of being a regular student. It seems impossible that he hasn't yet been unmasked, but it is also impossible that he has found Gemma – or Mya, as everyone now calls her – again, so he is content to exist in the realm of the uncanny. There are students who live off campus, many from the town in which he grew up, and no one has realised that he has no business being there. He enjoys the lectures and debates, and only wishes he had tried harder at school so he understood more. He likes most of Mya's friends, even though they're the sort of people his old crew would hate. When he's with them, joining in their marijuana-hazed discussions, where the philosophical and nonsensical slip through without filter, he feels content in a way he can't describe. They are young people figuring out the confusions and contradictions of life, and they're doing it together. They are not afraid to be honest, to be vulnerable. He thinks of how conversations play out among his mates from home: *Billy Bonds, total legend; Millwall, fucking wankers.* There is no room for debate. Any dissenting voice is a threat that needs to be crushed. Mya and her fellow students are not like that. They are supportive, earnest, interested. Even his most boneheaded contributions are mulled over, given due respect. The boy even starts writing his non-poetical poems again. He is climbing higher every day. He has a sense of a life that was once out of reach, now close enough to grasp. Even when Mya lets her secret slip, and then his own secret is swiftly revealed, it's of so little consequence it is almost laughable. Because who they once were doesn't matter any longer. They can both be different people. Better people, together.

The weeks slide into months and then become a whole year.

Everything starts to go wrong on his brother Roberto's stag party in Crete. The Malia strip glowing with febrile heat; the flashing signs outside the bars advertising free shots, good times, the world's greatest cocktails; the orange-skinned girls strutting along in tiny white dresses, pursued by boys with hairstyles that are ninety per cent hair gel. On their first night, there is a fearsome brawl between his friends and a group of young men from Newcastle. The next day no one can remember what the fight was about and the groups decide to unite. They're sitting around the pool with the Geordie boys, drinking and laughing and comparing bruises, sharing tiny bags of white powder. He hopes no one noticed that he played no real part in the fight. The week drags; each day and night merging into an endless stream of foaming lager. His Mohican hairstyle attracts a few derisory comments from the jackals of the neon strip, but he laughs them off. *You've gone soft on us, Marco,* Tony says, shaking his head. *Fallen hard for this one, aintcha? Beyond our help.* There is no malice in his elder brother's words, only fond regret. He misses Mya terribly. He buys the rounds of San Miguel more often than he should so he can hide at the bar and check if she has texted him. One night, his brother's best man Deano grabs the phone from his hand and starts reading out his messages: the florid words, the unabashed declarations of eternal love. The group is laughing. They're all laughing at him. A hand reaches out from the crowd to tousle his hair, then the grip tightens to give the pink spikes a spiteful tug. Playground nonsense, but it ignites a memory bomb inside his brain. He wants to destroy every one of the laughing mob. He will if he can. He hurts and he wants to hurt. Then everything goes dark.

He snorts some of Deano's cocaine before the flight back home – a misguided making-up, all-pals-again gift – and when he reunites with Mya he makes a terrible fool of himself. He offends her, he mistreats her, and he drives her away. As an act of penance, he slices up his arms with a broken glass and through this act of bloodletting – remembering the traveller boys at his boxing club who told him their grandads used to use fleams on lame horses – he expels the sickness inside him.

But it turns out that the cancer is not in remission. It's active again, hungry and growing, flooding his cells, poisoning his mind. Maybe, he thinks, he hasn't changed. It has all been a lie. He doesn't deserve Mya. He is more animal than man. He hates himself. If she stays with him, he will only bring her unhappiness. If she leaves him it will be the punishment he deserves.

The worst happens on the end-of-term night out. Something is wrong with Mya that evening, something he doesn't understand. She is standing on a ledge, teetering, peering down at an unfathomable drop he cannot see. He is frustrated at not being able to help her; she doesn't trust him any longer, and that wounds him more deeply than he can put into words. His thoughts darken along with the descending night. Too many drinks. They are in an underground club but Mya has disappeared. He is frantic with worry. Then he finds her at last, outside on the street in the rain, but nothing's right, she's damaged beyond measure. He's holding her, trying to help her. Then there is a confrontation with a young man he barely knows. Laughter, the sickly chime of mocking laughter that he remembers from his schooldays. *You got to admit it, mate, your girlfriend's a total fucking lunatic.* Through the alcohol mists a warped sense of chivalry raises its head. He needs to protect her. No one speaks to Mya that way. Nobody.

He remembers his right hand clenching into a fist. The anger explodes in a black bloom.

In a dream world, a dream timeline, he swings drunkenly and misses and Geraint, dodging away, slips on the wet cobbles and falls on his arse and hurts nothing more than pride and the crowd laughs at the slapstick comedy. Night after night he wishes that had happened. Instead he lands the most perfect punch he has ever thrown. The knockout blow connects and Geraint drops straight backwards and his skull crunches on the unyielding contour of the kerb. He doesn't get up. Blood begins to stream from his nose and ears. There is a high, terrified voice in the background that he cannot quite place: *What have you done… What have you done… What have you done…*

Down on his knees, he stares into the young man's face, cradling his head as redness stains his white tuxedo, weeping apologies. The rain falls into Geraint's open eyes.

What has he done?

38

New Beginnings

The trip to the seaside helped, at least for a while. Mya was smiling now. Perhaps a little too brightly; her laughter was turned up a few levels louder than natural. But she was trying. She held his hand and kissed him and loved him. She still intoxicated him, filled up his senses. Their days passed happily. They watched films, went for long walks. They cooked each other meals and she teased him about his ability to scorch onions and liquidise pasta. All their friends told them what a great fit they were together. She teased him and he comforted her. They enjoyed food and wine and sex and every pleasure of life. Oh yes, the days were fine, even wonderful.

But the nights troubled him. Once he had loved watching her while she was sleeping. Now her face was slack as if a puppet-master had sliced the strings on his marionette. Those morning sessions he once spent in reverie now passed in a grinding state of high anxiety. Mya seemed better but how long before the next Great Wave came? He didn't have the power to hold back that dark tide, and knowing that he couldn't help her made him burn with shame. Maybe next time she wouldn't have the strength to swim free of the waves.

★

Almost a month after Mya's fit of melancholy had passed, he took her to the christening of his brother Roberto's son. At the blessing reception at his family home, he was proud of the way she circulated among the guests. She talked, she laughed, she admired the vast three-tiered christening cake. He felt drunk with gratitude as he watched her. She was an exotic flower amid the shabby shrubbery of his family. He sipped his beer and gave thanks to a God he didn't truly believe in; he couldn't quite shake the teenage hangover of faith. Everything was almost completely back to normal. Mya was normal. She was just a little different ... no, quirky, that was the right word. Eccentric. Intelligent people were always just eccentric. Definitely not crazy.

He lost sight of Mya after being drawn into a conversation between his brothers. He wanted to find her, make sure she was still bobbing merrily on the surface. But every time he tried to break free there was another vitally important point about how the Hammers needed to sign a decent right-winger; or how Uncle Gi was causing a minor scandal by introducing poker schools to the social club; or how Sofia was sounding more Australian with every transcontinental phone call and their mother was frantic that her only daughter might never come home. He contributed nothing to the discussion but nods and *uh-huhs*. Eventually his siblings could take no more.

'Totally lovestruck, aintcha?' Tony chuckled, punching his arm lightly. 'There's no saving you. But that girl of yours ... yeah, tasty. Respect, my brother. You pulled that one out the bag.'

'Dark horse, bro,' Robbo agreed. 'Always the quiet ones, yeah?'

'What is she?' Tony asked. 'Like Arabian?'

'Half-Indian,' he said.

'The best half,' Robbo added.

'Dark hair, dark eyes,' Tony said, pursing his lips. 'Looks pretty damn Italian to me. Where's she gone, anyway?'

He shrugged. 'Mya's around somewhere. I'm not her keeper.'

'Bring her here to meet the brothers,' Tony said, with his familiar unchallengeable authority, raising his glass of red wine. '*Padrino* got to have words. Make sure she don't break your heart.'

Following his brother's orders, he set out in search of Mya. Robbo and Saskia's house was small and most of the guests had spilled out into the garden to enjoy the gentle haze of the September sunshine, but he couldn't see her anywhere. He was unable to move two paces without having his hand wrung or enduring a tickling kiss on both cheeks from an aunt. Everyone seemed delighted to see him, and ordinarily he would have submitted to their affections, but now he was worried. Mya had seemed happy that morning but he knew how quickly her emotions could change. He couldn't recall the last time he had seen her. She might have left at any time. He had been distracted by his brothers' meaningless conversation. Had he missed her slipping away?

The downstairs bathroom was locked. He decided that Mya was probably inside so he waited. After a few moments there was the sound of running water and the door opened. He stared into bright green eyes that peered out from under a fringe of hair so blonde it was almost white. This girl couldn't have looked less like Mya. It was the sister of Robbo's wife Saskia; he had met her at a few family parties but right now he couldn't recall her name. Anna? Hannah? He seemed to remember her husband was a tall Scottish man who had a mass of curly hair and a quick way with a joke, although he hadn't seen him with her for quite a while.

'You okay?' she asked.

He nodded, leaving her standing in the hallway, staring curiously after him with those piercing emerald eyes.

Taking the stairs three at a time, he could hear voices in his mother's bedroom, a hushed conversation. He paused outside the door. He could make out Uncle Gi speaking urgently. Then he heard Mya reply and let out a short gasp of relief. The door was ajar. Instinct stopped him pushing it open. Instead he listened.

'This is not right,' Giuseppe was saying. By his wavering tone, he knew his uncle was massaging his temples with his knuckles, the way he always did when a problem was troubling him. 'I seen it for months now and I kept my counsel, but there is only so much of this I can stand. It's not right. Is he happy? Are you?'

'Yes,' Mya replied. Her voice was soft but firm. 'We're very happy. We're incredibly happy.'

His uncle huffed irritably. It turned into a coughing fit. 'I hope so,' Uncle Gi wheezed at last, his breathing just about under control. 'I hope you really think so. I don't mean to intrude. It's simply ... I got responsibility for that boy. His father made me swear it before the cancer took him. He's the youngest. I made a promise. I need to look out for Marco.' At the mention of his name he froze, feeling sweat spring out underneath his arms. He knew he shouldn't stay, eavesdroppers never learned anything good about themselves, but he was unable to drag himself away. 'His brothers, they're fine men, but Marco is special.' Giuseppe's voice dropped to a pained croak. 'Marco used to be special, anyway.'

Now it was Mya's turn to sigh. 'He still is special, Giuseppe, very special. Don't be so dramatic. He's different in some ways. But, you know, maybe that's not so bad.' She let out a strange brusque laugh that jangled his nerves. 'Marco wasn't all sweetness and light before, you know? Trust me. I know him best.'

'Maybe I know him second best then. And that man down-stairs, he's not Marco. Standing there not saying much, grinning like he hasn't got a care in the world. You know who else grins like they haven't got a care in the world? Simpletons. *Cretinos*. It kills me to see him the way he is now, absolutely kills me. When you took out that part of him, maybe you took too much. You see?'

'This was the only way,' said Mya. 'Don't you understand?'

'No. I'm never going to understand this,' Giuseppe replied. 'He did what he did. So he takes his punishment like a man. Not like this. This is no prison, is a damnation.' He paused, his breathing ragged. 'How do you think he feels,' the old man went on, his voice cracking with emotion, 'being only half a man?'

'He doesn't know. He'll never know.'

His uncle grunted. 'Maybe I tell him then. The truth.'

'Not if you ever want to see him again.' Her voice was coldly furious. 'This is how things are now. This is us. Deal with it, Uncle Gi. If you want to keep him in your life.'

There was a rustling of fabric and the sound of footsteps. He ducked into the shadows just as Mya burst through the bedroom door. If she had looked around, she would have seen him, but her hands were clapped over her face as if trying to block out the world. He stared after her as she clattered down the stairs, feeling a sickly anxiety churning in his stomach, trying to make sense of what he had heard.

39

The Bleaklands (memory holes)

The room is stark and featureless. The walls are white. There is a brilliant light shining down on him. No sound but for a water cooler in the corner that gurgles at regular intervals. Clad in a grey tracksuit, he is sitting on a plastic chair in front of an empty table. His hands are free – he can still see the reddened abrasions on his wrists from the plastic tapes they used to cuff him – but a police officer is standing mutely in the corner of the room, his arms folded. He is thinking about everything and nothing. He wishes he could stop his brain. He wonders if he will ever see Mya again.

The door opens. He is expecting another counsellor or lawyer. Instead he's surprised. The man standing in the doorway is Mya's father. He takes a seat opposite and waves away the police guard. Gurdeep Dala's expression is grave yet his eyes glitter in the harsh halogen glare; a capering light in the depths of his pupils.

'You are wondering why I'm here,' says Mr Dala.

He nods. What is there to say?

'You did a bad thing, Marco. A very bad thing.'

He nods. He is a schoolboy again, being ticked off by a stern teacher.

'They tell me you are looking at up to five years in prison,'

Mya's father says matter-of-factly. 'Taking into account your age and lack of previous convictions. That is if the young man emerges from his coma. If not –' he spans out his hands to indicate an impossible length of time '– then who knows? Who indeed knows?'

The lawyer has explained this to him already but the repetition of the facts does not dilute their harsh taste. He cannot look at the father of the girl he loves. The shame is too great. A solitary traitorous tear slides down his cheek.

'Do you wish to go to prison, Marco?'

He manages to find his voice. 'Does anyone?' he asks rhetorically, striving for toughness, but his tone is high and wavery.

Mr Dala drums his fingers on the table. 'As you are aware, I knew all about your little subterfuge from the very start,' he continues. 'Nothing occurs at the Academy without my explicit understanding, you must know this. I saw you attending lectures, embroil yourself in debates both scientific and metaphysical, engage in every aspect of the lives of our students. I indulged you. I must confess that I found your fascination fascinating.'

He says nothing. He knows what is coming next.

'Obviously, I believed your ulterior motive was to grow closer to my daughter.' He stiffens. Then Mr Dala lets out a chuckle. 'I wish that I could blame you. But I was a younger man myself once, although this bald head and the wrinkles I see in the mirror convince me otherwise every single day. You found her but you found something else, did you not, Mr Pellicci? A latent thirst for knowledge. A desire to improve yourself. A wish to ascend.'

He tries to speak but his throat is parched, his lips cracked. Mr Dala fetches him a paper cup of water from the dispenser and he drinks and drinks. 'I wanted to be better for her,' he says at last. 'I did it all for Mya. I did everything for her.'

Gurdeep Dala nods approvingly. 'At the Meinhof-Dala-Smithson Academy of Science, Research and Learning,' he says, leaning forward, 'we are in the business of perfecting people. Changing minds. You, Marco, have so much potential. At this moment your potential is at great risk of being wasted.'

Once Marco Pellicci would have sneered at such talk. But now, trapped in this airless room, tormented by his guilt and fearful he will never see Mya again, he begins to feel a tentative stirring of hope.

'What we can offer you,' her father continues, 'is an opportunity. An opportunity for redemption. In a normal case you would expect a significant amount of time in prison to atone for your sins – and quite rightly so. But this is not a normal case. And you are not a normal person. That can be fixed. Everyone in the judicial process is aware of the work I do, the service I perform for this town. You are the chosen one, Marco. You can be saved. You can be given a second chance. All you need to do is ask.'

'What about Mya?' he managed to choke out. He will submit to anything. There is no strength left in those muscles he had once been so proud of; he is so frail, so weak. He will do whatever her father wants. He will do it to prove himself to her, to show that he can change. 'Will she ... does she ...'

'Mya wants what we want,' Mr Dala says, reaching across the table to clasp his hands. The touch feels wonderfully warming. 'Mya wants you to be the best possible version of yourself.'

The tears are flowing now and he concedes defeat. There is salvation in submission – and her father believes he is worth saving. He is worth a second chance. Anything for her. Anything.

The shocking-pink strands of hair litter the floor. The mohawk he loved – his suit of armour, his comfort blanket, his shield against the world – has been shorn. Denuded, his head feels weak and fragile. His fingertips trace around the bones of his skull, working at the temples where a monstrous ache is booming.

'How do I look?' he asks his lawyer, desperate for distraction. The pallid, middle-aged man stares back dispassionately. The man's suit is grey, his words are colourless. It is as if the life has been washed out of him.

'You look ready,' says the grey man.

They enter the chamber. He is conscious of many eyes staring down upon him. His family is sitting together in a neat row and briefly he glances upwards. Uncle Giuseppe is in tears. It looks as if every one of his seventy-eight years is weighing heavily upon his shoulders. His uncle's face is a tragedy mask of betrayal. He turns back to the dock, wishing that he hadn't looked.

At some point Gurdeep Dala stands before the judge. There are many words. The words relate to him but he doesn't recognise any of them. They could be speaking about a completely different person.

A plea bargain is entered and agreed. He realises that everything has been agreed long before this sham of a courtroom appearance. Mr Dala steps down and smiles at him briefly. There is an unsettling eagerness in the man's expression. The sentence is passed and there is silence in the court. Only now does he feel fear. Surely it can't be that simple? Six months in a low-security prison then out on probation. Providing, that is, he responds to the agreed course of treatment.

He is led away. On the way out he catches sight of a girl with red hair sitting very still and alone. It is Clare Key, Mya's best friend, the partner of the boy he almost killed. He expects to see anger but instead she holds him with a strange, speculative gaze. That frightens him too. Nothing is right about this moment.

Where's the punishment? Where's the atonement for his sins? The skin of his shaved skull begins to prickle.

As he is driven from the courtroom, he wonders what prison will be like. He has only ever seen jails in the movies. Instead, when he emerges from the white van, he is standing in front of a familiar building. The tower blocks out the sun. He has the sense of an unknowable monolith looming over him. He wants to ask his guard why they are here but fear has stolen his voice. He is led inside the Academy building. He is sat down on a sofa in a small, bare room. He is given a cup of cool water to drink and downs it in one, a balm to his cracked throat. It smells of a childhood sweet shop, something like aniseed. Almost immediately there is wooziness, a disconnection, a floating sensation. Is he walking or is he being carried? It's difficult to say. There is relief in having power stripped away. Now he's sitting in a chair and his hands and legs are strapped down and he wants to struggle and kick and scream but these feelings – the anger, the fear – are so very distant. Instead he sits and floats.

The room is vast and white. There are soft murmurings, hushed voices.

He wants out. There is no way out.

Gentle hands place a band around his head. The metal is cool, almost pleasant, as it encircles his cranium. There is a brief flare of pain. Too late, he realises that he needs to fight against the floating.

He thinks of all the punk songs he loves – the way the music fizzes through his veins and gives him lifeforce, makes him feel ten feet tall, able to conquer anything. He thinks of his family, his mother and his siblings and Uncle Gi. He thinks of Mya; how he was truly happy for the first time in his life when he was with her, how they are entirely different people yet they fit together so perfectly. He wants to see her again; he needs to see her again. If only to apologise – to tell her that she was the best thing that ever happened to him, that he's so sorry for his terrible mistakes. He can't bear the thought that this might be the end of them.

Then he recalls something Mr Dala had asked him during one of their meetings before the trial. What sacrifices he was prepared to make. What he would do for another chance. *I'd give up anything to be back with her,* he told Mya's father. *Anything and everything.*

Anything and everything. For her.

He wishes for a second chance.

The mask is placed over his face.

Then nothingness.

40

New Beginnings

A great roaring had filled the room, ripping him from sleep. Knuckling at his bleary eyes, he saw that Mya was dancing around his bedroom. A punk record was playing far too loudly on the stereo system. She was wearing his leather jacket over the top of his West Ham United shirt, and... what was she holding... surely not... why was she waving around his stone boxing trophies? It was difficult to shake the feeling that he was still dreaming.

'Happy birthday!' she yelled, leaping upon the bed. 'Look. Look! I got together all your favourite things.' She patted the onyx gloves together with a dull clink. 'Do you like it? Tell me you like it.'

'It's ... nice,' he said. 'Uh, thank you.'

She frowned. 'Nice. Your favourite things? Is that all you've got to say? Nice?'

'I don't...'

'What if... what if...' She held up a finger as if struck by inspiration. 'What if I was wearing a Millwall shirt? You hate Millwall, yeah? How would that make you feel? Would that piss you off? What if I was playing Barry Manilow or some Stock Aitken Waterman shit – that'd be annoying, right? How would that make you feel?' Her grin was manic, too wide. 'What if I...

What if I threw these boxing trophies out the window? What if I cut your leather jacket into tiny little pieces. Would you be upset? Would you be angry? Tell me you'd be angry.'

He shook his head slowly. 'Please, Mya. I don't care about anything like that.'

'Even waking you up so early,' she said desperately. 'For God's sake, Marco, give me something here.' The music was still blaring obscenely. She was an inch away from his face, a troubling intensity in her gaze, and he shrank back from her. 'Where's the emotion? Where's the spirit? Where's the life?'

He bit down on his lower lip. He thought of what she was asking; how her emotions zig-zagged wildly across the spectrum while his remained on a flat and straight line. He tried to summon up some response for her – anger or passion at least irritation – but despite the ignition key turning, the engine had no hope of catching fire. 'I'm sorry. I don't know who you want me to be.'

'Oh, this is hopeless,' she moaned. The stone gloves thumped to the floor. She padded to the music system and snapped off the power. She shrugged free the jacket and chucked it in the corner. The West Ham shirt came off next. She turned to face him. Her shoulders had sagged and she looked utterly bereft. 'I knew it wouldn't work. I don't know what I was thinking.'

'Mya, I'm so confused right now.'

'It's nothing,' she said. 'Nothing. I'm an idiot. I'm asking too much. Forgive me.'

'Mya, what is this … I don't …'

'It's nothing,' she said. Her tone did not invite further questioning. 'Please, Marco. Go back to sleep. It doesn't matter. Nothing matters.'

★

This boy was mad. His eyes were wide and stared at an indefinable point in the mid-distance. His breath came in ragged, plosive bursts. There was blood on his forehead and blood running out of his mouth, as if he had been chewing on raw meat.

They heard him before they saw him. A clang and clatter as he put the soles of his boots against every steel shutter on the high street. Then they caught sight of him staggering towards them. Drunk out of his mind, hurling obscenities at passers-by and thin air. They should have crossed the road to avoid him. He should have steered Mya away from the main street. Their paths were bound to intersect but he didn't realise in time; they had been drinking too and he was slow, too slow. Now the mad boy was standing in front of them. The stranger was skinny but every sinew was straining out of his neck and biceps, as if his body had been wound up too tight and his skin was about to burst from the pressure. He stared at his blond Fifties-style quiff, his jittery stance. The drunk man looked familiar. He had never seen him before in his life.

'Youse... youse...' The words forced themselves out of the stranger's throat, churning like a faulty engine. 'What the fuck youse want?'

A wave of unreality washed over him. The night couldn't end this way, surely not. It was his birthday and – with Mya's peculiar behaviour earlier that day almost forgotten – everything that evening had been perfect. The champagne with her father on the Academy building's roof terrace, looking out at the coruscating lights of the funfair in the distance as the sun gently died. Then a taxi to the little trattoria in the town square. Mya told him that she had booked the restaurant to put him back in touch with his Italian roots. The place was cheerfully buzzing, the waiters greeting them like treasured friends. The soft pillows of ravioli, the Amalfi lemon tart so gloriously sharp it cramped the taste buds. The wine, far too much wine. The bottles of Barolo that promised the taste of black cherries and leather. *Like spreading jam on my jacket,* he told Mya when she picked the bottle, and she laughed until she was overcome by hiccups. The wine coated his tongue with sticky-sweet tannins and turned every sentence into poetry. Then the shots of grappa on the house, then he was being helped into his bomber jacket by a waiter, then they were out into the balmy night, walking hand in hand towards home. He wanted to treasure the walk, having rarely felt so happy, but there was still a purpose in his stumbling steps.

'I didn't get around to buying you a present,' Mya had whispered as they left the restaurant, 'so I thought when we get home, you might want to unwrap me?'

Even when the mad boy was making his clanging, swearing process towards them, he failed to realise the danger. Because tonight was their night, and wonderful things had happened, and yet more wonderful things would happen soon, and nothing could possibly ruin it.

Even when the boy was standing in front of them – reeking of whisky and cigarettes, his fingers formed into fists – he felt no fear. Surely the young man would realise they offered no threat? The effects of the alcohol were hitting him in waves and he stared at the stranger with honest interest.

'Come on then,' the boy spat. 'Think you're fucking wide?'

'I'm sorry, what?'

'Talking all that shite about me, big man?' the boy yelled into his face. 'You dinnae ken who I fucking am.'

This was a misunderstanding. He realised that now. The young Scotsman was so drunk he thought he was someone else.

'I don't even know what you're talking about,' he said, hoping he sounded braver than he felt. 'Why don't you just—'

His words were cut off by a flat palm in the centre of his chest. The shove sent him backwards. He knocked into Mya, and heard her hiss of surprise and pain as she tumbled to the ground. Time was running in slow motion; he saw the man throw a clenched fist towards his face and twisted his neck so the blow only clipped his ear. The punch was nothing more than a bee sting. He only cared about Mya. He had to protect her. Dropping to his knees, he reached for her then gasped as he felt a boot lift into his ribs. There was still no pain. He saw that her black tights were ripped and the skin of her right knee was abraded. She pointed her finger in accusation. The man standing over him had made his girlfriend bleed. He had made her hurt.

He was eye to eye with Mya, kneeling on the dirty pavement in front of her, and there was a darkness in her expression.

'Hit him back,' she said, and he never knew if she had spoken or whether he read her mind. 'Be like you used to be. Do it for me, Marco. Get mad.'

His lips twisted upwards into a tight, predatory smile.

Turning away from her black glare, he leapt to his feet. He felt a coldness sink into his bones. The man had to pay; he had to pay for what he'd done to Mya. The Scotsman threw another punch and he easily side-stepped, then, running purely on instinct, he grabbed the flailing right arm. A left hook to the jaw would put him down, he'd never beat the bell. No, too easy. They were in a street-fight, not a boxing ring. Instead, holding on to the arm, he twisted the limb backwards into an unnatural angle. He could hear the joint creak and now the drunk man's eyes were filled with panic at the shifting of control.

It was so easy. Twist the arm further until the delicious snap signalled the joint had separated from its moorings. Then sweep his right leg against the back of the knees to bring the boy down to the concrete. After that, the combinations could begin.

A short left-handed jab to the mouth to loosen some teeth, followed by a strong right to turn his nose into a burst tomato. Then finally his hands around that chicken-skin scrawny throat, squeezing... squeezing... choking... the referee's waving it off, it's all over: Marco Pellicci wins by technical knockout and the crowd is on their feet...

He could do it. Mya wanted him to do it.

But he didn't do any of those things.

That cold anger ran out of him like water down a plughole. The strength drained from his muscles. He let go of the man's arm. His attacker stumbled backwards, holding his shoulder, wincing and swearing.

'I'm with my girlfriend,' he mumbled. 'Please... please just leave us alone.'

There was a clatter of feet and he turned, feeling incredibly tired, unable to cope with further confrontation. Two men had taken hold of his attacker's arms and were dragging him away down an alleyway. Had they been watching from the shadows? Why hadn't they stepped in until it was almost too late?

'Sorry, mate, I'm really sorry,' one of the strangers called back at them. He was wearing a T-shirt emblazoned with a monochrome print of a heavy-fringed male face and the word *Numan* stamped above it in capital letters. 'He ran off on us, gets like this when he's had a bevvy. Daft prick. I'm sorry, mate.'

Listlessly he waved a hand. Now he only wanted to sleep. His shoulders sagging, his posture defeated, he stared over at Mya. She was standing very still on the street corner, the traffic light painting her face with a sickly greenish glow. The blood on her knee was oozing down her shin.

'Why didn't you do it?' she asked. Her voice was quiet but carried clearly in the still night air. 'That man, that bad man, he hurt me. Why didn't you do it? Didn't you want to protect me?' Hopelessly he shrugged, unable to explain. 'Didn't you want to save me?'

'I couldn't,' he told her. 'I just … I don't have it in me.'

She breathed out, staring into his eyes as if seeing him for the first time. 'Okay,' she said at last, nodding. 'Okay then.'

They walked home in silence. She didn't take his hand again.

When he woke up the next morning, Mya wasn't there.

She was gone and he had no way of finding her. His head buzzing with a filthy red wine hangover, he padded around their flat, trying to make sense of anything, everything. He had rung her mobile three dozen times but his calls went straight to voicemail. He told himself that it was a misunderstanding. She could have gone out to pick up coffee and bagels from the hipster café down the road. Maybe it was a post-birthday surprise; Mya loved surprises. But he couldn't convince himself that the explanation was innocent. Before he turned the light out – no love for them last night, the distance between their bodies on the bed was a chasm – he had seen her face reflected in her bedside mirror. Her expression had been bereft. Her face was twisted, wracked with an unreadable expression that looked weirdly guilty, and he couldn't understand why.

He could go out. To the Academy or her family home, track down Gurdeep Dala – but he didn't want to alarm her father unnecessarily. Maybe he could tour the roads on his motorbike hoping to catch a glimpse of that slight figure, lost and wandering. But what if she came back to their flat and she needed him? Instead he stayed, pacing their little apartment like a caged beast, his nails gouging half-moons in his palms. It was on his fourth circuit of the flat that he noticed what had changed. He stared at the shelf of their bedroom wardrobe and his breath caught in his throat.

Those mysterious boxing trophies, the two onyx gloves, had disappeared. *Heavy as hell*, his voice echoed. *Heavy as hell*.

Then the mobile phone shrilled and his breath wheezed out of his chest. His fingertip hammered at the green *Answer* key. He held the phone to his ear in trepidation.

'This is my fault,' she said. Her voice was choked and breathless.

'Mya, please—'

'I don't want to live inside this head any longer,' she said. Her tone was almost apologetic, the words punctuated by a rhythmic rushing sound that he realised was surf lapping on a shoreline. 'I don't want to live knowing what I've done. I'm not strong enough.'

'Just come back to me,' he said desperately. 'Whatever you think you've done, I promise it's not a problem. You don't have to explain anything. There's nothing we can't beat together. But I need you here with me. We can make things better. I promise. Everything will be alright.'

Mya let out a small sob. Then she was silent. He could hear the manic cawing of gulls and the metronomic murmur of sea on sand.

'Find out what they did to you,' she said finally. 'You're not yourself, Marco darling. This isn't you. And it's my fault. It's all my fault.'

Then there was a crunch and a hiss of static. After that he could hear only the waves.

41

Mya, replaced

Shallow breaths. The greenish-blue sheets rising and falling. Her eyes were closed, she was at peace. Mya had been asleep for hours. Sometimes she slept for eleven or twelve hours at night, as well as a couple of catnaps during the day. He didn't mind. Mya could sleep for as long as she wanted. What mattered was that eventually she would open her eyes.

It had been three months since her trip to the beach.

She was barely alive when they pulled her from the water. A few stubborn gasps of breath were clinging resolutely inside her lungs, refusing to give themselves up. It was luck, pure luck, that she had lived. His onyx boxing trophies, which she had used to weigh herself down, had torn through the pockets of her nightgown. Her limp body floated up to the surface. A fisherman and his son spotted what they thought was a discarded bin bag. The man cast out his rod to remove the pollution. The hook had snagged through the top of her nightdress. He could not imagine the shock and horror on the kid's face as they reeled in their early morning catch. Another couple of seconds and Mya would have been lost. If the fisherman and his boy had been staring the other way, even momentarily, Mya would have died.

Instead, miraculously, she survived.

He spent three nights by her bedside, barely sleeping, until she woke. He was lolling in the uncomfortable hospital chair by the side of her bed, half dozing, his vision fuzzy with fatigue, his skin prickling. He didn't know why she woke up when she did. Maybe he had let his coffee cup slip from his fingers to bounce on the squeaky-hard floor, he couldn't remember. What he did remember was how Mya sat straight up in bed and her eyes shot open and her mouth yawped in a soundless scream. He jerked backwards in fright and toppled out of his chair, upsetting the drip plugged into her forearm, and a buzzer shrilled. Then everything happened very fast – the squeak of footsteps and a surging battalion of people in white coats – and he was bundled out of the room and the door was shut firmly behind him.

Hours later, pacing up and down the ward, the door opened again. Mya's father spoke to him outside her room. He would take care of everything. There was no need to worry. Mya would be fine. She needed a little time to recuperate, to be in a place she understood, a space where she felt safe. He didn't understand what Mr Dala was saying. Mya was safe with him, she understood him, she was happy with him. But no one was listening.

. She spent the next fortnight at the Meinhof-Dala-Smithson Academy. He was not permitted to visit for the first week. On the day that he was finally allowed to see Mya, he was taken deep into the centre of the complex by one of the security guards. First, they were walking along a corridor that grew darker and narrower the further they went, and the harsh lights dimmed to a pleasant pastel glow, and he realised the atmosphere had changed – the air felt warmer, moister, somehow comforting. Then he realised he was walking on soft grass. He could smell jasmine. He heard water babbling gently. The pathway sloped upwards and they pushed through an overhang of creepers. Now they were standing in a lush, sweet-scented garden. A small waterfall churned ripples through the stream that ran around the garden. Multicoloured blooms sprouted around the circumference of the lawn. A curving trail of flat stones led towards a wooden pergola.

A figure dressed simply but perfectly in white was sitting on a swinging bench beneath that intricately carved archway. He barely recognised her as the anguished, fractured girl she had once been. Her palms were folded in her lap, her posture was relaxed, her smile – as she turned to greet him – was dazzling. The guard who had led him to this quiet place had tactfully vanished. Now it was only himself and Mya. He took a seat on the bench next to her, his heart pounding. He could barely believe she was real.

'It's so good to see you, darling,' she said. 'Thank you for waiting for me.'

He mumbled a confused platitude in response.

'I'm sorry I've caused you so much pain, so much worry,' Mya told him. 'I can't believe how selfish I've been.'

Dumbly he shook his head. 'It's not ...' he started, without knowing what he would say next.

'I don't feel that way any longer,' she said, her eyes shining. 'I feel better. Happy. Fixed.'

She reached across the distance between them to squeeze his hand. The lights above them twinkled and it barely mattered that the stars were artificial. The scent of jasmine was all around, intoxicating. He could barely see her face; his eyes were too blurred with tears. He squeezed back.

'Fixed,' he repeated.

42

Mya, replaced

The weeks that followed were as good as he had ever known.
The physical recovery took some time – she was still very weak,
tired easily, needed to sleep often – but the mental recovery
was so complete he could scarcely believe it. Her father had
now furnished them with an apartment in the great tower at
the Academy. It boasted splendid views over the splendid landscape: a bedroom, bathroom, kitchenette and living area; and a
discreetly concealed panic button, just in case. Each morning,
while Mya slept, he prepared her breakfast silently, walking
around the apartment on tiptoes, as if a loud noise might shatter
this delicate bubble of contentment. But it really did seem as
though Mya had recovered. He had never heard her laugh so
much, never seen her so openly affectionate. It was as if she had
become a different person.

There was no sadness, no fresh criss-crossed cuts at the tops
of her thighs, no more endless days staring into space. It seemed
that the Great Waves had washed themselves out. Now there
were only calm seas and a gentle breeze. They had met with Dr
Frank Baumann, Mr Dala's colleague and old friend, a number
of times to assess Mya's state of mind. Dr Baumann – who
had now become Frank, just plain old Frank – was delighted

with her progress. Mya was happy. That was all he wanted from life – for her to be happy.

Mya was so content these days that he didn't even worry about the razors in the bathroom or the knives in the rack by the kitchen sink.

He told himself that she was better now – so he had to get better too. For her, everything for her. If she bore him any resentment for his paranoia, she concealed it well. She woke flushed with happiness, determined to make every passing day more joyous than the one before. He played along as best he could. Everyone said that they were the most perfect couple, just the loveliest people you could ever wish to meet. He remembered the way Mya had once been – sharp-tongued, reckless, open-hearted yet totally unreadable – and grieved privately for what he had lost in her. For his partner it had been a small sacrifice. She was adjusted, perfected, and he looked so much the worse in comparison. In the full-beam glow of her utter contentment he felt exposed, naked, his brokenness picked out by the spotlight. But he had become adept at concealing his faults and fractures. He tried not to let the cracks show.

It was far easier to say what she was not than what she was. Once she had been a jumble of contradictions, an otherworldly mess. She was beautiful but never cared for her looks, she was sharp-tongued but extraordinarily tender, she could be so very remote, yet he had never felt so close to anybody in his life. Before her trip to the beach, Mya had been anything and everything. But now, since her accident, he could only think of what she was not.

Disquiet tickling spiderishly down his back, he stared down at his sleeping girlfriend. She was so happy now, it seemed impossible that only a few months ago she had nearly succumbed to that Great Wave. He thought of the boxing trophies that she had used to weigh herself down, the carved hunks of onyx now buried in the seabed. *Heavy as hell.* If those trophies had been a few pounds lighter, they would never have ripped through her pockets and Mya would have been lost forever. Somehow he felt that the answers to his questions were in the boxing trophies. He couldn't remember winning a single one of them. He never remembered fighting; the thought of violence sickened him. It was another riddle that he was too stupid to solve. At nights, lying awake, he would press his fingertips harshly into his temples and will his sludgy brain to make the connections. Sometimes, when he was holding his breath and gritting his teeth, there was a sparking sensation that sputtered out far too quickly. He kneaded at his skull, his fingertips slipping into the tiny abrasions that had encircled his hairline for as long as he could remember.

Mya stirred and rolled over in bed, letting out a small sigh. There was a trace of a smile on her face. He wondered whether she knew he was here, watching her, his fumbling fingers failing to unpick the knot in the centre of his brain.

He wondered what she dreamed of now.

Later that day, basking in the friendly embrace of the springtime sunshine, the worries of the early hours seemed almost inconsequential. Sleep had claimed him until at last he woke to the scent of freshly ground coffee and fried bacon. Mya was in the small galley kitchen, the pan sizzling merrily. She was wearing one of his overlarge punk band T-shirts that hung to her upper thighs. He was certain she was wearing nothing underneath.

She turned and grinned, her dark eyes flashing. 'Hey there, handsome.'

'Morning.'

He licked his lips and she noticed. 'Do you like what you see?'

'The bacon sandwich, or you?'

'They're both yours to enjoy.' She pushed up on her bare toes to kiss him. He submitted for a moment then held her at arm's length. He stared at her T-shirt. A large white skull and the words in gothic script: The Damned. His brow furrowed as he attempted to work out yet another riddle.

She picked up on his unease. 'Is something wrong, darling?'

'Nothing much,' he mumbled, 'only—'

'Only what?'

'I've never heard of that band. The Damned. Never heard a single song. I don't know why I own that T-shirt you're wearing.'

'Funny,' said Mya. 'Maybe it once belonged to someone else?'

'Maybe it did.' He nodded, turning away. He didn't want her to see his troubled expression.

But those misgivings seemed very faint as they laughed together on the beach that afternoon, kicking up sand, listening to the happy shrieks of children playing in the surf. She wore a red-and-white striped two-piece swimsuit, a sarong wrapped loosely around her waist, and the scent of sun oil on her hot skin made him giddy. He had been unsure about taking Mya to the beach, the location so close to her suicide attempt, but Dr Baumann had insisted. If Mya remembered how she had felt that awful day, she showed no sign of it. They had brought a rainbow-coloured beach ball to throw around, and she had a fit of the giggles when a scruffy dog appeared out of nowhere, sunk its teeth into the ball and raced off with its prize. He gave half-hearted chase and she laughed even harder. He carried her into the sea – again, as Dr Baumann had ordered – and she laughed some more, kicking against him until they toppled into the shallows. She kissed him even as he spewed foam, his eyes streaming, and her lips tasted of salt. They emerged hand in hand and set up deckchairs at the furthest reaches of the waves so they could feel the surf against the soles of their feet, staring out at the calm expanse of the sea. They watched as two children – evidently brother and sister – marched past them, frantically licking ice creams before the sun turned them into a dripping mess.

'I'd love one of those,' Mya said. 'One day.'

'What flavour?'

She dug him in the thigh with a red-painted toe. 'I wasn't talking about the ice creams, Marco Pellicci.'

'I know you weren't,' he said, letting the warmth of the sunshine soak through his bones. He smiled and willed himself to relax. This was the best time of his life and he was with the best person he knew, and the Great Waves – not the mild, friendly kind nuzzling their feet – were only a memory. Gazing out to sea, there wasn't a single cloud on the horizon. 'Neither was I.'

'Good.'

'A boy would be great,' he said. 'I know the score. Take him to the football, let him get a cool haircut to impress girls. Easy, you know?'

Mya stared at him from over the top of her white-rimmed sunglasses. 'So if it's a girl you'll be disappointed?'

He shook his head. 'No. I'll be even happier. Girls are … girls are something different. Something unknown. Weirdly brilliant. I don't understand them. I don't ever want to. There's a word … there's a word I can't place …'

'Complex?'

He gave her the thumbs-up with both hands. 'Exactly that. Girls are complex. A puzzle.'

She let out a short laugh. 'I used to be complex too. I hated it.'

He shifted in his seat. 'You can't mean that.'

'Uh-huh.' Mya nodded eagerly. 'I don't remember how I felt before ... before what happened. I don't remember anything about it. But whatever I did, it must have worked out, in a strange way. Because now I don't feel that way anymore. I won't feel that way ever again.'

'What if it comes back?' he asked, his voice a croaking whisper. 'What if you feel like that again?'

'You don't have to worry, darling.' She laughed. 'I'm not who I was.'

He blinked. 'You're not who you were?'

'I'm a different person now. I'm happy. Free. Can't you see?'

He supposed that he could – or at least it was simpler to submit to her certainties. He reached for her hand and she squeezed back. He held her until she drifted off to sleep, her chest rising and falling in time with the waves. Gently disengaging, he sat with her – until the sun dimmed and the parents ushered their children back to the car park, and the light breeze had turned feisty – and tried to think of nothing.

But the words she had said to him kept echoing across the sea, filling his ears like a gargantuan wave, back and forth, back and forth, drowning happiness: *I'm not who I was ... I'm not who I was ... I'm not who ...*

43

Mya, replaced

It felt as if someone was watching him. Watching them. The feeling was strongest inside the Academy. The sensation dimmed only slightly when they went for walks in the surrounding flatlands, as if the great red tower was a radar mast and the signal scrambled the further away they roamed. He had tried to dismiss the feelings as irrational paranoia. But he couldn't shake the certainty that they were not alone. He knew Mr Dala and his team were looking out for Mya, to ensure her thoughts did not slip back into that dangerous melancholia that had almost killed her, but this was different. He felt there were ghosts all around them.

The proposal had been stupid. Irrational and badly thought out. A distraction tactic. She had agreed readily; surprised but delighted to see him down on one knee on the empty seaside promenade. At the time it had seemed important to offer her a grand display, a great showing of love and commitment. Later, too late, their engagement felt more like kids playing dress-up. They were talking about marriage and children while barely into their mid-twenties – what the hell was he playing at? Maybe he had believed that such an abject display of emotion, prostrating himself before her, would explode her back to her former self. The cheap ring on her third-left finger – all he could afford – held the reflected light staunchly, yet it did not glitter. That was the real problem, he thought: Mya herself had ceased to shine.

'What's the matter, darling?' she asked. He held her gaze and saw no duplicity, only an earnest desire to please, to help. Her innocence raked ragged claws through his conscience. 'Please tell me, Marco. You know you can tell me anything. What on earth's the matter with you?'

She wanted to help. She wanted to help him. It was a sick joke; throughout their relationship, at least in the days before she walked into the North Sea, he had thought Mya was the troubled one. He was the safe anchor that kept her wilder impulses from flying off into the ether. They had specific roles in their union: he was steady and dependable; she was unreadable, impulsive, mercurial.

Mercurial. *Mercurial?* He didn't even know what that word meant. So why had it popped into his brain? It seemed a perfect word to describe Mya's personality before her accident. Every syllable made sense so why didn't he know the meaning of the word? It wasn't the first time this had happened; barely comprehensible words and phrases echoed in his brain, like a never-before-heard song on the radio filtered through static. If he squeezed his eyes shut and let his mind drift, he heard unknown voices calling through the mire that was his mind.

He didn't understand. He didn't want to understand. He *needed* to understand. *I'm not who I was.* No, please, not that again. He squeezed his hands into fists. His molars gritting against one another, he willed himself to be brave.

'What happened to you, Mya?' he asked, the words coming as a plosive burst that left him almost exhausted.

She blinked. There was nothing but love in the depths of

her eyes and maybe that was worse. 'I don't understand,' she said mildly.

'When you ... when you ...' He had to stop. The thought of her limp body being pulled from the water, her dark hair saturated with saltwater, was almost too much to bear. But he hardened his heart and pushed on. 'When you walked into the sea with my boxing trophies weighing you down. When you almost drowned. When you tried to kill yourself.'

'I don't feel like that anymore,' she said in that same quietly drifting tone. 'I'd never do that sort of thing again, darling. It's all gone away.'

Anger flared inside him; the sensation was like an ancient machine, rusted with disuse, cranking into life once more. He pushed his nails into his palms, gouging at the flesh. 'It doesn't just fucking go away!' he shouted, hating himself as he saw her flinch and recoil. 'I'm not the brightest guy, in fact I'm pretty dumb, but even I know you don't go from suicidal to Miss Happy-Smiley-Well-Adjusted overnight.'

'I did, Marco,' Mya whispered. 'I did because I knew how much I'd hurt you. I knew I had to get better. For you.'

He slapped his forehead in frustration. 'That's bullshit, Mya,' he said. 'No one gets better just like that. There's no miracle here. It's not even a magic trick or some street conjurer's con job. It's all wrong.'

She stared at the floor. 'That makes me feel very bad inside.'

'I don't know what you're feeling. I don't know how much I can trust you.'

She tried to take his hand and he pulled back from her. 'Darling, I'm a little scared right now.'

The anger drained away as his cheeks lit up with shame. He reminded himself that whatever was wrong with Mya might be his paranoia, his confusion. He didn't understand why these depth-charges of madness kept floating up to the surface, exploding in the face of the girl he loved. 'Scared?' he mumbled. 'Of... of me?'

She shook her head but looked away. As a show of faith, it was unconvincing. 'No. No, no, of course not, darling. But... you've been acting strangely lately. I hope there's nothing the matter. I hope it's nothing to do with me.'

He let out a disbelieving laugh. 'Nothing to do with you? Jesus Christ, Mya.' He thought of the eeriness of her abrupt personality switch, how she might be better now but he was getting worse and worse. He was scaring her and the cruellest joke was that the girl herself had absolutely no idea how much she was scaring him too. 'Who are you?' he demanded. 'Really, please tell me. Who are you?'

'I'm yours,' she said simply, 'and whatever's hurting you, I want to help you beat it. Even if... even if it's painful for me sometimes. Because I love you. I got better, Marco. I want you to get better too.'

Defeated, he hung his head. 'How, then? How can I get better? How can I make these thoughts stop?'

Mya said, 'I think we need to see my father.'

'Tell me everything,' Gurdeep Dala said, spreading his arms open wide. 'We are all friends here. Don't worry about what you think I will or won't believe. I promise you, young Marco, that I have heard every expression of the human psyche within these four walls.'

Those four walls seemed to close in on him. They were sitting in Mr Dala's spartan office inside the Academy building, sipping paper cups of coffee. Despite his bonhomie, Mya's father had seemed slightly frustrated to be dragged away from his work. This meeting was an inconvenience. The man kept staring over his shoulder as if waiting for someone else to come in and save him from this charade.

He breathed out slowly. 'I think I'm going insane,' he told her father. The words had seemed ridiculous in his head, but out in the open, between the three of them, they tolled with a heavy weight. 'I don't know who I am any longer. I don't know who Mya is either. We're strangers to each other. I feel like a stranger to myself.'

Mr Dala grimaced, rubbing the back of his forefinger over his moustache. 'My estimable colleague Frank Baumann has been assigned to your case. From your presence here today in my domain, may I assume you find his pastoral care lacking?'

'No-no-no,' Mya said quickly. 'Dr Baumann... Frank... he's been wonderful. But I was worried about Marco this morning. So worried. I wanted to see you.'

Her father nodded. 'Perhaps I should be flattered. However, I confess that I'm more disappointed.' He took a swig of coffee and chewed at his lower lip. 'Frank led me to believe that the pair of you were blissfully happy.'

'We were,' he said miserably. 'Then things started changing. Some days I'm not sure what I can believe. Some days I'm not sure what's real.'

'So the fault is not that of my daughter?'

The measured words were tying his tongue up in knots. He was sure that wasn't quite what he had meant to say.

'When you tell me that you do not know what is real, Marco, do you mean—'

'What do you do here?' he broke in. Mr Dala's tufty eyebrows bounced in surprise. 'You brought Mya here after she was pulled out of the sea. You made her better, or so she says. So what is this place? I've been here more times than I can remember and I still don't know where I am. Is it a research facility? A convalescent home? A psychiatric hospital?'

A crooked grin slalomed across her father's face. 'How perceptive, young Mr Pellicci. In fact, it is a blissful melding of all three. A perfect point of confluence. I can show you, if you like.'

Taken aback, he glanced over at Mya. Her face blank and still. He wondered what she was thinking. 'You'll show me? Really?'

'Why, of course!' Gurdeep Dala boomed cheerfully. 'The grand tour. You must forgive me for rhapsodising at times, slipping into grandiloquence. A spot of boasting? A *soupçon* of self-satisfaction? Well, perhaps. You are looking at my life's work. My vision, Marco. Our future.'

44

Mya, replaced

Their footsteps reverberated along the empty corridor. Instinct told him that they were moving underground even though it was impossible to tell whether the walkway was descending. There were no windows in this white place. The walls were tunnel-like, curving. With every step into the bowels of the Academy, he felt more uneasy. His brain seemed to be in two places at once – a soaring chorus of voices was urging him back to Mya, even as a whisper in the furthest reaches of his thoughts told him not to trust her. The quieter voice grew to a great chanting: *She's not who … She's not who … She's not who … She's not who she was …*

No. She was his partner, his life and his world, and he loved her. He longed for her comfort. Logic told him that he was lucky she was indulging him on this mad escapade; that he had tested her love so sorely; that he would be lucky if she was ever able to forgive him. He could stop this nonsense right now. Surely it wasn't too late. Not yet.

Mr Dala came to a halt by what appeared to be a blank wall. Then he realised they were standing in front of a door. The frame was almost imperceptible in the whiteness except for a touchscreen pad set into the centre. He breathed deeply. For some reason, he thought of aniseed. There was a liquorice taste on his tongue.

'We have numerous promotional videos,' Mr Dala said, 'but I can tell that you are hungry for answers, not advertising.'

'I just want to know what's going on,' he said. A feeling of foreboding pulsed against his skull in jagged spikes.

'Everything shall be revealed most shortly,' Mr Dala said. He placed his fingertips on the pad. Green lights tracked around the digits and he heard a soft click. 'The answers lie within.'

The door swung open. He and Mya gasped in harmony.

Suspended in mid-air, they stared down upon the nerve-centre of the Academy. It took him a moment to realise they were standing on a glass floor and the ground was a storey below them. Giddily he dragged his gaze upwards. The roof was an endlessly curving dome that mimicked a twilight horizon, twinkling with constellations. Beneath that shining sky, at least a hundred workers in smart white uniforms sat at terminals or scurried between errands in a room the size of an athletics stadium.

'This is the nearest to home I have ever felt,' Gurdeep Dala said as he led them down the spiralling staircase, smiling and waving at his employees as they passed. The man's presence had electrified the vast room. 'I left my native country when I was six years old. My parents were being tormented, they had almost nothing. I saw the worst of the world. When I grew older, I realised how humans inevitably fall prey to their emotions: anger, sadness, mistrust, despair. However, there was joy, too. So much joy amid the atrocities. Tears of laughter falling upon the ashes of burned villages. To me, that was the essence of humanity. But couldn't we be more? How might we hold on to the joy – but lose the worst of our emotions?'

They passed the rows of terminals. They looked unlike any computer screens he had seen before; instead of the pastel shades of Windows or the harshly functional text of programming code, each screen was filled with a pleasant pinkish fog, out of which dark objects spun past, meteorite-like, at incredible speeds. He peered closer but could not understand what was happening on the terminals or how they were operated. The workers wore small headsets, but they had no keyboards or mouses and they did not touch their screens like tablet computers. Nobody noticed them as they passed by. Everybody appeared to be in a state of intense concentration or religious rapture. Eventually Mya's father stopped behind a woman in her mid- to late thirties with a ragged dark fringe falling across her face. He placed his hand gently on her shoulder.

She turned, shaking her head as if emerging from a dream, her eyes failing to focus. Then she stared up, truly seeing him, and her mouth fell open. There was awe in her gaze. The woman pulled off her headset. He saw a row of tiny spikes glittering on the silver band. The nametag on her lab coat read *Dr Ehrlich*.

'Mr ... Mr Dala,' she said. 'Forgive me, I never expected—'

'That's quite alright, Johanna,' he said. 'An unannounced visit. I'm glad to see you so engrossed in your work.' She nodded eagerly. 'Tell me, Johanna,' he continued, 'how did you come to work at the Meinhof-Dala-Smithson Academy?'

'I was a patient here.'

'Why were you a patient here?'

Dr Ehrlich stared at each of them in turn. 'I was ... I was sad. I was sadder than I could possibly tell you. Then I was sent here. And everything got better.'

'Johanna,' Gurdeep Dala said quietly, 'would you mind showing my friend Mr Pellicci here your arms?' Her lower lip quivering, she stared at Mya's father in mute appeal. 'It will only be for a second, I assure you.'

Taking a quick breath, the scientist pulled up her white sleeves. Mya let out a retching noise, gripping his arm as she tottered off balance. The scars on the woman's arms were deep; so deep that the cuts had distorted the flesh into twisting valleys that looked as if they could hold water. He felt a lurch in his stomach too. Then the sleeves were pulled back down and the horror was hidden. He was staring at a normal woman with a pleasant, open face. A woman who seemed perfectly happy and content.

'Thank you, Johanna,' Mr Dala said. 'How do you feel now?'

'I feel fine. I feel good. I'm a good mum for my children, Zelda and Ronnie. They need me and I need them.' Dr Ehrlich indicated the rouged swirls on the screen in front of her. 'That's why I asked to work here afterwards. To work with you, Mr Dala. To give something back. For everything that you gave me.'

'Thank you, Johanna,' Mya's father repeated. 'You may return to your work.'

Nodding in gratitude, she slipped the silver band back over her forehead and returned to her screen.

They were led away from the terminals, down the corridors, into an alcove that opened out into a small passageway. He smelled a familiar exotic, evocative scent. Then his feet were treading on spongy earth and the three of them were in the jasmine garden beneath the artificial stars.

'My Idlewild,' Gurdeep Dala explained, as if that word made sense, 'a tranquil resting place, where I can unwind from the stresses of my work.' He ushered them towards the pergola and motioned for them to sit down on the swinging benches inside. 'Dr Ehrlich was only one example,' he continued. 'One tiny success among thousands. As I told you earlier, I had grown tired of humanity being ruled by our worst impulses. So I made it my mission to change our foolish ways. We, young Marco, are in the business of perfecting people. Changing minds.'

The smell of flowers was overpowering. 'How?' he asked.

'The orbitofrontal cortex,' said Mya's father, reaching his hands forward to clamp gently upon his head, his forefingers tracking around the top of his skull, 'is associated with approach motivation and positive affective processes. Emotions, to put it bluntly. But this part of the brain... well, first it giveth then it taketh away. Through a process of cerebral cauterisation, we rid ourselves of the worst elements of our nature. You can witness the results for yourself. Our success. Our triumph. Look, Marco. Look and see. She's right beside you now.'

Understanding dawned on him. The garden pitched and yawed sickeningly. The words made sense now: *I'm not who I was.* Mya wasn't a different person. She was the same person. She had not been replaced; the girl sitting next to him was no doppelganger, no clone. But something had happened to her. She had been... she had been...

'Fixed,' Mr Dala finished his sentence for him, reading his mind. 'Mya had been broken for far too long. My fault. Completely my fault. Now, she has been fixed.'

'You messed with her brain,' he stammered through numbed lips, his whole body trembling. He was gasping like a fish drowning in oxygen, desperate to be told that the truth staring him in the face was a lie. 'You... why... you're her father...'

'The ends justify the means,' Mr Dala said. The man's voice was almost casual. He looked over at Mya but her face was unreadable. 'I am a widower, Marco. I had no desire to lose my daughter too. But there is no fear of that now. Mya is perfect in every possible way.'

She touched his hand. He couldn't bear to look at her. But he knew that she was smiling at him. She was smiling and his own mouth was open in a silent scream.

'It is you and I who are the flawed personalities here, young Marco,' Mr Dala went on. 'But you don't have to be. Of that, I give you—'

What Mya's father planned to give them was lost in a deafening chorus of sirens. The lights flickered on and off. First they were thrust into all-consuming blackness, then they were caught in the blazing glare of halogen spotlights. In the distance he could hear shrieks and shouts of alarm from the workers. He felt a rumbling beneath his feet like a localised earthquake. The sprinklers overhead turned on and within seconds his shirt was sodden. Mya clung to him, letting out a whimper of fright.

There was the sound of stumbling footsteps behind them. They turned to stare at the intruder.

'Guru ... oh shit, Guru ...' wheezed Frank Baumann. His tartan bow tie was askew and his face was waxy-grey. 'I think you'd better see this.'

45

The Bleaklands

We are forced out of the memory hole with a tremendous shunt and immediately the stones seal off the void in the harsh earth of the Bleaklands. Marco is sobbing, curled up into a foetal position. Clumsily I wrap my arms around his heaving shoulders and hold him as best I can; trying to be a comfort for him even as my brain throbs with the bawling voices of understanding, each one clamouring to be heard. It is starting to make sense now – some of it, at least.

The landscape has shifted. We are at the foot of a hill constructed from sun-bleached gravel. Perhaps at the summit I'll be able to see clearly.

We're not dead. I understand that now. We are somewhere else, we're far from home, but we're not dead. I'm so close to realising the whole truth and I'm scared of what it will reveal to me, to Marco, to us.

What I don't understand is this: I knew Marco as a child. I knew Marco when he was a punk with spiked pink hair and severe anger issues. The memory holes have told me this, so why doesn't my knowledge extend back that far? Throughout my time in the White Prison, I remembered him as a gentle and sweet-natured man who would never cause harm to anyone. But there is a whole fragmented history that I don't remember. A history where he was a different person – and I was a different person too.

Everything comes back to the Academy, back to my father's work. My partner was fixed. Mad Marco became gentle and malleable. Oh God, was I fixed as well?

Of course I was fixed. That's why my memories are so fractured. That's why I can't trust anything my brain is telling me.

We are in the business of perfecting people, my father was fond of saying. But I always thought he meant other people. Not me, not us. I'm so confused. I need more time. I don't remember being that girl. I don't remember fixing Marco. I don't remember those memories. It's all in my head but I'm struggling to let it out. I did this – this is my fault. I can't blame my father. I wasn't his stooge. I was his willing helper.

The complicity tastes like rancid meat in my mouth. I locked away the people in the White Prison. I don't know how I can help them now, Johanna and Alec and the rest of my father's victims. Maybe they are beyond helping.

But because I know what I did, I also know the entrances of this system – and the exits too. Which means I know how to set us free.

'What happened?' Marco demands, his eyes rolling sickeningly in their sockets. 'What's happening, Mya? I don't understand.'

How can I tell him? The memories are coming back to me now. Two words, medically impersonal and cold, reverberate through whatever passes for my mind: *cerebral cauterisation*. My father has removed the worst of our emotions. My sadness and Marco's anger, cut out of our personalities and stuffed into canopic jars. When I was younger, I even performed the procedure under my father's guidance. I'm guessing my own treatment was somehow botched because I'm still here. I am my true self in these Bleaklands of lost and scattered memories, but how far away am I from reality?

'You're not yourself, darling,' I tell him with a high laugh that scrapes a little too close to insanity. 'You're a construct of your negative emotions, your own worst enemy. But I'll get us back to how we used to be. I promise.' Drawing him close, I can feel our hearts juddering as one. 'You have to listen to me, Marco. Really, really, really listen to me. I know it sounds impossible. When I tried –' I feel my breath coming in wheezes and swallow hard, knowing that I have to be strong, for the sake of both of us '– when I tried to kill myself, when they found me floating in the sea, they fixed me. In a way, I was killed. Only it wasn't suicide, it was murder. They removed my nasty flawed personality and created a bright, fresh, new one.' I almost feel like laughing at the insanity of everything. 'And the old version of me – the real version of me – is right here with you.'

'Who did this to you, Mya? Who tried to fix you?'

'I reckon you've already worked that one out.'

He breathes out heavily. 'Your father.'

'That's what he does at the Academy. He's in the business of perfecting people. Please don't hate me, but I've been helping him. I used to love his work. I thought he was making everyone's lives better, fixing the damage caused by a bad life or bad luck, giving people a second chance.' I manage a rueful smile. 'I never thought I'd end up as one of his patients.'

Marco lets go of me. His hands clench into fists. The milky light of whatever sun shines on this blasted world glints in his eyes and, yes, there is that familiar flat blackness in the depths of his pupils. I'm scared, so scared. But I can't deny that I'm excited.

'I'll kill him,' he says flatly.

The Madboy. Mad Marco. The damaged boy who had so

much potential. My father and his colleagues drew the venom out of his sting, but in removing the anger from his personality, they destroyed his essential self. He was never meant to be safe. Neither was I. We're both bad people, we're both beyond redemption. But without the worst aspects of our characters, do we have any true personality at all? In my father's perfect future, we are just happy and mindless ciphers. I want to be me again. I want Marco to be himself again too. Whatever it costs, I want us to be free.

'Marco, there's something else I need to tell you.'

Using my forefingers, I tilt his head up until our eyelines align, wishing I didn't have to do this. It would be easier not to let him know. I tell him about the young man with a pink mohawk who crashed our study group at the Meinhof-Dala-Smithson Academy; the boy who could be so intelligent and charming but held a crazy grudge against the world. I tell him how this shy, troubled girl fell for that boy beyond measurable depth. How his confidence, his vivacity, shone a light on her gloomy life. How her grief and guilt at her mother's death slipped away when she was with him. How she felt unstoppable when they were together, how she didn't need to be afraid of the world any longer. How he lit a fire inside her and made her, if not a better person, then a bolder one. How she still felt the tremendous pressure of the Great Waves but now yearned to stay on the surface for him. Marco Pellicci, the man kicking furiously against the elements, did his best to keep her afloat. How he saved her without even knowing.

When I am finished, he has only one question.

'Did you—' Marco stops, trying to compose himself. I've already decided that whatever his reaction, I will stay here kneeling before him, my neck exposed for the lover's embrace or the executioner's blow, because I deserve both. 'Did you fix me?'

'Yes,' I tell him. 'Yes, I did.'

He blows out heavily. 'You fixed me.' The words are flat and echo emptily in this airless landscape. 'You messed with my brain.'

'Yes.'

My heart is thumping. The setting sun has splintered into fiery shards across the landscape, tinting the Bleaklands with prismatic hues. The entire spectrum of existence has been narrowed down to a boy and a girl, both bruised and exhausted and changed in ways neither of us can truly comprehend, kneeling opposite one another. Now it is his turn to tilt my chin with his fingers so I am forced to look him in the eyes. His gaze is impossible to read. I'm shuddering with apprehension and remember when I once trembled with desire for him, love for him. I try to remind myself that the person here with me is not the Marco I love; it's the worst of his character. He's still dangerous. He's still not himself.

'Why?' he asks. His voice is so, so soft. 'Tell me why you did it.'

How can I explain to him the horror of the weeks after the end-of-term party? The arrest, the court appearances, the crushing sense that everything had been my fault. Even though I couldn't bear to think of what my boyfriend had done, his senseless violence, I still pleaded with my father to intervene. I wasn't thinking of Clare, who had helped me so much in those lonely early weeks at the Academy. I wasn't thinking of that poor idiot boyfriend of hers. I was selfish; I was only thinking of myself and Marco. While Geraint lay in his coma, we concocted a plan, my father and I, to save Marco – even though we knew that by saving him we had to destroy his essential nature. *I just want him back without the pain and anger and aggression,* I told my father before the treatment began. *A regular, everyday guy.*

'You want to know why I did it?' I ask defiantly. 'I did it because I love you. Even though I wish I could hate you.'

A tic pulses in his jaw. He reaches down and sinks his fingers into the washed-out rubble of the ground as if trying to dig a memory tunnel of his own. Through the rips in his medical gown, I can see the veins popping out on his biceps. The silence draws out mercilessly.

Then, with a scream, he turns and flings his two handfuls of grey gravel across the landscape. Snarling, gibbering, he beats his fists against the ground over and over again until his knuckles are a bloody mess. I cower back, certain that this is the most control he can muster as the Madboy, certain that it is my face he wishes he was pounding.

At last he is still, collapsing in a tsunami of dust, his howls tailing off into ragged sobs. Tentatively, I reach across and place a hand on his shoulder. The muscles vibrate like a live cable.

'Where do we go from here?' he asks at last. His tone is thick and glottal, rasping with barely suppressed emotion.

'It's time to end this. It's time to be who we really are,' I tell him. This version of Marco is dangerous – but he could be useful too. I guess I'm manipulating him once again. There is a plan forming in my mind and I need him. 'We're going to find my father.'

If I can snap myself back to reality – even for a few moments – then we might have a chance. We are inside the nerve centre of the Academy. The mental storeroom that we used to call, with a certain grisly irony, the Brain Cell. The secret prison that houses the snipped-out emotions, the worst memories, of the Academy's patients. My father always kept their brain patterns, replicated on hard drives, for research purposes. He told me it was for legal reasons – in case a procedure needed to be reversed, or an operation was challenged in the courts – but really I know he just liked to play with these negative impulses. Like a child with a favourite toy; perfecting people, changing minds.

I am convinced we are close to the faultline of reality. The window shutters are sealed but there is a glow around the edge of the frames that I'm sure is natural light. I've jammed my fingers into the gaps in the rotten oak, pulled desperately until my nails split and my fingertips bleed. I can see the sunlight. I swear I can see the sunlight.

The sensations are far stronger than when I was staring at the video screen in the White Prison. They are so strong they explode my synapses, making me giddy with how close I'm coming to the real world. It's so much, too much, it's unbearable. I drink and drink and I'm still so thirsty. I'm going to break out. I'm going to live free again.

'What is that all punk rockers want to do?' I ask him, my tone almost goading. 'Smash the system. Right? We're going to smash that system. And I know just how to do it.'

'How?'

'Because I've been in the system this whole time. So have you. We're part of this. The worst parts of our brains were removed and replicated as computer patterns. We're formulae, algorithms. The brain runs on pure electricity – and that's all we are. Right now we're stuck in the furthest reaches of the computer system that connects every corner of my father's Academy. Hiding among forgotten lines of code.'

Again he glares darkly at me – twin coals burning out from beneath that stained and sticky gauze. 'I hope this is going to start making sense soon,' he says quietly, menacingly. 'This doesn't feel like I'm electricity in a computer system. My face is burned to the bone and that feels real enough, I tell you. It feels like my entire body is corroding. You and your dad have created a living hell.'

'That's why we need to go back,' I tell him rapidly. 'Back to the White Prison, or the Academy, they're the same place, only the colours have changed. The Academy is the only way out. So that's where we're going.'

He stares at me, aghast. 'That place? Again? You really have fucking lost it this time.'

'Oh yeah.' I smile against the fear. 'That way madness lies. But trust me on this one. We're too far away right now for me to do any proper damage. Currently we're hiding in some backwater of forgotten code. But back at the white place, I can start to destroy it all. Bring it down from within. There will be fireworks.'

He shakes his head. But he knows it's either my plan or be trapped here forever, his true personality slowly collapsing outside the cells that sustain it.

'You owe me,' he says. That simple statement sounds like the worst threat imaginable. 'So you'll take me back. Yeah?'

'Definitely,' I reply. 'I owe you your life.'

46

Endgame

The world has been broken up into fragments. But my mind is without fear and my head is held high. The journey back to the White Prison has taken us no time whatsoever. We are nothing more than electrical impulses shooting around a vast computer terminal. The idea is terrifying but oddly reassuring. Because as long as there is a spark then we have a chance.

I remember taking Marco – the new Marco, the one who had been fixed – home to see my father at the start of our second relationship. This innocent boy had believed he was meeting him for the first time. During dinner my father kept needling him about his emotions – trying to push him, flare up some of that old anger. I had been mortified and nervous; Dad was being so obvious, or obvious to anyone who hadn't had a vast section of their mind cut out. Marco suspected nothing, of course. In the eyes of Gurdeep Dala, Project Marco had been a tremendous success. He was in the business of perfecting people and now Marco Pellicci was perfect. His old personality, the rough edges and sharp snags, had been smoothed into an endless contour.

Weirdly, I had seen Marc's rebirth as a catalyst for my own reincarnation. I was tired of being mild and meek Mya, the sweet girl who had been blown away by the force of nature

301

that was Mad Marco. Maybe some of that passion, that rashness, that reckless confidence would work with me. It had been so goddamn alluring, I rather fancied seeing its effect on others. I wasn't a different person, I hadn't been fixed – not then, at least. I simply wanted to be someone else. My father encouraged it: *A fine idea ... I believe you should be assertive, Amaya, take the lead ... this Marco will be slower, maybe confused ... you can be the person you have always wanted to be ...*

Yes, I did want to be someone else. Not now, not any longer. I've seen the damage messing with the mind can cause. The brain isn't a computer that can be upgraded on a whim. What my father did was a crime against human nature. I promise – *swear down*, as Marco used to say – that when I've fixed everything for us tonight, I will make it up to everyone else. The people my father experimented on. Marco was the greatest and most horrific of his projects.

That was what drove me into my depression; the reason I tried to drown myself in the greatest of Great Waves. Because I couldn't bear to look at what Marco had become, what we had made him. It was my fault. I had killed what I loved.

But there are second chances in this world if you look for them hard enough. I have to hold on to that thought, hold on to hope. I'll make things right. Whatever the cost.

The White Prison has been rebuilt to sheening perfection. My little rebellion, my bomb and my fire, barely scratched the surface. There would have been a back-up file – my father leaves nothing to chance – and it would have been the work of minutes to upload another digitised recreation of the Academy.

There is no sound inside the building but for our footsteps. The corridors wind around in a spiral, eternally downwards. To think that I had once felt so safe in this place, so comfortable and at home, and now my heartbeat is racing as if I am trespass-ing on hallowed ground. Marco is limping badly. His body feels unnaturally hot, riddled with sickness. I wonder whether this is a corruption of his code and how much time I have left with his original personality. On our journey back he had stumbled frequently and I had to help him walk, gritting my teeth in delirious apprehension, half expecting to feel his hand slip from my shoulder and clamp around my throat. I don't trust him but I still need him. *Lean with me*, I told him, *so we don't spill.* More memories of long-ago conversations echoing around whatever remains of my brain.

At least I now understand the truth about my doppelganger, about the girl I thought had replaced me. I know this system because Dad taught me everything he knew and he built it himself. That was why I could spy on myself while I was in the White Prison. The television in my cell wasn't a video screen at all: I was accessing the Academy's security cameras, the miles upon miles of closed circuits threaded through the building, connecting to every part of the system. I was watching myself, watching Marco, as we lived our fixed lives, innocent and unquestioning and blank. The television screen that had been both my antichrist and my saviour came from my own head, my instinctive knowledge of this brutally beautiful system. I had been escaping from my cell for months – I just wasn't even aware I was doing it.

But now we are back here at last. At least this is the place where it ends.

'This is where I leave you,' I tell Marco as we stand beneath the grand arch of the atrium, at the entrance to the lift to the great tower. 'You know the plan. I have to do this alone.'

As I turn my back on him, he grabs my arm and yanks me backwards and I hiss in pain. Momentarily he looks ashamed, before the worst impulses take control again. Then he merely sneers.

'Let go of me,' I snap.

'It just occurred to me,' he says, his nails sinking into my forearm, 'how do I know this isn't a trap?'

I choke out despairing laughter. 'A trap inside a trap? Even for you, that's pretty damn paranoid.'

'I'm not sure I trust you.'

'Well, I could never totally trust you either. But I need you to do this for me. For you, too.' Prising myself from his grip, wondering how many of my mental resources are still remaining – I feel exhausted but oddly wired, and I can't afford to slip up now – I face him down. 'We've been through this, Marco. You create the distraction, burn the place up again. I deal with my dad.'

'What happened to doing this together?'

'It's my father. My mind. Why would I need you?'

'He's been outwitting you throughout your whole life, Mya. In what world will it be different this time?'

'Because now I know what he is. I won't fall for his tricks. I know them all.'

'Kind-hearted mothers write fan mail to serial killers,' he says. 'Think about it.'

'We're talking about my father here. Not some bloody psychopath.'

'Like I told you,' he says, the gore-stained paper mask creasing into an approximation of Marco Pellicci's cocky smirk that I used to find so fetching and infuriating, 'think about it.'

'He wanted what was best for me,' I tell him, striving for stridency even though I can hear my conviction wilting in the heat of his crazy certainties. 'He wanted what was best for you, too. He thinks he's doing good. Great good. He's just ... misguided.'

'I'm sure he sounds convincing,' says Marco. 'He'll tell you he only wants to save you from yourself. But so do I, Mya. And I'll admit it – I've been a bit of a bastard at times. But I'm not capable of his evil. That old boy blitzed his own daughter's mind. Trepanned her skull without a second thought.' His words are harsh but his eyes are moist and his voice is wavering. 'He mashed that incredible brain of yours into jelly. He ruined you. Didn't he?' He's starting to cry now, shaking, his expression childlike, his tone desolate. I'm sure he's not acting. I want to hold him, comfort him, but I know it would be dangerous to let myself believe that this is the Marco that I love. 'I can't lose you again. Even as messed up as I am right now, I know that much. I'm so broken. Please don't leave me in this place. You're all that's left.'

This is not good. In the real world, my father turned him from a wolf into a lapdog. Marco needs to be snarling at the end of his chain, not whining and cowering. I need him strong, I need him deadly. 'Remember the plan, darling,' I tell him reassuringly. 'You need to start breaking down the system to lure my father here. Smash it up. Do whatever you want, have some fun. Leave Dad to me. I promise that I'll come back to you. I'll meet you outside.'

'Outside?' he repeats uncertainly. 'I don't want to go back into that land out there again. I can't take any more horror-show memories.'

'No, the real outside,' I tell him. 'I'll meet you back in the real world. When we're both real people again.'

Marco tries to smile. A proper smile this time. 'I don't even know—'

'You don't know the first thing you're doing.' A new voice

pierces the air. Startled, we turn. Johanna Ehrlich is standing in front of us. She is barring the double door to the lift, blocking my path. Her entire body is trembling as if in fear but her eyes are cold emerald stones. 'I won't let you do this. I can't let you do this.'

'Jo-Jo, we need to—' I start.

'Don't Jo-Jo me, you bitch!' she snaps. She paces towards us. Her hands are hooked into claws as if she wants to go for my eyes. 'If you ruin this place, you ruin everything. My life's perfect now. So is yours, if you could only see, but you're too blind.'

I shake my head. 'This ... this isn't the answer, Johanna. My father, he's selling everyone false hope. You're not in the White Prison to get better. You're here to be experimented on. You're a lab rat. Unless you let us do what we're here to do, you'll be stuck here forever.'

'You think I don't know?' she screams. 'What do you take me for?' Then her anger dissipates and her lower lip begins to wobble. 'I'm not dumb. I know this version of me won't get better. But the Johanna on the outside ... she's happy, she's content, she's a good mother. I know that. I've always known that. Can't you understand? I want to help. I want to help others like me. This is where I deserve to be, where I can't harm anyone and I can't harm myself. You — both of you — you're just too fucking selfish.'

'That's right,' breathes Marco. He sounds freakishly calm. 'We are selfish. You can't spell *selfish* without *self*. And that's what we've lost. We lost ourselves, Johanna.'

She shakes her head. 'You only lost the worst part. Think of the damage you did, Marco Pellicci. Think of the damage you'll do in the future. Think of—'

Abruptly Johanna stops talking. She cranes her head from side to side as if picking up a distant sound. Her jaw drops and her eyes open wide and she lets out a whimper. She has definitely heard something. Then finally I hear it too: the sound of barking, slavering, growling. A sound that has haunted Johanna Ehrlich's dreams for almost three decades.

The dogs are coming. The bad dogs.

A sea of snarls rushes towards us. Huge black hellhounds with red eyes and teeth like sabres. She raises her hands in a hopeless bid to ward them off. But there are too many of them – hundreds and hundreds – and her worst phobia is converging upon her. She's so brave to stay for so long, guarding the Academy, fighting for what she believes in, as they circle her. The dogs pace ever closer with their serial-killer smiles. One lunges out and snaps its fangs half an inch from her ankle. Finally, with a defeated scream, Johanna turns and flees. As the pack pursues her, I see the fur flickering, misplaced heads and strobing bodies; glitches in the code that Marco has imagined into existence. Within moments the atrium is silent.

Now he is looking at me expecting approval, even congratulation. He's growing so much stronger now – physically he's a wreck, but mentally he is a powerful virus skittering through the computer system. Marco was always a fast learner. In the time it took for Johanna to confront us, he managed to flit to her file, rip out her nightmares of ferocious dogs, and turn the pack loose on her. No wonder my father wanted to play with his remarkable mind. His plan was genius. It was awful too.

'That was a dirty trick,' I tell him. 'You know she's terrified of dogs.'

'That was a simple solution,' he replies, unconcerned. 'Same difference.'

I blink. I don't know what to say. How can I blame him? I told him he needed to destroy the Brain Cell by any means possible, so we could lure my father into the system. By the time

I manage to conjure a response, he is already gone, limping away towards the main compound. Off on his mission of destruction. Oh God, what have I unleashed? But there's no time to think about what I have done.

I'm on my own now.

47

Endgame

The lift shoots me upwards with dizzying speed. The lights flicker through the floors as if I've just scooped the jackpot on a one-armed bandit. If I have no real body in this place, then why has my stomach performed a loop the loop? I am guessing it's like the burns on Marco's face and his collapsing muscles – enough of our personalities still remain to convince us we have a physical presence here. We still believe we're human. Holding on to our humanity was enough to torture us inside the White Prison. It could be enough to save us now.

The doors slide open with a jaunty dinging sound. At the top there is an open-plan office – a white-walled room dominated by a large boardroom table carved from darkly shining stone. Bifold glass doors lead out onto the viewing platform. This, like so much of the White Prison, is a spectral recreation of the Academy; my father used to entertain his sponsors and backers in this room, inviting them to admire the view before turning their attentions to his mission statement on the huge video screen that dominates one of the walls. With a certain inevitability, the black screen comes alive the moment I enter the room. I've had enough of screens – if I ever get out of here, I'll smash every screen I see – but still I cannot stop myself turning to see what is playing.

The screen is showing the inside of the Academy. The real Academy. There are no colours in the pictures but I can hear sounds of industry in the background. No, more than that – I'm sure I can make out a thrum of panic, maybe even a siren? My dad and Dr Baumann are huddled over a screen in the nerve centre. This is good, this is very good. Marco must have begun his work. I told him where to go, what plugs to pull, the location of the weak points between this version of reality and whatever passes for it outside these walls. Those walls are so thin; full of fault-lines and fractures. On my command he can rip those walls to shreds. Maybe more, as he showed in his little stunt with poor Johanna. There's no telling what he might do.

'When you informed me that you had the measure of this problem, I was inclined to believe you, Frank.' My father's voice is as clear as if he is standing next to me. 'After the last time.'

Baumann is trembling, plucking at his ridiculous bow tie. Is it a tartan day or a houndstooth day? I can't be sure in black-and-white. What I do know is that he is caught in an agony of contrition.

'I'm sorry, Guru,' he whimpers. 'Truly sorry. I don't understand. I thought we'd killed all the gremlins in this damn system. Now it's worse than ever.'

My father places a hand on his shoulder. 'No-no-no, dear friend. Accidents happen. This can easily be fixed.'

He stares upwards.

And he sees me. I'm absolutely sure he sees me. He's coming. He's coming now. I need to be ready for him. Leaving the screen, I pull open the glass doors and step onto the viewing platform and taste the delicious night air on my tongue. I can smell a mysterious sweetness drifting by but I'm unable to place the scent. It is twilight, the sun's orange glare splintering across the horizon. The flatlands seem to swoop out to the end of the world. The stars are twinkling so brightly, so perfectly. It's a pity they don't really exist. Nothing he created is true; everything is a beautiful lie. Especially me.

Rough hands take hold of my shoulders with a gentle grip and I jump, spinning around as the stranger catches me unawares. But I know who it is already. A familiar face stares at me. Dark skin roughened at the cheeks; a moustache speckled with silver; crinkle-cornered eyes that have witnessed the worst of the world yet wish only to improve it. I realise that I can't move. My dad strokes my hair away from my forehead, the way he always used to when I was a child. Then he draws me into his arms and I can't resist. There is only tenderness in his embrace, only love in his gaze.

'Hello, sweetpea,' my father says.

My lower lip quivering, I try to respond even though I have no idea what I'm saying. 'You got here fast,' I mumble weakly. I should have thought of a better line, to let him know I'm in control, to tell him that finally he's playing my game. I wish I could believe it myself.

'I'm so sorry it came to this,' he says. 'You must understand that I was only trying to help. All of this, Mya . . . all of this was for you.'

'How could you do this?' I demand. 'Why did you do this to us?'

A sad smile spreads across his face. His expression aches with melancholy, with lost hope. 'I can't tell you, sweetpea,' my father says. 'I have to show you.'

He touches his fingertip to the centre of my forehead. Suddenly we're not in the White Prison any longer.

★

There are soft voices. The squeak of rubber shoes on linoleum floors. My nostrils are assaulted by the reek of cleaning fluids. I can hear a metronomic beeping sound.

There is a girl lying in a hospital bed. Her eyes are closed. Her skin is tinged with an unpleasant, nearly dead greyness. Her black hair falls lankly on the pillow. The only sign of life is a rising and falling of the white sheet. She looks so close to the end. It would be easy – if the steady implosion and explosion of the lungs ceased without fanfare – to use the sheet to wrap that frail frame and turn the hospital blanket into a burial shroud.

She is me. She is a younger version of me. That unconscious grey girl is me.

'You don't remember this day, my darling Mya,' says my father. His voice is quiet yet amplified, booming as if he is broadcasting from inside my head. 'You are seeing what I saw.'

Staring down at my comatose teenage self, I grab blindly for his hand, my eyes blurred with tears, wishing only for his forgiveness. This is what I did to him. So much guilt, so much shame. I want it all to go away.

'I'm sorry,' I whisper. 'I wasn't—'

'You weren't yourself,' he finishes for me. 'That is what they told me, Amaya. An attempt to console the anguished father. You weren't yourself, they told me. Most certainly with the best of intentions. However, I knew differently. You were wired wrongly, my darling. Darkness was in your nature. Exactly like your poor mother.'

Then we are lifted from that sad little room, passing through the walls as if we are spectres, and there is a tremendous rushing sensation and the great tower of the Academy building is signalling us home like a lighthouse beacon. Only this is a siren's call, a cruel trick, and the ship will be dashed to pieces on the rocks.

Now we are inside my father's office. Dad is staring at a

double of himself, sitting on his swivel chair, slumped over his desk, his head in his hands. This version of my father is physically younger but looks somehow older; there are fewer flakes of snow in his moustache, the bald spot on the top of his head is penny-sized. But there are bags underneath his eyes like purple pillows and his face is slack with fatigue.

'What you're suggesting is immoral. I won't stand for it.'

Standing in the corner of the room, refilling his pipe, is Dr Frank Baumann. He is also younger. His auburn beard is scrubby and his paunch is less pronounced. My father always said that he hired Frank because he was the only person who dared talk back to him, a conviction I found odd considering the psychiatrist's endless compliance with the Academy and its work. Frank is talking back now though.

'She's your damned daughter, Guru. I'm simply asking you to think about what you're doing. To consider every alternative.'

'What is the alternative?' my father asks. He sounds so broken. 'You don't understand, Frank. You have no children. I have endured beyond comprehension, and for what? I have lost so much and each time I beg the world not to take from me anything else I love – that surely by now I have repaid whatever celestial debt I owe – and each time the world steals a little more. Soon I will have nothing left.'

'She'll get better. That's what the doctors say.'

The ghost of my father's memory is still for a moment. Then, with a sudden furious motion, he bangs his fist down on the table, over and over again until it feels as if the entire room is shaking. 'Fuck the doctors, Frank!' he almost howls. Startled, I shrink back. I can't remember hearing him swear before and I've certainly never seen him lose his temper. 'Mya gets better and she never gets better. How long do we wait until she does

313

it again? And then she gets better, and she does it again. Where does it end? With my daughter dead, that's where it ends.'

'There are moral implications here, Gurdeep. I don't think you fully understand.' Baumann rakes a hand through his coppery tangle of hair. 'We ... I thought the purpose of our Academy was perfecting people. The commission we had for the violent prisoners; I could get behind that. They were killers and we turned them into angels. Fine members of society. Or the army veterans ... we took away their shellshock, their trauma. Remember that? I'll never forget it. I went to bed happy for a year. I loved my work. I thought that's what we were doing here. Making the world a better, safer, happier place. Not some personal crusade.'

'Then leave me,' my father says. 'Go from this room right now and I shall always think well of you. And I thank you for your invaluable assistance.'

Dr Baumann steps across the room and places a hand on his mentor's heaving shoulders. Blinking, he stares around the office, his expression that of a rabbit caught in a snare. He is as trapped as we are.

'I won't leave you, Guru,' he says quietly. A tic flickers in his left eyebrow. 'What you're doing – what we're doing – is too good to lose. Too great. The impact on humanity could be ... it could be wonderful. We could save the world. But using your own daughter as a test subject—'

'Mya is no test subject. I have performed this procedure many times before.'

Baumann gnaws on the stem of his pipe. 'Not to this extent. If we wiped someone, there was no real harm done. Murderers, paedophiles, who gives a shit? They were gone anyway. But Mya ... she's eighteen, Gurdeep. Eighteen and she's the smartest person I've ever met, except for you. Think of her potential. If this goes wrong…'

'If the worst happens then I shall end my work,' my father says. 'Burn it all down. The fault will be mine alone. You shall be free.'

Frank Baumann hangs his head. He is defeated, resigned. 'I'm here for you, Gurdeep. Always. In whatever way you need me.'

'I shall be very careful,' my father says. There is such satisfaction in his tone, such gleeful anticipation, it makes me choke with revulsion. He is eager to get started. 'I will not be greedy, I will not cut out too much. Only enough. Enough to make her better.'

Then the scene splinters into nothingness and we are everywhere and nowhere, rushing through a vacuum into an impossible future. Two hearts in a kaleidoscope, and I'm melding into my father, our incorporeal bodies endlessly converging and I know everything about everyone. And I know I'll remember nothing when it's over and I don't care, I'm laughing and laughing. I'm a genius and I'm insane and I'm every point in between. It's all in my head, it's all in my head, it's all in my head. Euphoria explodes from deep within my soul as we ride this great unearthly rollercoaster and I know that I'll never be unhappy again because there's so much impossible beauty in existence. And I want to live, I want to live, I want to live no matter what it costs me.

The pace slows and that wild headlong rush veers into an achingly gorgeous swoop and I know that we are returning to that place where everything must end, swan-diving through a sunburst.

48

Endgame

I was fixed. I was fixed again and again and again. Whenever a Great Wave came, drowning me in depression, my father plunged into the swirling, sucking foam to rescue me with his vast knowledge. He was my lifebuoy. My saviour. And if he had to kill a little part of me each time to save my life, then surely it was a sacrifice worth making. Surely?

I remember the day that Marco was fixed. Lying on the gurney in his white smock, unconscious, he looked so small. Infinitely reduced. *Why did you shave his head?* I asked my father. *His mohawk ... he loved his hair ...* My father told me that a bald skull was necessary for the procedure, so the metal teeth of the band could trepan his skull without risk of contamination. *But that's him*, I replied. In that moment – only in that moment – I understood the consequences of what I had agreed to set in motion. *He was a punk, a man who walked on the wild side, anything but normal. Being different made him happy. You're not going to change every bit of him, are you?* I asked desperately. And my father said to me ...

'Only what is necessary.'

We are back inside the Academy boardroom, seated at opposite ends of that vast oblong table. I realise, in one of life's tragic little coincidences, that it has been carved out of onyx – the same heavy stone that I used to try to drag myself to the seabed. My father takes a sip from a glass of iced water and straightens his spectacles on his nose; even in this mirrored reality he still keeps up appearances. He stares at me, his eyes urging acquiescence, and I turn my face away. I can't bear to look at him, knowing what he has done – knowing what he has willed me on to do as his muse. Soon, after I have been fixed for the final time, there will be only whiteness. Will I wake up in my cell with the video screen on the curving wall, trapped once more in the depths of my head, or will there simply be blankness? He could go further, I know. He could cut much deeper than he has before. He could destroy every original thought in my brain. The worst thing about it? My father would kill me out of love.

'If I'm such a bad file,' I say slowly, 'why not just delete me?'

My father chuckles fondly, as if this is just another one of our great dining table debates at home. 'You are arguing for the death penalty – or at best euthanasia, Amaya. Instead we can save you, we can protect you, we can fix you.'

'Would you ever put the real me back in the real world? No matter how cured? No matter how fixed?'

Only for a moment, he looks away and that is all the confirmation I could ever need.

'Didn't you ever think,' I ask, picking my words with care, 'that before you changed someone's mind forever, they might change *their* mind?'

He shakes his head. 'Your depression – those Great Waves that tried to drown you – were a line of botched code, an error in the human program. Now *you* are that line of botched code. You are the error, Mya.'

'So you splintered my soul into who knows how many

fragments? That was your big fucking cure? Do you even know who I am anymore?'

'I suppose this concerns every part of you.' His voice sounds resigned – even weary. 'Wouldn't you like to meet the other Myas? They're all here, of that I assure you. There isn't only one Brain Cell, sweetpea. There are many. And there are many of you, too.'

I don't have time to contemplate whether or not he's telling the truth. Because there is someone else here with us. My father was too entranced in his self-justifying spiel to hear the pinging sound of the lift arriving, the door to the boardroom sliding open just wide enough to let a body sidle through. That shadow figure creeps around the broad leather backs of the chairs, keeping out of sight of his prey, more animal than human.

'Don't you want to see, Mya?' my dad asks, leaning forward eagerly. 'Don't you want to know who you really are? I can show you. We can see so far together. You are right on the edge of understanding everything. Realising and releasing your full potential.' He spreads his arms wide, embracing empty air. The shadow is behind him now – such a horrific and glorious vision that it takes a tremendous effort to keep my gaze on the beaming, genial face of my father, rather than the ruined one looming over him. 'Come now, sweetpea, there's no need for any great war between us. You've proven your abilities – twice, now! You have uncovered your traumatic memories in the darkest depths of our mainframe. You have befuddled Frank Baumann and caused astonishing damage to our systems. I applaud you.'

I need to keep his attention on me. 'What did it mean to you to see us that way?' I ask. 'Did it make you happy, secure? We were in a safe place – if you ignore the shackles. Your daughter a frightened rabbit cowering in a cage. And Marco – Marco a rabid dog on a thick leash.'

He rubs at his moustache.

'What happens when you can't control what you created?' I demand. Sickly charges of adrenaline are pulsing through my bloodstream. 'What happens when that leash snaps?'

The monster behind him takes his cue. Marco lunges downwards and wraps a sinewy, blackened forearm around my dad's throat. With his other hand he grabs hold of my father's right arm and forces it behind his back, pulling it upwards so brutally hard that I fancy I can hear the bones shriek outrage. My father lets out a startled caw, his glasses flying off his face and skittering away beneath the table.

'It's hard to applaud,' Marco growls into his ear, softly, murderously, 'when some mad cunt could break your arm in a millisecond. Isn't that right, Guru? Isn't that one hundred per cent correct?'

'Marco... Marco Pellicci... is that you? It *is* you, good grief. Please let go of my neck, dear boy. Even in this artificial world, it does make talking rather difficult.'

'I've been listening to your justifications. I've been listening for what seems like years. Makes me sick. Makes me fucking sick.'

'No doubt. But in this place, violence is entirely unproductive. Like dreaming you are falling out of an aeroplane. In the outside world, the physical effect would manifest itself as no more than a twitch of my eyebrow.'

'I'm not buying that,' Marco says. But he sounds uncertain.

'I am not intending to sell it. But you still have me, as they say, at a loss. You may release your chokehold and I shall still be entirely in your power.'

Marco glares over at me and I give him a terse nod and he relaxes his grip. We need to stick to the plan. My father has recovered his composure although his face is still puce.

'My wife died,' he says mildly, as if the two men are enjoying a pleasant conversation and an interesting thought has just struck him. 'She was murdered by her own mind. I could never risk losing my daughter the same way. Quite simply, that is my justification. Surely you can understand?'

Marco stumbles into a chair. My dad waits for him to formulate his thoughts, smiling benevolently. He has all the time in the world. Finally, Marco says, 'I do understand. I couldn't bear to lose Mya either.'

His words set my nerves skittering. My father's smile wobbles, then falls apart, and – despite everything, despite what he's done to us – it feels like my world is collapsing. The tears spill freely from his eyes. The guilt; oh, the guilt. I feel that I did this to him – and, somehow, I made him do this.

'We saw every doctor for Alice's condition,' he says. 'Every psychiatrist, therapist, head-peeper. They told her to meditate. Meditate!' He almost screams the word. 'A disgusting joke. Like trying to beat back an advancing army holding a handful of posies. Sheltering from a blitzkrieg beneath a paper bag. There was no solution. I failed. I failed her most abjectly. I promised myself I would not fail my daughter too.'

'Your solution,' Marco rasps, 'involves killing people's minds. Her mind. My mind too.'

'There is no ideal solution, I grant you that. How I wish Amaya had been capable of a full recovery without my intervention. Instead my hand was forced so many times. However, in your situation, your exceedingly complex situation, my hand was steered by the person most dear to me in the world. Mya and I decided – together – that the future we chose for you was the righteous path. Rotting away in jail, or living free? Free from the rage and hatred that weighed so heavily on your young shoulders. Free to love Mya with the purity you both deserved.'

He sounds so reasonable. Marco stares at him, captivated by his eloquence, his emotion. I can't let him be drawn into complicities like this – my Madboy might become compliant again. Malleable. Fixable. And my father is the best in the world at fixing people.

'You see, my bright young protégé—'

'Leave him out of this,' I snap, recovering my composure. 'What gave you the right to mess with his brain too? Who made you God? I started out with Sid Vicious and you left me with Forrest fucking Gump.'

My dad tuts under his breath. He is the teacher and I am the errant pupil. 'Sid Vicious murdered his own lover, I believe.'

'That's not the point,' I reply, even though part of me knows that it is the point, it's the exact point. 'He's ... you're ... we're not ourselves. Doesn't that bother you? Scare you? You're not perfecting people, you're destroying them. Creating a blank generation.'

'It saddens me to hear you say those words, sweetpea.' He shakes his head sorrowfully. 'I thought you believed in my work. I thought that you, out of everyone, would understand.'

'They're not humans. They're zombies.'

He flinches. Ever so slightly, my dad flinches and it feels like a victory. Is that a bead of sweat on his forehead? He doesn't like me saying that word. So I say it over and over again: *zombies, zombies, zombies*. It's an idiot mantra but it might be working. His knuckles tighten on his water glass. That relaxed smile has tightened and hardened into a grimace.

'Who's the real Mya?' I finish, almost panting with exertion even though my body hasn't moved an inch. 'Where's the real Mya? What have you done with your daughter?'

I need to make him understand. He is not insane. He is not an evil man. In many ways he's a better person than the pair of us because he truly believes he is helping people. But no one ever told him he was about to go over the edge. No one ever told him to stop. Not my mother, not Frank Baumann. Too late, far too late, I realise that it should have been me. I could have spoken, he would have listened to me; I might have pulled him back from the edge. But I never spoke. I never reached out.

And now…

'We have gone far too far,' he says. 'What's done is done. What must be done will be done. It is impossible to change anything now.'

'That ain't true,' says Marco, grinning painfully beneath the tattered flaps of his mask. 'Two people are walking around with our names and our faces. Those two ciphers. Bring them here. You've got no idea of the damage I can cause in this place. So bring them to us. Now.'

My father shakes his head. 'How needlessly dramatic,' he mutters. 'Very well, if it shall bring an end to this matter. I fear solace shall not come with the solution.'

His image flickers like television static and I realise he is somehow in two places simultaneously. Time seems to stop, then rushes forward with incredible speed. I beckon Marco over and he comes to me, wrapping his arms around my shoulders, sagging against me. Whatever he has done outside this room has taken a great toll on him. His heartbeat is booming against my body and his muscles are trembling. Despite everything, I'm glad of his touch. We've come so far. We need to face this together.

There is a fizzing, crackling sound and for a second my vision greys out. Then I see two people standing in the doorway. Hand in hand, so happy and innocent, a perfect portrait of devotion. Oh God, am I wrecking my life all over again? Am I wrecking his life all over again? I can hardly bear to look.

Everything we've been through, every one of our torments, and it comes down to destroying the existence of this contented, well-adjusted couple. Finally I look up.

And I stare into my own face. My doppelganger – although she was really me all along – stares back.

49

Endgame

'A word to the audience,' says my father. 'To the left of the stage, your heroes.' He casts his hand towards Marco and me. Then he indicates the couple framed in the doorway. They haven't moved, they look frozen in time. 'To the right, your villains.'

The inference is obvious. The replacement Mya is staring up at the replacement Marco. Her lips are moving but I can't tell if she is unable to speak or if she is afraid to voice the words she mouths. Then she turns to gaze at me. The other Marco's hands go to his face as if trying to block out the sight. Their movements are slow, achingly slow, as if they're swimming in formaldehyde. I stare at her eyes, her hair, her skin. She is beautiful and she is a mirage. She seems so divorced from me. I don't know if I can go back to being that person again.

But Marco decides for us.

'Make the transfer,' he orders. 'Switch us over.'

'Put you back?' my dad asks. 'Just the way you were?'

'Just the way we were.'

He sighs deeply. 'You, stuffed full of anger and resentment and bitterness? A lifeforce sustained upon dreams of revenge? I fear for your future, dear boy. And I fear more greatly for those closest to you.'

'Make the transfer,' Marco repeats. There's something cold and unsettling in his tone, something deeply wrong. My body stiffens beneath his grip. Then I realise the arm wrapped tenderly around my neck has now tightened into a constricting coil and I wheeze in fright, my heart battering against my ribcage, the blood roaring in my ears as my oxygen – or whatever passes for it here – is cut off. 'Do it. Or I'll kill Mya. Right in front of you.'

I try to speak, to plead or promise, but the pressure on my throat is too great. I know that tone: so flat, so stripped of emotion. He's serious. Oh God, he is serious. I'm struggling against him but he is too strong. Made powerful by the furies that never truly left him, the energy of anger. He's the Madboy now. He's not Marco, not Marco in the slightest possible way. There is nothing of the person I loved – and still do love, against all odds – in the man choking me.

'You can't … you won't …'

'Right in front of you. Swear down.'

'Then you will be trapped here …'

'I'm a fast learner, Guru,' he says, and I can hear the sick smile in his voice. 'Guess I know just as much about this system as you or your daughter. More, even. I've been to places you wouldn't believe. We're all wired together. Wouldn't take too much for me to destroy us. Blitz all our minds. Only difference between us is that I got nothing to lose.'

'This is not reality, Marco, I promise you …'

'Enough of her is linked into the system now for me to ruin Mya's mind,' he continues implacably. 'Dunno if she'll be left a corpse or a vegetable. Your call, Guru. You tell us you been messing her up all these years cos you can't bear to lose her. Well here's the thing – you don't get to decide any longer. If you're not really yourself, then you're better off dead. That's what I think anyhow. Want to know something else funny?

325

While you was distracted with your darling daughter, I pulled the plug on this whole fucking place. It's going to burn. For good this time. Every one of those poor souls you got trapped here, they'll burn too. It's over now. It's over.'

'Let her go, then,' my father begs. 'You can take everything I love but not her. Please.'

'Not until you make the transfer. Not until you put us back to how we were.'

'So this is the end,' my dad says, staring straight at me. 'The end of your brighter future.'

'No,' says Marco. 'You're wrong. I'm sure of it. This is the start.'

My father's eyes squeeze shut.

The impact hits me like the heaviest cloud, like a cotton-wool juggernaut. The spectral floating visions of the other Mya and Marco contract then expand then encompass us. White light, white heat. There is a sensation of immense pressure as my shattered soul is decanted into a new vessel. The feeling is the same as an operation under anaesthetic; your body is aware of the ripping and tearing but there is no pain. Now I can't even speak. I'm going, I'm fading, I'm falling away. Then conscious-ness returns. I'm back. In some elemental sense I feel a physical form. I feel the silver spikes digging into my skull from the jagged cradle around my cranium. I feel my memories reform and solidify, gasping as my brain adjusts with frightening speed. For the first time in what seems like forever, everything has fallen into place. I am Mya: unimproved, unmodelled, unfixed. I am myself again. Whatever that means.

My father's head falls into his hands. He slumps forward on the onyx table. I don't know if the work has exhausted him or if he cannot bear to look at me.

'Thank you,' says Marco quietly. 'Thank you.' He is shaking, his colour faint, his eyes wide, his expression pleading for reconciliation. He reaches for my hand and I don't have the strength to pull away even though his touch repulses me. 'I'm so sorry, for what it's worth. I had to ... I had to be my worst self to become myself again. That freak ... that Madboy ... it's not me. I promise it's not me.' He turns towards my father. 'I'll look after Mya. I'm a good person. I promise.'

I wonder who he is trying to convince. There is only silence between us. We stare at each other and turn to go. What else is there to do?

A snuffling sound comes from behind us. 'Please watch,' says my dad. 'Before the pair of you leave me, I wish to leave you with this.'

The video screen in front of us widens and widens until it fills the wall, then swallows the entire room. The solid floor has disappeared beneath my feet and I'm not sitting or standing but floating on an unearthly current of air. Now we are soaring and rushing, burning the years behind us, and we descend upon a chaotic scene. The muggy heat slaps me around the face, I'm choking in the clouds of dust. A train station. A steam locomotive packed with caterwauling children. A boy, no more than four or five years old, is leaning dangerously out of the carriage window, howling. Tears stream down his dirty face, creating clean rivulets on his skin. He is reaching out to a woman wearing a purple and gold sari and she is reaching back to the boy, her face a portrait of despair. I've never seen her before but I know who she is. I know who the boy is too.

The woman is pulled back by the guards in brown uniforms. She is struggling, kicking, screaming as she is ripped roughly from her son. Her foot catches one of the guards in his upper thigh and he hisses in irritation, swinging his rifle and driving the heavy wooden butt of the gun into her mouth. Her hands go to her face and blood blooms like a flower between the henna whorls on her fingers and she drops to the bare earth. The guard stands over my grandmother, his shoulders heaving. I feel the anger; the pointless, meaningless, mindless anger. I stare at the face of my father as a child. He is not crying any longer. He is silent, pensive. Contemplating a new and awful knowledge. So many questions yammer in his head.

What if you could take away that anger? Rescind those negative emotions? What if you could strip the inhumanity from humanity? What if you could start again, create perfect people, a perfect world?

The little boy's face warps and corrupts like a photograph set aflame. The train station collapses into a liquid spray and new surroundings are painted around us. My father is meeting my mother for the first time, and it's a first time for everything because this is the first time in his life that he has been truly happy. The beginning of a beautiful story. He has no idea how tragically it ends. He is standing at a bus stop, wearing his best three-piece suit from Marks and Spencer, grappling with his umbrella against the heavy Yorkshire rain. He is reciting his pre-prepared answers for the job interview under his breath when he sees the girl across the road. When he sees her face – pale, tinged with a beguiling melancholy – it feels as if his heart might burst. She is trying to keep her shop uniform dry with a soggy newspaper. Not even noticing the onrushing traffic, he runs across the road and holds out the umbrella for her to shelter beneath, while the downpour turns his favourite suit to mush. She smiles at him. The innocent hope in his expression breaks me apart.

The vision fades, the colours swirling into psychedelic patterns, until there is nothing left of the scene but a black-and-white photograph clutched in my father's hand. The three of us are back in the boardroom. He has sunk to his knees, prostrating himself, tears spilling down his cheeks. The room has begun to shake, huge cracks gouging themselves into the walls, the floor feeling rotten and spongy beneath our feet. The stars outside are flaming out in dirty-orange shades. The White Prison is falling apart.

'We need to get out,' I say, but I know it's useless. He is staying here. The captain will go down with his ship.

'Mya,' says my dad, turning to stare at me one final time, 'you should know—'

But his words are stolen by a horrendous creak and crash and Marco yanks me backwards just before a huge spike of metal plunges through the ceiling, dividing us forever. My father's head is bowed in reverie. Marco pulls me away and even though the building is falling down around us, somehow I know we are safe; we're in control now and the exit is whatever we make it. I suppose we have won. I wish I could feel some sense of triumph. The lift arrives with its mocking musical ding-dong and as the White Prison shakes and crumbles and we step forward and the doors slide shut, I catch a last glance of my father, broken, kneeling in the centre of his collapsing empire.

50

Endgame

This is reality, or whatever passes for it. I open my eyes, expecting carnage and chaos, and see that the three of us are sitting in a semi-circle inside the Brain Cell of the Academy. My father looks as if he could be sleeping; there is a half-smile on his face, he seems at peace. Marco has returned to consciousness, blinking and rubbing his eyes. There is a glittering silver band wrapped around his shaven skull.

Tugging the band from my own head with loathing – feeling its teeth, the metal receptors, remove themselves from my frontal lobe with a sickening sucking sensation – I try to snap it but the thin metal is surprisingly strong. Marco beckons me over, then sets both of our bands on the floor and pulverises them beneath stomps of his boots. His face is waxy. I can tell by his eyes – his watchful, mistrustful, brooding black gaze – that he is the person he used to be. What I can't tell is how that makes me feel. There are too many conflicting emotions. I suppose I should be grateful I have emotions at all.

'How are you?' he asks. He tries to smile and the charade is awful. 'Maybe I should say – who are you?'

'I'm fine,' I tell him colourlessly. 'I'm me again. Whatever that means.'

He pulls me into an embrace and kisses my forehead. I try

not to recoil from his touch. 'You know I didn't mean what I said in there, Mya, don't you? It was just a distraction, baby girl. Didn't it work a treat?'

'Oh yeah,' I say, 'that bit about you killing me. That was great, really creative. One to tell the grandkids.'

He rubs at his lips. 'Your father—' he starts.

'Don't,' I tell him. 'Just don't. I can't think straight right now. I only want to get out of here. Far away.'

'He's dangerous. He's a danger to us. He's a danger to the whole world.'

'So what are you suggesting?'

Marco stares at me. It's so difficult to tell what he is thinking, or maybe I don't want to even imagine. His lips purse, and I think he is going to speak and I dread what those words might be, but then the door bangs open and Frank Baumann appears. He is sweating, his face florid, but his expression is triumphant.

'We're good-good-good, Guru,' he blusters. 'We ended up saving most of the systems, damned if we didn't. Water damage is nasty, but we can rebuild. Every cell but yours is back online. Did you manage—' He stops in his tracks. He takes in the scene: the smashed metal littering the floor, the senseless smirk on my father's face. 'Guru?' he says tentatively.

Marco grabs him by the lapels of his tweed jacket and forces him against the wall. The back of Baumann's head connects with solid brickwork and he lets out a whinny of fright. 'You get in there and save your precious Guru,' he snarls. 'But when you do, you let everyone out of that fucking prison. Do you hear me, you fat shill? Every single person whose real personality is rotting in your cells. Johanna ... Alec ... Duane ... Tristram ... Anna ... they need to live free. They need to be themselves.' He takes hold of Dr Baumann's bow tie and begins to twist it tighter and tighter until my father's best friend hacks painfully

ANDREW EWART

for breath. 'Otherwise, I'll find out. That's right. I'll find out and come back and finish the job. *Capiche?*'

Baumann is squirming, struggling. He can't answer. Even if he wanted to, he couldn't answer. He's choking, near to passing out. I've tumbled from one nightmare into another.

'Marco … Marco, please,' I beg him, tugging at his shirt, trying to pull him away even though a treacherous part of my mind tells me that he will turn on me next, because he's the Madboy right now and this is my fault, all my fault, because I brought him back with me. 'We need to go. We need to leave right now. For Christ's sake, let him go!'

'Nearly done,' he says with a crooked grin, chuckling merrily into Baumann's swollen, purpled face. 'Ain't that right, big boy?'

'You're not yourself,' I tell him. 'You're not the man I used to love.'

My words shock some sense into him. But for how long? He relaxes his grip on the bow tie that has become a noose, and Frank Baumann sags to the floor like a bloated broken puppet. Marco sucks at his teeth, staring at the floor. 'You're right,' he says. 'I'm sorry. They messed with my head, Mya. They broke me into so many pieces.'

I can't tell him how many lives he broke into pieces too. The guilt is too great for me to comprehend. 'Let's go,' I mumble through numb lips. 'We just … I need … we have to get out, anyway.'

Walking quickly, not quite running, we descend the spiral walkways until we reach the exit. The Academy has been evacuated after the mess we created and nobody is around. The foyer is deserted and the automatic doors slide open and the fresh morning air catalyses my senses. This seems so easy it's almost uncanny. A punk rock rhythm plays in my head, a harsh and frenetic marching drum beat: *We're getting out, we're getting out, we're getting out.*

Marco lets out a crow of delight as he spots his Suzuki Bandit, almost concealed by the overhanging willow branches in the shadow of the building. The spot where a group of idealistic young students had once sat and debated everything and nothing; only certain that these were great days and they were great people, and these were the best of all days, and the days to come were so exciting it was almost unbearable. Everything would only get better from now on.

Swinging his leg over the Bandit's chassis, Marco gestures for me to climb on behind him. For a moment I think about leaving, running the other way as fast as I can, but where else is there to go? Eventually, obeying, I climb onto the back of the bike. I can't stop crying and I don't know whether I'm feeling joy or fear or pain or hope, or maybe an electric concurrence of every human emotion.

'So where do we go from here?' he asks.

'I don't know,' I tell him, trying to compose myself. 'Wherever. Somewhere new.'

Marco fires up the ignition and the motorcycle thrums to life beneath us. He guns the engine and the bike takes off, and we're racing with incredible speed, putting many miles between ourselves and the Academy and my father, and I won't look back at the tower. Our past is behind us now. But I can see no future.

Epilogue

In the months since the crash, I have recalled it only in fragments; a stained-glass window reduced to splintered shards, impossible to piece back together again. Marco was riding fast, recklessly fast, making a blur of our surroundings. Racing through the twilight, the Bandit's headlamp picked out the bushes and trees as we roared along the single carriageway. White on black, the world stripped of colour. The hair that had escaped from my helmet was whipping in the wind. I remember hearing him whoop with delight. He was free. We were free, or so he thought.

I felt like I was still trapped.

Then a vehicle with no headlights flew around the bend, far too far over our side of the road, and Marco let out a howl and wrenched the handlebars to the left and the dark car zoomed past us, inches away. I could feel us going over, propulsion fighting gravity, and I thought of what he had told me on our first ride together, what seemed like millennia ago: *You have to lean with me, Mya ... your body has to follow mine.* But I couldn't do it. I just couldn't go with him. I couldn't follow him any longer, because his path would only end in madness again. Instead I sat there, paralysed, as Marco fought for control over the motorbike he loved so dearly. Knowing we would spill, just as he had warned me. Then we were wavering and wobbling and he screamed my name and squeezed the brakes again and again and we were off the road and jouncing over bumps of earth and then the front wheel locked and we toppled forwards as the ground rose up to meet us.

Then I don't remember anything for a short while.

Somehow I made it to my feet before consciousness fully returned. The Bandit was about twenty feet away, lying on its side in a culvert, the moonlight glinting off the mudguard. One wheel was still turning lazily, so I couldn't have been unconscious for too long. A flock of starlings, startled into the trees by the crunch of the crash, begin to chirrup nervously.

Then my vision greyed out although I think I stayed on my feet. When I came back to myself, I was walking back and forth across a farmer's field, the dirt shifting beneath my shoes, calling Marco's name. The enveloping darkness meant I didn't see him until I almost stumbled over his inert form. His eyes were open. He was lying on the ground staring up at the constellations. The moonlight glinted off the buckles of his leather jacket. The pulse of a vein was flickering above his brow. His fingertips tapped out heartbeats on the soft ground.

It was at that point I saw his wound and realised – with a thundercrack of understanding – that nothing could be done for him.

I don't want to think about how he looked after the accident; his lower body shredded and broken, his stomach gouged by the handlebars. That furious lifeforce was ebbing away in a dismal field with the shadow of the Academy still looming over us. Those black eyes stared at me. He understood. His lips moved soundlessly. I rested my head on his chest and listened. I was prepared for his anger, his recriminations, his blame. I was prepared to gulp down a whole banquet of guilt. Because he had saved me, in his own way, and I had destroyed him.

Instead he told me he loved me. Over and over again, he told me he loved me. We held one another as best we could as the chill bit into our bones, and I promised I would never leave him and that night was both endless and gone in an instant. I couldn't leave because he kept telling me that he loved me. After some time, I realised the mantra was only playing on repeat in my brain and Marco Pellicci was gone. His chest had stopped rising and falling. He was still.

I can't remember how I found my way home. But I didn't stay there for too long. Spooked by the empty house – uncertain of whether my father might return at any moment or whether he was still trapped in the White Prison with his memories – I stuffed whatever I could carry into my rucksack and left that home forever. Left that house, left that town, left that life. Left everything I knew, or thought I knew, behind. That was four months ago. I haven't looked back.

Today I woke up halfway across the world from where I was imprisoned. It's a good place, a peaceful place. The walls of my room are white and even slightly curved at the edges, but outside I can hear the wash of the waves on the pebble beach and the shouts of market traders ready to start the day and the put-put of tinny car engines and the cackling caw of gulls. The sunshine cracks through the wooden slats in my window and the salt tang of the sea air dances on my tongue like an unearthly wine.

Most mornings I see a woman who walks on the beach pass my window. Her body bears the encroaching stoutness of middle age but she has a certain elegance, a gliding grace. She always wears long floral dresses and a large sunhat and I can never properly make out her face. She is barefoot and as she walks along the shoreline, you would expect the foam to pool around her toes, but it is almost as if she is floating an impossibly small distance above the waves. Each day she raises her hand in greeting and I raise mine too. I think we understand one another. Here we can float.

I do like it here but tomorrow I might wake up somewhere else, who knows? The truth is that I've been drifting for a while. Getting to know myself again. Realising who I am. It's tough – every day is a little struggle, a minor war, but I'm trying. I'm trying so hard. I have promised myself that I won't give up.

There are things in this world that can't be fixed. Marco was one of those things. But maybe in his memory I can build myself into a better person. I want to see the worst and the best of existence and confront it head-on. I want to be flawed and difficult and strange and endlessly problematic. I want to dive into the greatest of Great Waves and break it apart with the strength of my life and love, beat back the sucking currents and swim forever. I don't want to be perfect. I just want to be human. There is so much I want to do. There is so much to experience. There is so much to live for.

I want to live free.

Acknowledgements

The first full draft of *Replace You* was completed on Christmas Eve 2019. Putting down my fountain pen (actually closing the laptop lid, but that doesn't sound quite so romantic), I opened a celebratory bottle and looked forward to the bright dawn of a brand new year. As 2020 began to turn somewhat apocalyptic, writing a book about being trapped in a strange, bleak environment riddled with hidden dangers began to seem like a rather tasteless joke ... Being locked down in leafy Hertfordshire suburbia isn't quite as traumatic as Mya's White Prison, but the unusual circumstances certainly contributed to the paranoia and confusion that courses through these pages.

In such strange times, I was lucky to have the backing of a great team and the love of my family. Tip of the hat as always to my brilliant agent Harry Illingworth, his trusty assistant Rocket and DHH literary agency. Many thanks to Tom Witcomb for crucial work on the structure, Lucy Frederick for laser-guided editing and ensuring every scene sizzled, and Francesca Pathak for steering the good ship Orion. The design team created an amazing, disquieting, eye-catching cover. Also thanks to everyone who bought a copy of *Forget Me* or helped with its promotion.

I'm forever indebted to my parents George and Marjorie for never-ending love and support. Above all, my wonderful wife

Laura and incredible daughter Arianne have provided me with laughter, reassurance and – in the case of Ari – the best cuddles in the world. Sadly this book features neither space, dinosaurs nor space-dinosaurs for her. I can only apologise. Maybe next time.

Credits

Andrew Ewart and Orion Fiction would like to thank everyone at Orion who worked on the publication of *Replace You* in the UK.

Editorial
Lucy Frederick

Copy editor
Clare Wallis

Proof reader
Jane Howard

Audio
Paul Stark
Amber Bates

Contracts
Anne Goddard
Jake Alderson

Editorial Management
Charlie Panayiotou
Jane Hughes

Design
Debbie Holmes
Joanna Ridley
Nick May

Finance
Jasdip Nandra
Afeera Ahmed
Elizabeth Beaumont
Sue Baker

Production
Ruth Sharvell

Marketing
Tanjiah Islam

Publicity
Ellen Turner

Sales
Jen Wilson
Esther Waters
Victoria Laws
Frances Doyle
Georgina Cutler

Operations
Jo Jacobs
Sharon Willis
Lisa Pryde
Lucy Brem

Don't miss Andrew Ewart's first epic, speculative thriller...

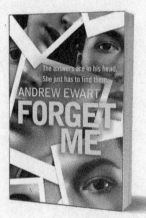

The answers are in his head. She just has to find them.

Your partner doesn't remember anything: how you met, your first kiss, not even your wedding day. An experimental treatment promises to recover the memories they lost. But some memories are better off hidden.

How far would you go to bring back the one you love? And what if the truth hurts more than the secrets...?